Something New

A Novel

by

Malena Lott

buzz books

ISBN13: 978-1-938493-05-8

ISBN10: 1938493052

For more information on the book or to schedule a speaking engagement, discuss a media opportunity or sales, please contact Buzz Books at www.buzzbooksusa.com.

Other books by Malena Lott:

Dating da Vinci

The Stork Reality

Fixer Upper

Life's a Beach (novella)

The Last Resort (novella)

Praise for *Something New:*

"*Something New* is something wonderful! Malena Lott understands love...and knows that it's ageless. Exploring the lives of four women and one barely functional family, she delivers a novel of remarkable wit and insight. This book is a treasure."
— Ellen Meister, author of *The Other Life*

"I am completely smitten with *Something New:* it's endearing, romantic, and utterly satisfying, with characters so well-developed they feel like old friends. Maeve steals the show, but I missed them all when I reached the end. Highly recommended for mothers, daughters, granddaughters, and sisters."
— Jess Riley, author of *Driving Sideways*

"Utterly charming, romantic, and beautifully written, *Something New* is the story of three generations of mothers and daughters struggling to define their relationships and to ultimately find their own place in the world. I absolutely loved it!"
— Maria Geraci, author of *A Girl Like You*

"Ego is to the true self
what a flashlight is to a spotlight."
—John Bradshaw

The apple never falls very far from the tree.
—Proverb

Chapter 1

Kelly

I'm going to be honest: I don't think it's natural to have three people present at a conception. Even a wild-eyed liberal like me moons for the picket-fence version of family, but damn if I didn't find myself laying there, legs in stirrups, with not one, but two people prepping me for conception—neither of them glistening with lust. Hell, one of them wasn't even male, though she did look an awful lot like Tom Hanks.

They say it takes a village to raise a child. In my case, it took nine bad boyfriends, three months of donor daddy research, one blue-eyed doc that looks like he plays one on TV, the manly nurse, and donor 61894—all to get a shot at conceiving one.

And I do literally mean "shot." The white liquid appeared on the ultrasound, a mushroom cloud of sperm that took the speedboat through the twin Venice canals that are my fallopian tubes and docked in my uterus. It was every sperm for himself in the final lap to my mature egg. By mature, we're talking thirty-five big ones, which in egg years means she's swapped her subscription of Cosmo for AARP. Only a dose of Clomid got the ol' gal out of her rocker for a trip to the port to meet the sailors. I prayed the 500 million swimmers didn't take a look at her and decide they'd rather die than hatch a human with her. It's not a complete exaggeration, since the aforementioned boyfriends all had come to that conclusion one way or another.

"You okay?" Doc asked when he was finished, peeling off his latex glove, his blue eyes shining with nothing but concern.

"It was good for me. Was it good for you?" The joke fell flat and the nurse raised her bushy eyebrows in mock horror. I know nothing about motherhood yet, but I'm pretty sure a good mother-to-be doesn't make sex jokes upon conception, unless it's with the father-to-be.

Doc grinned, then patted my knee, which felt more like a slap. I tried not to think about how much I wished the circumstances were different. How I wished the lights were dim from a romantic evening of lovemaking in the glow of candlelight and not an intra-uterine insemination with the glow of an ultrasound machine. I wished I were wearing a sexy black negligee instead of a white cotton wrap with pink flowers and a tie at the neck that even my grandmother wouldn't be caught dead in. I wished the doctor and I were doing it the old-fashioned way—if he were, say, fifteen years younger.

"Saw that you sold your house," he said, gathering up my medical file, and thankfully standing. TV Doc, who can regularly be seen chatting it up with the local anchors on camera on the topic of fertility, has a real name, Dr. Mont Spurlock. But to me, he's simply Monty, a neighbor down the street from the historic house I was about to give up in Crown Heights.

"We close today," I said, feeling the knot of sadness return. No white picket fence, but a historic home in Crown Heights, down the street from the doctor. I'd lived a few houses from the best fertility physician in Oklahoma for five years, never needing anything but a stick of butter from him all that time until my lesser half high-tailed it to Florida for greener golf pastures.

The "we" was a slip of the tongue. It's just me, the home in my name—a purchase I'd made for my thirtieth birthday in between men and overcome with liberation. I'd called it my declaration of independence, but compared to what I was doing in these stirrups, it seemed rather ordinary. When John had asked me to move in with him the prior year, I insisted he move in with me instead. The house had plenty of room for his things, and though I didn't voice it at the time, room for our future child. He'd agreed, sold his smaller house and moved in, yet as the months passed, we grew no closer to an engagement or condom-free, baby-making sex. He had no place in my mind as I conceived someone else's child, even if that someone was a faceless list of characteristics and attributes.

"Hated to see you move, but I think it's great you moved in with your mother and grandmother."

I nodded, letting out a small humph. Not sure "great" is the word for it. It's not like I'm the typical thirty-something moving back home like the articles you read about. I own my own business, but with the economic downturn, it would be nice not to make that big mortgage payment each month. Someday, when things looked brighter on all fronts, I would buy a different house without memories of John embossed in every square inch. And helping take care of my grandmother felt like the right thing to do. My best friend, Taylor Montgomery, called it a "rebound move" and my baby a "rebound baby," the two acts together combining like Kryptonite to keep any future heartbreak at bay. She'd been the first and only person I'd told about my baby, my way and swearing off men for good. My family, my judgmental thou shalt not conceive out of wedlock family, would have to wait.

"Your mother holding up okay?" the doc asked.

"It's safe to say we Apple women are falling to pieces all together," I told him, wondering if this was too much information. But then, the man had been romping around in my cervix. Surely I could confess that my mother may have some internal angst about her and my father's divorce after nearly forty years of marriage. If it weren't for my parents' divorce and my grandmother's Alzheimer's and my John's "Dear Kelly" break-up the night before I'd left for Hawaii for my biggest event of the year, then no way in hell we would all be living together again.

My sister, Gwen, who hates to be left out, brought her huge wardrobe, including two hundred pair of designer shoes, and the camera crew (more on that later) with her. So much for some peace and quiet. She's getting hitched in three months and living with her fiancé is strictly forbidden due to the Family Reputation. Unless that is, you're over thirty and the family figures you're a lost cause, as was the case with moi. I'd already broken the thou shalt not co-habitate rule, so why not go for broke? I doubt they'd give me such leverage on the baby-out-of-wedlock issue, which is why there was no need telling them until the last possible moment.

Doc says IUI has a 20 percent chance of success, so why get the Apples minced up about something that may not even happen? Better to let them think I'm on the road to spinsterhood than motherhood.

"Lights on or off?" he said as he opened the door to leave me in privacy.

"Off. Shy egg," I joked again, and fortunately, this time he laughed. Gwen was the natural jokester, but if I couldn't laugh at this situation, then when? Better to laugh than to cry, which seemed the only alternative.

The screeching fluorescent lights from the hall pierced a shard of light into the room. "A nurse will be in shortly to check on you. And congrats on being named one of OKC's Most Eligible Bachelorettes," he said, motioning at the OKC Insider magazine in the rack next to the bed.

Not a single note of sarcasm in Doc's tenor voice, yet all I heard in my head was a screeching "nooooooooooooooooo," with the image of me being shoved into a dark and musty dungeon that smelled of cat piss and afghan blankets, where the city stuck all the old maids. Honest, I don't mind a bit being 35 and single. This is the new millennium, after all. If I hadn't felt the urge to have a child so badly, I could not have cared less about the number of candles on my cake. Didn't mean I wanted to be the poster child for the unmarried thirty-something businesswoman, either.

Besides, what OI didn't know is that I most definitely was not one of OKC's Most Eligible Bachelorettes, because I had taken myself off the market. Permanently. I hadn't planned on issuing a press release with this tidbit, but I was certain when my bump became apparent, if the IUI were successful, my official position would be obvious. I was done with men, done with their false promises and philandering ways. Done with their allergic reactions to commitment, dirty dishes and steady employment.

I'd waited for my knight in shining armor as long as I could. Hell, I hadn't even found a knight in rusted armor. Not even close.

In Hawaii, I'd had my last sexcapade with an unbelievably hot Polynesian masseuse. The Mojo in Maui conference – and likely the island itself – had worked its magic on me. I did suspend my heartbreak over John long enough to make love to another man, and decided I would go through with finding a suitable father. (Fine, suitable father's sperm, details!)

"You don't need love," my grandmother Maeve told me in her ritual post-break-up pep talk after we'd scarfed down an entire bundt cake together. "All you need is a good facialist, good stylist and a hefty bank account."

But who was she to talk? She'd been married to my grandfather for fifty-five years before he passed on, and she'd married well—as in, son of an oil tycoon and state senator, future governor and U.S. senator well. She had no business talking about unrequited love because she'd had her proverbial wedding cake and ate it, too. He wasn't just a knight; he was friggin' king. But I took her advice about the facialist, stylist and hefty bank account. I was a lonely, 35-year-old business owner with a peachy complexion, shiny reddish-blonde tresses and plenty of my own money, but I'd give it all up for this.

Thing is: I was of no age to wait two more years for Mr. Maybe to come along in hopes he'd love me, cherish me and give me his DNA.

I may still need something to believe in, but it sure as hell isn't love.

"You rest now. And give my best to your family."

"Thanks, Doc." I looked at him over my foot in the stirrup as he gathered my medical chart and the empty vial and left me patiently waiting for the mating ritual that was XX plus XY equals baby.

No, this was not the honeymoon in Jamaica I'd imagined when I was 25 or making love in Breckenridge on a cold winter's night I'd hoped for at 30 or making a romantic evening of candlelight and Marvin Gaye with passionate procreation I'd wished for on my 34th birthday. This is what you get when you're last hope flees to Florida and your biological clock has nearly ticked its last tock.

You do what you must to keep the dream of a child from slipping through your grasp like every man you've dated. You need one sure thing and the only way you're going to get it is with a quickie from a sperm bank you paid way too much for. You think of all those used condoms that were tossed away like pieces of garbage, but you didn't really want a baby with any of those men, anyway. You'd rather have it this way, you tell yourself: with a handsome, faceless donor who gave you the finest gift on Earth and expects nothing in return. Not picking up his stinky socks or making him waffles or putting down the toilet lid for the jillionth time that month. You never worry he'll leave because he was never here to begin with.

I inhaled slowly, wishing medical facilities allowed candles, so at least the moment would've felt less clinical. Just because it lacked a partner didn't mean it wasn't worth celebrating, yet I let my curiosity get the best of me and plucked OI out of the rack to find the Apples had made the cover once again.

In Oklahoma, you get to be a celebrity one of two ways: one, you move far, far away and do something fabulous and return for fundraisers and gala events that people will pay big money to be in your now-celebrity presence, or two, you're rich and keep your residence here and scatter your vacation homes in Colorado, New Mexico, Arizona and beyond. You are a doctor, lawyer, business owner or a blue blood like me. Four generations of social, political and business influence meant the Apples would be considered "society" for generations to come. I am, by all accounts, descendent of Oklahoma royalty. The Apples are golden in these parts.

As I lay there, I thought of what I might tell my child about the conception. Forward thinking and progressive, I would tell my child the truth, but most likely leave out the part about the nurse who was a dead-ringer for Tom Hanks. I loved you so much from the moment you were conceived. So much it hurt.

I lay my ringless hand on my abdomen and wondered if this was the moment that would change everything. If this was the first of thousands of memories I would have with my child. I thought of humming a lullaby to mark the occasion, but the only song that came to mind was one Gwen had been singing incessantly the last few days: Madonna's '80s hit, "Like a Prayer." I couldn't remember all the words, but it was far more fitting than "Papa Don't Preach" or even "Like a Virgin."

It would do.

Six hours later, I arrived at my mother's loft, officially the only place I could call home.

"Maeve? Mom?" I yelled out as I plunked my

keychain down in the crystal bowl in the foyer of the loft in downtown Oklahoma City. In truth, I'd moved in not only because my mother needed help taking care of my grandmother where dozens of home health aides had failed, but because I had to get away from the memories in that historic home—every room full of John and his false promises for a life together—and being one block away from my event planning business would at least be convenient. I could go from being a run-of-the-mill workaholic to a pathetic workaholic.

My mother Bess air-kissed me on her way out to an evening social event, something arty or musical or otherwise do-gooderish. Fridays were another day of the week for me, and since most business engagements were held earlier in the week, Fridays were solidly Girls Nights In for Maeve and me.

"She's been mulling around in the attic," Bess said as she swung the door open. "Playing dress-up again. Don't forget to lock both locks when I leave."

"Will do." I nodded dismissively, as I settled into the modern black couch in the living room, opened my black laptop and wondered if the Wi-Fi waves could hurt the baby, if there was a baby at all.

"Maeve! It's almost time for Deal or No Deal," I shouted, clicking on the flat screen while not taking my eyes off of the computer screen. They were re-runs, but it didn't matter because Maeve couldn't remember watching them the first time around. I reviewed the notes for my newest article for WIRED on how to be popular on the social networking sites.

"As the premier event planner in the Midwest, my advice has always been it's who you know. Getting the right people to back your causes, give you referrals and attend your events is critical to climbing the corporate and social ladder. So how did I get more than 5,000 people Linked In within two months? How do I use the 2,237 "friends" on Facebook to make a difference in my life?"

I groaned. If I'm so "linked in" and have so many "friends," why the hell was I watching a TV show at home on a Friday night? I could use more IRL (in real life), but reality sucked.

I looked up, noticing Maeve's absence. What was taking her so long? And why, oh why, couldn't we choose what to remember and what to forget? If only I could pluck John from my hippocampus, I was certain my life would improve immeasurably.

"Maeve! Seriously, Howie is calling up the first contestant!" I shouted again. I don't know why Grams loves this game so much except it is a game of chance, unlike so many game shows she used to love that required her to tap into her memory bank to answer. I don't love watching the show, but I do love watching Maeve shake her balled-up fist at them when she thinks they are being too risky with their money. "Take the deal!" she'll tell them before it's even reached the $50,000 mark. She has forgotten she's Queen.

My iPhone buzzed from its place in my left bra cup where unfortunately there was plenty of room for a phone. Mother. Thanks to the ability to dedicate a ringtone to the caller, before I even reached for my breast, Elvis Presley, Mom's teen heartthrob, forewarned me of her call. Had she really been gone an hour already?

"Forget something?" I said, my brain still on the fascinating inner workings of itself.

"I meant to ask you how the closing went."

"It went. It closed."

"Did they seem like nice people?"

"Nice enough." John-less, I'd handed over my keys to an adorable little family of three: husband, wife, Buddha-esque baby. I overheard them telling their realtor they would convert my office into the baby's room, which had been my plan all along. The thought brought tears to my eyes and the crushing weight in my body. I no longer cried over men, just baby-sized versions of them.

"That must make you feel good, then. That they're nice, I mean. What did they look like?"

"What difference does it make what they look like?"

"Because. You want your house to go to good people, that's all. Forget I even asked."

"I will. Are a bunch of your friends there?"

"Depends on your definition of friend," Bess said sarcastically. I'd noticed a sharp drop-off of those "friends" since she and my father had separated. Mom knew all the right people, though she wasn't nearly as business-inclined as me or as social as Gwen. "Please tell me I'm not one of these people," she added.

"You're not one of those people." I sighed. She was so one of those people.

"Thank God for that." She laughed. "How is Maeve?"

Maeve? Shit.

"Deal? Or no deal?" Howie asked a short, excited woman onscreen, and I realized the contestant had gone through half the cases and Maeve still hadn't appeared from her bedroom. My heart thudded, thinking she may have fallen—or worse. I hoped for the best—that she'd gotten carried away with her make-up again. We'd taken away anything really dangerous—like nail polish, which she used as brow liner the week before, or a curling iron, which she used to burn off several curls when she first moved in.

I hung up with Bess, accepting her offer for Chinese take-out on her way home. I swear if people didn't remind me to eat these days, it wouldn't happen.

"Maeve!" I shouted in my best singsong voice. I stopped in front of her door, open, the room empty, and I spun around staring at the front door. The locks! The door was shut, but certainly I would've heard if Maeve left the loft, wouldn't I?

The front door squeaked as I opened it and peered into the hall, an antique chandelier illuminating the concrete floor where a linen cream envelope addressed to Maeve was left behind like bread bits from Gretel's hands.

Chapter 2

My eyes widened. Raised black letters on personal stationary. Expensive stuff. Arthur P. McGuire, a famous playwright. I glanced back at the postmark date on the envelope. Two days prior, yet hadn't Arthur died earlier in the week? Huge news articles had flooded the press about his life and times. Depending on when he actually wrote the letter, this could very well have been one of the last pieces of communication before he passed on.

My heartbeat quickened. The envelope had been opened, the card still tucked neatly inside. I pulled it out.

Dearest Maeve,

I have but mere days left on Earth, courtesy of colon cancer, and in all my down time, I've had nothing to do but reflect on my life. As a playwright, I've preferred creating new stories than reliving my own, and yet, what else can I do? I cannot merely think; I must write. So you know, I am only writing three such letters. One to my only nephew. One to my surviving sister, and one to you, the one that got away.

I write not because you may not remember how much I cared for you in our brief time together, but to let you know that as much as this surprises me, I still feel as strongly today about you as I did when we were scrappy kids from the wrong side of the tracks. Upon reflection, I realized it was the unrequited love I had for you that spawned my entire life's work: twelve Broadway shows, two novels and untold years of wondering "what if?"

I do not send this to make you feel uneasy about your decision. I know the truth about what happened, and knowing my own pain about not getting the joy of spending a lifetime with you, I wanted to say I'm sorry things didn't go as planned for you, either. I also know you had to do what was right for you at the time. I'm sorry I was not the door you chose to walk through.

Now that I am on my deathbed, I realize I probably should've written a memoir. My agent begged me to, but I've never liked writing about myself. You, on the other hand, I could've written about forever. Know that you will always be my Princess. My last purchase was the old theater where you sang your heart out for a month. I have bequeathed the Orpheum to my nephew, with strict instruction to renovate it and bring back "Princess and the Pauper" as the first production, on the anniversary of the original in July. I have also instructed him to leave the chair on the third row center where I watched each and every rehearsal. I hope you will be in good enough health to attend opening night and maybe even give the audience a final encore.

I die not with a broken heart, but a full one. Thankfully the memories watching you on that stage shine brightly still. I hope I fall asleep dreaming of you. That, to me, would be heaven.

All my love,
Arthur

A love letter from beyond the grave. Goosebumps pricked my skin. If that wasn't the most romantic thing I'd ever read.

I quivered as I placed the card back in the envelope. Of course the playwright naturally had a way with words, but it was more than that. It was those two men — or maybe more? — had loved my grandmother. Had I ever had a man pine for me? Ever written me a single love letter? Don't even have to think about that one. Big fat N-O.

I panicked trying to recall my mom's words before she left — the attic, Maeve playing dress-up. Had the letter's arrival tripped the wire in Maeve's brain to dig up her old princess costume? Had she decided to go back to the place where her stage career ended?

After a quick call downstairs to confirm Maeve wasn't in the antique store, I grabbed my bag, and then did a quick Google search for the Orpheum. Six blocks away. But if Maeve could no longer remember every day things, how could she possibly remember how to get to the Orpheum?

And how in the world could I be a good mother if I couldn't even be a reliable sitter for Maeve?

Seven o'clock on a busy Friday night in downtown. Sexy singles and dolled-up dates strolled the streets in hopes of fine dining, pricey booze and whatever came after. Humidity stuck to me like a wet blanket, the threat of an oncoming rain sending sporadic lightning strikes in every direction behind the massive buildings. The ominous air chilled me to the bone as my car squealed into the space marked "No Parking" next to the fire hydrant right behind the patrol car. I'd called the one beat cop I knew by name and he agreed to meet me at the Orpheum even though he was off-duty. If she wasn't there… but God, I couldn't think like that. She had to be.

The Orpheum stood like a queen turned bag lady on Grand. While much of downtown Oklahoma City had been renovated, the Orpheum remained a forgotten theatrical dynasty until Arthur had decided he would resurrect her.

The main door to the Orpheum swung open, chains dangling and rattling in the Oklahoma wind. Someone had gotten in. I prayed it was Maeve.

A dark cloud sent sheets of rain pouring down as I scrambled to the entrance, soaking my clothes within seconds.

Stepping into the darkened foyer, I heard her before I saw her. Maeve, stage name Mae Moore; our shrinking dahlia at 85, still drawn to the lure of the stage like a bug to light. I followed her voice, breadcrumbs leading me back to her.

There she stood on what was once the largest stage

in the state, shimmying her ample bosom and sashaying her round hips in a come-hither move I'd seen in photos of her from the late '40s when she'd been, as she liked to put it, "hot to trot." As I suspected, she wore her emerald-green princess costume she'd found in the attic. Despite her shifting body weight, the dress still fit her — baggy in some places and stretched tight in others.

I felt like I'd beat the banker at his own game and sold the contents of my one-dollar case for a quarter million. Jackpot. Maeve would be okay. This time.

The officer in plainclothes and his very pregnant wife stood in the front row, next to a tall, handsome man in black cycling shorts, a yellow-and-black cycling shirt and calves big enough to feed a pack of hungry wolves. They wouldn't even have room left to devour his biceps. Dark hair, peppered with gray, thick and curled at the end, with neatly trimmed sideburns and sexy stubble. Not your typical downtowner.

The trio didn't rush the stage, and clearly Maeve was performing for them. I shook the officer's hand, then stood next to the stranger, clasping my chest in relief.

I smiled at the stranger, despite wanting to turn on my heels and run to the other side of the room. Maeve. What was he doing standing in an empty theater listening to my grandmother?

Yet he stood there all cool and collected, like a sporty member of the famed Rat Pack. Like Dean Martin if he'd retreated to the mountains without his grooming products for a month. Because of my quest for a man to father my child, I had gotten very good at sizing them up.

Height: 6'2"
Build: Athletic
Complexion: Olive
Origin: Something Mediterranean. Greece, perhaps?
Style: Devil-may-care, wash-and-go good looks
Normally, I'd dismiss a guy like him before we even

exchanged a word, but something felt different about this one. Not only his looks. How to explain it? That familiar, oh crap feeling. One heart-thumping vibe.

The man turned toward me, a large smile on his angular face. Light eyes, nearly the color of ice. "My uncle said the place had been abandoned for decades. Imagine my surprise when I find the Maeve Q here as if she'd never left." He was amused. Well, that made one of us.

Maybe in her heart, she'd never left. That as her memory drifted off, this is what remained. I offered my hand, slightly wet from the rain, but the man didn't falter if he'd noticed at all. One could say I shake hands for a living for all the networking and business functions I attend, but this wasn't your average, ho-hum, nice-to-meet-you handshake. As soon as my firm grasp met his, mine turned to butter. He didn't simply shake my hand; he held it, then gently squeezed, sending a tingle up my arm before letting me go. Wow. If he could do that with one hand, imagine what … no I'm done thinking about men and their body parts altogether. Get a grip, Kell.

"I'm Kelly Apple-Barton. Maeve's grand-daughter."

"Edgar McGuire. Arthur McGuire's nephew. Pleased to make your acquaintance."

"Edgar. I haven't heard that since..."

"Sophomore English Lit?" Edgar finished with a smile.

"Shakespeare or Poe?"

"A bit of both, I suppose. My mother was a voracious reader – all the classic stuff people typically only pretend to read - and King Lear was my uncle's favorite. Like most dads, my father didn't have a say in the matter."

Not what I expected in a famous playwright's nephew at all. I'd assumed he's be more of the small glasses, bow-tie sort of aristocrat. Somebody my father would sneak a cigar and bourbon with behind closed doors. "Heir apparent to the Orpheum," I added, swinging my arm out at the dilapidated seats. "Lucky you. Think you can pull it off?"

Edgar shrugged. "If my uncle's will hadn't been so implicit that it open on the anniversary, then I'd say 'yes' in a heartbeat. But giving me under three months to do major renovations and pull together the whole cast?" He raised his left brow and sighed.

A man willing to show a sign of weakness, a moment of doubt. So rare these days. I smiled. "You basically need a miracle."

"Several of them in fact. You in the miracle business?"

"Nope. Your basic blood, sweat and branding. Branded event planning, mostly."

Edgar nodded, notably impressed. "Even planning, huh? I've been so busy thinking about recovering the seats I hadn't thought about the fact I need people to pay money to see the blasted thing." He paused, then straightened his shoulders, turning his whole body toward mine. "Can I call you, then?"

"Excuse me?" I knew Edgar McGuire, sexy guy in a dark theater, had not asked me out. Especially not after I'd asked for my own miracle earlier that morning in the doc's office. After I'd sworn off men of all sorts, even extremely handsome ones.

"Call you. About branding the Orpheum. Marketing the show." He nodded, hopeful.

Work. Of course. Why would my life be about anything else?

"I look forward to it. So what's with the biking ensemble?"

"First time in OKC. Best way to take in a place is on a bike. You ride?"

"Yes. When I was ten. Though I do cycle at the downtown gym. Actually, that sounds like I do it regularly. I cycled at the gym twice, but my legs were pissed at me for a week, so I never returned."

He grinned. "We'll have to get you back on a real bike then. No better way to see the world. At least on land, anyway."

What an un-asshole, I thought. "Sure, I'd like that," I found my mouth saying, though my body laughed hysterically at the prospect of making it more than a few blocks before passing out from exhaustion.

My mother and sister burst through the doors, but not even their frantic entrance disrupted our star.

"What on earth?" Bess said as she stared up at her mother, whose booming voice echoed in the theater.

I marveled that Maeve could remember all the words, as natural to her as breathing. Out of the corner of my eye, I marveled at the officer's wife's pregnant belly, I thought, I want to look like that. Huge big belly, full of baby.

The officer glanced at his little notebook. "Says she's meeting Canty here. Something about a musical. That a friend of hers?"

My mother shook her head. "Canty? Never heard of him."

"She seemed pretty adamant she was to meet him here."

I explained the letter I'd found from Arthur McGuire, and Edgar filled in the gaps.

The officer continued. "So she wasn't confused after all. Said she was gonna rehearse here and then, bam, she burst into song. Think we should stop her?" The officer closed his notebook and crossed his arms.

We stared at my grandmother, mesmerized by her siren song for whoever this Canty was, if he actually existed, or like the Orpheum, existed once a long, long time ago.

"Oh, my God," Gwen gushed. "Grams was Princess from Princess and the Pauper?" Gwen asked, mesmerized by our grandmother's performance.

Bess sighed. "Still is, apparently. Arthur started the show here and then moved to New York to make it a big Broadway hit. Your grandmother always said he had a thing for her."

"He was her muse," Edgar said softly.

I marveled that Arthur would've shared that with his nephew. Grams may have been the queen of Oklahoma society, but she'd always thought she was meant for bigger things. We'd assumed she hadn't gone to Broadway because she'd fallen in love with our grandfather Henry, choosing him over stardom.

Bess shook from relief, the anxiety of yet another "episode" pouring over her. Her worry glistened in her eyes. She could've been hit. Could've been killed. What was she thinking? But, of course, the answer is that she hadn't been thinking. Maeve's primal desire to leave took over, her judgment sadly a thing of the past. Her facilities may be failing her, but her vocal chords continued to deliver on key, despite a wavering note here and there.

I thought that's what Grams would've wanted. She would rather sing than think any day.

We stood back—my sister, mother and I—Maeve's biggest fans, staring adoringly like any star-struck groupies might.

In the last few months, we Apple women had bonded as a search-and-rescue team, finding Maeve Apple time and again. We had tried to lock her in, but the bigger danger is that her mind has locked her out.

Damn Alzheimer's.

While my mother was more concerned with Maeve's survival, but I was more concerned she would hitchhike to Vegas where she'd been telling us they were always looking for experienced showgirls. We'd lose her to phony Elvises and all-night buffets, though I knew deep inside she was lost to us already, but we couldn't admit it. Besides putting Maeve in shackles, what more could we do?

Nausea curdled in my gut, but I blamed it on the stress of the day. I didn't feel pregnant yet, though I wanted more than anything to feel the fertilized egg split into the cells of human life, like dominos tapping each other on their way down.

When Maeve sang her last note, we clapped and Edgar whistled and hollered enthusiastically—a good sign he might show some enthusiasm for the project. If the show had meant something to Maeve, then it meant something to me.

"Do you hear that? They love me," Maeve beamed as Bess took her into her arms. Maeve presented her cheeks for air kisses and seemed to be looking for a gift, like a dozen roses or perhaps searching for Canty. A quick scan revealed only a Doritos wrapper at our feet and a crushed Budweiser can.

"Oh, thank you dah-ling," Maeve said batting her eyelashes, with one false eyelash hanging precariously from her thin eyelids, threatening to blow away from the breeze of the storm coming through the open door.

With all the Apple women safely buckled in my black Lexus, Edgar came around to my open window, the light rain dusting his fitted cycle wear. I tried not to look down at his ... pelvis. "You going to be okay?" he asked with genuine concern.

My throat caught. He didn't mean me, but us. Maeve. "We'll be fine. Good luck with the renovations," I said.

"See you at rehearsals, Arthur," Maeve said, reaching out from the back seat and rubbing his arm.

I gulped. Maybe Edgar resembled his uncle. Simple mistake. He handled it with class.

"Great performance, Maeve." He tapped the car door, then met my eyes.

"It's not Maeve, darling, it's Mae. You were the one who gave me my stage name!"

"Of course," he answered. "I'll be in touch, Mae."

As we pulled away, I couldn't help but watch him in my rearview mirror, confident stride, wide back, tight backside. Then he turned around, as if he could feel my eyes drinking him in, and waved one last time before mounting his bike.

Gwen leaned up, her sultry voice in my ear. "How fab is that? He's hot and he's going to call you."

"I suppose," I said nonchalantly, but whether or not he called me to help with the musical, I had to keep my focus on my primary goal, becoming a mother. I'd leave the romantic notions to people like Gwen and Maeve. Bess and I were much more practical, which was definitely the safe way to go.

Bess grabbed a Kleenex from the glove compartment and settled into the front passenger seat. I could see she tried not to cry, her fists balled up like she could punch something, and I had a feeling when she got home she'd walk through the rows of trees in our park and let out a good wail. I thought how nice it would be to join her for a cry, but I've never been a crier. I would go home and make a to-do list of possible solutions to keep this from happening again.

Out of the corner of my eye, I saw the manila file folders on the passenger floorboard. Crap. I left in such a hurry I forgot to hide the files in my briefcase. Fortunately for me, my mother was too preoccupied to bother being nosy.

In the rearview, I watched Maeve and Gwen singing, "Cell Block Tango (He Had It Comin')" from Chicago, happy as larks. Gwen and Maeve were two peas in a pod. Sixty years apart in age, but you wouldn't see a day's difference looking at them together. I felt another pang of jealousy that they had this connection. They even shared the same body type, Jessica Rabbit curves all over the place.

Gwen has never liked her body, wishing for smaller hips and breasts like me, but I think she's got it all wrong. I think God must've given her that body for a reason, though she doesn't see it. At the very least, her hips are perfect for baby making, but I know its purpose reaches beyond even procreation. She's always trying to hide it, cover it up, wearing shawls and squishing her breasts and forcing herself into tight body huggers underneath her clothes.

I got an eyeful of it every morning, since we were roommates for the first time in our lives. Growing up, we had our own rooms, and at 35 and 25, we were no better suited to handle the others' quirks than we were when I was 15 and she was 5. My mother said it's our age difference that kept us from being close growing up, but seeing she and my grandmother together, I know it's not age at all. It's chemistry. You either have it or you don't.

"To the Skirvin, driver," Maeve said, tapping on my headrest. "I'm on in thirty and I desperately need a stiff one before I go on. And I'm not talking about a drink."

She cackled, and my sister howled with her, causing me to stifle a laugh. I'd heard my grandmother was quite the catch back in the day. Every eligible man in Oklahoma City had been after her—and even some that weren't eligible, but were still willing. Maeve had hinted she'd had her fair share of men before she'd settled down with my grandfather, but she'd never elaborated. Her theatrical past was just that: the past. And an Apple woman never discussed sex in the open.

"You're encouraging her, Gwen," my mother said, pushing my folders around the floorboard with her feet. I hoped for a red light so I could move them before my mother beat me to it. I'd put them in the car to take them to my office to shred since I'd made my selection, but as usual, I had gotten knee-deep into a project and forgotten all about them.

"Who's the sourpuss?" Maeve asked Gwen while pointing to Bess.

"Oh, God. I can't take this," Bess said, digging her

nails into my arm.

"Dr. Haunschild said it would come and go."

My mother nodded, blinking back tears, and whispered. "So many times I wished to be anyone other than her daughter, and now ... I never thought it would come to this."

"It'll pass. You've got to admit, it would be a little funny if it weren't your own mother. Can you believe she can still belt it out like that?"

I wheeled into the parking lot behind Apple Antiques, which was a gift from my grandfather to my grandmother back when she needed a place to store all of the pricey antiques she shipped over from Europe. Henry convinced her she should sell them, be her own woman.

One streetlight cast ominous shadows on the vacant asphalt. Behind the lot was the Apple Urban Park and Tree Farm, an experiment my grandfather, Maeve's husband, started in the '50s to ensure plenty of natural beauty in downtown, around the same time he's started his urban planning company.

We shipped trees all over the state. If anyone other than an Apple owned it, I'm certain urban sprawl would've downed the trees decades ago, but even though it took up two acres of prime real estate downtown, it had become a landmark, and my mother loved it. More than three hundred couples had gotten married there, and hundreds of more remembered it as the place of their engagement. The whole park buzzed with an energy field of love. I think it was the trees more than the prospect of living downtown that gave Bess the idea for converting the abandoned apartment above the antique store into a cool loft.

"All the hip kids are doing," Bess had said, days after my father told her he was leaving her for another woman – a family friend, or so we thought.

Maeve unbuckled herself. "Damn contraptions," she huffed. "Let's hurry to see if Canty is still there. Maybe he'll buy us a drink before his set."

My mother and I exchanged looks. Again with the Canty talk. Canty. Now that's a nickname.

"Mae, remind us what role Canty is playing," I asked sweetly.

"Is she kidding, this one?" Maeve asked Gwen. "He's the pauper, darling! But he'll always be the prince in my heart. How's that for a love story?" Maeve asked, clutching her chest and giving us a dramatic sigh.

"A fling,'" Bess said, dismissing her mother's statement. After all, Bess was the only child of Henry and Maeve, and her parents had a storybook life. "She never spoke of Canty to me," Bess whispered.

A silver Mercedes pulled up and idled in the parking space next to mine. Gwen and Maeve had given us their final note, and burst out in laughter, obviously pleased with their own performance. My grandmother had officially lost all touch of reality, and was having one helluva good time.

"Your chariot awaits," I said, referring to Victor, Gwen's fiancé. I heard a sigh escape my sister's red pouty lips. Her strawberry blonde hair fell in big curls around her slender shoulders, pointing to her cleavage. "What, Juliet not want to shack up with Romeo tonight?" I said, sarcasm intended.

"I think I should stay and get our star to bed."

"Bed? The night is early, fair child," Maeve said. "We'll party on the horizon and hitch a ride on the sun on its way up."

"Lord help us," Bess said. "I think her new medication keeps her up at night."

Maeve's pink tongue darted from her mouth in lizard fashion. "The fuddy duddy's not invited. Besides, she's a little old for our crowd."

My mother flinched. Maeve had slipped between the cracks of time, and whatever age she believed she was, it was obviously younger than her daughter, maybe even granddaughters. We didn't press her when she made those mistakes. Better to ride it out, let reality fade back in.

Tired of waiting for his princess, Victor exited his car and opened the door for Gwen. "If it isn't the Apple-Barton ladies in waiting."

I cringed. It seemed everyone in OKC loved Victor – except for me.

"And how are you, future Mrs. Prescott?" He leaned in to kiss Gwen.

I take that back. I can't think of a single thing I like about Victor Prescott. Not his prestigious name or his perfect hair or his personal trainer-trained body or his Cheez-Whiz charm. His name gets him VIP access anywhere he wants to go in town and to the middle of the invite list to all the best parties. And obviously a silver Mercedes at the ripe old age of 28.

As much as I disliked him, I felt the pang of jealousy again, thinking about he and my sister's obnoxiously golden genes coming together like Fred Astaire and Ginger Rogers. Their babies would be gorgeous, smart and, if the child gets my sister's vocal chords, damn good singers.

My stomach gnarled, and I realize those pangs may not have been pangs of jealousy at all, but simply pangs of hunger. I hadn't eaten since that asiago bagel during my branding "mind map" session with the downtown urban planning committee that morning before my procedure and closing. Another side effect of workaholism: I tend to forget to eat. My sister, forever on a diet, wished she had this problem.

"What's this?" My mother picked up the files at her feet, illuminated by the open door.

Panic rose in my throat. "Oh, nothing. Work stuff. Let me have those."

"They're baby pictures," Bess said as she thumbed through them. Another downfall in living with my family again. Think they have to know everything going on with me, and normally this isn't a problem. Normally, I have nothing to hide.

"Boring work files." I tried to grab them from her manicured hands, but she was too fast for me.

Victor had left, pretending he was upset his betrothed wouldn't join him at the hottest clubs downtown. Right. But that meant Gwen was in my business, too, only it wasn't business at all.

"Is this for a new event? Why would you need old baby pictures?" My mother kept her door propped open to give her more light to look at the babies in the folders. I knew them all by heart. Marcus the Investment Banker; Simon the Crazy-High-IQ, All-Star Athlete. Dave the Serial Entrepreneur. The photos of their baby selves. Itsy bitsy, tiny, coo-coo-cachoo babies.

My guy's paperwork has been hole-punched and put in my baby binder for safekeeping, and his photo has been cut out and framed in a pewter 3½" x 5" frame in my bedside table drawer. Privacy policy, you know. I could only imagine what they might look like as adults.

"Let's get Maeve in," I said and ripped them away from my mother, save for one, which she promptly opened. Ah, that one. One of my favorites. Thomas the Nuclear Engineer, with his chubby baby cheeks and marshmallow thighs. I have a thing for fat babies. I was a fat baby, and look at me? Thin as a rail—but then, I do forget to eat.

"Genetix!" Gwen shouted right into my ear, and my mother gasped. I so wish Gwen hadn't gotten Lasik for Christmas. The girl has super-human vision. I could see the Genetix logo on the folder, plain as day, and Gwen was familiar with it because she works at Apple Developments, an urban planning company started by my great-grandfather after the Depression.

Calm down. They know it's a client. Stay cool. I got a lot of crap for taking Genetix on as a client, naming them and launching their brand and a regional, press-worthy launch. Genetix built a corporate office downtown three years prior, causing much shock and awe among the state's conservatives, including my own.

Bess's blue eyes locked with mine. "That's the sperm donation company, right? Where you can cherry-pick the kind of child you want?"

Gwen squealed—half-drunk, I was certain. "Whatcha' doin'? Fishing for a baby daddy?"

Maeve, whose mind I thought was completely gone, seemed to have remembered who I was again. "Ooh, Kelly. Don't leave out the screwing part. That's the best part of making a baby."

A regular cuss-bucket grandmother. Nice.

I squeezed my eyes shut and when I opened them a moment later, my mom's eyes were closed, her mouth slack. I thought I killed her. Instant heart attack. So much for being the good girl, the responsible one, the one that never rocks the boat or shakes the Apple tree. I am relieved when she opens them again and takes a deep breath. I couldn't tell them yet. The stress from their reaction alone might hurt the baby. I'd wait until it was safe, until the first trimester was over. But before I knew if it worked? No way. Besides, they'd never understand. Every one of them was used to getting what they wanted.

If my grandmother wasn't making my mother crazy, then I would tip her over the edge.

Chapter 3

*Why not upset the apple cart? If you don't,
the apples will rot anyway. –Frank A. Clark*

Gwen

The buzzer to the back door jarred me from the hypnotic trance gazing over the hideously gorgeous brides in the glossy pages of Society Wedding, which had been left there by Skylar, my new nemesis who only thought she was trying to "help."

Only three months to my "big day" and I still hadn't decided on a dress (I'd look nothing those skinny bridal beyotches and it's sadly true the camera adds, like, twenty pounds), the cake (the richer you are, the more tiers you are expected to have) or floral arrangements—my family owns a nursery, so you'd think this would be a no-brainer, but alas, it makes the choice much more difficult. Roses? Gardenias? Lilies? Really, aren't flowers , well, flowers? God, don't let our gardener, Samuel, hear me say that.

And this was the tip of the iceberg. A million other details demanded decisions, yet I could barely stammer a single one. The decisions were all the more pressing because I was on a production schedule in addition to a countdown. A year ago, I'd agreed to let *Luxe Weddings*, the hottest reality show on RLC, follow us around for nine months to tape all the "big moments" in wedding planning culminating with the wedding and reception.

At the time, I loved the idea of being on camera (forgetting the part about looking heavier on TV). And though I'd told my family and my fiancé that I wasn't doing it for the money (a $100,000 pay-out after the final guest at the reception left the party), they had no idea how much debt I was in. Fifteen credit cards, all maxed out. When Victor had asked me how much debt I'd be bringing into our union, I'd lied. He would assume, because of the family I'm from, that I'd have no debt, but my dad is Mr. Budget. He doesn't realize the importance of Chloe gowns or Dior shoes or Gucci handbags. I'm too ashamed to admit to Victor that I'd gotten so carried away, and I swore to myself I'd have it paid off before our wedding.

Even though I work for the family for the planning and development company, I'm a project manager. Not exactly a lucrative gig, and quarterly work bonuses were a stingy $1,000 if I met my goals. A far cry from the six figures I needed.

They say opposites attract, but I don't think they had in mind this one: Victor, like my dad, is the saver. I'm the spender. And I'm really, really good at it. What started with a few simple credit cards in college turned into accounts at some of the major department stores, jewelry stores and designers around the world. It's amazing what you can get away with when you have a big name. So I'm $90,000 in debt and there's no way Daddy can bail me out of this one. *Luxe Weddings* is my ticket out of debt, and if I'm lucky, maybe I'll be the next reality-star-turned-journalist on The View. Anything has to be better than a cubicle-slave project manager.

The producers were more than a little miffed that I kept changing my mind about wedding plans until they decided to work my indecision, and my struggle to lose twenty pounds before the big day, into the storyline. Should weddings even have a storyline? And if so, I don't like "bridezilla" and "struggling fatty" being mine.

Yet the public, of course, is eating it up. Supposedly my bitchiness and bulge makes me most popular. Yay! So why do I feel so crappy about it?

Luxe Weddings features three luxury weddings into the ongoing series, so starting in January the crew practically set up cots in the loft. My sis, Kelly, is miffed because she doesn't want to be on camera, even though as my maid of honor, I think it wouldn't kill her to say a few nice things about me to the world, even though we've rarely said more than two sentences to each other at one time our whole lives. She doesn't like to shop or party (or eat for that matter) and I don't like to talk about work. The only plus is that she's one of the most connected women in Oklahoma, so when I need to know who to go to for what, she always has an answer for me at the tip of her tongue. And being an event planner, she has gotten me into some pretty bitchin' parties.

It's only April, and the other two weddings, one on the East coast, one on the West, are kicking my butt in the planning department. (I know, as a project manager I should be kicking tail!) My competitors know exactly what china they want to register for and picked out their wedding dress and bridesmaid dresses by episode 3. We're on episode 12 and I still haven't a clue. Supposedly, my "bridezilla" tendencies—I swear I'm not a monster, I don't know what I want—have caused ratings to skyrocket. People can't wait to tune in to see how I'll screw up next or if I've given in to eating Cheetos, which I swore off in the first episode. (Yeah, you're welcome for that free product placement, Cheetos!)

One might think this rise to semi-celebrity would be welcome—icing on the proverbial wedding cake—on top of an engagement to the best catch in Oklahoma. *So why the hell do I feel so completely unhappy?*

Mom's more than a little fed up, and I don't blame her. Last thing I'd want to do when my husband asked me for a divorce is to plan my daughter's wedding, let alone be filmed arguing with me about the wedding. My brain boiled thinking about Daddy dumping Mom for what seemed no good reason to me. Hell, if they, Mr. & Mrs. Damn Near Perfect, had a Crap Marriage, then what kind of chance did Victor and I have? Huh?

It wasn't just the divorce. There was something going around with the Apple women, though nothing as obvious as a cold virus. It felt stronger, hereditary, or like the cycle of the moon, yet I'm not sure if we were waxing or waning.

The buzzer growled again at the same time my cell phone rang.

"Mom wants to know if you decided between the Skirvin or the Colcord," Victor said in place of a hello. "As does Skylar."

Skylar, the producer of LW, aforementioned nemesis. Apparently 'hellos' were for the unbetrothed. We were way, way past hellos. Years past such niceties. "Nope. Haven't decided."

"We can't keep asking both of them to hold the date. Even if you are an Apple. Even if one of them will be featured on national television."

"Like I'm doing it on purpose," I said. I didn't tell Victor that Bess had said we were already $10,000 over budget. It wouldn't exactly be a *luxe* wedding with a skinny budget, now would it? When I'd come out and asked my mother if we were suddenly poor, she corrected — only cash restricted (she refused to use the term cash poor.) We still had investments, money market accounts, real estate, but there had been some bad investments, some losses, and the economy didn't look like it would bounce back before my big day.

Bess agreed to take over as wedding planner because my first two planners were pushy and controlling in addition to being expensive and my sis refused to take me on as a client, with a deadpan: I don't do weddings.

So much for sisterly love.

Daddy sweetly recommended I start forking over some of my decent salary towards the wedding, but he didn't know I was already using every cent of it to keep up with the minimum balance due on all those credit accounts. Why else would I have agreed to move into the loft with my annoying sister as a roommate? We didn't even have adequate closet space.

The buzzer sounded again, this time as if it got stuck, or what was more likely, someone laying on it because I wasn't moving fast enough.

I checked on Maeve, who was sitting at her vanity fixing her hair up into a '40s hairdo. Grams always had to wear the latest hairstyle, so I kinda liked seeing her go all retro. "Fine," I said to Victor. "If the show needs a decision now, then you pick. I don't care."

"Dammit, Gwen. I know you care and you're leaving the decision to me so you can complain about it later."

"No, I'm not." I huffed. So what if I couldn't decide between two gorgeous reception halls? And what if, maybe, I'd meant what I said? But the reception was as, if not more, important than the wedding ceremony on the social spectrum. So I very, very much should care, but a nice luxe reception at either place would run a cool twenty-thou when all was said and done. No, I wasn't keeping up with the Joneses. I was keeping up with the Goodmans in California and the Haverly's in Nantucket. In Oklahoma, I was the "Jones." This city kept up with me, but they had no idea there were chasing the styles of someone who was also being chased by creditors. Oy.

I'd have to work up the courage to ask Victor to start forking over some of his big salary to our big day. He works for my dad, number two manager, but on the more lucrative oil and gas business.

Racing to the back door, I sweetened my voice. "Really, honey. Let's throw your mom a bone. She hasn't been too happy I haven't gone her way on a few other things, so let her pick. It'll be like a peace offering. Make for great TV drama. She might even weep," I said, nearly tripping over an ottoman.

"You can't be serious."

Maeve hummed a tune from Princess and the Pauper (she'd told me hotly when I told her I'd never heard of it) and looked at me, perturbed. As if I were interrupting her little solo rehearsal. I whispered. "Trés serious. Love and kisses. Gotta go."

I hung up. Apparently, we never said goodbye anymore, either.

"Are you going to get that?" Maeve asked as the buzzer sounded again. Last delivery of the day, and for the sake of my growling stomach I would've preferred it were pizza instead of furniture. Though, at the moment, I was hungry enough to eat a nice seventeenth century hutch. In the last stretch and in a desperate attempt to take off fifteen pounds before the wedding, I had to give up every single food that gave me pleasure, which was basically the only things I liked to eat anyway: ranch on everything, pizza, burgers—and did I mention the ranch?

Note to world: the universe has a predetermined weight range in mind for you, and mine seems to be somewhere between not-skinny-enough and Marilyn-Monroe-in-her-bigger-years. If having a camera stuck in your face—or worse, at your behind—doesn't cause the pounds to melt away, then honey, it ain't happening.

Truth be told, losing fifteen more pounds seemed as likely as Cinderella's godmother appearing to do the work for me. But, hey, I'm the optimist in the family. Everybody says so.

I made my way through the dark storeroom, flicking on lights. The buzzer rang again, this time, longer, ruder, more insistent. "Coming!"

I punched the garage door opener and watched as the old, heavy door lurched and squeaked upwards. His shoes appeared first, tall black riding boots, stitched to below the knee. Next came black leggings over muscled thighs, topped with a chain mail shirt and black scabbard that held what looked like a real sword, clasped by a strong hand with shiny nails, while his other fist jutted into his pinched waist. Didn't our regular delivery guy have a beer gut? Stork-thin legs?

I blinked my eyes twice and held my breath, wondering if I had gone back in time. A medieval knight topped with an unforgettable face, wide smile, triple dimples and blue eyes under dark eyelashes and crazy, loose curls that fell chin-length. Golden brown skin, so beautiful he looked like he was lit from within. Native American? Hispanic? Hell, he could've time-traveled from ancient Rome for all I knew. His eyes held a mischievous glint that told me he was trouble, uncaged and wild. I swallowed hard, my mouth suddenly dry. No way this was real, yet for a split second, I was sure my knight in shining armor had come to steal me away. My grandmother's stories had gotten to me.

"May I help you?"

The stranger grabbed the top of the garage door as it stopped above his shiny hair. His eyes swept over me as if he'd touched me everywhere he looked. A slight shiver went through me despite the heat, and I wished I'd rethought my Saturday ensemble.

A fitted T-shirt and jeans. I hadn't even bothered with my appearance when mom said it was time to watch Maeve. Nonetheless, the medieval cutie smiled at me, those dimples and superhero chin making me weak.

"Hope so, m'lady. I'm Ax. Ax Ellis." His voice low and sweet, with a lilt at the end, reminding me of recordings of Sinatra from recordings from his early days. He ended each sentence with a short burst.

"A-X??"

"Short for Akocha. Got the nick-name Ax playing football." He shrugged. "You look like you were expecting someone else?" He leaned in, inches from my face, the smell of a musky aftershave wafting into the room. Whatever it was, it worked its magic because I caught myself trying to inhale him.

I feared one brisk breeze and he'd land right smack onto my anxious lips, so I backed up, nearly falling over yet another ottoman. "Sorry. It's just you don't look like our regular delivery guy."

"How would you care for me to look?" Half-smile, one dimple on full duty. My heart nearly leapt off the platform.

"How would I...?" Unbelievable. A guy that made me stammer. Self-assured, typically, I supposed standing in jeans and a T-shirt in a storage room wasn't exactly my element. And I'd never been in the presence of a knight before, even a pretend one. If this is what they did to women, I favored bringing back the style.

"You mean I'm not supposed to wear my armor to deliver here?" He looked over his shoulder at the husky older man unloading the delivery truck. "Damn you, Hank. You made me look like a fool in front of the gorgeous broad."

Broad. Why didn't it sound sexist from his mouth? Perhaps because it had followed the word gorgeous? Something I hadn't heard in a while. The loops called me a lot of things, but gorgeous wasn't one of them. "So you're the new guy, then?"

"Jeeves didn't give you the 4-1-1, eh?"

"Jervis."

"Jervis. Right. So where would you like this dining set?"

God, I'd nearly forgotten. Work. Here for work and not to flirt with me. Those dimples had completely made me forget my place. Or time. Hank looked like a delivery driver should—jeans threatening a plumber's crack, sweat rings around his underarms and chest. Ax didn't have a single drop of sweat on him.

"That corner will do."

"Righty-o." He winked and hopped down the steps onto the pavement and joined Henry.

I placed my hand over my stomach, willing the butterflies to take a rest.

"What's the real story behind the lingo and the costume?"

Ax blushed. "Sorry. The costume is getting into character. I figured it would be big news around here that Princess and the Pauper was coming back. Bringing the musical and the theater back to life."

"I did hear something about that," I told him, not wanting to confess at the moment that my grandmother had played the original princess. My sister was the name-dropper in the family, not me. Unless it was a designer name, but that's totally different.

"Figured dressing in character can't hurt my chances, anyway. Better get used to wearing this. Not exactly comfortable. Arrived two days ago from the reservation."

I shook my head in disbelief. "Hold up. A reservation? As in Indian reservation?"

He smiled. "Yeah. I teach theater at the school. I live in the Chickasaw Nation."

Ax unleashed his smile, turning me to putty. "But as much as I'll miss the kids, it's not every day you get to be in an Arthur McGuire production. And it's high time I play the leading man. Besides, Princess and the Pauper is an amazing story."

I raised my brow and he continued: "King sends out a notice to all the land that he'll marry off his only daughter to the richest man in his kingdom. So the princess has to sit through all these uncomfortable, stuffy meetings. Then one day she goes to a jousting tournament and sees this handsome jouster and tells him he should come to the court. She gets him on the list and it's the best visit she's had, but of course by this time, the King has found out the jouster is a pauper. Penniless. He gets kicked out, but not after she's already fallen in love."

I held my breath. "I have a bad feeling about this."

"So, she gets forcibly engaged to this total asshole rich kid who leers at her whole court. She's so upset by the news that she's to marry him that she steals away in the night and rides to the remote village where the pauper lives. He builds her a tree house and she hides in it when there's word the king's men are looking for her. Otherwise they do normal couple kinds of things. Fishing, hunting, archery."

"Sounds romantic except for the fishing, hunting and arrows bit." I laughed.

Handsome shook his head. "City girls."

"So don't keep me hanging. Do the king's men find her?"

"Of course. She's taken back kicking and screaming, and she and the new prince have the most glamorous wedding the kingdom has ever seen."

Sounds familiar. "Ugh. Don't tell me she becomes Queen Lonely Hearts and chops off her own head."

Ax grinned. "No. Even better. When she and her new husband leave in the carriage to head off to their honeymoon at the country estate, guess who the carriage driver is?"

"The pauper. Don't tell me. The three of them live in the tree house happily ever after?"

"Close. They tie the prince up to that tree surrounded by wolves. Steal the dowry given to the prince's family and live modestly and probably have bundles of babies."

I smiled. "I like it. Full disclosure. My grams was Princess in the original. Not on Broadway. Well, here in OKC."

Ax looks surprised. "This her place?"

"Among other things." I instantly liked that he's an outsider. That he doesn't know about Oklahoma politics or, it seems, recognized me from *Luxe Weddings,* which meant he's probably not gay.

"So you want to be the asshole prince or the kick-ass pauper?"

"Who's in the title?" He beamed.

"Gotcha." I started to bite my lip, my eyes blurring from the vision in front of me. But I nodded, longing to find out more about the musical, and maybe this actor, too. Seeing Maeve up there had made me yearn for the spotlight again.

A born star, the university paper had proclaimed about my starring roles in college and community theater. But Vic and my family considered it a hobby, something I'd outgrow when we got married. I hadn't been in a musical in two summers, and I wondered if the itch I felt might have something to do with not performing, too. I'd satiated my lust for the spotlight with weekend karaoke performances, but it was harder and harder to fit singing into my busy weekend schedule with Victor.

I had been good, but I didn't tell anyone how much I'd loved it, how thrilling the lights and the applause had been — far better than the temporary high of a shopping spree or upscale soiree or even being on camera these last months. One taste of the stage and I understood why Maeve would've picked that time in her life to relive again.

Maybe I could pop in with Maeve and watch the auditions. Edgar said we were welcome anytime. "So you're a sort of Ax of all trades, huh?"

"Sense of humor. I like that in a city girl. Helping out wherever I'm needed, I guess. I'm also a freelance photographer – I also teach photography back home - and I got hired to teach swing dancing on the weekends."

"A jitterbug and a shutterbug? You're a busy guy."

"Whatever it takes." Ax resumed his gig; carrying two chairs up the ramp and then set one down in front of me and one across from it. He twirled it around and sat on it backwards, leaving Henry to finish the load. "So what do the young 'uns do in this town for fun?"

Young uns. Ha. I may only be 25, but I hadn't felt young and carefree in a very long time. He fluttered his eyelashes, long and gorgeous. I could imagine our kids having them someday. Where the hell had that thought come from? I didn't even want kids for eons. *And, Jesus, I wanted them with Victor!*

"Let's see. Great martini bars. Some cool clubs downtown. " I nearly mentioned the social mixers I either hosted or attended every weekend, mostly upper-crust mixers disguised as philanthropic fundraisers, which this teacher from the reservation had to think was pretentious. I added, "And the Museum of Art is wonderful."

Ax laughed. "You sound like the tourism department."

"Close. Urban planner. Well, project manager, but someday I hope to create something...wonderful."

"You don't look like an urban planner."

"Not sure if that's a compliment or an insult."

He winked. "Compliment. I doubt many urban planners are hot."

My blush deepened. Did he mean I'm hot or, like other urban planners, I'm not hot? He had me so rattled, I wasn't sure. I hadn't seen a guy flirt like that, since ... well, let's say I hadn't been on the other end of it.

"Ax. Four legs, man. You want to get us fired?" the deliver guy gruffed.

"Sorry, man. Old habits die hard."

Rehearsals for auditions, huh? Damn. Victor and the engagement party we were supposed to attend that evening. Not our engagement party. An engagement party for someone in our wedding party (out of seven bridesmaids and seven groomsmen, the odds are high that you're going to have to return the favor).

Your twenties are a parade of endless wedding

showers and baby showers, followed by the endless parade of birthday parties and play dates followed by spoiled teenagers and rounds of Botox in my forties and … no, no, no. This began sounding eerily like someone else's life, someone else's road map, someone I swore I'd never be anything like. I had inadvertently jumped on the same track as my mother and look what it got her? Divorced at 60. Effin' alone.

I felt like someone had tossed me in the spin cycle and left me there. No martinis. No musical. No Ax. I'm sorry, I wanted to tell him. I'm apparently tied up for the next forty years or so. Can we hook up again when you get your social security card? Forget this. I swallowed my disappointment and leaned in, our elbows nearly touching. "So you must sing, dance, act?"

Maeve appeared from behind, placing her hands on my shoulders. "All of the above. The best in the West. Hello, darling. I thought we were meeting at the theater?"

Ax's brows rose. "Pretty ladies like you deserve a house call."

Maeve batted her lashes. Really batted them. "Have you been introduced? Gwen, this is my special friend, Canty. Canty, this is my roommate Gwen."

Ax opened his mouth to correct her, but I shook my head quickly, vowing his silence. Play along. "Canty, of course! I've heard so much about you."

He held out his hand for me to shake. Warm, soft, an actor's hand. I didn't want to let go. "Pleased to make your acquaintance, Gwen." His voice lowered. "I suppose I'll be whomever you want me to be."

Ax tilted his head and retreated down the ramp to help carry in the eighteenth-century dining room table. What a cocky guy. I crossed my arms, noticing I hadn't worn my engagement ring. A rock, all right. Two carats. One look and people knew I was marrying into money. No wonder he'd thought I was a safety flirt. Maeve grabbed my arm, the look of unmistakable love in her eyes. "Isn't he a dream?"

"He's one interesting cat, alright."

Maeve laughed, but her eyes narrowed. "You know if you try to make a play on him, I'll scratch your eyes out," she said sweetly.

Getting out of the engagement party had taken major skills. I used Maeve as an excuse (which was partially true, even though Bess was supposed to take over at 6:00 p.m.) I had to promise Victor a late-night visit (i.e. booty call) after I put Maeve to bed. I didn't mention Orpheum to Victor—he could've stopped by after the engagement party, but from all my years on the stage since Victor and I had been together, I knew auditions and rehearsals were the equivalent of watching paint dry for my all-business fiancé.

Bess made me promise not to let Maeve out of her sight (even to the bathroom) or do anything embarrassing, but I didn't see the big deal. We'd go and watch a little singing and acting. Maeve would get to relive her past and I'd get to see Ax again. Seemed pretty tame to me.

Thanks to a multimillion-dollar influx into downtown, the city enjoyed resurgence with the creation of the Bricktown Canal, our first downtown skyscraper, Devon Tower, and the hippest restaurants and stores flocking to set up shop in downtown and Midtown.

To avoid the streets, we took the canal for safety, to blend in with the real characters on the canal, street performers and the like—and because Maeve had insisted on wearing her Princess costume, we fit right in.

A fire breather juggled flame sticks and the smell of kerosene overpowered us. I led Maeve to the other side of the bridge to avoid the fire. Protecting Maeve had to be my number one priority, even if I did hope to get a few moments alone with Canty, er, Ax.

"Did you notice Canty wasn't wearing his wedding band?" Maeve said as she took my arm as we crossed the river's bridge.

"How long has he been married?"

"Three years too long," she said, with a smile. "They were neighbors in a small town, so it was a marriage of convenience more than anything.

"So where did Canty get his nickname?"

"His musician friends nicknamed him. Used to say there's nothing that man can't do. And, boy, he could go all night long."

TMI, Grams! I nearly blushed for her. Man, this real Canty fella must've been something else.

I squeezed Maeve's hand. "We won't let anything spoil our night. But I'm shy, so can I stick close to you?" Of course this was a huge fib, but Maeve hadn't seemed to remember I was her granddaughter and I needed her to stay within arm's length.

She tossed her silver shellacked hair, her curls smaller than mine. In the evening light, her stage makeup looked too harsh and settled into her wrinkles, but she was still beautiful. Still a knockout.

"Stick by me and you'll get the pick of the litter. Men will flock to us like flies to a picnic."

I smiled, hoping I would have that confidence when I was her age.

We stepped inside the Orpheum and I got goose bumps. Built in 1903 as the Overholser Opera House, the place became the Orpheum in 1921, and boasted the largest stage in the West, perfect for the rowdy musicals that became popular after WWII. As entertainment swarmed to the coasts, the Orpheum closed in the mid-1960s. The Civic Center Music Hall became the local bastion for orchestras and musicals. Ownership of the Orpheum changed hands, but fell short each time. I knew to do the renovation right would require big money, the kind that Arthur McGuire brought to the table.

I'd often wondered why my grandmother had not wanted to renovate it, as it had been the place of her last performance. She'd never talked specifically about Princess and the Pauper; only that she had once been an actress and jazz singer and had aspired to become a Broadway star before common sense and reasoning set in. Instead she had focused her patronage of the arts with the Civic Center and smaller theaters across the state.

The place smelled like a time warp — old movie-theater musk meets dank men's locker. The doors at both ends were open, an attempt to air out the joint. Even in its lackluster condition, the space gave me the chills. I'd never performed on such a large stage and had wanted a peek inside since I was a child. In two weeks, renovation had been completed on the stage with a shiny wooden floor and red velvet curtains gleaming in front of dated lighting. The seats had all been removed and the carpet stripped. Amazing what Edgar had already accomplished in such a short time.

A dozen or so actors swarmed near the stage talking and reading over scripts. I imagined the mice and spiders were none too happy with our intrusion on what had been theirs alone for forty years.

Maeve didn't seem to notice the dirt or decrepit state, and when she entered — regally, always regally — the young actors drew in their breath at the site of her. Maeve was a legend, not because she was the original Princess of Princess and the Pauper, but because she was figuratively crowned the Queen of the Arts. She loved artists, her loyal subjects, and so they loved her in return.

The city knew of Maeve's dementia, but few had laid eyes on her in years. The dance instructor took to the stage and the actors followed. Thankfully, Maeve didn't make a move to get up. Surely the walk alone had tired her.

"Where's Agnes De Mille?" Maeve asked, watching the beautiful dancer explain the first act.

From my theater classes in college, I knew Agnes had been a famed choreographer who fundamentally changed musicals forever after. Chorus girls were replaced with professional dancers, elevating the quality of the musical. Maeve had told me on more than one occasion that she'd been taught to dance by the best. I, on the other hand, had relied solely on my voice and acting ability to get me through high school and college plays and musicals, carefully avoiding any number with too much dancing.

Out of the corner of my eye, I saw Edgar wearing khaki shorts and a tank top with flip flops and a raggedy Lakers cap going over fabric samples with a decorator. He looked ready to mow the lawn, not reprise a theatrical legend, yet he was the guy who would bring all the housewives out on their front porches come mowing time.

I wanted to head over and give him a heads-up that Maeve was in the house. I pulled a pretty young actress over, introduced her to Maeve, and slipped off.

Dr. Haunschild says it's our call about Maeve's lapse in time. Either we continue to tell her that it is not 1949, since the world around her clearly is not, or we go with the flow. Going with the flow has never been easy for Apples. Well, not for the typical Type-A Apples. But for Apples like Grams and me? Flow is a piece of cake. We'd go wherever the Oklahoma wind blew us if we didn't have the safeguards to keep us in place.

As for Edgar, you don't get very far in business without knowing one of my grandfather's Golden Rules: I scratch your back, you scratch mine.

"Thanks for letting Maeve be a part of this," I said sweetly. "I'd be happy with helping you with whatever you need. Reliable contractors, food vendors, you name it."

"I'll take you up on that," Edgar said evenly, relief washing over his face. "I may have to start working 24/7 to get it all done. I've been trying to call your sister about handling the opening, but she's always on another call or out on business."

"Show up in person." I grabbed my little notebook from my purse and scribbled her address on the pad and handed him the sheet. "She typically works through lunch and stays late at the office. Oh, and weekends, too. I guess she basically works all the time. If you're persistent, I'm sure you two can connect."

I got a quick thrill at the prospect of them together. Her life seemed so, well, empty. She was always so lost in her work—even when work was parties. And Edgar was so different from her usual suit-and-tie frumpsters. A girl could dream, couldn't she? If she left things up to me, she wouldn't be a bachelorette for long. We spun on our heels to face the auditorium. "Shit."

"Excuse me?" Edgar asked.

"My grandmother. She's left. I wasn't supposed to let her out of my sight."

"She couldn't have gone far."

Geez. Had he not remembered how he'd met her in the first place? We rushed backstage where we could hear a group of singers behind the closed red door. I swung it open, relieved Maeve stood among the tenors singing about the princess. The room was full of testosterone. Their big, booming voices nearly knocked me over as soon as I stepped inside. Maeve the Floozy, eh? We hadn't been here thirty minutes and she surrounded herself with handsome men. She leaned against Ax as if she owned him.

"There you are, Arthur, dah-ling," Maeve said, proceeding to air-kiss him. Whew. Disaster averted. I'd keep that to myself.

Ax raised his brows, looking me over as he continued to sing, and winked hello.

When Maeve wasn't looking, I winked back.

Chapter 4

Kelly

I'd never been so happy to throw up.

Nausea is an early sign of pregnancy and I had a feeling I was pregnant. By donor 61894.

In the end, I decided to go with a balance of athleticism, intellect and achievement. I wanted a well-rounded baby daddy, though the phrase made me shudder. I have his chart memorized by heart. I only wish I'd met this guy in real life, but it doesn't matter. I've planned it perfectly. I silently thanked "him" for not rejecting my aging ovum. Hell, with a 20 percent chance of success with the IUI and my lazy ovaries, I only needed to sweet-talk one squiggly guy out of millions to mate. Good little ovum. Plus, I'd picked wisely, and I do mean Mensa-wise.

Ethnic Origin: Swedish, English, Norwegian

New Donor: Yes (I preferred to think my baby might be one of the first from the donor, though certainly not the last.)

Open Donor: Yes (Meaning Daddy is willing to meet Child at least once when Child reaches 18 years of age.) And perhaps, so, too, will I?

Hair Color: blonde

Hair Texture: wavy

Eye Color: blue

Height: 6′ 0″
Weight: 175
Blood Type: O+
Skin Tone: Medium
Years of Education: Occupation: Business administration, music
Kiersey Temperament: Guardian
Baby Photo: Chubby and adorable with baby blues that hold on and won't let go and a heart-shaped mouth you want to kiss all day long with equally kissable, marshmallow cheeks and wispy blonde hair that curled up on the ends.

I'd never even remotely dated anyone with those physical attributes. John was more Mr. SDH (Short, Dark and Handsome), though far from gorgeous. He looked like any regular guy, and I'd been attracted to him precisely because I thought he looked like someone who would be a devoted husband and father in his cozy sweaters and worn denim. (Note to all: Don't judge a dude by his duds.) He ended up being as smarmy as the smarmiest I'd dated, and believe me, I've dated some doozies.

I promised myself looks didn't matter, but this was my child we're talking about. The donor had to make up for my physical shortcomings. My eyes have never been "dove into," though they are hazel. My hair is flat as a board, and the same reddish-blonde as my mother's, though my grandmother and grandfather both had dark hair. I have sprinklings of freckles, only because I don't let myself get out into the sun to turn me into one big freckle head to toe. My sister got the creamy white, non-freckled skin. Grams says the Irish comes from her paternal parents though they were deceased by the time I was born. My mouth is an ordinary mouth (and from my dating record, apparently not so kissable).

I needed to get upstairs to get under my bed into the box where I'd hidden the pregnancy tests for confirmation of what I know is true, but Maeve will be awake soon, and by God, she won't slip out on my watch again.

Trying to be quiet (unlike my retching), I gently closed the bathroom door and found Maeve standing in the hall, arms crossed, waiting for her turn. She scowled, her '40s hairdo mushed to her head from sleep. "Just what we need. Two knocked-up broads," Maeve said. She scowled and pushed me out the way and bee-lined for the toilet where she threw up, too.

Puzzled, I pulled out my notebook and jotted down, "vomit, 8:10 a.m." I'd given Gwen and Bess each a notebook so we could track Maeve's episodes and pass on pertinent information when our shift changes ended. Hopefully, Maeve would return to something closer to "normal" and we'd be able to hire a nurse's aide, but when Mom had tried that at her and Daddy's house, Maeve went through six of them in less than a month. She didn't want them there and even kindly nurses don't care for Patients from Hell.

I added "pregnant" in my notebook and then tucked it in my linen pants pocket while my left breast buzzed with the ringtone of a siren from my phone in my bra. With my paranoid clients, everything was an emergency. Unfortunately, this client, by far my biggest, was also my dad. I appreciated how he'd grown Apple Urban Developments and sat on the board of Apple Oil & Gas and given me a start when I was a fledgling business, but I kept hoping he'd be less of a hands-on client.

When he wasn't calling me with an emergency, he had Victor do it. It wasn't that I didn't mind taking orders from family. It was that they assumed because we were family (and Vic soon-to-be-family) that I should do what they want, no questions asked and put their needs at the top of the list. If I didn't need the money so badly, I'd fire them in an instant.

I let it go to voicemail.

Bess was late again, but I heard her coming down the steps then saw her, barefoot as she emerged with two pots of flowers in her hand, her fingers covered in black dirt. "Which one do you like?" Bess asked. "I want to decide before the crew gets here."

"Both," I said. "But it's not my wedding. Thank God."

"What is that supposed to mean?"

"Nothing. Why aren't you wearing shoes?" I asked. Bess never let us roam around barefoot when we were kids. One of a long list of don'ts.

"Bunions."

"Is that hereditary?"

"I'm going to ignore that you asked that. Besides, it feels good."

My siren blared again, Paranoid Client trying to rattle me before I've even had my second cup of coffee. Coffee! With a smile, I realized it would have to be decaf from then on if nausea meant what I thought it did.

"Got to get this. We'll talk about her later," I said, motioning to the bathroom door, no time to share with her Maeve's "knocked-up" comment, and I didn't want Bess questioning me until I went to Doc's office and confirmed mine, either.

Jervis strolled through the back door and waved as I headed towards the front. I heard him ask my mother, "What's she so happy about?" before Bess launched into the same old story: "Kelly never was a happy child."

She was right. I wasn't a normal, happy-go-lucky child. I don't think I'd ever been this happy. Ever. Even Phillip's call couldn't unnerve me. Until he told me he'd need to cut the new downtown mall project's marketing budget in half. Which strangely coincided with the salary of my creative director, hands down the best illustrator in Oklahoma City. Every great event needed a killer logo.

Of course I blamed my sister's extravagant wedding. He cut my budget to give his little princess the wedding of her dreams. Dammit.

An hour later, I heard my account manager, Justin, plop the bagel box on the conference room table and I identified the high-pitched coo of my sister while I peed on two sticks in my private bathroom outside of my office. Bagels. Couldn't I cut bagels and coffee from the company budget and keep Levi around? Without Levi on board I was no more than an event planner with a penchant for details. He was the one who turned my vision into reality. I would fire no one. Not yet. I would concentrate on something other than work.

Two sticks. Couldn't trust the results of just one. I'd bought a box of pregnancy tests for the office in case this happened. Really, I lived at work more than I lived at home, anyway. I'm nothing if not prepared.

Antique-thin walls meant I could hear Justin and Gwen talking (or flirting, as the case may be) while hopefully all they could hear was the sound of water running in my bathroom sink.

So that's what Phillip had to talk to me about so urgently besides the budget debacle. He'd given Gwen the ice rink project. Her first senior project manager gig. Not only did I have to put up with her messy ways at the loft and Skylar and Shadow (the camera dude) following us around like puppies, I had to work with her. Joy.

We needed to name it, come up with a logo, create the image. The whole thing would naturally be a disaster with Gwen in charge. My sister has never been my direct client before. I am certain she will be far worse than my father or uncles or cousins or even her fiancé have ever been. She's probably been waiting for this day all of her life — to finally get to boss me around for a change.

I stared at the tests on the edge of the sink, eyeballing them back and forth. All I needed was for that second pink line to appear, confirming my vibe. My heart caught in my throat. One of the tests began to turn pink. My God, I'm pregnant! My blonde-haired, blue-eyed, curly-headed angel was on her way. Or his way. My destiny was nine months away.

Or not.

The other test refused to budge from its negative state. Not even a pinkish cast to the second line. No second line. Dammit. I'm not pregnant. Destined to be a shriveled-up cat lady with no Guardian. Good thing there were plenty of strays in downtown. Maybe I'd corral them up and get a head start. You can't officially be called a cat lady if you have a child, even if there's no daddy.

My eyes became drier as I chunked the tests into the trash.

"Where the hell is my sister? She's the one who always yells at me for being late," Gwen shrilled.

I took one last look at myself in the mirror, wondering if my blue-eyed baby would always be a fantasy. If I'd ever be a mother. I inhaled and tried to keep from weeping. Either I'd had a false positive on the first test or a false negative on the second. Either way, I didn't know now and I had to get to my meeting. I'd been so sure. I'd have to get more tests and try again later. Normally I'm very good at delaying self-gratification. I'd waited thirty-five years to do it the old way, hadn't I? Thinking each time I went to the supermarket or to a business networking event that I'd find the father of my child? My mistake had been trusting that John was the one.

"Coming!" I entered the conference room to find my sister looking like a buxom pinup from a WWII bunker. Her hair, her outfit. Her posture, even. All changed.

"Bagels? You know I can't eat carbs," Gwen said as she tossed her Louis Vuitton into an open chair. She slit her eyes at Justin, whose eyes did the equivalent of licking her head to toe. Her hair fell in deep red curls and her new suit accentuated her hourglass figure. She wore four-inch heels, which I've never had the guts to try. The word "bombshell" came to mind.

"I think I prefer the '40s fro," I said, motioning to her locks. I'd never had the guts to dye my hair before, either. I'd figured you should stick with what you're born with, even if the color was miles from va-va-voom.

"I love the red," Justin gushed.

"What made you do such a thing? Jacques talk you into it?" I don't know why I cared what her hair color was, except that we had even less in common. It had been the one thing that made people realize we were sisters.

"Jacques did color it, but someone else mentioned I'd look great as a fire engine redhead." She bit her bottom lip, and my vibes kicked in.

"Who is he?"

"What?"

"Some guy, probably a cute guy from the look on your face, told you to go red and you raced to the salon to do it."

"Alright, if you must know, it was Canty."

I shook my head. "The Canty Maeve was waiting for at the Orpheum?"

"Not that one. Well, yes, Maeve thinks it's that one, but he's an actor. Whole Sinatra thing—sing, dance, act, cause women to fall at his feet. Ax Ellis."

"Please tell me that's a stage name."

"His real name is Akocha. Native American."

I sighed. A long, exasperated sigh. "I thought you'd put the stage behind you. And Grams plus some hot Native American bring you back in." I drew in my fist for emphasis. "Grams thinks this Ax guy is her long-lost pauper?"

Gwen nodded. "It's perfect. Ax and Edgar are kindly playing along. Said she can hang out there all she wants. And you should see how the young actors adore her. She remembers all the songs. Isn't that amazing?"

"Considering she can't remember how to dress in matching clothes, yes. Like a small miracle."

I could practically hear the pitter-patter in my sister's chest. I shuddered and reached for my notebook to write it down. Maeve had slipped further into the well and who knew if we could bring her back. "Do you think it's a wise idea to indulge her fantasy?"

"I'd say it's better than sitting around letting her put fingernail polish on her eyebrows."

Point taken. "I still don't think it's a smart idea."

Gwen pushed back her chair and furrowed her brow. "Excuse me for caring about Gram's welfare. And who says she doesn't have a right to sing anymore? She may be losing her memory, but she's still got her voice."

"And what about Ax?"

Gwen rolled her eyes, but I could see how her body stiffened, on alert, talking about him. "I don't like him in that way. It's not just Ax. It's the whole place. It's the energy of bringing back a legend. To be a part of history. I'm thinking I should audition.." She raised a perfectly waxed brow.

Since when did my sis care about history? She'd always been Ms. What's Next. "I didn't think you were interested in theater anymore?"

Gwen sighed. "Victor didn't like how time consuming it was. Takes up so many evenings and weekends. Can't get away and play with him if I'm in a play. But, yes, I love it. I miss it. I have to convince Victor. And the story is so romantic and funny and the dancing is modern and funky. They're modernizing it, but it's still so effing romantic. And you should see what they've done to the Orpheum already. Ooh, and Edgar says he's been trying to hook up with you, so call him back for godsake."

I groaned. Already so overloaded, and from what my best friend Taylor told me, pregnancy would zap whatever energy I had left. I was working longer hours for less pay. But maybe this was the ticket to keeping Levi on the payroll a little longer. "My staff is already so busy with this ice rink project."

"Ice rink? Oh, Edgar would melt that ice rink in a red-hot minute. You can't say no to him. And I think he'd pay top dollar. Not be stingy like some accounts I know."

"You're talking trash on your own company," I said, trying not to smile. "Your own family."

"Well, come on. Can you believe Daddy has me on a budget for Luxe? And not even a good budget. I'm going to be the laughingstock of the country."

"If it means that much to you, then tell him you'll pay him back when you get paid for the show after the wedding."

Gwen's eyes flickered. "I can't. I need it. For, for starting a new life with Victor."

"Sounds like Cinderella's in a pickle. I think it's ridiculous to blow a bunch of money on a wedding, anyway"

"So you've said. Look, I could use an influx of cash. Something that doesn't involve illegal drugs or prostitution."

I looked down at her feet, at the funky multi-colored buckled, chunky-heeled shoes. "They had to cost, what, $450?"

Gwen blushed. "They're Dolce & Gabbana."

Which meant nothing to me. I've never paid more than a hundred dollars for a pair of shoes. "So it's more?"

"More or less. That's your big plan? Stop buying designer shoes?"

"Not buying more is smart, but I was thinking you could sell the ones you have."

Gwen's eyes widened and her hand instinctively flew to her cheek as if I'd slapped her. I suppose I had.

I rolled my eyes. "What? You hardly wear them. I should do you a favor and count them for you. They get out of their box with less frequency than a werewolf waiting for a full moon. You could probably at least make half your money back.""

Gwen shook her head. "Nope. No way. Sorry. Not that I'd ever consider selling drugs, but selling my shoes sounds just as awful."

"You are such a spoiled brat, you know that? This is OKC, not NYC. I know you're the star of a reality show, but with three months until your wedding, you won't even get to wear your whole shoe collection for the cameras. Let alone all those clothes we've stuffed in Gram's closet."

Gwen stuck out her chin and pouted, something I was used to. I could see I'd struck a nerve.

"I think it's a terrible idea, but I appreciate it nonetheless. I hope you won't be charging the company for it." She winked and opened her notebook.

"Well, you'll think of something. You always do." As for me, I could most certainly say no to Edgar. Even with his tanned features and icy blue stare. Maybe the old me couldn't, but the new me? Ironclad will. "Since Edgar looks like some rugged movie star, he'll want nothing to do with me and he's probably slept with hundreds of women and has diseases the CDC hasn't even classified yet."

Gwen shook her shiny hair. "You always were the pessimist in the family."

"Realist. I see how the world really works, Gwen. And it's not always pretty. And not everyone gets a glamorous wedding and the hunky, rich fiancée and the stupidly expensive shoes."

"Wow. Bitchy much? I think Mom was right. We must all be on the same cycle already. Besides, I refuse to think like that. It can be different. Don't you ever want a change? Something new and big to happen in your life?"

I thought of the tests and had to choke back the knot of disappointment. Of course I knew. I wanted a new life as much as she'd wanted a new hair color. I had to change the subject. "Well, Maeve thinks she's pregnant. Threw up this morning."

Gwen's green eyes widened. "You're kidding. She hasn't mentioned it, though she has been acting strange the last few days."

"Is that what you call it? Come on, she went back in time sixty years."

"But what if she is reliving what really happened? And why isn't she talking about Papa? They were dating in '47. Hell, they got married in '47. Bing, bang, boom. It was a very good year. So you think she had a shotgun wedding then?"

"You're her best friend. Her fellow stage rat. Find out. But don't upset her. Remember what she did last time she thought Grandpa was alive?" Her bedroom at Mom and Dad's house in Gaillardia had been destroyed, like a scene from a movie. She'd broken every breakable in the room and cut herself in the process, requiring 20 stitches, plus a heavy sedative to calm her down. "Maybe she's blocked out Papa because it's too painful."

"I don't know, but you should see how happy she is around Canty – Ax. I've never seen her like this before. I think we should try to find Canty. I mentioned it to Edgar and he thought it would be great to do a sort of reunion on opening night. Though if his event planner would ever return his call, he could talk it over with her."

"You mean the real Canty? You don't even know if he's still alive. You don't even know his last name. Or his first name, for that matter."

"It's got to be in the records, right? Won't be hard since he starred in Princess and the Pauper on Broadway, too. And you don't know that he's not alive. What if he's somewhere thinking about her, too?"

"You're having your movie moment. It's very sweet, Gwen. But finding Canty would serve no purpose other than upsetting Grams. She may not even remember him. She thinks he's Ax because Ax must resemble him a little bit. But an 85-year-old Canty would look totally different. She's not in her right mind. She's sick. We mustn't forget that. She tried to eat three breakfasts yesterday."

Gwen crossed her arms. "I know her short-term memory is shot, but her long-term memory is fine. Okay, except for remembering that any of us are her family. At least it's fine when she thinks it's 1949. I want to find Canty. I have to. I have a feeling about it."

My lips twitched. "Like a vibe?"

"Yes, dear sister. Like one of your infamous vibes."

"Don't you think you should concentrate on your wedding? The show? And your job?"

"I'd rather find Canty." For the first time in long time, my sister lit up. As red-hot as her hair.

"Like anything I can say would stop you."

Justin returned and waited at the door for my approval. I nodded. Gwen turned on her 100-watt smile, pure flirt. "Jacque calls this color Ruby Twilight." She leans over the table, two inches of her cleavage rising as she breathed. "What do you think, Justin?"

The poor boy nearly panted out of his seat. "I like it very much."

I couldn't help but interject. "What does your fiancé think?"

She avoided contact with me, still focusing on my excited employee. "Oh, he barely noticed. Had to point it out to him. Nice, huh?"

How could a man not notice my gorgeous sis? I hated how the Ruby Twilight made her eyes even greener. Like a cat purring for attention. I slapped the table with my palm. "Ice!"

The two stared at me. "Remember? The ice rink? Purpose of our meeting here?"

I grabbed a bagel and smeared on cream cheese. No more forgetting to eat. Maybe I had someone else to think about for once. Someone who depended on me for every cell to multiply. Suddenly the blue eyes and big boobs and ice rink didn't seem very important. That bagel? Way more important. I had to nourish my destiny in case one of those tests was right. So far I had a 50/50 chance, which was a lot better odds than I went in with.

For a split second, I felt sorry for Gwen. My sis, the one who never invited me to her cool friends' parties, the one who made me feel old for not being married when she was 22 and I was 29. The one who always looked impeccably polished. Underneath that shiny new hairdo, the poor thing looked miserable, trapped. Her eyes, the green gems flecked with gold, gave her away. She hated being here, and I only made it worse. I couldn't imagine going to work if I hated it with every fiber of my being. She shouldn't be a project manager. She should be a star. A very humble, down-to-earth star. Ha.

"I do like your hair," I said. "I was just jealous. And I think you should go for it. The Princess thing."

"Justin slip you a truth serum in your coffee this morning?" Gwen's cheerleader grin returned and she winked, her eyelash extensions cartoonish under the fluorescent lights. They reminded me of a moth stuck in a jar, fluttering to break free.

I needed some way to melt the familial wall that had been between us since we were born. But how? And after so many years of letting our distance be okay. Something we could do together that didn't involve her wedding to Jack Ass.

I opened my planner to begin the meeting, the solution clear. "Fine. Now let's find a name for this bad boy."

Gwen shook her shoulders, triumphant. "You mean for Canty?"

"Ice rink, first. Canty, second."

12:08 p.m. Private bathroom at Appleseed Branding & Events

The aggressive knocker at my front door was damn persistent while I'd hoped to pee in private on stick number three. The rest of my staff was out to lunch, and I didn't want anyone screwing this thing up. Yet the knocker was doing his/her best.

"Go away," I muttered, placing the stick on the counter. The last pregnancy test in my stash. I hadn't shed a tear in all my life, save for the time I broke my arm trying out for cheerleader my freshman year in high school, my one abysmal attempt at high school popularity. It was the universe's way of telling me I was the last person on earth to be rah-rah. I actually shed a single tear when the pain shot through my arm from my failed back flip.

Since then, dry eye. Drier-than-the-Mojave dry eye. Yet strangely, I felt a tear tugging behind my eye as I waited for that stick to tell me whether or not I'd be a mother. I pushed away the sad thought that there would be no excited father on the other side of the door awaiting the result.

The knocking increased followed by a male voice yelling through the glass. I began to think something had happened to Maeve. Could it be a police officer?

I left the stick to work its magic and stepped into the foyer of my office where through the glass Edgar stood leaning on the frame of the door. My door. Sadly he wasn't wearing his nylon-fitted cycling uniform, yet he was still Mr. Athletic, a Men for an M.S. Marathon t-shirt over running shorts and Nike running shoes. Still not clean-shaven or cut, with only the slightest glint of sweat on his forehead, and it was a good eighty-five degrees out there. I opened it, feeling a twinge of guilt that I hadn't returned his calls.

"I normally don't have to beat down someone's door to give them business,"

Edgar said, annoyed.

"It's lunch, or hadn't you noticed? You running or working?" I stepped aside to let him in, a smile pressing at my lips.

He looked down at his sports wear. "I run at lunch

when I'm training for a triathlon."

Should've guessed. Means he also swims. I couldn't remember when I'd last even stepped into a pool. I'd always been more of the bookworm in the shade type.

"I hear you work through lunch, so I thought it was worth a shot to swing by." He held his hand out. "You haven't returned my calls."

I shook his hand and a warm tingle shot through my arm and straight to my chest again. Second time. Strange. In all the boring business functions I'd attended, my body had never reacted so instinctively. "I've been very busy. I'm sorry. Returning your call really is on my list."

"Way down on your list, apparently. I've Googled you. Quite an impressive portfolio of clients. Saw that you have an article coming out in WIRED. Sounds like you're pretty connected online and off."

"In my alternate reality, I'm a star," I said with a wave of the hand. "My avatar wears a crown," I joked.

His brow rose. "Ava-what?"

"Avatar, you know, a digital person."

Edgar shrugged. "Not really up on all that. My business partner has been trying to get me on the Internet for years."

I nearly choked. "You're not on the Internet? What does that mean—you don't have a computer?"

Edgar shrugged, sticking his hands in his pockets and surveying the framed promotional posters of events I'd planned on the walls as if he were at the Museum of Art. "Nah. I mean, I do at the office, but I try to avoid it. It's like a vacuum that sucks you in. I'd rather live out here."

"So you're saying you don't get your e-mail messages when you're away? Or check the stock market on your cell phone or have a Facebook or a Linked In account?"

Edgar looked surprised by my reaction. "I've heard of them, don't get me wrong. I get WIRED because I have interest in a few tech businesses, but," he shrugged again, "not my thing. I text if I have to – but I prefer talking," he added, "in person."

I nodded slowly, trying to digest his words. My last three boyfriends were e-addicts, but I couldn't exactly complain that they were checking their e-mails before and after we'd made love, because I'd done the same thing. I'd once joked to John that he was tweeting, "Imma copulate and BRB." (Be right back.) He wasn't amused.

Edgar was different, all right. Not old school as in he didn't know how to use the Internet or e-mail, but that he didn't seem to give a damn.

Through with studying my agency's captivating illustration for "Wine, Women and Shoes," a fundraiser for breast cancer that my sister actually supported (she bought twelve pair of shoes), he seated himself on the butter-yellow leather chair against the wall and I took the one opposite.

I grabbed the notebook from my pocket where I'd written pregnant. The test! It would be developed. If I could excuse myself to take a peek. Wouldn't work. The news would either send me attempting a second back flip or send me to the top floor to jump. Either way I couldn't find out until Edgar left. Besides, I didn't want this stranger to be the first person to know I was having a baby, even if he was a very striking one.

"The renovations are going well for the Orpheum. Producer, set decorator, and choreographer are working with the potential cast. So everything seems to be moving along except for the branding and event planning. You could say I'm in desperate need of your help, like yesterday."

The nerve. I'd seen clients like him before. Clients that expected you to drop your other clients to work on their project 24/7. Just like my family. To meet ridiculous deadlines that not even a superhero event planner with a speed-laced IV drip could meet. On the one hand, I needed the money. On the other, the stress could be harmful to my baby, if there was a baby. At least my family's accounts could get me by.

"I had hoped I'd be able to help you, but after reviewing my current...calendar...I'm not taking on any new clients right now. Especially ones who demand super-speed. Perhaps for your next production."

"Like I said, I'll pay whatever it takes, as long as it's fair."

I laughed and leaned forward, my elbows resting on my knees. "I barely have enough time in my day to get done what needs to be done. I'm not sure I could devote enough time to get you launched by July. Taking care of my business and my family, my grandmother, is my life right now. There's no room left for a theater, even if it was a special ode to my grandmother. I'm sorry."

Edgar did something I'd been waiting for man after man in my life to do. He got down on bended knee. "So you know, I ran four miles uphill and this is killing my thighs. So the sooner you say you'll take me, the better."

I, Kelly Apple-Barton, take thee, Edgar McGuire— screech! That's not what he meant. He wants me to take him on as a client. I tried really hard not to think about his burning thighs.

He held out his hands. "Your grandmother, whom you claim is your life, is the lifeblood of the show. Surely that matters to you."

"What does that have to do with us working together?"

"Well, I'm sure Maeve wouldn't like it very much if we spent all this time on the show and no one came to see it."

My mouth dropped open. "I'm certain another agency can help you."

Edgar smiled and rested his forearm on his bended knee. "Like you said, I've done my research. The biggest agency in town works for my competition. And my assistant tells me you're the most Linked In executive in Oklahoma."

I tried not to smile that he'd been checking up on me. "If your strategy is family guilt, then it won't work. Maeve shouldn't be at the theater, anyway. She can come on opening night like Arthur wanted, and that be that."

"I'm going to be honest, I don't know the slightest thing about opening a show. I'm a real estate guy from California. An entrepreneur. Whatever stage bug my uncle had didn't pass along to me. I don't think I have a creative bone in my body, which is why I need someone creative like you."

For a second, I thought he said he needed a creative body like mine, but I'm certain I heard wrong. That seemed to be a common theme when I was around him. Maybe he was trying to do right by his uncle to make Princess and the Pauper the best it could be. And he was being nice involving Maeve. "Tell you what I can do. I'll give you a referral to another planner and a publicist. She's the real deal, very in with all the journalists. She'll get you the nationwide attention your uncle's show deserves."

He stood, his hands on his hips. "I don't want anyone else. I want you."

My heart skipped in surprise. This man wouldn't take no easily. Gwen had been right about that. But could I refuse him?

"I appreciate your enthusiasm, but I meant what I said. I really don't have the time."

He reached out and grabbed my hand. Why did this still feel like a proposal and why, oh why, was my heart beating out of my chest? "What are you doing now? It's lunch. Can't I buy you lunch?"

I let him hold my hand longer that I should have. "I don't eat lunch. As you stated, I work through lunch."

"Which is exactly what I'm proposing. I'll buy you lunch and pay you double your normal rate for as long as it takes to get the campaign ready."

Lunch, every day with this attractive man? I gulped. It would never work. I couldn't get anything done with him staring over my shoulder. Besides, he was only being nice to get me to say yes and then he'd turn Creep in no time flat. My zillionth Client from Hell, only it would be Cute Client From Hell. Yet I should start eating a good, well-rounded lunch for the baby's sake and having it brought to me wouldn't be such a bad thing. "Restaurants are too loud and takes up too much time getting in and out."

"Give me the menus to your favorite places and I'll bring it at noon sharp every day. The crew takes a break then, anyway. I'll be free."

Bingo, only I hadn't counted on him staying through lunch. "I like to be alone," I said, but even as I said it, it rang false. Could he tell it was a lie? I hated to be alone. I'd been alone for so long. John had left me emotionally before he'd left me for good.

"You're a tough nut to crack, aren't you?"

"Not a nut—an Apple. But, yes. I suppose I am."

"Tell you what. You take me on and I'll tell the director to let Maeve do an encore performance of 'We Did It' on opening night if we can find the original pauper to sing it with her."

The romantic duet closed the show; both Princess and the Pauper saying goodbye to the past as they pledged their love and new life together. If Grams could remember the lyrics, she'd be overjoyed with the offer. It was her final chance to be in the spotlight.

"How did you know we were looking for Canty?"

"A little birdie."

"A bird called Gwen, I presume. But isn't that risky to bank on a woman with Alzheimer's?"

"A risk I'm willing to take. I have a good feeling about it." He smiled, his face brimming with confidence. "Don't you? Surely they'd want to get together for old time's sake, don't you think?"

Canty and Maeve, together again? The original Princess and Pauper reunited. That alone could be some good PR. "I'll think about it." There. At least that should bide me some time. Get me away from his smile and unsettling presence.

"Good, cause my knees and thighs are killing me. I'm not as young as I used to be." His phone rang from his pocket. "Excuse me."

He answered it, his voice going soft while I tried to guess his age. Forty? Forty-two? He was so in shape he looked younger and no receding hairline or hair plugs that I could see. Then I listened in, or I should say I couldn't help but hear every word. "Hey, Leslie, how are you?"

Leslie. Of course there's a Leslie. There's always a Leslie, isn't there? From the coo in his voice, Leslie was someone that mattered. I conjured up a bleached-blonde California girl, taut, tanned and well-titted. Probably a tri-athlete who marathons in the sheets with him.

"I'll call you back in an hour. I promise. You take care now."

So much for fantasizing about working lunches in bed. For the best, because I didn't need any temptation to keep me from breaking my personal vow to Keep Away. Especially from dangerously attractive men like Edgar. That's it. I'd take him on as a client to keep me from sleeping with him, because I'd never sleep with a client.

He hung up and stared at me evenly, daring me to look away first. I didn't, but I can't say I wasn't put under his spell. I rambled on. "You'll have to do your part. Respond quickly. Make decisions as soon as I've presented the options." God, I was crazy. Why couldn't I say no? N-O. Come on, Kelly, you can do it. Stand up to this ridiculously sexy chump.

"Responding quickly won't be a problem. I'll be right here. And besides, my office is two doors down."

He Cheshire-grinned me, the bastard.

"In the vacant insurance building?"

"Not vacant anymore. I'm living in the loft upstairs and working downstairs while I look for a new place."

I placed my notebook back in my pocket, not a single new word written. Lunch. Every day. With Edgar McGuire. Either I was a huge idiot or it was the best man-move I'd made in a long time. Which would be fine and safe because he had this Leslie person and I, hopefully, would soon have my baby.

I'd get a client that didn't share my last name and lunch everyday. I'd need to eat for the baby's sake. Grams could get her final bow in the spotlight and maybe, maybe we'd find her pauper to join her on that stage. Everybody wins, right?

I found myself reaching out for him, extending my hand to touch him, to feel that electricity again. I left him with one word I hoped I wouldn't come to regret: yes.

Thinking gooey thoughts of him all the way back to my office, I caught the light from the bathroom flickering (bad electricity) and I couldn't believe I'd forgotten the test for even a second.

I raced the four steps to the door and closed my eyes. I couldn't look. I had to look. Don't be disappointed, Kelly. You can always try again. You're still young. Thirty-five is not ancient, despite what your sister says. Another egg will eventually drop, drugged or otherwise. If it's negative, it wasn't meant to be.

I opened one eye, but the test was too far away for me to make it out. My legs felt like cement columns. I couldn't move them, but I leaned my body forward, my left hand still on the door handle, when I lost my balance and fell towards the sink, my hand slipping on water on the counter's edge, causing me to knock my head on the way down and send the test spinning through space until it landed on my chest, upside-down.

Blood trickled down my throbbing head, following

the trail of a person's tears. I wiped the tear away and stared at the test on my flat chest as if a spider were sitting there instead. Gingerly, I exhaled and reached and turned the test over.

I stopped breathing. My life, my world, suspended in time. My freckles crested like snowy mountaintops. My vision blurred through the salty tear rimming my lashes.

I was no longer alone.

Chapter 5

"When the apple is ripe, it shall fall." — Irish Proverb

Bess

I've never been anything but a mother, a daughter, a wife.

My whole life has been determined by my relation to someone else in it. Wife of, daughter of, mother of. Now that my daughters were grown, they no longer needed me, yet strangely I found that I needed them more than ever. Perhaps this is why I proposed they move in with me. Why I decided, against my better judgment, to be Gwen's wedding planner on the reality show, a final attempt to keep us close together while there was still time. Time, the evil beast that has already kidnapped my mother. I wondered how long I could keep running before it caught me, too.

Since *Luxe* came into our lives, I felt no more than Mother of the Bride, which I'd looked forward to for so many years. But I hadn't planned on it being under the microscope of a million viewers.

Since my mother Maeve no longer recognized me, and even worse, didn't seem to like me at all as a stranger, I felt abandoned, motherless. Funny thing is I'd never felt that mothered in the good sense when she'd known who I was, either. With the "wife of" only a signature away from disappearing from my identity, I felt more alone than ever. Who was I, really?

As I opened the vanity drawers in mother's dressing room in her Nichols Hills estate, the scent of Oil of Olay wafted in the air, and my mind reeled back, to Mother sitting in the same spot, the dainty gold and green settee, while she sang feverishly into the lighted mirror while I stood at her right side, transfixed by the raven-haired beauty and the silkiness of her voice. I had no idea how a freckled, pale girl like me came from such a glamorous, olive-skinned woman, but I felt lucky. Proud. I'd thought at the time she looked and sounded like a star, but I would never utter those words. I was afraid she would agree with me, and leave me to join Lauren Bacall and Bette Davis on the big screen.

The pride quickly turned inside out. Our ritual, me watching her get ready for an evening out with my father, meant, of course, that she would be leaving, anyway, and as an only child, I would be alone in this big estate with a babysitter who preferred to gossip on the phone than play dolls with me.

All this time later I learned how much she had loved the stage, that maybe she would've preferred a larger audience than one. Which is why it wouldn't hurt to work with the girls to find her old co-star. At this point, I didn't expect her to remember I'm her daughter, but I would love to see her remember something she had loved. Someone she had loved.

The main curse of being an only child was being left to care for mother and her estate. My heart thumping loudly in my chest, I opened up every drawer, every cabinet, every closet. Full, jammed to the gills, as my father used to say. My mother's past lay before me in boxes and bags and hangers. It was all too much, and this was only the dressing room. I'd have to deal with the bedrooms, the linen closets, the kitchen, the garage, still full of daddy's tools, and storage throughout the massive home.

Even though she's my mother, it felt like an invasion of privacy. What secrets would I uncover going through her personal belongings? Would I find a diary full of an inner life I knew nothing about? Details of the past and this "Canty" she raved about? Do we ever really know our loved ones?

As for the estate itself, Maeve and I had discussed passing it down to the girls. Mother wanted it to stay in the family, but as our walk-through with Skylar and Gwen indicated moments ago, it would take a lot of renovation to get the house ready for a reception, let alone updated enough for today's standards.

Mother was never very good with money, and she insisted she had "people to deal with that" after my father passed on. Had I done any better? I didn't even know where Phillip had kept the checkbook. I had a check card and credit cards and that was the beginning and the end of my understanding of my finances. I knew it was time to buck up and take control—both of my own life and Maeve's.

All the homes in Nichols Hills were being remodeled. Gone were the parquet floors and painted cabinets. The traditional-style homes were being remodeled to look like Old World masterpieces full of granite and stone and hand-scraped wood floors. The day before a remodeler and decorator had estimated $250,000 for the remodel—on the low side, they'd added.

Most of my friends in the inner circle wouldn't blink an eye at such a cost. After all, it was still a hell of an investment since the property wasn't in my name until Maeve's death, but Phillip had told me in no uncertain terms that we wouldn't be using "his" money.

My concern went beyond the money. I certainly didn't want to move in to such a large place alone, renovated or not, and Maeve's suggestion that it go to one of the girls seemed too lavish, especially knowing the kind of money that the new owners would have to pour into it.

I could sell it, even if that went against mother's pre-Alzheimer's wishes, but the saying about what makes a house a home also makes it more than a real estate property. It fuses itself to you—you within it and it within you. Yet for whatever reason I felt more comfortable in the still half-finished loft than I had in my Old World style estate in Gaillardia or even this childhood home. I hadn't cared much for living in the Governor's Mansion, either.

I'm not sure which was harder—saying goodbye to by parent's things, or eventually having to do the same in Phillip's and my home. I'd only taken the bare necessities with me to the loft for a reason. I couldn't deal with packing up and moving out. That would make it all so final. But as my mother used to say when she remembered she was my mother, "Get a grip, Bess."

Gwen bound into the dressing room and stood with her mouth agape at the opened drawers and cabinets. I'd nearly forgotten she and the crew were in the other room, talking strategy for the next day's shoot. Flowers, which I was looking forward to because it meant we'd be featuring my childhood friend Samuel, who had been our family gardener since he was a boy. "Looking for something?" Gwen asked.

"I suppose," I said, setting down mother's hairbrush she'd used to brush my hair fifty strokes every evening before bed, even when I was a teenager. I had a feeling I could rummage through all day and not find what I was looking for. "I believe it's time to sort through the house." I studied my daughter, the same bundle of energy she'd always been, yet I had to admit she was all grown up, and about to leave me for good.

If there's an art to letting go, mine would be scribbles in crayon.

"I'll help you. It'll be fun," Gwen said. "The four of us. Wouldn't it be great to see if Maeve remembers any of it? That her things might spark a memory?"

I thought of the hairbrush. I could never throw it away. It would take me weeks, months to go through it all. I had to pick out those things that mattered most, but I was afraid most of all that I couldn't part with anything. "That would be lovely. You okay with having the reception here?" Gwen pulled up a stool in front of me and I instinctively turned her back to me so I could brush her hair. Some things we couldn't — or shouldn't — say on camera.

"I think a reception in the gardens would be totally cool," Gwen said. "I'm sure Samuel will have a good plan."

"I know he's been thinking on it since you got engaged." I smiled at the thought of Samuel sketching in the notebook he kept in the greenhouse. His passion for flowers inspired me to spend more and more time in the gardens.

"The pool probably needs some work, though."

I cringed. The pool renovation alone would be $30,000. Definitely not in the wedding budget. "Perhaps we can cover it with lilies and floating candles and no one would notice," I suggested.

Skylar knocked and popped her porcelain head into the room. "Sorry to interrupt, ladies. We're taking off. Loved what we shot today. Using the china settings from the past three generations of Apples is a great idea. Nice to add some history and heart to the show. Think we can get some photos of you all with Henry from his days as governor and then Senator?" I nodded, then just as quickly, she was gone. Just like her to pop in, give me a long to do list and leave. I'll admit that the day Skylar and the photographer were out of our lives couldn't come fast enough.

"We'll go through the albums before we leave," I said. I purposely hadn't looked at old photos for a long while. Too painful to remember how things were.

The history and heart of my past broadcasted as a wickedly superficial look into the lives of the Haves, though I had a feeling we fell into a sub-group: the Used-to-Haves.

The last thing I'd planned on doing in my sixties was being a part of a national reality show, yet Gwen was certain it would make her a star, a household name, and she really got me with the "saving our memories for posterity" line. She knew how to get me. With Maeve's memory gone, and mine a question mark, I loved the idea of us capturing this special time in our lives for a day when it might all seem fresh to me.

The episodes I'd seen of me so far made me cringe and want to hide underneath my comforter. High definition television is far harsher on one's appearance. My pores looked the size of Rhode Island, my wrinkles, like the Colorado River. Don't believe the beauty ads telling you that you can look young again. I've tried everything but the knife. Though my friends were the primary clientele of the best cosmetic surgeons, I couldn't bring myself to do it. Every inch, even the sagging inches, belonged to me.

What hurt most of all about my image wasn't what was there, but what was missing: the glimmer was gone from my eyes. But it's not youth I want to recapture; it's the feeling that goes along with it. To feel like life is a playground again.

Gwen shook her shiny head of hair. I could practically feel the electricity course through her. "I think the reception here is fantastic. I used to run around in the gardens as a girl dreaming of being a bride," Gwen said. "Besides standing on the patio pretending the roses and orchids were my audience, as I belted out New York, New York."

"You and my mother," I sighed. "Never without a song on your lips. Kelly mentioned you might want to audition for the musical. Have you given it serious thought?" This was a trick question, normally asked so that my daughter would give something serious thought. So often, it seemed, she made rash decisions. Also like my mother.

"I guess it's hard to keep things from each other when we all live together."

"To say nothing of the TV cameras."

"Right. It's weird. Sometimes I even forget it's there. Did she say anything else?"

"About what?"

"Oh, nothing. I need to talk it over with Victor, but I'm sure he'll be supportive."

"Aren't you afraid you're doing too much already?"

"Like you should talk, Ms. Chairman of the Board of Boards."

I stood up and began shutting the cabinets and drawers. Someday. But not then. "Well, believe me, I've been wondering how I got into this mess. I've inherited Maeve's positions all over town, and I'm a poor replica. I should've said no." Dare I give it all up? It was my duty after all. My legacy.

Gwen nodded, then bound up to her feet and followed my lead. "In that case, I should definitely audition. I love the stage a helluva lot more than work. Dad was talking about promoting me to Senior Project Manager as if that's a good thing." She groaned.

I shook my head. "You should know they're grooming you for the top positions in the company. Of course you're father is a traditionalist. He'd rather see Victor take over the company someday and you stay home and raise his grandkids." I'd never worked outside the home, but the idea that Phillip would make that decision for her inflamed me.

"No, thanks, Daddy-O," Gwen said, giving herself a once-over in the mirror and sucking in her stomach. "I know a lot of my friends are having babies, but I'm so not ready for that. 25 in Oklahoma City is like 35 in New

York, you know? And land development and oil and gas? Bor-ing!"

This relieved me, somehow. "Well, your grandfather – and great grandfather's – hard work have made us who we are."

"Not so sound ungrateful, but is it really who I have to be forever?" Gwen said, putting her arm around me. "Sorry. I'm being dramatic. Seriously, off camera, how do you think my big day is shaping up? Especially compared to my east and west coast beyotches?"

"Must you use that word?"

"Fine. Bitches. Is that better?"

I laughed. One couldn't help laugh at Gwen. For a second I saw her at three, same bright eyes and teasing tone. Overcome, I grabbed her and hugged her close. Never one to cry, I sobbed like a baby.

"Mom, Jesus. Are you okay? What did I say? Shit. It's because dad is divorcing you, right? I'm a terrible human being to put you through this right now."

Not wanting to let go, I whispered. "Don't ever say that, Gwennie. You deserve all the happiness in the world. All of it."

"I love you, Mommy." And the way she said it, it was sincere, unlike the times she had come to me wanting something. She's always had two ways of saying "mommy." Honestly, I didn't care if she ever called me anything else. I hated the leaving part of our lives.

"I love you, princess. In light of what's happened, perhaps I should amend that statement. What I meant to say is that you only get one big life. As far as marriage, I suppose your mother can't give you any advice on that. Who's to say this will be your only one?"

"Mother! You love Victor."

"Of course I do, dear. I'm sorry. Like I said, I can't be the champion for marriage right now. As long as you work as hard on your marriage as you are on your wedding, then I'm sure everything will be fine. And as long as you understand that in the grand scheme of things, the napkin rings you choose for your reception don't matter."

Gwen scowled, then kissed me atop the head. With her three-inch heels, she was always taller than me and I could no longer pretend I could wear those damn things anymore. "I get it. Now come on. Let's rifle through the kitchen."

"Hungry? There's nothing to eat in there, though the liquor cabinet is stocked."

"When in Rome," Gwen said. "It'll take the edge off having to go through Gram's things."

When I needed a little push, I could always count on Gwen to shove me. Her lime green heels clicked as she walked across the parquet floor I'd played cars on with my cousins so long ago, the very floors the designer had called, "déclassé," the day before. Screw her.

We took pictures and inventoried everything in the kitchen. Maeve never was much of a cook, but she certainly had the cookware. The bar alone would take an entire afternoon to sort through. I'd thought we'd postpone packing anything for another weekend, but when Gwen jumps into a project, it's headfirst, so we found a stack of boxes in the garage and a roll of duck tape in my daddy's tool box and started packing up.

We could parcel out some of the cooking utensils among us and donate loads of boxes to shelters and women's homes. The thought of giving them away cheered me. Mothers and daughters and fathers and sons breaking bread with the silverware, filling the pumpkin candy dish at Halloween and the Santa cookie jar at Christmas. Though Kelly was far from a cook, we labeled a box for her and gave her the basics as well as a few special entertainment pieces.

My big save? The sunny yellow kitchen timer my mother had used on rare occasion to make me chocolate chip cookies. The sight of it and the sound of the clinking bell brought the very real smell of fresh-baked cookies in the kitchen. I tucked it in my purse, and happily handed over the Kitchen Aid mixer to Gwen, who insisted we take it back to the loft and make some of Maeve's favorite baked goods. I didn't remind Gwen that nothing on Maeve's favorite list was on Gwen's diet though I could care less if she lost another pound.

As Gwen taped up the boxes to donate to the women's shelter, my cell phone buzzed. I barely knew how to use the thing, but ever since Maeve's health went south, I couldn't be without it.

I groaned. Phillip the Bastard.

"I called about the papers," Phillip said, his voice cold and distant.

Papers? Papers. What papers? My mind was gone lately, but I blamed it on stress. My throat caught. *The divorce.* That alone could account for a good bit of that glimmer. Phillip always had impeccable timing, except for in the bedroom.

"Of course. Those papers. The ones that say we're no longer man and wife." The papers were back at the loft on the kitchen desk, sitting ominously in the corner. We'd been separated for three months already, and I'd signed the papers weeks ago, but for whatever reason, I couldn't manage to put them in the mail. Every time I tried to pick them up, they weighed a ton. I wasn't strong enough, but I knew it was all mental. Why couldn't I? I definitely didn't want to be married to a man who no longer loved and cherished me. Had he ever, really?

"I heard about Maeve's stunt at the Orpheum," Phillip said.

"Stunt? It wasn't a stunt. You make it sound like she's a teenager sneaking out of the house." Amazing how protective I felt of her, fluctuating between wanting to hug her and never let go and sending her off to another home.

I could make jokes about Maeve's episodes, but not

him. He no longer had the right. From here on out, Phillip would no longer have a say at all.

"Fine, then, Bess. The banker and estate attorneys will be calling you to finish out the legal matters. Bunch of Maeve's things to go over. May as well do it now so you're prepared."

I knew what he meant. Prepared for her death. Yet how could I deal with the death of my marriage and planning for the death of my mother all at once? I'd rather not know, pushing every bit of it to the last possible moment. I didn't want to see the will, to start dividing up property and sentimental treasures, though I'd survived the kitchen with only a few tears.

I didn't want to journey back on Memory Lane with my husband or my mother. Phillip cared nothing of our past and Maeve couldn't remember hers, so why bother? My only saving grace was that she hadn't given me anything yet, which meant nothing would belong to Phillip. He'd leeched on the Apple name long enough. A black worm wriggling its way to the core.

"I canceled the wedding credit card," Phillip said. "I'm not writing one more check for that wedding. I've got my magic mall investments and alimony to deal with. If the wedding account is overdrawn because our daughter can't stick to her wedding budget, she and Victor will be responsible."

My voice cracked, so I dared not say what I felt. Phillip had lived happily in the lap of luxury thanks to my family's money all these years and sat at the head of my late father's company, yet he could so easily turn off the financial faucet where our daughter was concerned? He's the one that insisted our girls get the best of everything, and I hadn't argued. I'd grown up that way, especially being the only child. Did he really think he could unspoil her?

What would Victor's family say when they found out we wanted our children to pay for their own wedding? It would be all over town in an afternoon, let alone on those dreadful online message boards and maybe even fodder for the show itself

"As I recall, you were the one that thought her participating on *Luxe Weddings* would be good for business. Give the Apple businesses and Oklahoma City more of the spotlight. Help your silly magic mall concept. I refuse to have the Apple name humiliated on national television. Goodbye."

Who was I kidding? Is that all that was left? My name? Words on a piece of paper? I set the phone down, my hand shaking as I spun around and stared at the five-foot-high painting under the stairs of my parents after they were crowned King and Queen of the Nichols Hills Country Club in 1962. I'd passed by that painting a million times as I went up and down the stairs, thinking someday, someday I'll get a guy as good as daddy to love me as much as my father loved my mother.

I hadn't even let go of my maiden name when I'd married Phillip—something he'd agreed to all too eagerly. He was as proud of my Apple name as I'd been. He hadn't even made a fuss when I'd said we should hyphenate the girls' names. He'd thought it cute I was being progressive, yet I think I was really being safe. I knew life would be easier for them with the Apple in place.

But with no apple beside me on the family tree, no mate on the branch, what would I possibly do hanging there by myself? Two names could not even define me any longer. Our marriage had caught a disease and it slowly spread until one day we shriveled in our unhappiness. Our union was what had become rotten and black and fell from the tree.

Without Phillip and the comfort of a pretend good marriage to the outside world, I had no clue how I would spend my retirement. Would I spend the next twenty or thirty years alone? Would I never feel the exhilaration of love again? Would I be forced to gather up the crumbs of others' joy and make them my own?

If I hadn't cared all those years, then why now? I'd been content to live a shadow sort of life versus a spotlight life like my mother. So what was eating at me? Stress? It had to be stress. Surely it would pass like the hours and the days.

As Gwen began flipping through the photo albums in the sunken living room to pick out her favorites to feature on the show, I heard the mower on the back lawn crank to life and stood by the back window, watching Samuel and his crew begin to work. God, if things were as bad as Phillip made them sound, would I have to let go of Samuel, too?

I'd found myself working more and more in the nursery behind the loft, not only because it had become our back yard since we moved into the loft, but because digging in the dirt—cutting, pruning, shaping, seeding—became therapy. Some days I worked for hours alongside Samuel, our gardener since we were classmates, and the manager at our tree farm. He had tended my parents' gardens in Nichols Hills for 40-plus years—ever since he was a boy with a lawnmower and a dream.

The handsome widower had always been real and genuine, and I didn't have to stop and think about what to say to him when we worked in the gardens together. I think I may have looked forward to our exchanges more than he did, though I'd never ask. So nice to have a friend again, totally removed from Phillip and this wedding business. Funny how I'd transitioned from awaking with the dreadful thought of being alone and hating Phillip to looking forward to something again.

I walked through the back door and waved Samuel over to talk about how to make the gardens, and more specifically the outdated pool, look great on camera without a pricey renovation. I hated being surprised on camera. My husband—ex—may be the king of the magic malls, but Samuel knew real magic—he held Mother Nature in the palm of his hands.

"I know the perfect thing on a budget," he said, with the tip of his hat, and we walked around the pool as he laid out a vision plucked neatly from his imagination. We would go vintage. Do a retro-modern theme for the tables, lounge chairs, pots and simple flower arrangements. Pared down. Simple, but elegant.

"It's perfect," I told him, as I patted his broad back, and when he looked back at me, I saw something I hadn't noticed in the past. The gold flecks in his eyes were the color of a sunrise, and I felt something rising within me as I fell into his gaze.

A moment later (had I even breathed?) my phone shrilled again. My cousin Deidre, the only niece my mother had liked before her diagnosis, was on the line. "Don't panic," she said in a panicky voice, "but when I came back out of the bathroom, your mother was gone."

Chapter 6

Back at the loft, I raced through the empty rooms, screaming both my mother and Deidre's names. I felt the panic of new motherhood, the fear that something would happen when I turned away for a single moment. Like when I'd been talking to the vacuum salesman while not a foot away Kelly stuck her barrette in the electrical outlet or the time that I'd been doing dishes and looked down to find Gwen drinking the dishwasher detergent. Yes. That's exactly what this was like. I hadn't been a great mother the first time around. I seemed to goof up what other mothers did with ease. I could never get my Rice Krispie treats right for one thing, let alone make a decent Halloween costume like the other moms. How strange to feel that again after all this time.

"Maeve!" I sang out as I trampled down the steps, light-footed and heavy-hearted. At the bottom of the stairs lay a black rose like the one in Maeve's hair the night before. Like Cinderella had dropped her magic slipper.

With a lineman sort of tackle, I pushed the old door open to the antique store, where the waft of furniture polish and centuries-old aromas from around the world welcomed me. This place smelled more like home than any home I'd ever lived in. For better or worse, it smelled of my childhood.

The memory of furniture shopping in Paris washed over me. I was only 3 or 4 years old at the time. While Mother negotiated a deal in French, I'd caught sight of a stained-glass blue jay in the window, spinning from the air conditioner above it. Two or three feet away. So close I swore I could touch it. The bird whistled, beckoning. I left Mother's side to take a closer look, but the bird turned out to be much farther away than it had seemed. After I had wound around the tall bedposts and china hutches and sofas, I finally reached the bird and stood up on my tiptoes to take a closer look. The air conditioner vent provided the whistle I'd taken for song, but when I spun around, my mother had vanished. Lost. For a brief moment, no longer than the space between two heartbeats, I feared she had run away from me.

"Mrs. Apple. How do you do?" Jervis asked from behind the counter, looking down at my bare feet. "Missing something, are we?"

Deidre rushed at me, her whole body tense as she raised her arm pointing to the Early Century department. "Seems she's found a cozier spot. I should've known she'd try something when I refused to run lines with her. Is she in some musical?"

I gulped back a cry. At least she was safe. "Yes. No. I mean, she thinks she is. Princess and the Pauper is being revived."

Deidre clapped her hands. "That explains it then." She looked at her diamond-encrusted Fendi watch, a pretentious pairing with her track suit, and air-kissed me before a good long look into my eyes that made me feel more like her child than her cousin. "Don't you think it's time, Bess? She needs to be in a good home."

"This is a great home," I defended, though I certainly knew what she meant. Round-the-clock Alzheimer's care. Losing Maeve wasn't just irresponsible, it was dangerous.

"Is there a reward?" Jervis' raised his salt-and-pepper brow above his tortoise-shell frames. He smiled and pointed toward the Early Century department. I hustled through Renaissance and English Tudor to Early Century, where all the furniture one would find in a home in the early 1910s-1940s could be found.

My heart still racing, I eased onto the corner of the bed, contemplating whether or not to wake her. Outside the antique store window, cars whizzed past on Sheridan to the high-rise law firms and downtown shops. Amazing the morning rush hour hadn't awoken her. You never knew what you were going to get when you woke her up. Maybe I would be Maeve's daughter again. I'd see if she'd like to go to the Skirvin to sample menus with Gwen and I later, though it was risky with the LW crew in tow. No telling what she would say on camera. At least it wasn't live. The Skirvin had been around in the '40s and she still loved to give the world her opinion about everything.

Irked that Gwen had let Victor's mother select the reception hall, I banged my head on the headboard. If she wanted Catherine's opinion so badly, why didn't Catherine take over all the wedding coordination?

My back ached from running and I lay beside Maeve, next to the dresser with two hurricane lamps and an old black-and-white photo in a pewter frame beside a voluminous spring floral bouquet. I stared at the happy couple in the picture, the woman wearing the same costume as my mother had at the Orpheum. Upon closer examination, I saw that it was my mother—my drop-dead-gorgeous mother, dressed in character as Princess.

No wonder so many guys had been head over heels for her. The man to her left wore a costume, a chain-mail shirt and elbow and kneepads made of metal. Must've been from the scene when the pauper had pretended to be a knight to win the favor of the king. The man held an open-faced helmet in his left hand, his right hand around my mother. His mouth open, caught mid-laugh. Handsome as all get-out. Definitely someone the girls would flock to the theater to watch.

I plucked the photo from the table and held it inches from my face to get a better look. Lord almighty. A gasp of air escaped my lips. The chemistry between them had been caught on camera, captured for all time. Maeve, her arms around her co-star, flirting with the camera. I thought I'd seen all of Maeve's photos. In fact, I'd spent an entire summer five years earlier putting them into albums for mother's 80th birthday. So where had this one come from? Did Maeve have a secret stash somewhere? A secret, period? I hadn't any photos of her final performance, for after I was born, she left the theater stage for good, immediately transitioning to a patron of the arts.

Using my nails, I pried the cover off the back of the frame and slid the photo from the glass. I expected to find mother's handwriting, but instead I found the large scrawl of a man's: *To my sexy little songbird Mae-by. I'll never forget you. Love, Canty*

So he had a nickname for her, too. Mae-by. Please. So this was Canty, the she'd hoped would give her a "stiff one" the week before? The one she'd mistaken the young actor for at the Orpheum, the dirt on Maeve that my daughters were bound and determined to dig up — hopefully, only figuratively. I thought back: sixty years and not one whisper of this Canty fellow until tha point? Everyone knew she had loved musical theater and had performed since she was 16, but she hadn't talked in depth about it. Almost as if that time in her life hadn't existed at all.

I settled in next to her. I had practically leapt from my bed at home into Phillip's, and he hadn't been a cuddler, even in our early days of marriage. He claimed I was too hot after lovemaking, and he hadn't meant it in the complimentary sense. And that was decades before hot flashes ensured he wouldn't get close to me, either.

I felt the tears hit the pillow before I even felt them on my face. I couldn't believe I was 60 years old and missed my mother — yet she was only six inches away from me. May as well be six thousand miles for all the good the proximity did. Everyone thinks about the fantasies mothers have about their daughters, but truth be told, we are daughters first.

Children, even ones nearing social security, have fantasies about their mothers, too. If we liked our mothers, we hope we can spend more time with them as we age, doing the things we never had time for in our youth though it would've been nice to do them when our bodies cooperated. If we didn't like our mothers when we were younger, we hope we'll grow to like them or that old age will turn our mothers a little softer, a little kinder, a little more loving; a lot more loving.

We missed that boat. She hadn't softened before Alzheimer's took her from me. I'd always thought "mother love" was unconditional, that if everything else got stripped away you would cling to that tiny seed of maternity. The final thing to go. The love that remained when the ashes were swept away. I'd always hoped love was a spirit, not a memory.

The snoring got louder and then stopped. I turned, fearing she had stopped breathing. Her eyes were open and for once I saw in them the flicker of recognition. "What are you doing up so early, baby? Have a bad dream?"

Baby. She hadn't called me baby, since ... Since I don't remember. Had I ever been her baby, even when I was one? Had she returned to present day? I cleared my throat, putting on a happy voice.

"Time to rise and shine. Got a to-do list a mile long, though it doesn't seem right to deal with a divorce and plan for a wedding at the same time. Phillip has all our money tied up in some new development deal and you seemed to give away most of what Henry had saved for your retirement. Not that it's not very generous of you, of course, Mother, but everyone in town believes our toilets are made of gold. I'm afraid to meet with the banker and the estate attorney to see what's left. Anything you need to tell me?" I rushed to get it all out before the wire in her brain tripped again.

Maeve smirked. "If it makes you feel better, Phillip is a boring prick."

She's back all right. I exhaled. "How can you talk about your son-in-law that way?"

"Now that he's an ex I can say any damn thing I like about the man, not that anything would stop me before. And as for money, I'm sure I've taken care of you and yours?"

I held my tongue. No use explaining real estate rich and cash poor. Worst of all, I wondered if there was even enough left to care for Maeve.

I hated how accustomed to this lifestyle I'd become. How I'd cried when I'd moved out of my estate in Gaillardia to live in the loft downtown, though I could've kicked Phillip out instead. I couldn't stand being there alone. Not in the huge house with the golf greens he played every morning and the country club he liked to dine in every night. If I'd stayed, I wouldn't have truly gotten away from him. We would have more than enough cash on hand if Phillip agreed to sell our home there and downsize himself, but he'd said he'd rather be struck by lightning than to sell that house.

I keep praying for a storm.

Maeve raised her hand to her throat. "Why do I sound so hoarse?"

I debated whether or not to tell her she's been singing at the Orpheum every night helping the young starlets. It might be like telling someone the ridiculous things they did while sleepwalking. I chanced it. "You've resurrected Princess Mae."

"I don't sing anymore," she said stiffly, removing her hand from mine. "And I don't want to be called that name. Ever."

I handed her a cough drop from the dresser. So much for warming her up to talk about Canty. I tried to ease into it. "You got a letter from Arthur McGuire two weeks ago. He bought back the Orpheum before he died."

Mother's face hardened. "Arthur died?"

Which made me the Bad News Bitch again. "He's asked his nephew to oversee bringing *Princess and the Pauper* back. You've been going to the rehearsals, overseeing things."

"Arthur never forgave me for not following him to New York."

I'd heard the story only once, a long, long time ago. Arthur had offered to give her the part on Broadway, which would've made her a national star, a household name. Instead, she married my father and gave birth to me while another unknown actress hitched herself to Maeve's star.

I thought of telling her I'd read the letter, that Arthur had more than forgiven her and still loved her with his last breath. "But the actor that played the pauper went on, didn't he? This was on your dresser," I said, holding the photo of she and Canty closer to her.

She flinched, as if I'd cursed or slapped her. Obviously, she couldn't remember that she'd mentioned him the night we found her on the stage. She thought she'd never uttered the man's name before, let alone slipped up and let a photo of them together be found.

Her eyes rested on the photo and her brows rose. Her eyes glossed over with tears. "Where did you get this? Have you been going through my things?"

My body tensed. I knew I shouldn't have brought it up, but my own daughters had taken it upon themselves to try to find this guy for mother's sake, some sort of "going away gift" they called it, wanting them to duet again, but it wasn't a good idea, not knowing how she really felt about him. Why the secret? If he was a fling, then why hide it at all?

I strained to keep my voice calm. "No, Mother. I said

it was right here on your dresser. I'd never seen it before. Canty was more to you than a co-star, wasn't he?"

She stuffed the photo underneath her pillow like a child might whose lost a tooth and waits for the Tooth Fairy to take it away in the night. Maeve said nothing, but her eyes remained open, staring out the window onto the busy street, thinking. Remembering. "Canty was every note in every song I ever heard. I can't listen to music without thinking of him."

"Is that why you gave up singing? Why you didn't go to New York?"

Her lips pursed. "You're why I gave up singing." Gentle, tinged with blame.

I could feel the rocks in my throat. "But you loved him, didn't you?"

Maeve flinched again. "What does it matter now? If I had to do it over again, I would've ...."

"Would've what, Mother?"

"Oh, it's no use now. What's done is done. But now that I'm old, I see things clearly. I should've been honest when I had the chance. Before it was too late. Now it's in the past, where it shall remain."

"You said in the end it's all we have, remember?"

"It's too painful to think about. Do one thing for me, Bess."

"Anything."

"I know I should've said this to you sooner, but don't live a life of regrets. No matter how painful. And don't make promises you can't keep." Her voice cracked.

"So you want me to promise never to make promises?"

"You're a brat, you know that? A brat disguised as an angel." Maeve huffed.

I smoothed the blankets over the curve of her spine. "Mother, please. I'm trying to have a conversation."

Maeve patted her pillow, then pulled the frame out from under it. "What the hell are you thinking putting a frame under my pillow?"

"I didn't, Mother. You did. Less than a minute ago."

"What do you take me for? An imbecile?" She tossed the frame onto the cement floor, the glass breaking and shooting across the room. She turned away from me, shutting me out. "And I'd appreciate a little more room. Don't you have a bed of your own? I don't need a goddamn bed-warmer. If I did, I'd get a dog. You're hot as a volcano."

The anger rose within me, as sure as the sun. I wanted to shake her, to scold her, like a child. Instead, I knew what I'd do. I would carefully pick up every sliver of glass, sweep and mop to make sure she wouldn't get cut when she got out of bed in a few hours. As usual, I would get cut in the process.

As I swept the photo of the young, carefree actors into the dustpan, I plucked the photo from the wreckage. I decided I'd keep it myself. I studied Canty's face, the curl at his forehead, the dimples on his chin and cheek, the confident smile that seemed to say he had the world by a string, and surely this woman's heart, too.

The thought hit me like a sour note. She didn't love my father the way she'd loved Canty. She was too bruised from loving this man. This married man. God, my mother, the adulterer. A sick feeling crept over me. What would she have done differently? How was she dishonest? What was her regret she was so willing to take to the grave?

If he was every note in every song she ever heard, how could I not find out more about him? Phillip and I were always off-key, two different melodies trying to play the same song. But Canty had set my mother's world on fire before I'd come along and I had to know what he'd done to extinguish it. Had my father been her second choice, her back-up plan?

I thought I knew everything about her. What if this one thing could explain it all? Explain her whole life after? Not surprisingly, my girls were absolutely right. Finding Canty had to be a top priority.

With the photo in hand, I bee-lined through the store, holding my breath, holding back the tears until I'd reached the outdoors, and let them escape into the spring air. Samuel's tall, athletic frame appeared from behind the Empire Blue Butterfly bush, concern on his face.

"You want to talk about it, Bess?" He removed his gardening gloves and ran his hands over his worn denim jeans before adjusting his Australian cowboy hat. The man embodied the word "comfort." Some girls may relieve their stress with comfort food, a nice dish of ice cream, a piece of chocolate, or even a martini. All I needed was a heaping scoop of Samuel's husky voice, a solid minute of staring into his Godiva-colored eyes and the lightest touch of his arm brushing up against mine.

But then, I'd never tell him that, would I?

"I'm fine, Samuel" I said, but the slightest tilt of his head told me he didn't believe a word of it.

"Come sit a spell," he said, motioning to the bench in the middle of the nursery.

"I don't want to be a bother," I said hesitantly.

"You're anything but. Besides, I'd like your opinion on some things I was going to go over in the taping tomorrow. I'm a bit nervous."

A man who wanted my opinion? My daughters may not want it, but he did. I flushed with joy, forgetting all about Maeve's behavior for the moment. "Alright, then. If you insist."

Thank goodness he did.

Chapter 7

Kelly

"I can't perform without it," Maeve said as she brought out an intricately carved jewelry box I'd never seen before as we rummaged through the dusty attic above the loft. After only a few moments of the Present with Bess a couple days before, Maeve had returned to believing she was twenty-five again, which made me her gal pal who she didn't think was all that fun. "My daddy made it," she said lovingly.

Looking for a piece of Maeve's past, a tiny heirloom, proved as difficult as finding Canty. You'd think in this day of instant Googling, we'd find Canty and already have them united by now. Yet with privacy concerns, it was still very possible to stay hidden or at least make the hunt difficult for the hunter. If we couldn't find him, Maeve wouldn't get her final performance, and I so badly wanted to see her on that stage, doing what she loves. We still weren't giving up—not on Canty or her lucky pin.

After a half-hour of digging, Maeve's eyes gleamed. "There it is," she said, pulling the green and blue butterfly pin from the box. "I can't believe I'd forgotten where I'd put it."

She placed it in her hair while I studied the rest of the contents of the box. More hairpins, a strand of pearls and a simple platinum band with three small emeralds. I picked it up, but Maeve snatched it from my fingers. Definitely not pieces I remember playing with as a child rummaging through Grams' things. I wondered why she'd stored them here instead of in her home.

"Engagement ring?" I asked fingering the beautiful ring.

Maeve snorted. "The engagement ring from Henry has a carat on top of it. I haven't said yes, you know that." She snatched it from my hand and slid it on her ring finger. "Canty gave it to me for my birthday, hours before Henry proposed to me. I must be crazy to love it more than the big diamond one. Don't they say diamonds are a girl's best friend?" Her tone was thick as syrup.

"Two rings," I said softly, then added, "Some birthday." Grams' twenty-fifth birthday party became an Apple legacy. The evening Henry Apple asked for her hand in marriage, after having only dated a few short months. Of course there had been no mention of another man in the picture—a married actor at that—and it had taken her several weeks to finally say yes to Henry's proposal. What had prompted her change of heart? Had receiving this promise ring from Canty caused the delay?

Thinking back to my 25th birthday, I not only did not get two rings from two handsome men, but my boyfriend had forgotten my birthday altogether. I kept thinking he hadn't mentioned it because he had a big surprise in store, but the only surprise was that he could remember every important date in Sooner football history, but couldn't remember one day concerning mine. He had tried to make it up to me the next day, but can you really?

My grandfather had joked that Maeve wanted to drive him crazy waiting, but I had a notion she had been waiting for something else—someone else.

Maeve could see the question hanging in the air between us. "It's a promise ring. A promise he'll come for me. A promise he'll love me forever." No maybe, possibly, we'll see. Stated as fact. Solid as stone.

"So he's leaving his wife." I obviously knew the

answer, or thought I did, but I was so fascinated with her steadfast conviction. She believed in this guy. Believed love would conquer all.

"Unhappiness is not reason enough for divorce in this day and age, is it?" Maeve said. "You know as well as I do that men don't leave their wives if they've any morals or scruples. Besides, his wife is expecting their first child soon. He can't very well leave a pregnant wife now, can he? His musical career would be canned. He wants to star on Broadway. As do I."

I nodded, wishing I could tell her that Canty had in fact starred on Broadway. Her pauper pretending to be a knight had become the world's favorite Pauper and leading man in a dozen movies and musicals thereafter. He'd even been typecast as the swashbuckling hero adventurer, which fared well for him while he was still young. But I didn't tell her. We did everything we could to keep from confusing her, and what would happen when she found out that she didn't become the star she'd dreamed of? Best to keep the bad news at bay while she was in the state of the past.

"Let's get changed so we won't be late," Maeve said.

Earlier that day Maeve had selected a cool Katharine Hepburn-style pantsuit from her vintage makeshift closet of clothes from the '40s my mother had picked up at a pricey thrift store that wasn't so thrifty. I've never been much of a dress kind of girl, never wanted to feel feminine. I insisted I wouldn't wear a dress, yet Maeve insisted my modern-day pants ensemble looked "dreadful." (You're one of those women, Maeve had said with a quick nod of her head. The kind that doesn't wear dresses, doesn't eat lunch and doesn't make babies the old-fashioned way. Yes, Maeve, I'm one of those.)

"Even though you'll most likely be sitting in the darkened theater, I'd appreciate if you would at least appear stylish when the lights come up," she had said. Thank God for Hepburn's insistence on wearing pants.

Frankly, I loved it. If Gwen could change her hair color, the least I could do is change my pantsuit.

A working night out. The only kind for me, right? Otherwise I'd be curled up on my coach eating Nutter Butters and watching an old Doris Day flick, hoping inspiration struck for the naming of the ice rink and the downtown magic mall, the latest project for Phillip to dump on me. Only called "magic," because it was supposed to feel like a shopping and dining fairytale.

It would be weeks before that run-over-by-a-truck-feeling would dissipate, but I promised myself I wouldn't complain about all the first trimester stuff like a lot of new moms-to-be. I wanted this baby, and I was determined to be strong, nausea and all. Baby names slipped into my brainstorming sessions with more frequency. Old-fashioned and traditional? Unisex? Or something crazy like Apple Apple. That one made me laugh out loud.

While I waited for the end of the first trimester to tell my family, I had to tell someone, so I told my best friend Taylor my big news. She'd been the one person I'd introduced the three final candidates for daddydom to, and she'd agreed I'd picked a prince on paper. God, it felt good to say the words! *I, the workaholic, sucky-luck-with-men Kelly Apple-Barton, have a tiny Apple sprouting!*

Yet why did she pause a good two seconds before telling me how thrilled she was for me? I mean, come on, let's face it, the woman does most of the child rearing anyway, right? Her hubby Jake wasn't exactly on board with the whole daddy thing until the squirt materialized. And Taylor admitted he wasn't Über-Daddy. But he was a help. Okay, her exact words were: I think I'd shoot myself if he didn't take over every now and then.

If Taylor had paused, my family would most likely faint. I had to come up with a strategic plan first. One couldn't blurt it out over spaghetti on a Sunday after church. I could just imagine what they'd say about my unconventionally produced child. And that I'd done it on purpose? I'd probably be plucked off the family tree for good.

Work first. I could always count on work to be there to squelch any emotional wallowing, though Edgar's presence over lunch had been more distracting than I liked. In four days, he'd convinced me to walking lunches next to the river. We brainstormed about the Orpheum and the musical, I got some much-needed exercise (was that a calf muscle on my lower leg?) and we ate after.

Edgar, I had no trouble Googling. There were more than a hundred articles on him.

McGuire Raises Three Million for Breast Cancer Foundation...Entrepreneur Starts Dollar Zone Franchise...McGuire Finishes Third in Iron Man Triathlon

And oddest of all:

California Business Tycoon Opens Executive Adventure Tours

Not only does Edgar swim with giant squid, he gets people to pay *him* to swim with them, too. And sharks. And skydiving in the Alps. And hot air ballooning across the Grand Canyon.

The Edgar I ate lunch with everyday, the guy who preferred ripped jeans and flip-flops to a business suit, a tycoon? In my world, no tie meant no tycoon. Even more, he never talked about himself or any of his ventures or adventures. Instead, he asked about me. My family. And we talked in depth about the musical, which he loved way more than he would admit. As a producer, he was a natural, but he seemed like there wasn't anything he wasn't natural at. If only he wouldn't look at me. If he would keep his eyes anywhere but on me, I'm a hundred and ten percent certain I wouldn't fall for him.

I blamed any sexual feelings on the surge of hormones and not any signals he may be emitting that he was attracted to me, too.

Maeve put a bumblebee hairpin in my hair, something she hadn't even done when I was a child. "I've been trying to shift Arthur's attention to Gwen, but I think he might be more your type," she said.

"His type?" I tried to hide the surprise in my voice. She was talking about Arthur from 1949, not Edgar, yet it still felt like a compliment.

"I mean a working woman. A secretary."

The most logical choice out of the traditional nurse, secretary, teacher choices from her time. I did practically live at my desk.

"So why aren't you interested in Arthur?" I asked, wondering if Arthur had the same easy charm that Edgar possessed.

"When you are choosing a husband, you must look at his past. Far too many girls don't follow this bit of truth. If a man did something once, he's likely to do it again. Don't think for a minute that you can change him. See, Arthur's first wife left him because he doesn't love taking creative gambles. And when he's the most creative, he happens to be the most drunk. And when he's the most drunk, he happens to fall in love with whatever girl is within arm's reach. Get my drift?"

"Like a tidal wave." Maeve had been right. Arthur had gone on to marry four more women after he'd arrived in New York, and became the serial philanderer and hard drinker Maeve had prophesied. His reputation was legendary, and I wondered if Edgar was anything like his uncle in that respect, too.

"But Canty is married, and … "

"Cheating on his wife with me. I know." Maeve shrugged. "My head is telling me to get as far away from him as possible, but my heart, my dear, says something else entirely. Not to mention what other parts of my body demand."

I thought of Edgar again, and how we hadn't talked

about our past relationships, which was for the best. I don't want to hear about all the women he's left broken-hearted after whisking them away in hot air balloons or camping with in the Amazon. He had to be a womanizer. Look at him. Then there's Leslie, whomever she was.

In the end, Maeve had made the right choice then, hadn't she? She picked the stable one, the leader, the one who would never cheat or leave her. She chose Henry and lived a grand life. If only she could remember it.

I reassembled some of the piles in the attic, knowing Mom would have a fit when she saw how we'd torn up the place. I would write in my notebook what we'd done to remember to tell the others about it. Lucky hairpin. Promise ring. At the very least it told us how serious Canty had been for Maeve, though it didn't tell us what changed their minds.

Maeve stood in front of an oval antique pedestal mirror, one that wasn't in the showroom downstairs. Another broken heirloom. She rubbed her hands over her swollen belly, her pooch the result of the shifting of body weight brought on by old age.

"Do I look pregnant?" Maeve said, trying to suck in her gut to little avail. Two inches, maybe.

"Not at all," I said, which wasn't really a lie since the rest of us believed she looked like an 85-year-old woman with a potbelly.

"Good. I'll have to start wearing jackets, I guess. Let's get on with it. I promised Gwen I'd teach her the dance moves before the rehearsal begins," Maeve said. She began descending the stairs to the loft with surprising agility, her voice bouncing up the stairs behind her. "I swear the girl inherited two left feet."

My phone vibrated, tickling my chest. A text message appeared in the green bubble. Edgar. Tiny bubbles popped in my head.

What about dinner after we take in the theater? Edgar wrote.

Can't. Client from hell.

He can't be that bad. Brownies?

Must stop feeding me.

We'll paddle it away tomorrow on the dragon boat.

I had to read it again to make sure I understood. Had Edgar asked me out on a Saturday morning date to dragon boat? I'd been to and planned more than a hundred events at the Chesapeake Boathouse on the Oklahoma River, but hadn't ever been on the river or in a kayak or dragon boat. I hadn't even rowed a canoe since I was a Girl Scout. My heart flip-flopped.

Planning on sleeping in.

Ha! Doesn't start until 11. See you in 30.

A man who knew the way to a woman's heart was brownies, but what about adventure? I wasn't sure if he was the anti-executive executive or just a charmer so smooth I couldn't sniff out the sleaze yet. Surely paddling wouldn't be bad for the baby though I had a feeling it would be a killer on my thighs. It wasn't a real date. He was doing what he does best—getting people to add adventure to their lives. For him it was as common as a morning commute.

Besides, plenty of agencies go golfing with their clients. Edgar wasn't the golfing type. Too mundane for him. So I supposed I could suck it up for some dragon boating.

I put the phone back in its bra-holder and took one last sweep of the attic, trying not to over think the invite. Edgar didn't know anyone here, that's all.

A stack of framed black-and-white photos underneath a flour sack caught my eye. While the bag had holes from mice, the pictures were in good condition—no warping and only slightly yellowed. The top photo showed the exterior of the Orpheum, the second photo of the cast, the male actors chivalrous and handsome surrounding their star Princess with her long, flowing dark hair. I'd seen the photo when I was a child, but I had no idea the man standing to her right, the one with the crazy curls and wide grin, had not only been her character's lover, but her lover in real life.

"Maeve!" I called.

She looked over her shoulder. "What is it now?"

I held up the group photo. "Look what I found."

Maeve tilted her head. "I can't believe it's framed already. We took the photo last week."

"Canty sure looks happy about something."

Maeve leaned her frame on the banister. "He'd better. We'd made love in the coat closet 30 minutes earlier."

What do you say to that? Go Grams? I remembered the question I was supposed to get answered for our mission. "Where do Canty's people live?"

Maeve thought for a moment. "He's got kin in Tulsa. Why ever would you ask?"

Because I'm going to find him. To find your co-star. The one with enough morals and scruples not to leave his wife for you so long ago. "No reason," I said. "I can definitely see the Irish in him."

"Why do you think they have to cake so much makeup on him to make him look darker on stage? He's so white he'd practically blind us under the lights!"

So that's why she thought Ax, who was a Native American, was Canty with makeup on. No way of knowing if Maeve's timeline was accurate. How would I know if she'd been dating Canty and my grandfather at the same time? She couldn't remember to put shoes on before we left the house, let alone specific details of her past. Or did she? Was 1949 the one time from her life that her memory was clear?

With the stack of frames heavy in my arms, I descended the steps carrying the past with me. I only brought down the theater photos, leaving behind the photo Maeve believed hadn't even been taken yet: the engagement photo of she and Henry, a photo I'd never seen. Perhaps she'd never hung it because she wasn't smiling, the light completely gone from her eyes. What happened in the space between those two photographs? Had she gotten "knocked up" by grandfather, as she so eloquently put it? Is that why the wealthy heir had asked her to marry him so quickly, after a few months of dating? Out of obligation? If Maeve's timeline was correct, was my mother the product of a shotgun wedding and not the "honeymoon" creation she'd been told?

Had Maeve decided to settle for the one sure thing?

Chapter 8

Gwen

Sex with Victor was hotter than it had been in months, thanks to the triple-dimpled Ax. Like most women, I've fantasized about other men, usually celebrities, and lately I'd gone retro. Hollywood heartthrobs pushing up daisies, to be exact. A few cases in point:

1. Early Elvis (Lord, what those hips are capable of!)
2. Marlon Brando (They don't call it Streetcar Named Desire for nothing.)
3. James Dean (He's a rebel with a cause in my little black book.)

The trick to making fantastic fictional love with a celebrity (dead or alive) is to watch the star's movie within two hours prior to lovemaking with (insert living male here), and if you have a very good imagination, you can even insert yourself into those black-and-white scenes. Their voices, movements and even the smell of their skin seemed oh so very real. (Elvis smelled like the beach and suntan oil like Hawaii.)

So you can imagine my surprise when I'm in the throes of near-passion with Victor (he doesn't last long, so I have to be ready at the first sign of liftoff) when my fantasy switched midway from Cary Grant to Ax Ellis. Not dead. Not a celeb. Yet there we were on the stage singing the final number where Princess and the Pauper pledge their undying love to each other, and thanks to the corset, I'm looking thin, with my ample bosom sitting perfectly atop the emerald green dress. Only there's no one in the audience, no fellow actors on the stage. When he comes in for that final kiss before the curtains go down, his hand slides from my back down to my bottom, our chests rising and falling with the powerful notes as he comes closer, the kinetic energy between us nearly combustible, our eyes locked. His hand squeezes my ass and he pulls me into his erection, which is as stiff as the cold armor at my chest.

"I'm getting close," Victor moaned, pulling me from my dream to his bed in the historic district.

"Hold it," I pleaded, but I knew he couldn't hold it much longer. I'd nicknamed him Quicksilver long before I'd even known exactly how long a man could reasonably last in bed.

I closed my eyes again and returned to the stage where Ax was busy untying my corset to get to the flesh within, as his red-hot lips tasted mine.

"Damn," Victor grunted to a finish.

"Damn," I muttered. I'd have to pick up where we left off next time.

I smiled in the dark, surprised that an imaginary kiss on the stage was all I'd needed from Ax, and feeling slightly guilty that I wanted to find out if the real thing was anything like make-believe. I was sure it was nothing. My typical overactive imagination getting the best of me. Nothing at all to do with the handsome guy breathing heavy next to me, or nerves about our upcoming nuptials.

"Thanks, baby." Victor turned over. That was it. Not even married yet and he'd given up pillow talk, nearly my favorite part of our lovemaking, that intimacy you can only get from groping and bringing each other to climax. Or one of us, at least.

I slapped his back. "God, we're already like an old married couple. Sex then Snoreville. Soon it would be Snoreville minus the sex. You've heard the penny jar theory, right?" I asked.

"I don't like the way you refer to 'old married couple' as if that's a bad thing."

Victor clicked on the 32-inch flat screen, but instead of watching CNN like I expected, he turned to RLC where a re-run of that week's *Luxe Weddings* was playing. I groaned and hid my face under the sheets. So not in the mood to see my big fat ass, on a widescreen no less.

"Finally an episode where the focus is on the groom for once," he smirked.

I raised my head like a turtle coming out of its shell. I hadn't seen this video. I'd nearly forgotten Skylar and the crew had been following Victor around to get the groom's perspective. This should be interesting.

"I look pretty toned, don't I?" He asked as he turned his wrist, flexing his tricep. "Should I be tanning? I'm looking a little pale."

"No, honey," I said. "You look hot." And he knew it. Out of the three grooms on *Luxe* that season, Victor was the best looking, got the most attention on the message boards.

Skylar, with her dark straight hair and Mediterranean features, positively glowed in his company. In addition to the producer, she was one of three co-hosts on the show. She'd told me early on that she wasn't thrilled she got the "Heartland" wedding out of the three choices, and frankly, I wasn't surprised. Most folks don't think they'll like Oklahoma City before they visit it. Once they do, they're won over. But from the looks of her chemistry with Victor on screen, she's not minding it one bit.

That week's episode was on tuxes so Skylar followed Victor and his best man around to three tux shops where they did a fashion show and Skylar commented on each one. She tells him he could be a runway model and instead of feeling proud, my skin feels hot.

"She's totally flirting with you," I said, but Victor wore a stupid grin on his face (matching the one on the screen) and didn't even look at me. "It's show biz. Oh, you're coming up."

My turtlehead retreated under the safety of the sheet. I hated to see myself on screen, though people tell me I'm photogenic. I hate to hear my voice unless I'm singing. But on *Luxe Weddings*, I'm sitting in a designer tux shop downtown next to Skylar awaiting Victor's first trip down the mock red-carpeted runway. My legs look humongous in those Ann Taylor shorts. Thunder thighs, hear me roar! All these weeks I've deluded myself with the idea that it's that the camera adding pounds, but seeing myself sitting right next to Skylar, who looks stick thin on camera, I feel sick.

"Maybe you should tan, too," Victor said. I wanted to remind him that I am a rare blue-eyed, redheaded woman who gets a slight bronze glow that he'd need to be happy with, but he's sitting up in bed like a boy watching Speed Racer. "Here I come."

They'd narrowed the tuxes down to the three Victor, and apparently Skylar, liked the most. Victor struts down the runway and gives his best-exaggerated model pose. Hamming it up for the camera isn't Victor's thing. He looks like an accountant trying to karaoke. He even flips his tux tail up so the camera can admire his firm, round behind, which had all the girls on the loop atwitter with excitement. I watched myself watching him, noticing I wasn't looking at him at all, but the wardrobe. I didn't look like I was having any fun. In fact, I looked a tad bored. Bored!

After a lot of hemming and hawing, I'd picked a tux, and surprisingly it was the one Victor and Skylar liked the most, too. As we did at the close of every show when a decision had been made, Victor and I popped open a bottle of champagne and celebrated being one step closer to matrimony.

If only it weren't so steeped in *matrimoney*.

Victor clicked off the TV and the light, satisfied he'd

both orgasmed and seen his handsome self on screen. I should've taken full advantage of the good mood. Spill the beans about the debt and wanting to audition for Princess. "Honey, I've been meaning to talk to you about something regarding the show."

He humphed, hitting his pillow.

"About the talent fee, in particular. I know you said you wanted to invest it in the mall concept, but I was thinking it would be a wise financial move to, um, pay off some of my, um, credit cards."

Money was one of Victor's favorite topics. He turned over and faced me. "Sounds good. How much do you need? A thousand? Two?"

I swallowed hard, couldn't even speak. I nodded, though in my head I couldn't believe he'd ever assume it would be so little. I mean, doesn't he know a thousand dollars barely covers one good handbag? Did he really think my family had that much cash lying around? He must really think I'm a spoiled brat.

"Tell you what," he said. "Why don't we invest half the earnings in the mall, invest half into our house savings account minus what you need to pay off the debt." He hadn't ended it with a question mark. His questions were always statements, and he had to always be right.

I nodded again, stupefied. *Tell him you what you owe, Gwen.* Even after we moved in together, it would take me several years to pay off all that debt. Then again, if we kept separate accounts, then maybe he wouldn't have to know at all. What he doesn't know won't kill him, whereas I'm afraid if I tell him the truth, he could drop dead of a heart attack right then and there.

Victor kissed me; proud of himself that he thought he'd solved all my problems. "Oh, yeah. I also dropped some papers off from the bank to start our joint checking account. I thought we might as well start pooling our money. I know you don't have any expenses since you're living at your mom's loft, so why not, right?"

"Joint checking?" My voice shrilled. "How positively quaint, honey. But I'm using my money right now to help mom and dad with the wedding." I lied. Okay, a hundred percent of it was going to pay credit card interest and the miscellaneous great buy, but I'd nearly spent every dime in the wedding account Phillip had set up and we still had weeks of wedding shopping to do. Mom had told me he'd cut me off, as in cut up the card.

"I guess we can wait until after we're married then," Victor said. "But I've set up a meeting in three weeks for our financial planner. Gather up all your financial records and savings accounts and bring it to the meeting."

I felt like Dorothy had thrown water on the Wicked Witch of the East—me being the witch, not Dorothy. I melted into the bed, nearly dissolving into one big tear. So he wasn't marrying the rich girl he thought he was. Didn't mean I expected him to pay off all my debt. As long as he let me use my money to do it. I wasn't marrying him to solve any problems, yet why did it feel that way? After all, it was the marriage, wedding specifically, that would land me that reality show fee.

Crushed, I grabbed my iPhone, which buzzed with a new text message. Skylar. I swear the woman never sleeps.

Don't forget. Meeting with the travel agent at 5 p.m. tomorrow to discuss honeymoon options.

"That should be fun," Victor said, checking his message at the same time.

God, luxury honeymoons were expensive. "Should we discuss budget first? I mean, we don't want to commit to anything on TV that we wouldn't want to spend."

Victor smiled broadly, his face glowing in the white light of my iPhone screen. "I think it's great you've finally taken an interest in finances, Gwen. Could your shopaholic days be a thing of the past?" He crossed his fingers. He wished.

"I'm really working on it." Which was true. Unless I came across a really, really good deal that I'd be an idiot to pass up.

"Good girl. But don't worry about the honeymoon. We'll pay my savings account back after we get our show fee."

What happened to "our money"?

"Maybe that won't be an issue at all. We could postpone the honeymoon for a little while. I've decided I'd like to audition for *Princess and the Pauper*."

Victor looked at me as if I'd told him I wanted to adopt a kid from Borneo. "You can't be serious. Opening night is the same night as our wedding, isn't it?"

"I've thought it all through. We can move the wedding up to an afternoon wedding, still have a wonderful reception outside at Maeve's estate, and I'll have plenty of time to make it to opening night. If I even get a part. Which is a really big if."

He clicked on the lamp, obviously so I could see how his face had reddened. "We've already booked the church, the reception, the limo. Already sent out the godammed 'Save the Date' cards."

"Yes, but I'm sure anyone who wanted to see us get married in the evening will still want to come in the afternoon."

"But afternoon weddings are for the middle class."

I huffed. It would save us loads of money. No dinner to serve, only appetizers, and no dancing for sure. But Victor was right. *Luxe Weddings* typically happened at night with a full dinner, open bar, dancing under the stars. Hell, Nantucket was even having fireworks. "I feel like I'm supposed to be in that show."

His eyes seemed to scream that I'd lost my mind. Maybe I had. Did I seriously want to be Princess more than Mrs. Prescott? And why couldn't I be both?

"Hell, Gwen, why not go all out with a Medieval theme? You get married in your Princess dress and I'll put on some armor, how does that sound?"

Well, on the upside, that would clear up my bridal gown dilemma. If I looked half as good in that dress as I had in my fantasy, that wouldn't be so bad. I rubbed his arm, trying to soothe him. "I think that's the best idea you've had all week. Don't you think the show's a little stuffy, anyway? Let's shake things up."

"You're not marrying a shake things up kinda guy, remember? Did you not see how great I looked in that tux? I'm not dressing up like a weirdo for my wedding."

"Fine. I didn't think you would, anyway. Look, I know we're on a reality show, but the wedding's not the important thing," I said softly. "The important thing is the marriage itself."

"Wedding not important? Christ, Gwen. I'm about to call the cops and report you missing. You don't sound like yourself at all." He slipped on his glasses, the ones that made him look like a sexy model from a Calvin Klein eyewear ad. Maybe we could have sex again and I wouldn't think of anyone else, dead or alive.

Victor was right: I wasn't acting like myself. I'd wanted to be on the show, to have an evening ceremony, the big reception, the whole kit and caboodle, but something clicked, like a great big switch within. And it wasn't me. He'd changed, too, but I couldn't put my finger on it. We rarely talked anymore and making love felt more like another tedious to-do in our planners. I was tired of only talking about wedding plans. Of having to watch what I say around him because cameras followed us everywhere. When we did get any time alone, he only wanted to talk about work. And I don't care if work happens to be my family's business. Work already monopolized his life and he hadn't even made it to senior management yet. What then?

I rolled to face him, inches from the face I'd fallen in

love with in high school. We'd practically grown up together and now we were officially grown up - he was 28 and obviously ready to settle down, and it scared the hell out of me. I did want to grow old with this man, didn't I? "How do you know we'll last, Victor? How can you be sure?"

Victor rubbed his thumb along my jaw line. "I get it. The show is stressing you out and you're upset about your parent's divorce. Is that what you and your mom were talking about earlier?"

"No, we were talking about finding Canty. Okay, and napkin colors."

"The long-lost Pauper?"

I smiled. "Seems he and Grams were a secret item. He's all she talks about now."

"So your mom's actually in on this grand scheme to conjure up the old coot?"

I slapped his bare abs and his muscles contracted. "Don't call him that. And yes, she finally agreed it would be a nice gesture to find him, and Edgar thinks it would be great for the show, too. His real name is Clarence Russell Shaw. The Internet Movie Database gave us his birth date, wife and only child's name, but he hasn't been in a movie or a musical since the '60s. But the important thing is he's still alive. Somewhere."

"Somewhere. Do you know how difficult it can be to find someone who may not want to be found?"

"Come on. He was a star, and when does a star not want to be found? Maybe he still holds a flame for Maeve like Arthur did. She told Mom he was every note she ever heard. Isn't that the most romantic thing ever?"

Victor grunted and rolled over. "Sounds very Hollywood to me. Let me talk to Skylar about the wedding time changes and see how we can announce it on the show. And I'll tell her you need a little more time to yourself. Maybe I can take over some of the wedding planning. I think it's kind of fun."

Because he gets to be on TV. Well, sure, why not. Statistics show grooms are more involved than ever with the wedding planning. And at least that way the message boards would be talking more about his butt and less about mine.

"Thank you. I do want you more involved. And thank you for being understanding about the musical. I know it throws a kink in the plans, but it's what I need to take my mind off Luxe and work. But I still think we need to shake things up on the show."

He kissed me goodnight. A peck on the cheek. "That's my Gwen. Always shaking the Apple tree. Goodnight." He turned his back to me, but my mind continued to spin.

"But it begs the question. If my parents, who seemed to have a rockin' marriage for nearly forty years, couldn't last, what makes you so sure we can?"

He yawned. "The only certainties in life are death and taxes."

So not the answer I hoped for. How effin' romantic. Cue the violin! He knew I wasn't satisfied with that non-answer.

"Look, I don't know why it didn't work out. Your mother married your father because it was right at the time. Don't they say women usually marry men that remind them of their fathers? Your grandfather was a businessman and politician. Your father is a great businessman. Stable, secure, with an entrepreneurial spirit like her father. It's evolutionary psychology. You can't fight it."

Oh, God. Victor nailed it. My father was a lot like my grandfather and Victor Prescott was a lot like my father. They even wore the same outfits to golf in and drove the same cars. A shiver went through me. Was I seriously like my mother-in-law?

Fancy haircut from upscale salon? Check.

Renowned for throwing great parties? Check.

Busty and curvy? Check.

I jumped off the bed as if it were suddenly in flames. I grabbed my underwear and designer T-shirt. "You're marrying your mother!"

Victor shook his finger in the air. "I'm definitely not marrying my mother."

"You are. Admit it. We're marrying our parents and we're going to end up like them. Divorced and lonely at 60!"

"My parents aren't divorced," he argued.

"But you're father cheated on your mother when we were in high school," I said.

"How did you know that?"

"Please. It's a small big town. Everybody knew he was screwing his secretary. And the only reason your mother didn't leave him is because she'd never worked a day in her life. She'd be deserted. Lose her position in the community."

"You don't know that. Come back to bed. What are you doing?" He raised his hand, but didn't bother to get out of bed.

"I can't breathe. I need some air. I'll be back."

"Don't do this, Gwen. This isn't like you."

If Victor's evolutionary psychology bit was valid, then it all started with Maeve's decision to marry "up," to change the course of her family's history forever. She and Canty were two star-crossed lovers—one married and the other destined to marry a future governor and lose the love of her life in the process.

Did I have to find my grandmother's lost love to find me in the process?

If this wasn't like me, then I had to find out why before I made the biggest mistake of my life.

Chapter 9

Bess

The blood trickled down my finger, pooling in the web of flesh between my index and middle fingers. I debated what to do—wipe the gooey red appendage on my jeans, the only ones that didn't make my butt look like mashed potatoes; suck away the blood streaked with fertilizer, risking sudden death or vomiting; or make a run for the loft leaving droplets of blood along the way à la Lil' Red Riding Hood. I could hear my mother's voice in my head: "Stay away from the rose bushes, Bess. Their beauty is a trap."

"Here, let me help you with that." Samuel came up behind me and took my hand in his own, cleansing the wound with a sterile pad and then wrapping it in a large bandage from a first-aid kit he kept in the greenhouse. The tenderness of his gesture and the warmth of his hands made me unsteady. Or perhaps I'd lost too much blood?

"Thank you." I withdrew my hand; catching myself thinking how nice it would be if he held it for a while. Phillip had given that up years earlier, preferring his pockets instead.

"I could ask you what you're doing pruning rose bushes without gloves on," he said gently, "but you're the boss. You can do anything you like."

"Thought I'd relieve some stress by working in the garden," I said. "I think we need a warning sign that reads, Don't Garden While Angry."

"Wedding stuff again?"

"For a man, you're awfully perceptive. Gwen has decided to audition for the musical and in case she gets the part, she's moving the wedding from evening to afternoon. They're going to announce it on the show next week. So I guess we won't need candles on the pool, but the flowers will be beautiful." I could feel the tears pulsing behind my eyes.

"Changing it is as easy as resurrecting the Titanic." Victor grinned.

I laughed. "Exactly. Of course *Luxe Weddings* didn't mind it half as much as I do. They think it adds drama to the show. Watching poor me run around town trying to fix everything and negotiate with the vendors."

"At least money is no object," Victor said matter-of-factly.

"I wish," I said, then realized my slip of the tongue. I never talked about money, especially revealing that what I did have was dwindling. I tried to cover it. "You went through two weddings with your daughters. How did Alice survive it?"

"Well, our budget mandated a simple wedding. And my daughters' both got their mother's personality. Low maintenance."

"Neither of my daughters even know what the word means. Here I thought a wedding, and living together, would bring us all closer together, not tear us apart. Kelly said if she hears ones more thing about crab cakes or a lighting plan, her head would explode."

"Did you say lighting plan?"

"Don't even get me started. When we thought it was a night wedding, it was important, now it seems we have to decide if we want an outdoor wedding under a canopy, but it'll be a hundred degrees out so we're researching noiseless fans. Ridiculous, right? Things were much simpler when you and I got married." I blushed. "I meant when we married our spouses."

Samuel cocked his head. "If I recall, your wedding was a pretty elaborate affair in its own right."

"Oh, I suppose. But nothing like what Gwen's doing. I think it's a lot of hullaballoo for one day. But kids today are so much more ..."

"Difficult."

"You're two for two. I hoped things would turn out differently for me and my girls than they did for Mother and me."

"How so?"

"How you can know someone your whole life, but not really know them? Know what's truly in their heart? Canty is a perfect example. Mother never confided in me that she had loved another man before Father, and definitely didn't share any regrets she had about not going to Broadway. I'd hope that I can be more honest with my daughters and that they can do the same with me."

Victor scratched his chin. "I don't know, Bess. I'm sure it's different with mothers and daughters, but in the end, we do what we do to protect our own. Protect them from heartbreak. I think sometimes dishonesty seems like the best way to go at the time."

I considered it. What a hypocrite I'd been. I hadn't told the girls there were problems between Phillip and me, let alone the money problems. We'd kept our unhappy marriage to ourselves to protect them, which is why it felt like such a slap in the face to the girls when they found out. No wonder they were shocked. But had I been any less shocked? I thought one could reasonably live unhappily ever after and still lead a good life. How could I expect my daughters to be authentic with me when I wasn't even truthful with myself?

"Thank you for listening, Samuel. And for the bandage." I studied his handsome face. Samuel. Another example of knowing a man, but not knowing him. We'd been in close proximity all of our lives, yet I hadn't taken the time to get to know what he loved besides gardening because he was the gardener, and who has a friendship with the gardener? In my circles, you don't. He'd been on the periphery of my life, all this time, and something inside me wanted to bring him in closer even if it was against the grain.

He smiled down at me, his blue eyes shining under white brows. His full head of hair showed more salt than pepper, but because he worked out in the sun, he had a year-round bronze glow. I think he'd grown more handsome over the years, though he'd never had any trouble getting dates before he'd married Alice. I wondered for a split second if he thought I'd lost my looks.

Samuel put his leather Australian cowboy hat back on his head, topping off his fitted black T-shirt and jeans. Courtesy of manual labor, his body stayed in healthy, athletic shape, unlike most men his age. They either wilted and lost all their muscle mass or else their weight repositioned directly into their middle.

He tapped my elbow with his playfully and pointed to my finger. "Didn't you know life comes with some pricks along the way?"

"Namely Phillip," I said, rolling my shoulder back and laughing.

My joke caught Samuel off-guard. He knew I wasn't the witty sort, either, and he joined in on the laugh. Maybe I was finally lightening up.

"Good one." His eyes searched my face, perhaps rolling back the years, thinking of all the pricks I'd dated in high school and beyond before I'd settled down with the biggest one of them all.

He crossed his arms across his barrel chest. "Phillip wasn't half as bad as Bobby Frey."

I conjured the image of the young Bobby in my mind, before he'd wrinkled and shriveled and lost all his hair. "Bobby was a good kisser. I had no idea he was kissing the entire cheerleading squad."

"Not kissing from what I hear."

"My, my. Seems someone knew more about gossip than I did."

"Only because I wanted to warn you about him is all. Not that I would've ever gathered the courage to actually approach you," he said.

"Why ever not?"

"Hell, I would've fainted straight away. You were so far out of my league. You know I had a crush on you something terrible?"

"You did not." My face surely turned as crimson as the blood on my finger. Why did my voice raise so? I sounded like Minnie Mouse on helium. "I knew no such thing. How would I?"

"I tripped over my tongue every time I tried to talk to you. Nearly cut my foot off not paying attention mowing one day when I tried to steal a look at you in your swim suit in the pool in your back yard."

"I can't believe you'd admit that." My cheeks flushed. What was I supposed to do with this information? "I guess I assumed you were too busy working to talk to me."

"You were never short on suitors. And believe me, I noticed every one of them. Haven't forgotten, either."

Imagine. Samuel Whittier paying more mind to my dates than I did. They weren't lined up at the door, but I'd had plenty to choose from. Though they wouldn't admit it, most of them were set up by my parents from their inner circle. Why had I chosen Phillip? Out of all the men, he'd seemed the one that fit most naturally. I'd been hypnotized by his charm. Whatever that meant.

"I know a lot of people took my shyness for something else."

"Oh, I never thought you were a snob. And being the governor's daughter couldn't have been easy. No real chance to rebel."

"Rebel? The thought hadn't occurred to me."

"You're kidding. You never wanted to sneak out of the governor's mansion and go get wasted by the creek?"

"Obviously you did." I did remember his black leather jacket and the pack of cigarettes hanging out of the back of his jeans. He always knew how to wear a pair of Levi's. Still did. Thankfully he'd given up the cigarettes when he was young.

"All I'm saying is if you couldn't cut loose then, you've still got plenty of time to do it now."

"I have no idea what I'd do. Maybe I'm still scared of what my mother would think, let alone the rest of this town." I laughed, but really, was I kidding?

My finger stopped throbbing, yet I still didn't want to leave. With Samuel, I didn't have to do anything. I had to be.

"Thanks for fixing my finger," I said, holding it out into the setting sun and wagging it. "I don't know what I'd have done with out you."

"Don't mention it. It's been nice talking about old times with you. And new ones."

I gave him a long admiring look. His wife had only been gone a year. Or had it been two? Samuel fanned himself with his hat, and then did the same for me. "What's on the agenda tonight?" he asked.

"I rented a chick flick, but Gwen insisted the way I get on Maeve's good side would be to watch the rehearsals. Now that Gwen's a part of it, too, I may as well get in on the action."

"Maybe I'll stop by after I clean up." He raised his hat where it rested high on his head.

"I'd like that," I said, feeling a strange twist in my gut.

I watched him walk away, his gait long and sure. I liked the idea of his company outside of the garden, out in the real world. If I'd been blind, my eyes were opened. I wouldn't live a day longer with them closed.

First, rehearsals. Next, a mother/daughter road trip, scarves flying in the wind, fancy sunglasses on our sun-kissed faces and an imaginary banner flying across the trunk which would read: Canty or Bust.

Chapter 10

Gwen

"You call that dancing?" Maeve shouted from her seat in the theater while I tried desperately to learn the dance moves for the opening number. If I didn't get them down in a week, no way in hell I'd have a chance of landing the role of a lifetime — of my lifetime, anyway.

The choreographer Tabby agreed to come early to work with anyone who needed extra assistance, yet out of the twenty girls auditioning for Princess, I was the only one taking her up on the offer, the only one with lead in my feet and a voluptuous body, to boot. Up against stick thin ballerina-types with big voices, long legs and killer résumés. Crazy or not, I'd never wanted anything this badly before, not even the hard-to-get, insanely expensive Fendi love letter bag.

I'd even lied to Skylar about the rehearsal time because she thought it would be a good idea to capture some of it on camera to show the audience what was so important I had to change my wedding plans. But not yet. Who knew what kind of a bumbling idiot I'd look like?

"It's not the moves," a male voice shouted from the audience. I squinted and peered into the seats where Ax sat next to my grandmother.

"Excuse me?" I shouted.

Ax bound up the stairs and stood in front of me, wearing stretchy jeans and a fitted long-sleeved retro

Crush T-shirt, made masculine by his firm biceps. I drew in my breath, thinking he looked twice as sexy as any man I'd ever seen, especially in an old T-shirt. "It's not the moves. You know the moves, Gwen. You're not feeling it."

"I'm not? Because my legs, butt and arms are most definitely feeling it."

"Not there," he said, "Here." He pointed to his chest, then to mine. "You know what's at stake here, don't you?"

"Humiliation? Fame? Love, life, the whole ball of wax?"

He smiled. "Not for you. For the princess. You're still thinking like Gwen. You need to think like Princess, sing like Princess, talk like Princess, dance like Princess, make love like Princess."

I gulped. Had he said made love or were my ears playing tricks on me? "Method acting?"

"Call it what you want. But before you can ever play Princess you have to get her. Understand her motivation." He put his palm over my eyes and I could smell the musk on his body. "Close your eyes and think about her. Forbidden love. Being forced to marry a man she doesn't love. Feeling like a prisoner in that castle. The freedom out in the wilderness with the one she loves. Who is she and what does she want?"

I conjured Princess, imagining me as her, dressed in that fitted emerald dress, standing on the hillside, waiting for her secret meeting with the pauper. "Her heart is racing with anticipation. She's been thinking of him all day." My mouth went dry.

"What is she most worried about?"

"She's worried she'll never see him again. That he won't wait for her. That she'll be lost without him. She can't imagine a life without him."

My own heart raced as I took Ax's hand and pulled it away from my face, but with his other hand, he wiped away a tear. How had that gotten there?

"That's right," he said, with the smile I'd looked forward to seeing all day. "I think you get her now. So prove it."

I proved it. Tabby played the CD for the first duet, "Intoxicated," which takes place in the woods at night. Tabby turned the stage lights down, dimming the room. Princess has snuck out of the castle to find the pauper, the moon her illicit guide. She finds him waiting for her deep within the darkened woods. He can't believe she's come, that she would risk the crown for him. To give up royalty to live in rags.

Ax and I spun around the imaginary trees, a mating dance of sorts as I imagined losing layer after layer of clothing as the script called for, until I am no longer princess. I am woman stripped bare to a nightdress, my heart as exposed as my skin. I was no longer acting vulnerable; I was vulnerable, practically quivering with emotion. When the Pauper and Princess finally touched, palm to palm and then chest to chest and glided around the room, I thought: I am Betrayal. I am Lust. I am Passion.

I sang of love, which could never see the light of day. Of night's blanket covering the sin of what we were about to do, yet powerless to it.

Our bodies responded to the music, our hands, feet and hips swaying, bending and jerking to the beat. Ax took my left hand and spun me toward him, out and under and back again, our skin pressing and releasing frenetically. "You'll never ever know what you have done to me," he sang.

I whirled around him again, my body anxious for that beat when he would pull me into him again and our hips would sway together, right, left, right, release. "The stars and moon bear witness to our destiny."

When Ax and I fell to the floor in the final note of the song, his body splayed against mine, I was more certain than ever that I had fallen in more ways than one and couldn't get up again. I sure as hell didn't want to.

Ax locked eyes with mine, and for a second I thought he might kiss me, but I couldn't remember if that was called for in the script or not. I'd been so busy concentrating on the dance moves that I hadn't memorized my lines, but it felt very much like the handsome pauper should kiss Princess as the curtain closed on the first act. I was ashamed to admit it felt very much like Ax should kiss the suddenly sensual Gwen Apple-Barton. I Am Lust. I Am Betrayal. Yeah, yeah. I so get it.

While still on top of me, Ax whispered, "That's what I'm talking about," and he peeled his body off of mine.

"You two made me a little hot watching you," Tabby said, playfully hitting Ax. "If that was acting, then great job."

If. Ha. If. I laughed, trying to read Ax's face for an expression, but his friends had arrived and he was off to be with them, done with helping me for the moment. One actor helping another get to the top of her game. Professional, dedicated guy. I remembered: he was a teacher. He taught students how to be better actors. That's all it was.

The group whistled and clapped, including Kelly in a cool retro pants suit sitting next to Edgar and Bess and Samuel sitting behind Maeve. I couldn't believe I'd been so lost in the spotlight that I hadn't noticed we'd had an audience. Skylar and the camera crew walked into the room, in time to miss my heated moment. Perfect.

Maeve slit her eyes at me from her seat in the audience as I slipped behind the curtain and released my breath with tears that came from absolutely nowhere. If only I'd been acting. If only.

Social in his own right, Ax picked a jazz club hosting swing night, and I don't mean the kind where you switch sexual partners, either.

I invited Victor to join us, but he preferred to go to a late dinner with Phillip and some prospective business partners who were in town from New York to discuss the magic mall. I tried not to let it hurt my feelings that he chose work over me. If I'd learned anything from my mom being married to my dad for so long, it was get used to it. I couldn't exactly complain when he'd given in to the afternoon wedding switcharoo and had agreed to take some of the burden of the reality show off my back. He was a great guy, all in all. I had to keep reminding myself of this. Handsome. Successful. Dependable.

At the club, I was the only one in the group who didn't know a thing about swing dancing, but there was Maeve cutting up the floor with Edgar while my sister made notes in her iPad at a corner table. Really, I wish that thing would short-circuit, like apparently her brain had. Why couldn't she relax for a half a sec? How we're even related is a mystery to me. Fine. Let her be the wallflower. I, for one, was in the mood to make that little dance fantasy starring Ax turn into a real-life encore.

By the second song, "Zoot Suit Riot," I got the hang of it, and stopped kicking Ax in the shins quite as often. "Love the hair, doll," Ax whispered when he pulled me in again, and before I could say thank you, I was gone again. Tap, tap, jump, kick, twirl. The Lindy Hop kicked yoga's ass as far as I was concerned.

Out of the corner of my eye, I watched Samuel with his John Wayne kind of swagger. He wasn't dressed like a gardener at all, but a sexy widower out on the town. Black dress pants, black dress shoes and a pressed dress shirt with sleeves rolled up three-quarters. So nice to see Mom out having a good time for once.

At the bar for a cool down, I tried to control my panting, but I wasn't in nearly as good a shape as I'd given myself credit for. Ax on the other hand, seemed barely winded.

"You singing tonight?" Ax asked, then downed a Seven and Seven with extra lime before I could answer.

"Me? Why would I be singing?" Pant, pant, pant. Would he catch me if I passed out?

"It's amateur night. Stage is a free-for-all. Thought you might give it a whirl."

"That's what I've been doing. Whirling, I mean. And I think rehearsing wore out my vocal chords today."

Ax sucked on the lime, his face puckering up. "Tell you what: You sing and I'll accompany you."

Ax Ellis tickling the ivories for me? But what would I sing in front of all these strangers? Maybe they wouldn't even notice me up there at all as long as I didn't butcher the song. "What do you recommend?" I asked.

"Gotta be jazz. Know any Ella?"

I racked my brain. Jazz. Ella Fitzgerald. Grams played it non-stop in the antique store, and because she'd forgotten she'd already listened to it, she played the same song over and over. "I think I know a little Ella."

He raised his glass, full again, and winked. "Good girl. I'll meet you on stage."

Ax jaunted off to the band, while I paid Chris for another round. "Looks like the cat ate the canary. What gives?" Kelly said, coming up behind me.

I jumped, nearly falling off the barstool. "Damn, you scared me. What gives is I'm having fun. Might try it some time." God, I had to admit she looked pretty damn cool in the '40s Katharine Hepburn get-up. "Let me buy you a drink."

"Can't," Kelly said, sidling up beside me with her oversized black leather folder in her hand and her tiny blue notebook peeking out from inside of it. If someone could possibly look like a geek in a bar, she'd pulled it off. "Working."

I groaned, looking over my shoulder where Edgar stood talking to Maeve. "Is the folder a hundred percent necessary? People probably think you're going to poll them or start passing out homework."

"Some of us take our jobs very seriously." She winked.

"So what do you think of the musical and the Orpheum? Think people will come?"

Kelly cocked her eyebrow—her usual you're a moron reply. "Of course they'll come. I've got a VIP list together for opening night and my team is finishing up some ideas for the campaign." She thumbed through her folder. "Check out these photos of the Orpheum I found from the '40s."

She pulled the photos out of the folder, several 8x10 black and white glossies. Even without color, you could tell it had been the place to see and be seen. Champagne in the lobby. Suits on the guys and glamorous gowns on the gals. Really, society living would've been much more fun back then. Elaborate chandeliers, silk drapes, richly carved woods.

"I get it. You're recommending he restore the Orpheum to its original state? Copy the past?"

"Not copy. Emulate. Revive a downtown legend. Imagine the PR we'll get. Maybe not quite as big as the Skirvin, but it'll be huge." Kelly stuffed the photos back in her folder, perturbed at my lack of enthusiasm. She continued, undeterred by my lack of interest. "Maeve is filling me in on the details. Said she wondered why Arthur had let this place get so shabby."

I motioned to Edgar. "So I take it you've enjoyed working with Edgar. I told you that you couldn't say no to him."

"It's lunch. Working lunches. And I'm doing it for the business. Nearly all my clients have slashed their events budgets. And he promised Maeve could sing a duet as the encore if we find Canty."

I wiped my forehead again with the cocktail napkin. "I have a feeling about this. I think Canty is out there somewhere thinking about the good ol' days like Maeve is."

"I'm certain he doesn't believe he's back in 1949, though it must've been a very good year. They were hellcats together."

"Edgar would be quite a catch, don'tcha think?"

"What makes you think so?"

Ah, she likes him. Good. Proof at least her eyes aren't all business. "He's never been married so you don't have an ex-wife to deal with. Never had kids so you don't have step-brats to deal with, and he's a successful entrepreneur so you don't have to worry he's marrying you for your money." Last part? Slipped out.

Her eyebrow shot up again. "You think that's what Victor is doing?"

I cringed. I didn't think I'd ever have this talk with my sister. Never tell her something you don't want her to diagram and present a solution to within 24 hours. I squirmed in my seat. "Well, we're getting ready to meet with the financial planner in a couple weeks and he thinks I've got all this money saved, and has no idea I have any debt."

"You're kidding right? You practically wear a new outfit every day and he doesn't think you'd have debt?"

My stomach knotted. I hated that I cared what my sister thought about me. She'd always made fun of my shopaholic ways, warned me of the danger of trying to stay a step ahead of the fashion pack, but I hadn't listened.

"How bad is it?" Kelly asked, matter-of-factly.

It would be good to get it out. Practice for telling Victor. "Less than a hundred thousand," I said, off-handedly.

She laughed. "I'd certainly hope so! That's a three-bedroom house in Oklahoma! Seriously. How much?"

"Ninety," I mumbled.

"Ninety hundred? As in nine thousand?"

"Thousand, right," I said.

Kelly shook her head; her eyes popping out like a zombie. "Ninety thousand dollars!"

"Give or take."

"Oh my god, Gwen. That's some serious dough. That's way more than selling a few designer shoes on eBay."

"And I plan on paying as much of it off as I can with the earnings from *Luxe Weddings*. But Victor thinks we're going to invest it."

"Jesus, Gwen. You have to come straight with him. And if he loves you like I suspect he does, he'll forgive you and you two will work it out. That's what couples do, right?"

I nodded. How would I know? Mom and Dad didn't work it out. And Victor thinks he's marrying some sort of heiress, not a walking-talking financial disaster.

I gulped back a cry. Before I had time to gulp back another martini, Ax took his seat at the piano and waved me over. I couldn't take my eyes off of him. "Shouldn't I have complete faith in us?"

Kelly squeezed my shoulder. "That's generally the idea in getting a life partner." Her face grew serious, and exhaled. "You have to be honest with yourself before you can be honest with him. Don't get into a marriage thinking it will solve all your problems."

"Ha! Like I'm doing that." I rolled my eyes, but even with our age difference, Kelly knew me better than I knew myself. I'd been sweeping my problems under the rug for so long. I thought being on the reality show would make things better, but all it did was dig me deeper into debt. And once you're on the inside of planning your own wedding, it's not nearly as much fun as watching someone else do it on TV. They edit it down, make it look like some damn fairytale where there's an endless budget and perfect cakes and perfect dresses and perfect relationships. So *not* reality.

Kelly was right. I had to take control of my life

before it took control of me. Who said I had to keep up with the Nantucket and California weddings? Why couldn't someone have a luxury-like wedding on a budget? Like I'd ever let anyone tell me what to do before. But was it too late to change? The show? My relationship? Me?

Kelly nodded sympathetically. "You're creative. I trust you'll find a solution."

I smiled, seeing Ax wave me over. He was on the stage like a gorgeous specimen under a white-hot microscope. He leaned into the microphone, the spotlight lighting his face. "Ladies and gents, eyes up here and tips in the jar. It's time to meet our next vocalist. She's as frantic as the Atlantic. As terrific as the Pacific. And I think you'll agree the sexiest redhead we've ever had to grace this stage—Gwen Apple-Barton."

He called me sexy. Into a microphone, no less. I couldn't move, but Kelly yanked my arm until I could propel on my own. I climbed the steps and looked out at the two-dozen patrons sipping their drinks and only occasionally looking my way, though I noted the men's eyes lingered longer still. Suddenly, something weird happened: I didn't feel frightened at all. Instead I wanted all eyes, every last one of them, on me. When I put that microphone in my hand, the world became mine alone.

The mic's magic transformed me into more than a caption in a society page photo. More than the city's favorite shopaholic or the bride-to-be deliberating wedding wares. I had something to say, something to sing. I imagined Ella, with her big deep voice and sultry persona and began, "The poets say that all who love are blind..."

My voice took over; my body calm as the song escaped like a prisoner breaking free. By the time I hit the chorus of "I've Got It Bad (And That Ain't Good)" my voice had reached down and grabbed them by the ears and refused to let go. Every head in the joint turned my way. I had them captured, enraptured, and even when the last note breezed by, I wanted to catch it and hold on to it a little longer.

The audience clapped; a few men, probably drunk, whistled. Kelly gave me a thumbs-up sign and Maeve stood stage right behind the curtains, watching me suspiciously.

"Smashing, dollface," Ax said as I brushed by him to exit the stage. He reached up and squeezed my wrist, causing me to jerk back. He pulled me down and kissed me on the cheek, lightly, then let me go and began playing for Maeve. Before she put on her plastered stage-face smile, she glared at me and shook her head, obviously displeased with Ax's kiss, and bumped into my shoulder when she sashayed stage center and sang a rousing rendition of another Ella classic, "You Can't Take That Away From Me."

I'd gone backstage to get Maeve's things she had left in the dressing room thinking, as usual, that the place was hers. When she wasn't in a play "back in the day," she had night-owled at various jazz clubs around town. She'd taken over the lone vanity in the dressing room, her makeup scattered, crumpled tissues with excess rouge and her tiny purse propped against the mirror.

"You joining us, Gwen?" Ax swung his jacket around his shoulder and held his hat to his chest. Apparently, Ax, the social director, was still on the clock, and the night was young.

I hadn't stayed up this late in years. Actors/musicians, it seemed, can go all night. Maeve had fallen asleep an hour ago at her table; face down next to her virgin martini—100% cranberry juice. Her mind may have believed she was 25, but her body knew the truth.

"Who's asking?" I asked as I gathered up the tissues and threw them in the trash.

Ax stood inches from me as he retrieved his pocket watch. His cologne may as well have been blinking a neon sign that read, "Jump me."

"Me and the gang," he said with a smile.

"Don't see a gang."

"You got me, doll. They've already taken off. We get burgers and head out to the Crossing to drink and dance."

"Crossing? Never heard of it." If it were cool, I'd be informed.

"It's a place out in the country. Not a light for miles. Spotlight is the moonlight. Stage is the red earth. You game?"

My stomach growled, answering for me. I hadn't eaten a cheeseburger in eons. Surely I'd danced off enough calories, right? I deserved it. And what was one more hour? Victor was probably asleep already, anyway. He could take a trip to Snoreville without me.

"I'm game." I picked up Maeve's vintage black handbag handles, causing the contents to spill onto the counter. Lipstick. Age-old cigarettes with a photo sticking out the side of the package. I slipped out the yellowed photo and turned it over. Those eyes. Those dimples. That curl. Canty. I smiled.

"Who is it?" Ax asked, leaning in so close I could kiss him.

"You."

"Me?"

I showed him the photo. Definitely a resemblance. Especially if your eyesight had deteriorated like Maeve's had. "The real Canty, Clarence. Cute, huh?"

"So you're saying I'm cute?"

"Maeve thinks so."

"What does Gwen think?" He leaned in even closer, his hat pressed against his chest, the only thing separating our bodies.

"I think I'm famished."

He flipped the hat on his head. A literal hat trick. "I was trying to be a gentleman pretending I didn't hear your stomach growl. Let's roll. I'll drive."

Splendid. If I tried to find this mysterious Crossing, I'd probably get lost, anyway. Maeve and I never knew our way.

When I stepped outside the back door, I gasped. One lone car in the parking lot. A vintage something or other as if it had been transported from a showroom floor from the past.

"You like it?"

I ran my fingers over the curvy cream-colored body and leaned against the sexy chrome grill. "I can't believe you drive this. It's gorgeous."

"Stick with me. I'm full of surprises." We eased into the tan leather seats, his camera bag between us, and as the engine purred to life, jazz pumped from the speakers.

"You know it?" He asked.

"Enlighten me."

"Duke Ellington. 1944. 'Wanderlust.'"

"Is that so? I like it." Why did I like jazz even more in Ax's company? Listening to anything else with him would've felt plain wrong.

"I'll play it for you sometime," he said casually.

"I'd like that." Maybe too much. Maybe I should rethink that cheeseburger alone in a cool convertible with a sexy musician. But my stomach got final say.

"You really surprised me tonight, dollface," Ax said as he wheeled into Irma's Burger Shack drive-thru. I let the wind whip my hair in all directions and let it fly free.

Ax handed me the cheeseburger, larger than my hand, but the usual carefree look on his face had been replaced with something else — serious and curious at the same time. "Maybe it's time I get to know the Gwen underneath the big fancy last name."

I unwrapped the cheeseburger and bit down, the juice dripping down my chin. One thing was for sure. I wanted to get to know him, but did I really want him to get to know me? I was a lie, a sham, a designer-coated great pretender. I tilted my head toward the camera between us.

"You first. What do you take pictures of?" I asked.

"Whatever they tell me to. People, places, things. Have to make money somehow."

"Well, I'd love to see them sometime. If you're half as good a photographer as you are a swing instructor, they must be something else."

"And I don't get kicked in the shins nearly as often. My turn. Tell me about the Gwen no one else knows."

I nearly choked on my cheeseburger. Wasn't my life an open book, aired at 8:00 p.m. Eastern every Tuesday night? People saw me in the society pages, watched me on national TV. People knew about my weight struggles, my eccentric wardrobe, my historied family. What did no one else know, and why was I thrilled Ax seemed to care so much? My pedigree may be worthless to Ax.

One look seemed to say he got me—and I didn't even get myself.

One cheeseburger. One drink. One song. One hour out in the country under a starry sky. One night never killed anybody. Never ruined an engagement or changed a life.

Did it?

Chapter 11

Kelly

"Where the hell were you last night? I waited up until nearly 3:00 a.m. and Victor said you weren't answering your cell phone." I sat on my sister's bed, nudging her to wake up.

Gwen smiled a dreamy smile, which could only mean one thing. "What did you do, Gwennie?"

She stretched and squirmed, her vintage hair do and makeup smeared and wild. "I ate the most fantastic cheeseburger last night."

"You're trying to tell me you cheated on Victor with a cheeseburger?"

Gwen's eyes snapped open wide. "What? No. Hell, no. I didn't cheat on Victor. Me and the gang went out to Crossings and drank and sang, and God it was magical."

"'Me and the gang'? What's gotten into you? And don't tell me you're just having fun, either."

"But I am. I'm living in the moment. Carpe diem."

"What about carpe Victor?"

Gwen held her pillow tighter. "One night away from me won't kill him. Besides, he's going on a business trip with Dad this week, so I should get used to being apart from him. It's not like we need to spend every waking moment together. Maybe being apart will be good for us. You know, see how much we miss each other. Or not."

"Random thought here, but why don't you go with him?"

"Believe me, I tried. He's going to New York for three days, but he says they'll be in meetings the whole time and I'd have a terrible time. I think he's worried I'd shop the whole time. Which I would, if he left me his credit card, but he says he'll be in long meetings and schmoozing. Besides, if I hear the words 'magic malls' one more time, I'll scream. I'm going to use his time away to spend rehearsing."

What had happened to my sister? Someone had snatched my designer-loving sis and replaced her with a jitterbug. Maeve's lapse in time was sucking Gwen in like some sort of time warp. "You're serious about this theater stuff, aren't you?"

"As a heart attack. Ax said he'd work with me on the dance moves around his freelance schedule. Auditions are a week away."

"Is this about Ax?"

She tucked the sheet under her arms, the dreamy look on her face returning. "Ax? Why would you say that?"

"Let's see. He's gorgeous, single and multi-talented. Any other talents besides singing, dancing, acting and playing music I should know about?"

"How would I know?" She smiled coyly.

"Good answer. Look, I may not be a huge Vic fan, but you've found a guy who loves you and wants to spend the rest of his life with you. You don't even know how lucky you are."

"Believe me, I know. I swear this isn't about Ax — or Victor. When I sing, I feel like a completely different person. I feel like it's what's been missing in my life."

I eyed her suspiciously. "I would've never guessed the girl who has everything had something missing."

"Yes! I couldn't put my finger on it until I got up there on that stage and sang again. I've felt like I had this huge hole in my soul and I didn't know how to fill it up. I tried with power shopping and parties, but it never worked."

I looked around the room. Where most people had baseboards, our room had rows of shoes. Nearly half of them were turned around, facing the wall. She seemed like my sister, but something wasn't right. "New system you got there?"

"The ones facing the wall are the ones that I'm selling. I'll give credit where credit is due. It's time to scale back. The sale is the beginning. I was thinking I could also sell my Beemer. You know what I've secretly always wanted?"

"I couldn't even guess."

"A cute Volkswagen Beetle. Red, like a ladybug."

"You're yanking my chain."

"Am not. I totally swear. Wanna go with me to the dealership?"

"This I've got to see to believe. But if you're serious, and want some help listing your shoes, maybe we can do it after we pack at Maeve's this afternoon."

"You'd do that for me?" Gwen gushed.

"Don't look so shocked. I already took some liberties." I grabbed my notebook from the nightstand. "I went through the closet and half the stuff in there isn't even worn. You have a hundred handbags, two hundred thirty seven pair of shoes — sixty of them black — and twenty-five pair of sunglasses. Don't even get me started on the costume jewelry. It's like a treasure chest from Pirates of the Caribbean in there."

"I get your point. Think you could send a shout out to your Facebook list about a designer sale? And maybe I could get Skylar to let me promote it on the show. Mom wants to have an estate sale at Grams when we finish going through the house, so whatever doesn't sell could go into the house."

"Now you're thinking. And what about telling Victor about your debt?"

"As soon as he gets back from New York. I'm going

to talk to Skylar about a new direction for the show, too. Well, at least my part. How to pull off a luxury wedding without spending a fortune."

"And how exactly does Miss Shop-Til-You-Drop know how to do that, may I ask?"

"With your connections, I do. And I'm dropping the whole storyline about my weight, too, which is why I'm marching down there to tell Skylar I'm not going to the weigh in. I know the whole country's had a big laugh over my inability to lose more than five pounds in six months, but I don't need to lose twenty pounds. I'm gonna stand up for all the brides that aren't a size 4, 2 or 0."

"Wow. That must've been some cheeseburger. I've been craving one myself."

"I'll take you there." Gwen jumped out of bed, and to my shock, she made her bed, a first since we'd roomed together again. I wasn't even sure she knew how.

"Since you're thinking about a new direction for the show, I think you should know that none of those bridesmaids dresses we fitted a few weeks ago are going to work for me anymore."

Gwen shook her head. "You were the last bridesmaid I expected to go diva on me."

Bess knocked, but didn't wait for an answer before entering our room. Just like when we were kids. "I thought Saturdays were the peaceful day of the week! Skylar is fuming that you're keeping her waiting, and she's flirting up Edgar, who arrived. Maeve is crying in her room that Canty didn't show up to take her to a picnic and refuses to come out of her room. Yet I see your morning is peachy." She looked down at the bed and back at Gwen. "You made that? I should go get my camera. Or better yet have Shadow put it on tape for posterity."

"Ha, ha, Mother. Things were starting to look up when Kelly was about to tell me why her dress, which was selected by a nationwide TV vote, won't work for her anymore." Gwen crossed her arms.

Bess covered her ears with her hands. "I don't think I can bear to hear it. I'm so fed up with dresses, I could crap taffeta."

"Mother!" We said to her at the same time.

"Let me finish! The dresses are fine, but the winning dress won't look the same after it's been altered. You both better sit down for this."

Bess looked at her watch one more time, then joined Gwen on the bed, while I stood in front of them, pacing. I'd wanted to tell them separately, but this would have to do.

"I need the dress altered, because I'm expecting."

Bess shook her head. "Expecting what?"

Gwen's brows furrowed, then her eyes and mouth opened wide. "Not a baby!"

"Indeed. A baby. I'm eight weeks along." My face crept into a smile, waiting for the realization to kick in. One, two, three …

"No way." Gwen's eyes darted around the room. "Is this some kind of prank for the show?"

Bess clutched her chest. She closed her eyes and nodded three times as if letting the words sink in. "You're pregnant on purpose, I gather?"

I laughed nervously. "Do I look like a 17-year-old who forgot to use a condom?"

"Good point," Gwen said.

"I didn't think you even wanted children, Kelly. I thought you were a career woman," Bess said. She began fanning herself with a magazine plucked from the bedside table. "I think I need to lie down." She put her head on Gwen's pillow, her feet sticking off the side of the bed. "Maybe I'll wake up and this will all be a dream."

"See? I knew you'd be upset." I watched Bess cross her hands over her chest in funeral casket pose. Her eyes were closed.

Gwen shook her head in amazement. "You're for real? But how? I mean, I didn't even think you were having sex!"

"As crazy as it sounds, you don't technically have to have sex to make a baby these days," I told them.

Bess's eyes shot open. "I'm not sure if that's supposed to make me feel better or worse."

Gwen gasped. "I know you're not talking a virgin birth here." She snapped her fingers. "Genetix. God, I was drunk that night, but I remember those folders in your car. You really were looking for a baby daddy?"

"Please don't use that phrase, but yes, I'd had the insemination earlier that day," I said.

"Why couldn't you confide in us?" Bess asked, her voice shaky. "In me? I'm your mother. You should be able to tell me anything."

"If I'd told you what I was planning on doing, would you have tried to talk me out of it?"

"Yes," Gwen and Bess answered together.

"See? I needed everyone to be supportive, therefore I didn't tell anyone. I was going to wait four more weeks until the first trimester was over, but I couldn't wait any longer. I'm too excited. And I'm nauseous. Living together and all, I figured I had to give up the goose, as Grams' likes to say."

Gwen choked up, her face turning bright with surprise. "I would never have expected this from you in a million, kajillion years." She lunged at me, and rocked me back and forth in a hug. "I may think you're nuts, but you're our nut."

Bess sat up and hugged me in a python grip. "I'm sorry you didn't feel I would've been supportive," she said. "Once I recover from the shock, I'm sure I'll be thrilled for you."

I laughed, relief washing over me. "Good, because I have a feeling the rest of the clan won't be as kind. Dad, especially."

Gwen stuck out her bottom lip. "Does this mean Edgar's off the table?"

My heart screeched to a halt. "He was never on the table. Or anywhere else."

Gwen's face scrunched into a scowl. "Damn. I really wanted you two to get together."

"That's my hopelessly romantic sis. I love your optimism. But as sexy as Edgar may be, he's totally wrong for me. He's this big world adventurer bachelor and I'm ready to settle down. Besides, I don't need a man. The only person I want to fall in love with is my baby, okay?"

"Oh, dear," Bess said. "We're in for quite a ride, aren't we?"

After two hours of running lines with Gwen and singing on our way to Tulsa, we spoke like true countesses from the Middle Ages.

"We've arrived, sweet ladies," I said in a thick bard accent.

"Shall we see if the master is home?" Gwen asked as we viewed what would, by modern standards, be a peasant's home — a small, white clapboard house with black shutters and quaint landscaping. Summer foliage, bright and pretty. Someone cared about this place. Could Canty be behind that door?

"Maybe we should come back later," Bess said, losing the accent. "He's probably at church."

"We don't even know if this is his house," Gwen said, "let alone if he's churchy. I'm going." She got out of the car and we tumbled out after her, walking up the cracked sidewalk to the porch where a terra cotta pot was filled with purple petunias and cigarette butts.

"Great. He's a smoker," Bess said. "Mother can't be around cigarette smoke. Let's turn around and leave."

"She cried all night," I reminded her. "And you don't know that it's his butts. Maybe he has a caregiver."

"Not much of a caregiver if she smokes," Bess said indignantly.

"We're on a quest to find our pauper and we're not letting a few cigarette butts get in our way," Gwen said, rapping hard on the door because the doorbell had a taped sign that read "broken."

We heard the rumblings of a TV show inside, then someone's voice and footsteps.

"He's coming," Gwen said, her hands clasped in front of her.

We held our breath. The door swung open and an alarmed older woman with disheveled, wiry gray hair with random strands of red, stood in front of us in her cotton gown with dingy slippers on her feet. She hadn't shaved her legs in a very, very long time. Same went for the slight mustache above her yellowed teeth. Please tell me this isn't the Mrs.

"What do you want?" The woman barked, then coughed a few times. Definitely her butts.

Bess and Gwen looked to me to speak. Apparently, we were dressed like we might be selling something, at the very least spreading the Good News.

"Hello. We've driven in from Oklahoma City. We're actually looking for Canty. Er, I mean, Clarence Russell Shaw. We have this as his last known address."

"Who's looking? He owe taxes or something?"

So he is still alive. And perhaps a tax evader.

"No, ma'am," Gwen said. "Nothing like that. My name is Gwen Apple-Barton and this is my sister Kelly and our mother Bess."

The woman eyed us suspiciously and coughed again. "You kin to the late Governor and Senator Apple?"

"He was my father," Bess said.

The woman's wiry brows rose. I could tell Gwen was

itching to get her hands on them and pluck away. The woman's suspicion subsided. "So what would you want with that old coot anyway?"

Interesting choice of words. Old coot. Perhaps this woman wasn't his second wife after all. Thank God for that. Was Canty a handful in his old age?

"It's a long story," I said, suddenly needing the bathroom very, very badly.

The woman leaned her freckled, sausage-like arms on the doorframe. "I've got nothing but time."

I shifted from my right to my left leg. "I'm sorry to be an imposition, but if I could use your restroom, then we could sit down and talk it over."

The woman shrugged. "Why not? Got nothing better to do."

We entered her house, and I was pleased to find it as neat as the landscaping on the outside, with the exception of an ashtray next to her La-Z-Boy filled with cigarette butts and one cigarette burning itself out, the smoke spiraling to the yellowed popcorn ceiling.

I kindly asked her if she could not smoke, as I was with child. She obliged, congratulating me and telling me she could never have children of her own. On my way back from the bathroom, I surveyed the frames on the walls, pictures going back decades, as evidenced by the fashion of the times. Eighties big hair, seventies big collars, sixties big headbands until the pictures lost their color, replaced by classy black-and-whites. There. The last picture on the wall, across from the bathroom. I'd recognize those dimples anywhere. But something about the picture didn't fit. In the bathroom, it dawned on me: The wedding photo didn't look right because the woman next to him wasn't my grandmother.

When I returned to the hall, three pictures remained farther down on the wall, but it was too dark to see, so I reached down and clicked on a lamp on a credenza. What I saw made me suck in my breath so hard my chest hurt. The people in the pictures somehow looked familiar. Had I seen them somewhere before?

I heard Gwen cheer in the other room and my mom thank the woman. I raced back in the living room.

"He's got a daughter, Anna," my mother said. "She's been twenty minutes from us this whole time!"

I exhaled in relief. Sometimes the answer is right under you nose.

Chapter 12

Bess

I'd been robbed.

Papers were strewn across the hardwood floor like something you see in the crime dramas on TV. Only a few checks later (diamonds, purse, flat-screen TV), I realized I hadn't been robbed at all.

Upon closer inspection, the papers littering the floor were the contents of my Apple reunion and Apple-Barton/Prescott wedding planner. The den looked like an Oklahoma twister had struck an apple tree, sending the red, green, pink and blue fruits across the floor. My Apple tree! My perfectly cut and laminated Apple apples. Ruined! It would take me hours, days to put it all back together again.

The worst part was I didn't feel like doing it. The woman we'd visited in Tulsa told us Canty had a daughter, Anne and lived in a northern suburb of Oklahoma City. She'd said Canty lived in a retirement community in Oklahoma City (though she wouldn't say which one). That's all she would say. Whatever business we had with Canty, she preferred we deal with his daughter.

We were so close to the finish line, to finding Canty. But after a few phone calls, we discovered Anne was out of town on vacation, and not knowing about Canty's health, I was still no closer to knowing if he would remember Maeve or want anything to do with a reunion.

His relative in Tulsa believed he still played in a band, but couldn't remember the name of it. Not much to go from.

Why did I want this so badly for her? Or why, oh why, couldn't she come back to present day and be my bossy mother again?

No, there was no twister during the night. For once the June sky was brilliant blue, not a wall cloud in sight.

The only possible culprit for the mess had to be Maeve, our own personal F-5 tornado. Oh God. I could only assume she began reading the family tree complete with photos, old and new, and timelines and notes on achievements of the family. She probably freaked out and took it out on my binder and then the poor Apple tree board. More than 60 hours of planning down the toilet. That planner was the only way I was going to pull off an up-to-snuff reunion for the picky Apples, not to mention a ritzy wedding worthy of national attention. Especially when I'd had to switch things around for the reunion and the wedding when Gwen changed the wedding time.

My stomach dropped. I was being selfish and knew it. My work meant nothing compared to Maeve's feelings. I could only imagine how upset this could've made the Early Maeve, who hadn't yet accepted my father's proposal. The last thing she'd done before slamming her door behind me was to call me a witch, which made sense upon finding this disaster.

I followed the echoes of sobs coming from Kelly and Gwen's bedroom. Thank God she hadn't attempted the steps in her fury.

Inside the room, I found her splayed out on Gwen's bed, hugging Gwen's Snoopy plush she'd given to Gwen for her fifth birthday. The funnel seemed to have dissipated.

"Get out, you wretched witch," Maeve said, holding Snoopy out as if he were her guard dog and could protect her. "I don't know who you think you are writing about me like that. Telling such lies."

I stepped inside the room and took a deep breath, the sunshine pouring through the bedroom window. May as well lie out the god-awful truth. "I know this must be hard for you to understand, but I'm not your landlord. I'm your daughter, Bess. I was born in 1949 to you, Maeve and Henry Apple. When I was a teenager, your husband became governor and then a United States senator. He and his family own a lot of downtown Oklahoma City and several businesses. You became a passionate socialite and philanthropist until Daddy passed away. You have Alzheimer's, which is why you can't remember anything you read in the family history book."

Maeve shook her head, sobbing. "Stop lying! I would've never married Henry. Never in a million years, do you hear me? My heart belongs to someone else. And he swore he'd come back to me. A promise is a promise." She held out her hand where the promise ring shone on her finger.

I could feel my knees weaken beneath me, my heart weighing my body down. So that's what she meant by never make a promise you can't keep. So she did remember and love him in her old age. This was her greatest regret? Not waiting around for some philandering actor? No way.

The room began to swim. I sat on Kelly's bed across from Maeve. "I'm sorry about that Maeve. I know how much you loved, love, Canty. I'm sorry things didn't turn out the way you wanted." I nearly added, that I didn't turn out the way you wanted.

Twisting Snoopy's ears, Maeve looked around the room at the photos of Gwen and Victor and Kelly and Phillip. Seeing his photo made my stomach curdle. So join the club. Not everything turned out as I'd planned, either. Did Maeve not remember that months earlier she'd told me life sucks and then you die? No, now was not the time to remind her of her wisecracking personality.

Maeve wiped her eyes. "You've got it all wrong. I'm going to be a famous singer. Arthur is going to make me a star on Broadway. Everyone will know my name."

"Everybody does know your name. You're probably one of the most famous women in Oklahoma history."

Maeve's right brow rose, a skill Gwen had inherited. "I am?" Her eyes danced mischievously. "You're putting me on."

"Girl Scouts' honor."

"I don't know whether or not to believe you."

Could I? Should I? It seemed dangerous to expose her to the elements, to the big scary world she'd been locked away from for so long. Besides her accompanied trips to the Orpheum, Maeve hadn't been anywhere where people could see her. Most of all, she wouldn't recognize them. But maybe that didn't matter half as much as them recognizing her.

"Come on," I said, holding out my hand for her. "I'll show you."

Samuel, who had been working in the greenhouse on special hybrid roses for Gwen's wedding, agreed to drive us around town. I needed to check on the progress of the house, the renovations nearly complete.

My parent's house was the one thing that would've belonged to me if we weren't passing it on to Gwen. Maeve wanted it to stay in the family. Everyone assumed that she and I would move into the estate when renovations were complete. The only benefit I could see was that if we got mad at each other, we'd have plenty of room to separate us.

How do you prove one's existence? I felt like the host of *This Is Your Life, Maeve Apple*, only without the hidden cameras and guest audience. If the news

clippings and old photos hadn't been enough to convince
her she'd lived a noble, big life, then what would? And
even if I succeeded, how long would it last? A few
minutes? Hours? Days?

I have often wondered: is it the mind that keeps
memory of the place, or the place that keeps the
memory? Does the place await your return to hand it
back to you as a gift? I hoped walking into the spaces that
made up my mother's life might do that — hand her the
missing jigsaw pieces of her past.

With Samuel's help, I carefully selected our stops.
She would tire quickly. She took to morning and
afternoon naps in addition to an early bedtime. This is
what happens, isn't it? We slowly revert back to needing
the care that we did when we were infants.

We pulled into the driveway of Mother's sprawling
Nichols Hills estate. The 5,000-square-foot house had
been built in 1960 when I distinctly remembered having a
crush on President Kennedy. What girl at the time
didn't? Like most fashionable women of the time, Maeve
had tried her best to copy Jackie Kennedy's signature
style, which meant there wasn't anything signature about
it for Maeve.

If any place held her memories, surely the home
where she lived for nearly 50 years would. Victor turned
off the engine of his truck and the three of us sat there,
staring at the two-story home with the Greek columns
and massive fountain in the middle of the yard.
Contractors buzzed around us like bees. Samuel rolled
down the windows, allowing the breeze in.

I'd purposely placed Maeve in the middle of us so
she couldn't jump out of the truck if she took a mind to,
though some days I thought she might push me out the
truck with her. She never let anyone get in her way of
what she wanted. Except maybe this.

Except perhaps her whole entire life replacing the
one she would've preferred.

The place had to be renovated throughout, which wasn't cheap. And the more I spent on the house, using Mother's nest egg, the less egg there would be left for me. But keeping up with the Joneses in Nichols Hills was expensive. One could get away without granite countertops in the '60s, but not these days. Granite, marble, travertine tile, a new pool and deck updated lighting and on and on. You updated one thing and it made everything else look so out of character, you had to change that, too. I hoped on my visit that no one would spring any surprises on me. No plumbing disasters or grand ideas for the master bath.

More than anything, I hoped bringing Maeve along might jog her memory; that the sheer power of the house she lived in so long would fight back against the disease.

My heart began to sink the longer we sat there. How could she not remember the grand parties and the Easter egg hunts in the front lawn, first when I was a child and then with her granddaughters? Or how she'd let more than a dozen family members get married on the property? A lot of love happened here. A hell of a lot of love.

"Who needs to live in such a big house?" Maeve said finally.

"You did," I told her. "And Samuel used to mow this lawn for you when he was a boy until he was old enough to take over all the landscaping."

Maeve looked to Victor's kind face. "Child slave labor?"

Samuel laughed. "No, Mrs. Apple. You paid me and I very much needed the money. You and your husband paid my way through college at OSU."

I caught my breath. He had never told me that. Nor had my parents. But why would they? I'm sure it was one of a long list of random acts of kindness they never let the world know about.

Maeve nodded that she heard, but not that she

remembered. "My husband Henry, huh? Education is important. I sometimes wonder if I should've gotten my degree."

"You did," I told her. "You were 35. We'll stop by the music school."

"Don't tell me. The place is named after me?" She scoffed sarcastically.

"It is," I said matter-of-factly.

Maeve put her finger up in the air. "The problem, you see," she said slowly, "is that all those places that bear the Apple name aren't named for me. I'm a struggling actress from a poor family. I've got more Indian blood in me than anything else. We were treated like dirt. I swore I'd change who I was, where I came from. I swore I'd make something of myself. If I became royalty because of a husband, I don't think I can really get any credit for that. Anyone with a big checking account could donate enough money to get their name on a building."

"It's not the money, Maeve. It was how you used it. Yes, you had lavish parties and the best of everything money could buy, but everybody loved you because of your personality. You were always fun to be around. The life of the party. And you cared about taking care of others."

That last part was somewhat true at least. She seemed to love the philanthropy work more than I did, and I often thought she loved it more than she loved me. She definitely spent more time on it.

Maeve rubbed her belly and stared at her swollen abdomen, then looked at me and opened her mouth, but closed it again and watched the laborers. "Let's go have a look then, shall we?"

We stepped inside the marble foyer and Maeve gasped. The winding staircase and crystal chandeliers were breathtaking. I remembered every stage of the construction of the house. Maeve would drag me over and explain in detail why she had selected the wood, the paint, the lighting, and carpeting. How could she not remember that she personally picked out every stitch of the grand estate? She eschewed the interior designer's advice and went with her gut instinct

"I do love all the intricate details," Maeve said. "It reminds me of a mansion I saw in a magazine once when I was a little girl."

So that's where she got her inspiration. Making a little girl dream come true. For the third time, I told her, "You did all this, Maeve. Every bit of it was your idea. Your brainchild."

Maeve shook her head as if she still didn't believe me. "But who needs such a big house for only one child?"

I'd often wondered the same thing. "You couldn't have any more children," I reminded her softly.

A worried look passed over her face. "I can't believe Henry Apple became Governor," she said as we stared at the five-foot-high painting of she and Daddy when they were named king and queen of the Oklahoma City Golf and Country Club in 1964. "He doesn't seem that ambitious," she said. "His daddy sure is. Must've pushed him into it. I told you that's how we met, right?"

I shook my head. She had to be remembering wrong.

"Wesley is a hard drinker and an ass pincher," Maeve said of my grandfather, to which Samuel suppressed a chuckle. I elbowed him.

Maeve continued. "Wesley was a regular at the Orpheum, a patron of the arts," she said. "He'd come to opening night and to the after parties. He'd hit the liquor fast and hard and grab me and pull me down on his lap. He'd find out where I was singing around town and come hear me. Best tipper I ever had. Always had the best cigars. So one day, he says, 'If I can't have you, then the next best thing is for my son to have you.'"

"He did not," I said, my heart beating a little faster.

"Most certainly did. Next thing I know he starts bringing in this good-looking meek man in a business suit in after work. Henry can't hold his liquor like his Pops, though, and usually ends up in the bathroom throwing up by nine o'clock. Finally Henry gets the courage to ask me out. I say yes because as I said, Wesley is my best tipper and Arthur could've never put on Princess and the Pauper without the help of people like Wesley. Believe me, I knew where my bread was buttered."

For some reason, I felt like a child again and wished to run up those stairs and slam myself down on my childhood bed. This wasn't at all how I expected my parents to get together and certainly not how I pictured my grandfather. But I'd asked for honesty, hadn't I? Which meant hearing the things that had been until then left unsaid.

Samuel rubbed small circles in the middle of my back, comforting me. How did he always know what to do exactly when I needed it?

"But then you fell in love with Henry, once you got to know him?"

Maeve looked at me blankly. "I'm getting to know him, but I can't say there is much attraction there. He's nice enough looking, but dull as a doornail. When he asked me to marry him, I was shocked. This may sound silly, but it's almost as if his father put him up to it. Like his father said to make it as a politician, you need a charming wife. Like my personality would make up for Henry lacking one."

My father, dull? The last word in the dictionary I'd use to describe him. Maybe he wasn't flashy like Canty and couldn't play instruments, but dull? I told myself this wasn't the Maeve talking who had spent 50-plus years married to the man. This was Early Maeve, who still thought she could lasso the moon. I resisted the urge to shake her until her senses came back. I'd never hated her disease more than I did in that moment.

Samuel moved us along. "Let's see the garden," he said.

"Splendid idea," I said, my voice cracking. "You spent a lot of time out in the gardens." I never knew what she did out there all alone. Thinking? About what? Canty? Wishing she were here with him instead of my father? Or better yet off to city after city on tour—Paris, Vegas, Broadway.

"What's all the construction for?" Maeve asked as a couple of big guys passed us with a sheet of granite on their shoulders between them.

"We're renovating the house as a surprise wedding gift for Gwen and Victor." Saying the words out loud made me sick. As mired as I was in Gwen's wedding, I still couldn't believe my little girl was getting married. And giving newlyweds such a big gift somehow didn't feel right. Like they needed to earn their wedding stripes before taking on such a big house, such a big future. Of course Skylar was in on the surprise. Back when Phillip and I were still unhappily married, we'd told Skylar we could present the house keys to Victor and Gwen on the pre-show before the ceremony. Skylar had gone nuts. The world would get a tour of the grand old house, which meant it could no longer look old. I wondered how much of my spending on the home had to do with it looking good enough on national TV?

Depending on how the estate meeting went, I debated what else I could let go of. The antique store? I already had willing buyers just waiting for the word. But that meant the girls and I wouldn't be able to live in the loft together much longer. My heart hurt.

Maeve scratched her head. "The clumsy girl with the big voice is getting married?" She asked her voice thick with suspicion.

"That's Gwen, your granddaughter. She's getting married in a few months."

"Here I thought she was after my man," Maeve said in relief.

"After Canty?"

"Have you not seen the way she looks at him?"

I thought back to the weekend and the swing dancing. The man Maeve took for Canty was Ax. He seemed born to play the dashing pauper who stole a princess' heart. Very handsome, indeed. A real throwback. I supposed I hadn't noticed any special attraction, but then I hadn't really paid attention, and Gwen had always been a flirt, from the time she was a little girl, much like her grandmother. As soon as Samuel had shown up at the club, he was all I could think about, though I'm embarrassed to admit it. And not making a damned fool of myself dancing.

"She's in love with Victor," I assured her. "They think we're renovating the house to sell it after they host the reception here. But Gwen has always loved this house."

"Some dowry," Maeve said, gawking at the lavish interior.

Dowry. Such an old-fashioned word. Well, it wasn't as if I were paying Victor to marry my daughter. Giving the house had been Maeve's idea, suggesting it in her early stages of Alzheimer's. She was adamant we keep it in the family. "All the homes in Nichols Hills are being renovated," I said, not wanting to hurt her feelings, and not telling her that, sadly, many of them were being torn to the ground and replaced by much bigger homes.

Maeve sucked in her breath as we entered the gardens, Samuel's greatest masterpiece. The terrace looked down on the gardens, complete with a path that completed the letter A. My friends and I used to run the maze as a kid and we'd wind up in the middle where a fountain with stone birds shot water to the sky.

"You sat right here," I said, patting the wicker chair. Every morning. Every evening. When I looked for her, I knew where to find her.

Maeve plopped down, her knee popping in the process. She closed her eyes. Samuel and I waited for her to speak, to remember. I felt the compulsion to grab Samuel's hand and squeezed it. I did. I don't know why, but we were in this together. I think Samuel wanted Maeve to remember his gardens as much as I did.

He squeezed my hand back, yet instead of letting go like I thought he would, he held it. The warmth of his touch spread all the way to my throat where I was sure I would cry out.

Had she fallen asleep? Falling asleep in chairs was common practice these days, even for me. Yet her eyes opened a moment later.

"All I remember is that I'm due at the Orpheum for final rehearsals at 7 p.m. sharp," she said. "Auditions are coming up. And I have a date with Henry immediately following, though after what you've shown me I'm not sure I want to go on the date."

"Do you think you can change the future?" I asked hotly, letting go of Samuel's hand.

"The future being my past?" Maeve said, mocking me. "You're the witch. Or the ghost of the future. You tell me if I have any power to change it. All I know is that as grand as this place is, I'd still prefer to become a star on my own. I can't believe I'd give up singing. I'd rather sing than breathe. It sounds to me like I gave up the stage for acting out an entirely different life than the one I'd rehearsed. Sounds like I became an even better actor than I thought I was if I pulled off this charade. Don't show me anything else. I don't want to see it. Now take me back."

Tears pulsed behind my eyes. A charade? How could she be so hardheaded? Was my coming into the world so traumatic for her that she chose to erase it altogether? I had to shake myself out of it. It was the disease, nothing more, nothing less. Wasn't it? But what bothered me most was the question floating between us: if you had it to do over, would you make the same choice?

I wanted to tell her I had one final gift for her — that I was looking for the life she had left behind, the man she had loved and lost. We were so close. A few more days and Anna would be back in town and she would lead me to her father. As much as her not remembering hurt me, the thought that I couldn't do anything to make her pain go away hurt me more. I couldn't stand to see her unhappy the rest of her days.

When we returned to the loft, Samuel went back to his greenhouse and Jervis agreed to watch Maeve over the lunch hour so I could make it to Choral Society meeting downtown. When I moved from Gaillardia to the loft, the society agreed to move the meeting from the country club to Nonna's downtown, where we reserved a room.

After our episode that morning, going to a Choral Society meeting appointed only because I was Maeve's daughter felt like the last thing in the world I wanted to do. If Maeve couldn't fathom her future, yet couldn't change it, then why couldn't I change my future while I still had the chance?

I hated meetings, especially ones that were disguised as "lady lunches." There was an agenda, even when it wasn't declared. Mother wanted me to love my position in society as much as she did, but we both knew it could never be. I was an interloper. A fake. A phony. I don't care what my last name dictated — it was time for the real Bess to show up and take a stand.

I arrived a few minutes late, yet the women, whose perfume overcame me as we entered the private dining room upstairs, greeted me with hugs and air kisses. Not one of the eight women there had stopped by to see the loft. Not one loaf of banana nut bread or bouquet of flowers. Not one personal visit to see how I was handling the divorce. Maeve's disposition had rubbed off on me. I wanted to give every one of these pretentious ladies the middle finger and leave the meeting as soon as I arrived.

I had a better idea.

Thank God Phillip's new girlfriend wasn't in attendance. That would've surely sent me over the edge. OI's Grapevine column had said Diana and Phillip had been dating for months. The proof was in the pictures. Social affairs all over town together. Holding hands, her fake boobs sticking out of designer dresses, her Botoxed face rubbing up against Phillip's. I may not want to sleep with my ex-husband ever again, but that didn't mean I wanted an old backstabbing friend sleeping with him, either.

To think, I'd made her blueberry muffins every time she'd divorced one of her husbands.

I sat at the head of the table, the last place on earth I wanted to sit, yet the women always saved it for me. Kelly loved to sit at the head of the table, sure and confident, but as for me, I was ready to retire to the corner, declare my wallflower status.

The women chitchatted about upcoming jaunts to Africa for safari and Europe for summer shopping and Mexico for beaches. Suddenly, I was relieved none of them asked me about Phillip or the divorce. I was afraid I had enough tears held back to flood the room if I let them.

Instead they talked about *Luxe Weddings*, each throwing in their own two cents about what I should consider for Gwen as we finished out the shows and ideas on diets that might work for her. "You're so lucky Gwen is letting you help," Betty Smithton said. "My Tara wouldn't so much as let me pick out my own mother-of-the-bride dress."

Because Tara's a spoiled brat, I wanted to tell her. But could they say any different of mine? Just because Gwen had gotten fed up with the wedding planners the show had thrust upon her (she was the first in LW history to fire a celebrity wedding planner on the show) and she trusted me; didn't mean I was lucky. If it weren't for the show, I'd quit myself. But if I balked at even one pricey napkin ring, I'd look like a bad mother on TV.

I realized I couldn't have a real conversation with these women. We talked at each other, not with. I couldn't share with them how I'd felt my whole life had been stolen from me. How I pretended to have this great relationship with my children when we still kept secrets from each other. How I had no idea why women I'd never seen before were coming and going from my loft with brown paper bags and a big smile on their faces. Gwen said they were "friends," yet I swear one of them was older than me. I'd even rummaged through her drawers looking for drugs, until I realized I had no idea what sort of drug it could be. Was she selling uppers to tired suburban moms? Party pills for the socialites? I hated that I suspected anything awry with my own flesh and blood.

Sonya Berkenshire coyly poked her fork in the air my way. "I heard you went swing dancing with your gardener last week. Tell me it's not true, darling?"

"Bess always was kind to the help," Candy Prince added.

My mouth went dry, and I took a drink of water. Betty interjected. "Bess knows better than that. We should all think of the most eligible gentleman we could think of and get her married properly before it's too late."

"Too late? For what? The Botox to stop working?" I laughed. For once I understood why Kelly had been so ruffled with the Top Bachelorette title. No one wants to think you need help finding a mate, let alone the horrible feeling of being discarded after you'd served your purpose.

The women stopped chewing, the room suddenly silent. "I don't want anyone setting me up. If I do want companionship, I'll find it myself. As if it's any of your business, I did not go on a date with Samuel. That's his name, Samuel. You all should know his name by now. He's outfitted your flowerbeds for years. He's a talented, warm man and he deserves more than to be called 'the help.'"

Sighing and rolling of eyes and nervous laughter churned around the table. "Like you need any advice from us," Betty said. "You're an Apple. And what an Apple wants, an Apple gets."

How right she was. Most Apples got what they wanted. It was high time I started thinking like a Bess Apple-Barton, and not within the group dynamic.

Betty began the meeting as we chewed our blue cheese and almond salad with edible flowers, something Nonna's was famous for.

"Now about that additional funding for the summer concert series," Betty said, eyeing me with a twinkle that I'd recognized often over the years. Whenever any club was short on funding, they came to an Apple to meet the goal. The Choral Society wanted to bring two additional concerts in at a cost of $25,000, yet we already donated $250,000 for various music programs across the state. We supported starving artists, people like Ax (and I assumed, Canty) so they could live their dreams.

But when had I ever expressed myself? When had I selected a charity of my own choice to donate money to? Answer: never. Music and theater was my mother's thing. Urban expansion and development was my father's thing and then my ex-husband and soon to be son-in-law's thing. Not my thing. And what these women could never know is that we didn't have piles of extra money lying around begging to be spent.

After Henry died, Maeve had taken liberties with the money he'd so carefully stored away. Since hearing about my grandfather's gambling problem, I understand why my father was a saver, but my mother loved to give, in addition to her love for shopping. She acted like money was a well that simply never ran dry. God love her for being so generous, but I had to protect what was left of it.

"Do we really need two more concerts?" I asked dryly. The women, well, some of them, gasped as if I'd asked if we really needed to believe in Jesus Christ. "Attendance at the four we had last year was pretty dismal, if I recall." A bunch of blue hairs, not that I had anything against blue hair, per se.

As I opened my mouth to explain myself, Diana walked in the door, wearing what looked like a new suit, new high heels and the waft of guilty-as-sin. Don't even think about air-kissing me. My mother had it all wrong. I wasn't a witch. Diana was a witch and bitch all rolled into one—a bwitch. Sharing all those turkey dinners with us over the years when each of her husbands left her for younger women, and there we were to console her, and what do I get for it?

She air-kissed me. The bwitch! "I know where those lips have been," I said aloud.

Eyes widened, breaths exhaled, and Diana stood as still as the Statue of Liberty. An uncomfortable moment later, Diana laughed, causing the other women to follow. Not me. I wasn't eating an edible flower and I sure as hell wasn't laughing. "I wasn't joking," I said, to the room, then to her. "I'm sure I'm not the only woman around the table to read OI, though we'd never admit it."

Diana patted my back, a poor-sugar gesture that made me want to smack her overpriced, shellacked head of hair. "Perhaps we should stay for a drink after," Diana said firmly, then smiled. "Sorry I'm late."

"It's a long drive from Gaillardia," I said, tapping my pen on my notebook. You see, Diana doesn't live in Gaillardia, but I am certain she's staying in my former abode and all the women probably knew it. Who needs a private eye when these women gossip as effortlessly as they breathe?

Betty cleared her throat and the women shifted uncomfortably in the oversized chairs. Let them shift! Let them be uncomfortable! How comfortable do you think I am with this bwitch in my presence? "Diana, you can come sit down here, Sugar."

Oh, so they were making room for the Judas. Well, we'll see about that.

"Now about that additional funding," Betty said sweetly.

"Yes, does anyone have any ideas?" I chirped, thinking instead where I wanted that $25,000 to go. Not so these women could lounge in the park with their paws over other people's husbands, that's for damn sure.

I wanted the money to go to women who truly deserved it. To women literally beaten down, thrown out, discarded like used garbage. Children unwanted and abandoned. I wanted to give people second chances, not an evening of music in the park. That's what Mother wanted, and God bless her for it. She expanded minds. I simply wanted to protect and clothe and feed them. I wanted to help people with Alzheimer's. Men and women who may not have a caring relative to help take care of them.

"Oh, I see," I looked each of them in the eyes, sweeping the room with my gaze. "You assumed I would fund them?" Of course they thought this. The way it had always been. These were friends through purse strings only. "You all should be the first to know. I'm shifting some support," I told them, my voice growing more confident with each word. "Mother spent liberally before I became her trustee, but I can't afford to be frivolous." I nearly choked back the words. Me, the mother-of-the-bride on *Luxe Weddings,* giving a speech on saving? Where was this coming from?

Too bad these women didn't see it that way. Their smiles fell flat, then turned into frowns.

For the rest of the ladies, the air may have felt stifling

in the room, but for me it felt like the wind on the beach in Waikiki. Refreshing. Liberating. I shrugged my shoulders, put my pen and notebook back in my briefcase and scooted my chair back. My finances were none of their business, and I shouldn't have to explain myself. Men sure as hell don't.

"Unfortunately, I must retire my position on the board," I said. "I appreciate that you all ask me to take my mother's place, but I've got some things I need to do on my own. And since Diana is doing my husband— excuse me, ex-husband—I'm sure she can also fulfill my role as head of the committee from here on out."

I began removing my clothing on my way down the stairs, beginning with Mother's Hermes scarf, the Chanel jacket I could barely breathe in, and the high heels I should've given up long ago. I walked in my bare feet the two blocks back to the loft, but instead of checking in on Maeve, my usual first stop, I marched around to the nursery and headed straight for the greenhouse.

Samuel's muscular frame bent over the roses. I unbuttoned the top two buttons of my blouse. From then on, I vowed only to sport wash-and-wear clothing. Cotton. I would live and then die in a cotton T-shirt and denim.

I studied Samuel's body, his thick calves and strong thighs and round firm bottom. A baseball player's butt.

A hunger swelled within me, but it wasn't for food. I'd been missing the key ingredient Oprah's gurus say humans need for survival: sex. Seems we can't be truly happy without it, and I'd been without it for more than a year, when I'd made a last attempt at communion with Phillip, which had only ended with him sputtering to a climax and me lying there exhausted at the effort and not even close to orgasm. I'd told myself for years that my expectations were too high, but perhaps they'd been too low. Much, much too low.

I'd denied myself for so long. For pleasure. For

happiness. For love.

Samuel's head bopped back and forth, listening to his earphones from his iPod I'd gotten him for Christmas.

After a long moment, he noticed me, or else felt my presence. How could he not after I'd stared at him so long? He took one ear bud out and looked down at my bare feet. "What is it with you? No gloves when you prune. No shoes when you're outdoors."

"I want to feel," I told him, moving closer. "Feel the prick of the thorns and the earth below my feet. To feel, period."

Victor raised a brow. "Did something happen at that stuffy meeting?"

"Yes. I told them to stuff it."

"You didn't."

"I did. I'm going to start asking for what I really want. So I thought I'd start with you."

"With me?" Even with a tan, the man still blushed.

"Have you ever thought about kissing me, Samuel?" I asked, stepping even closer, the concrete of the greenhouse cool beneath my feet. I stopped when we were arm's length apart.

His eyes became fixed, his mouth soft. "When have I not thought about it, Bess? Many years of thinking about it."

"No way." I smiled coyly.

"I helped you carry your things up to your room from that trip to Paris. You were 12."

"My father tipped you a dollar. I thought you were trying to make a buck."

"More like trying to make a move. You were my first crush. You probably thought I was a dirty, scrappy kid."

I put my hand on his forearm and slid my palm down to his wrist. "Even the rich boys have a little dirt behind the ears."

Samuel swallowed hard, his Adam's apple bopping up and down. "I think I may faint right now. Not something a former quarterback likes to do."

"I'll catch you," I said, lifting his hand and putting it on my breast. God knows I'd never done that before. Good girls don't make the first move.

"Bess." Victor's voice was throaty, sexy. I couldn't stop looking at his mouth. The mouth I wanted so badly to be on mine. I hesitated, but thankfully, he didn't. He wrapped his arm around my waist and pulled me into him.

It was my turn to get lost, get carried away. All the girls in school talked about what a good kisser Samuel was. Finally I got to find out.

Yes, girls, I would tell them. Samuel is still one helluva kisser. In a flash, I hoped Alzheimer's would not steal this moment from me years from now.

I never wanted to forget what it felt like to get something you never knew you needed in the first place.

Chapter 13

Gwen

With Victor in New York City on business with my dad, and Skylar and Shadow in tow to learn more about the most popular groom ever to grace the show, I felt like I'd gotten a free pass. The prison door had been left open and I'd been able to walk right out.

Three whole days with no camera crew following me. Three days to be me and not the bride-to-be. I hated that I loved this freedom so much. I told myself it wasn't because Victor was gone. I nearly convinced myself all my anxiety was a by-product of the TV show. But I had another show to worry about, one I began caring about far more than *Luxe Weddings*.

Princess and the Pauper.

Freedom can take you in unexpected places, such as the middle of Nowhere, Oklahoma, and it's exactly where I wanted to be. Across from Ax at 2:00 a.m. outside his beat up RV where BB, Rogue and Taz were sleeping, leaving Ax and I alone outside. Living on the cheap seemed to come pretty easily to these actors. I think if I lived in the middle of nowhere and didn't have Internet access, I could kick my shopping addiction easy peasy.

Ax and I had rehearsed late and I wasn't in a huge hurry to get back home and listen to Kelly's snoring, especially when the moon was especially kind to Ax's sexy figure in the dark.

He propped a bottle of Pabst Blue Ribbon on his knee, dressed in soft denim and an old T-shirt.

"You've come a long way, baby," Ax said in the low, smoky voice he seemed to get after singing and dancing for hours on end.

"Think so?"

"Ever think about making a demo?"

"You mean besides the one I made on my Barbie karaoke machine?"

"Yeah. Besides that," he said.

"Let's say my family had a different plan for me, and I sort of jumped on the track and haven't had the courage to jump off."

"Well, it's obvious you love it up there on stage. I'm serious about the demo, Gwen. You're really, really good. You've got this amazing presence on stage, so whether or not musicals are your thing, you should definitely pursue a musical career. Your voice is original."

"How so?"

He leaned forward, resting his elbow on his knee. "I get goosebumps as soon as you open your mouth and the first note comes out."

And I get goose bumps just looking at your mouth. Hell, hearing you talk about getting goose bumps is giving me goose bumps. "You really mean that?"

"Don't look so surprised. Come on. You've got a bit of Ella and Norah Jones topped off with the charisma of Bublé. I think you'd do well on radio."

"Michael Bublé? No way. I love him. Maybe I could duet with him someday. Sorry, that sounds silly." I shook my hair; the big princess curls falling around my shoulders.

"Doesn't sound silly at all. Anything can happen, Gwen. You can never dream too big for yourself."

"Right now my dream is to be your princess," I said, nearly choking from the bitter taste of the beer. "On stage, I mean. You know you're a shoe-in for the pauper, right? No one even comes close to being so perfect for the role."

"I'm definitely living his life off stage," he said. "And

you're as close to the real-life princess as it gets. Think about it. Your dad is marrying you off to the best match. From what the papers say, they couldn't pick a better mate for our beloved Gwen."

I squirmed in the lawn chair. Hearing him say it out loud made it sound like an insult. But Victor had always been a great choice for me. So what if my family approved? That was a good thing.

"One big difference in me and the princess in the story is that I'm sure my dad would let me marry who I wanted. He'd support me in whatever I decided to do. In fact, I've been gathering up the courage to tell him I'd like to quit the company and take up acting for real."

"For real?" Ax laughed. "So auditioning for Princess isn't real enough?"

"I guess I'd have to get the part to know I could really do it."

Ax shook his head. "That's not the way it works. Some actors spend years auditioning and perfecting their craft before they get a big role. Why do you think I'm a teacher back home? It's tough to get work. Especially if you're not connected."

Ouch. That stung. But he was right. I used my connections where I could. "Not this time. It's not Edgar's choice, even if my grandmother was the original Princess. I won't get the role because of my name," I said.

"I wouldn't be so sure."

"I need to get home." My voice strained. I was afraid I'd lose it. It was too much to hope Ax could like me for me, and not see me as my family name. I got up and tossed the beer in the trashcan.

Ax grabbed my hand. "Hey, I'm sorry. That was a low blow. I've seen it happen time and again. I may be bitter because I've never had anything handed to me. I've had to work hard all my life. But you're getting judged enough with the reality show and the audition. The last thing you need is for me to judge you, too. I'm sorry."

I bit my bottom lip and squeezed his hand "Fine. But that whole thing about not judging someone 'til you've walked in their shoes? It goes for people like me, too."

"Then I have a real problem. I could never walk in those things." He stared at my stilettos. "What do you say we have a last dance before you take off?" His smile appeared like a crescent moon in the dark.

"Do people ever say no to you?"

"More than I'd like."

I nodded, and pulled Ax up. "One dance."

Famous last words.

Dean Martin crooned on the iPod. Ax pulled me close, and then closer, as I felt his chest against my chest, thighs against thighs, and his warm breath on my cheek. My whole body felt engulfed in desire.

"No matter how things turn out, even if I don't get Princess, I'm glad we met," I said, my arms around his neck. "I wish we'd met in a different time."

He took a step back and looked into my eyes. "You mean in the Middle Ages? Or 1949? Or, sometime before you had that rock on your finger and starred in the biggest reality hit of the summer?"

My mouth dried up. All of the above. Anytime but now. "Never mind."

Ax lifted my chin and our eyes locked. "You've got the world by the string, Gwen. The last thing you need is some actor messing things up for you. Trust me on this."

"So you feel it, too, don't you?"

He looked up at the stars. "I'm going to have to let you go."

And he did. I stepped back, hurt. "Now or always?"

"If I'm going to be honest, I haven't been helping you to be a nice teacher. But this isn't good for either of us. It may look like you have everything to lose, but I have this." He tapped his chest with his finger.

I choked back a tear. Could this really be happening? Is this what Maeve heard all those years ago? Did she let

Canty go, choosing grandfather over him, or was it the other way around? Was it Canty who had the change of heart, choosing to stay with is wife and taking her with him to New York so he could pursue his dreams on Broadway? Had he said something like, "One of the wealthiest men in Oklahoma wants to make you his bride. Don't waste your life on me. A nobody. A drifter. He can give you the world on a string. I've got nothing to give you but my heart."

In life, we usually don't get the gift of hindsight, but in this case, I'd seen how Maeve's life had ended up. A glorious, well-lived public life, for sure. But in the end, all she wanted was the one thing Henry could never give her: Canty's love.

Two days later, Ax was the still the main attraction in my head. I hated that I had feelings for him - that I thought about him first thing in the morning and last thing at night. That cliche. I wanted to miss my fiancé. I wanted to be madly in love with my "Prince Charming." I wanted... but what did it matter?

Okay, very, very first thing in the morning I thought about how much I hated that Kelly's pregnancy had given her rhinitis, which meant she snored all night long. If she weren't preggers, I'd seriously consider smothering her with my pillow. And if she yelled at me one more time about picking up my crap, I swear I was going to burst. Sometimes she made me feel ten again. Yet I had to admit we were trying. I think we could even be friends. She was helping me through the painful process of going through my closets to find things for the designer sale, packing up shoes in brown sacks and slowly making cash so I could pay off my debt.

As I headed to the shower passing by the long row of shoes that lined the bedroom and hallway to get ready for another mind-numbing day at the office, I couldn't stop wondering if Maeve and Canty's love had survived the test of time, especially after that painful night with Ax in the country. If Maeve's passion still burned, could that mean my infatuation with the stage and a certain jitterbug could be much more than that? Could my feelings for the stage and for Ax be real, everlasting? Would I have to suppress the real me for the life laid out for me?

"We're going to take the world by storm, Gwen," Victor had told me on the phone from New York, but I wasn't a part of the we. He and my father were going to take the world by storm. He most certainly wanted to spend the rest of his *business* life with my father. Why couldn't I be certain he wanted to spend his personal life with me? Why did I feel like if we took the business out of our equation, we would add up to nothing?

Chapter 14

Kelly

"There's only one problem with this list of names," my father said as he scanned the 50 options I'd given him for the proposed downtown ice rink.

"Which is what?" I said, leaning forward, and feeling the rubber band on my waist stretching to the point of nearly snapping. I'd love to have credited the extra weight gain on the baby, but it had to be all those lunches with Edgar. I'd finally moved into the hungry-horse stage. I was a walking, talking, cattle commercial. Beef—it's what's for dinner. And lunch. And late-night snacks. Which was my second, but most important, reason for coming. Announce names for the ice rink, and then announce that I was with child.

"I don't see one name with Apple in it," Phillip said, frowning.

I let out a *ha*, before remembering my father didn't make jokes when it came to business. "With more than a dozen other companies in the metro with the name Apple attached, I recommend we go with something different," I said.

"People associate the Apple name with a solid reputation, high morals, hard work and character. You said yourself that the Apple brand name is like gold in Oklahoma. So why wouldn't we want to use it even more?"

"We've discussed the inherent problems of using a real name for a company. If something happens with the family, it could reflect poorly on the businesses."

Phillip nodded, but handed me back the papers. "Kelly, nothing bad has happened with the family or the businesses in a hundred years. Sure, old man Apple had some drinking and gambling problems, but that was nothing that couldn't be swept under the rug back in the day. Since then, peachy keen. Smooth sailing. Hell, we're practically the buckle on the Bible belt, wouldn't you say? No, I think we should go with Apples on Ice. Nice ring to it." He swept his arm over his desk to emphasize how it might look in say, blaring neon.

"Got it." He snapped his fingers. "How about Arctic Apple Ice Rink? Yes, I love it, don't you? You work up the logo. But make sure it's got an apple in it. You know, with icicles and frost and such."

I hadn't spent ten hours brainstorming unique names to have them all swept under the proverbial rug where my great-grandfather's secret sins laid to rest in two seconds flat. And as I told my father, "I don't do cheesy logos."

"Not cheesy. You know, something classy."

"A classy apple with icicles on it? It'll end up looking like freebie clip art."

"Not with your best illustrator," he said.

"No." I crossed my arms.

My father frowned, his right brow arching to the heavens. "What did you say?"

"I said, no. That won't work for me. I have a reputation to keep, too. If you want a cheesy name and a cheesy logo, then I'm sure you can find some cheesy agency hack to do it for you, but this gal ain't it." I stood and gathered my things. Not like I could re-sell my great names on eBay. All that brainpower down the drain when I could've been watching Bewitched reruns, or maybe even reading a novel for once. I'd already discounted my price, again, for my family. He was running me over and there was nothing left of me to squish. God, I was tired. My bones, my brain, every inch of my body.

Phillip's phone rang, but instead of answering it, he kept staring at me. "Does this mean what I think it means?"

"It does, Dad, er, Phillip." I stuck out my hand, disbelieving what I was doing. How badly I needed what was left of the money in the budget, how badly I needed the business because two more of my clients had recently cut their summer spending. But enough is enough. "I really do appreciate everything you've done for me, but I'm officially retiring the Apple account. All of them."

"But you can't do that, darling. We're family."

"I certainly can. And I will. In fact, I already did. When I've joked about having Clients from Hell, I was talking about you." I inhaled as if an ocean breeze filled the air. "Wow. That felt really good. Good luck with the ice rink and the mall," I said. "And this isn't the way I wanted to tell you, but I do have another project that will most definitely bear the name Apple-Barton." I swallowed hard.

"For the mall development project, I hope," he said.

"No, Dad. It's for my baby. My baby that will be here in a little over six months." I put on a smile. "Congrats. You're going to be a grandpa."

He shook his head. "But...how?"

"Do I need to sing the fertilization song?"

"Kelly, for God's sake, please tell me you're joking. About all of it."

I rubbed my hand over my belly. "Nope. I waited all of my dating life for a knight to come and sweep me off my feet, but I think the whole thing's a terrible consumer plot to sell a bunch of makeup and sexy lingerie to desperate women. If you think of it the way I do, then you'd be proud. You raised a smart, confident woman who doesn't need a man to be happy. All I needed was a donor."

He raised his hand, palms out, in a stop motion.

"You're having a child with someone out of wedlock? Not even a someone, but a vial of sperm? I'm sorry, but all those things I said about the Apple brand applies to you, too. You're an Apple, through and through. I cannot allow, scratch that, I will not allow for you to do something to disgrace the Apple name."

Phillip sat back in his chair, an icy stare cooling me all over. The shame shot like daggers. "I don't know what to say."

Tears threatened behind my eyelids, but I had to stay strong. "You don't have to say anything. This is who I am. I'm sorry if you don't like it, or the investors don't like it, or if I'm getting coal in my stocking this year. I'm not going to be like Mom and live my life trying to please her parents. You know I'm not a 'whim' kind of girl. So I hope in time, you'll accept it. And if not, then that's okay, too."

He shook his head. "There will be repercussions, of course. What's your story? Something the public will swallow. You know, something sympathetic and conservative?"

"Dad, I'm not a politician. My pregnancy doesn't need spin."

"I'll call Richard Hunt and we'll take care of everything." He put his hand on the phone, and I leapt to my feet and put my hand over his.

"You'll call no one, and you'll take care of nothing. This is my personal business. I'll not have a PR hack like Richard Hunt thinking up ways to make my pregnancy palatable to the public. Or to your goonies at the country club."

Phillip put his other hand over mine. "You don't understand, Kelly. When you're an Apple, there is no such thing as personal business." He shook his head slowly. "Honey, it's not that. It's you. It's the baby. I know what it's like to grow up without a father around. I'd never wish that on a grandchild of mine. Ever."

When I arrived back at my office, Edgar was waiting for me, the smell of bacon wafting from the bags he held in his hands. I wished my heart didn't do that funny tick-skip-tick thing when I saw him. My father's words stuck in my head. I'd never intended to take something away from my child before he or she was even born. Maybe I had made a hasty decision, so mad at John that I didn't think a father was mandatory, not that a father didn't matter. Of course it did. But I'd been thinking of the baby. And me. Selfishly, of me.

Yet the father would never up and leave as Phillip's father had because there would be no father in the first place. Would it be worse never knowing who the father was? Never getting to know and love someone and then have them ripped away?

"You look like hell," Edgar said, leaning on the frame of my office door. My assistant had taken off, and the staff had started treating Edgar like "one of us." I wanted to tell him he didn't look like hell, he looked sexy as hell, but I didn't. He wore a thin baby blue v-neck with butt-hugging jeans and flip-flops. Sexy feet, too. I couldn't believe the Orpheum grand opening was four weeks away and that would be the end of it. The end of Edgar and me, whatever it was we had. We had lunch. We had an account. We had business. Always business.

"Well, hello to you, too. A rough meeting. Nothing I can't handle." As nice as it was to see him, I wanted to be alone. To crawl under my grandmother's afghan and sleep the next six months away. I'd escape and have my child in secret and not have to go deal with my family or the public. What happened to my confidence? I'd stood up to Phillip only to leave there feeling he had a point. But when didn't he? It was my decision, so why should they even be a part of it?

Why did I want to run into Edgar's arms at the sight

of him? A part of me wanted to tell him everything. That lunch, a former non-hour in my life, had become my favorite part of the day. That I looked forward to his presence, his voice, his laugh, much more than the food.

I motioned to Edgar's attire. "A little casual for Monday, don't you think?" I couldn't rush to him, couldn't tell him my personal life. Food and double hourly billing was all I could handle. I had to stop things from getting more personal. I didn't want to know Edgar McGuire like this. But, he wasn't Sexy Client anymore. He was Real Man with Real Past. And he ended up not to be the phony jerk I took him for at first. My attraction, the vibe, had been genuine.

"Playing golf after lunch," he said. "You know them, actually. Phillip Barton and Victor Prescott."

I shook my head, and sat on the couch with a huff. "Never heard of them. Oh, wait. They used to be my biggest client."

"Used to, huh? Tired of working for the fam? I can imagine that might be precarious."

"Don't even get me started," I said, tearing into the bag and smiling at the huge BLT inside. Taylor had told me about the Salt-craving stage, and I wasn't complaining a bit.

"Think they're hitting me up for something?" he asked.

"Most likely they want you to head up some position for the Downtown Chamber of Commerce. And give money. They'll position it better than that. They'll call it a sponsorship and tell you you'll get your logo on some stuff. Likely starting with the ice rink project I gave up."

"Maybe I'll say yes. I'm actually looking at a few other properties down here. I like it here. The people, too."

I smiled. "Does this mean you're going to stay in OKC after the musical ends?"

Edgar shrugged. "I was thinking of moving into

those lofts over on Sheraton when I heard the developer was selling. So instead of buying one loft, why not buy the whole building?"

Rich people. I swear. "The Get Laid Lofts?"

"Excuse me?"

"Yeah. That's what people are calling them. They're for sexy singles on the prowl. Happy hour every evening on the roof. Pretty convenient to get drunk and then take some honey back to your room. At least it avoids the whole drunk-driving issue."

He folded his arms and frowned, and leaned back on the couch. I loved when he scooted his body down like a plank and tapped his feet together like that. No, I hated it. I definitely hated how comfortable he made himself in my presence or how I thought I could straddle him in that position. No, I'm probably like the sister he never had. I straightened my posture hoping he would do the same. No such luck.

"Then maybe I shouldn't buy the Get Laid Lofts," he said. "I wouldn't want people thinking I'd bought property to get laid."

"Like anyone would think you have trouble in that arena. And I think that's TMI, don't you? Crossing some boundaries."

His face crept into a smile. He loved playing along. "You should know by now, Ms. Apple-Barton, that I enjoy pushing boundaries. But since you are so opinionated, do you know if there are any Old Fogey Lofts available?"

"Ask my father. He'll know. When I was in his office ten minutes ago, I saw a folder from the Get Laid Lofts on his desk. He either wants to talk you out of it or into it with him. He's a low risk guy, though divorcing my mother was pretty high risk, if you ask me. I love him, but I'm pissed. I'm pissed he's divorcing my mother and yet he's still in charge of most of our businesses because he's a man. For all I know, he married my mother for her money, for her family name. And a generation later, my future brother-in-law could be doing the same."

"I wouldn't have any idea, not ever having been married. And being a man who makes money on his own."

"So does that mean we can't have an opinion on matrimony, or that we're simply smarter than everybody else?"

Edgar laughed. "I'd like to think the latter. And I've never let not having done something kept me from intelligent discourse about it."

I smiled, but I didn't want him to make me smile because a part of me wanted to stay mad at men, every last one of them. I hated that he said things like "intelligent discourse" and asked my opinion instead of telling me what to do like a lot of clients did.

Edgar turned his body, his elbow propped on the top of the back of the couch, his head on his palm. "Do you want to know what I think?"

I shrugged. "Humor me."

"I think marriage is the biggest risk of all. It's so complicated. Scares the hell out of me. So when I read articles on what a risk-taker I am with my adventure business, I want to look at that reporter with the ring on his finger, and say, 'No. You're a bigger risk taker than I am. It's the one thing I'm not sure I could ever do. What about you? Have you ever taken big chances in your life? Besides firing your family?"

"That does go high up there on the list." I wanted to tell him my biggest risk, to blurt it out, starting a family on my own. But I couldn't. He'd know soon enough. In a couple of weeks, I'd be starting the second trimester my baby bump would be apparent.

"I take calculated risks. I'm in favor of a game plan," I said, starting in on the salty potato chips.

"A plan for everything."

"Typically."

"So you wouldn't be up for accompanying me back to Sonoma this weekend?" He cocked his head, studying me as I felt the tomato juice from my sandwich drip down my chin. He leaned over and wiped it off with his finger.

A piece of bacon got caught in the back of my throat. I coughed and took a swig of lemon water. "What about the musical?"

"Auditions are tomorrow. Producers came in from New York today. They'll cast and I get a weekend to think about something other than crystal chandeliers, Persian rugs and the insane price of chain mail in modern day. In other words, hell, yes, I need a distraction."

"You. Want me. To go to wine country with you this weekend?"

"For business, of course," he stammered. "I own some property there and have a new wine that will need some event marketing at trade shows in the fall."

Wine. God, I missed wine, but I wasn't thinking about wine. I was thinking about the romantic getaway with Edgar that wasn't supposed to be romantic. Gwen had joked once that I was like a shrimp: with my heart in my head. Gwen hasn't said much that makes sense to me, but that stuck. "I don't drink wine," I said flatly, adding in my mind, *at the present moment.* "But I could refer you to someone."

"Someone who drinks wine?"

"Someone who could handle your events for your wine."

"Why is it you're always trying to pass me off onto someone else? The first time was hard enough, but do I need to get down on my knee again and beg? You don't want me?" he asked.

My face felt flushed, so I fanned myself to make it seem as though the rising heat was the Oklahoma humidity and not the tug of attraction. My friend Taylor had warned me about coming into another stage, too: the

Sex stage. I was horny and I missed sex, period, but dating was out of the question.

I snapped myself out of it. Edgar was in love with the Leslie person I often heard him talking to on the phone. I was sure of it. And I couldn't bend my will because of a few hormones. No men for life. I could do it.

But doing event planning for a wine label – and getting to continue working with Edgar – would make up for me firing my family. Edgar seemed to sense my hesitation.

He leaned over, his face inches from my shoulder. "Even workaholics like us need a holiday." I resisted the urge to run my fingers through his peppered hair, massage his temples. My whole body lit from within. I shot up out of the seat before the compulsion overcame me.

"You said it was business," I reminded him.

"Out in wine country, business is pleasure."

And for Apples, business is personal and personal is business. I get it. My iPhone sang the witch tune from The *Wizard of Oz.* Great. Richard Hunt.

"Richard Hunt here." King of connected old fogeys. He handled PR for my family's businesses.

Edgar ate his BLT and I walked backward, watching him eat, again resisting the temptation to rip that sandwich from his hands and put my mouth where the bacon was. Crazy hormones. I'd bet if the bald, fat mailman came in right then, I'd have jumped him, too.

"Richard," I said, causing Edgar to look up from his meal. "How can I help you?"

"Your father seemed to think I could help you."

My face burned red. How dare he call Richard after I told him not to? "What did he tell you exactly?"

"Just that you had an issue you'd need some help with is all. No details. Said you'd provide me what I needed. Shall we meet for a quick coffee this week? Or knowing your work schedule, better make it this weekend, eh?"

I didn't take my eyes off of Edgar.

"Sorry, Richard. I'm going to be tied up this weekend. A new opportunity in Sonoma Valley."

Edgar cocked his head at me and smiled. I little vacay from my family was exactly what I needed. They were suffocating me. The Sonoma air would be good for us. Both of us.

Chapter 15

Bess

Thanks to Alzheimer's, I kissed Samuel in the nursery in my bare feet. I don't think I ever would've looked beyond my failed marriage had it not been for Maeve peeking into her past for one final performance.

I stopped whining about her. She may never love me the way I wanted, or ever remember that I even existed, but I was tired of trying to please both her Early and Present selves. My anxiety did nothing to endear her to me.

I stopped whining about Phillip. High time I saw him for what he was: a workaholic who loved the good life better without me in it. I think he loved me once and we had some good times and two great kids. I would be forever grateful to him for that.

I stopped whining about Gwen's wedding and the family reunion. I learned my lesson. If Kelly ever got married, I'd kindly offer to pay for a Hawaiian ceremony on the beach. No way I could be a part of planning anyone else's wedding, ever. Especially not family.

I was tired of being the Don't Mom.

The Don't Wife.

I declared from then on I would become the Do Mom, the Do (dare I say it?) Grandma, the Do (dare I say it, too?) Lover.

Like that Nike slogan, I had to "Just Do It."

I wrote in a thin purple Sharpie in my blue notebook while waiting for Jervis to call to tell me Maeve was awake and on her way up for coffee.

Do what feels right.
Forgive Phillip.
Let go.
Move on.

I flipped the page. One of those damn "find yourself" books my old neighbor in Gaillardia always yapped about, instructed you to write down the things you loved most in your childhood. The idea proposed that remembering and rediscovering your youthful self could reignite passions you've suppressed since then. When she'd told me that, I'd thought she was a bored housewife with too much time on her hands, and really, no one is going to feel sorry for someone living in those large estates, but for the sake of my own discovery, it wouldn't kill me to try it, and it wouldn't cost me a dime.

My list:
Riding my bike.
Riding my horse Louie.
Hiking in Colorado with my grandparents.
Boating with my Aunt & Uncle.
Reading in the rose garden.

After a moment staring into thin air, I added:
Baking with my mother.

Satisfied, I did a quick to-do list (wouldn't Kelly be proud!) to get to the Doing. The list seemed pretty simple. Could it really be my route to happiness? I no longer owned a horse (Daddy sold the horse farm when he became governor), and Phillip never liked cold climates, so we tended to travel to warmer locales with the girls, and he was never very physical, so biking or hiking was never a couple's activity. I hadn't read for pleasure in months, but I had a rose garden and much more right in my own backyard. Maybe Samuel would teach me how he made those hybrid roses.

I made a quick grocery list of all the things I'd like to bake: sugar cookies and apple pie and strawberry tarts and oh, Lordie, I better do more physical stuff if I planned on eating any of it. Would Maeve bake with me?

I told myself not to let it hurt my feelings if she turned me down, though I'm sure it would. Mother thought she'd toughened me up, but I wonder if she'd done the opposite of her goal? Made me too soft. I wouldn't bake with Maeve with a goal in mind. We would do it for the sheer pleasure. Not about the past or the future, but living in the present. The Now. It's all we had.

The phone wrangled me from my thoughts, followed by the quick footsteps of Maeve bounding up the stairs.

"What the hell are you looking at me like that for?" Maeve growled as I poured her a cup of coffee (decaf, though she didn't know it) and she plopped down into her chair.

Every morning Jervis would call to tell me Maeve was headed up, and except for a few questions, the antique shoppers didn't mind that an old woman haunted the floor in her night robe with curlers in her hair. It's as if they were the ghosts. She never waved hello to the customers, or, thankfully, yelled at them to get out of her house, as she had to Jervis and I that first day we'd found her in the Early Century department.

If they were locals, most had heard that the Maeve Apple lived in a loft above her precious antiques. Some said to guard them. Others said they believed she wanted to die there and then haunt the place for real.

OI had scooped that Maeve's Alzheimer's had gotten worse and that she'd started hanging out at the Orpheum where she had starred in the '40s, but no one had told the press that Maeve believed she was 25 years old. "Am I late on the rent again?" Maeve asked with her right brow pointed to the sky in indignation. "I haven't seen a paycheck from Arthur in weeks. In fact, I'm going to ask him for a raise. Who does he think he is not to pay his star?"

"You're not late on rent, Maeve," I said cautiously, wondering if she had forgotten our trip through *This is Your Life, Maeve* the day before. She hadn't liked what she'd seen, but could one night sleep sweep away the years again?

"I suppose you're going to tell me that you aren't charging me rent because I'm your mother?" She pursed her lips and stared at me evenly.

"That's right. You're living here for free."

She set down her coffee and crossed her arms. "Then I think you should know in case you wake up one day and I'm gone, when Arthur asks me to go star in the show on Broadway, I'm going to say 'yes.' I'll be moving to New York."

Maeve's face was set, her jaw tight, her eyes slit. Whether or not she believed it was possible, Maeve had made up her mind.

I swallowed the lump in my throat. "So you're going to choose a different door this time?" I asked quietly.

"That's right. I'll send you a postcard when I get to New York. But you'll have me for a few more weeks, until the show wraps here."

I inhaled deeply and exhaled slowly, like I'd learned in yoga class. Be transparent. No wall, no resistance. I'd let her anger pass right through me. My hands began to shake, so I hid them under the table. "That would be lovely," I said. "You'll adore New York."

Maeve exhaled. "Thank you for understanding. I can't believe I ever considered giving up on Canty and marrying a man I don't love." Tears streamed down her wrinkled face and I wanted to brush them away, but I held back. I tried to take myself out of the mix, but how could I? I was her child. I couldn't believe she could say such things about Henry. She loved him. I know she did.

I got up and refilled my coffee. "You're so lucky to have been given a second chance," I said. "We don't always get one. But I do know what it's like for things to turn out differently than you planned. I'm not saying it's to the same degree, but my husband left me after thirty-seven years together."

Maeve stopped crying momentarily. "The bastard. And you're sure you're my daughter?"

I handed her a napkin and she dabbed her eyes. "Damn sure," I said. "You're not the type to take in a child dropped off in a basket at your doorstep. You'd never even let me get a dog. Come to think of it, I never let my kids get one, either."

"Lord, Bess. Every child needs a dog. Who doesn't know that?"

"Us apparently. I've been thinking about getting one," I said. A dog would never ask me to pick out wedding invitations, either.

Maeve sighed. "I never planned on being a mother. I was dreadful at it, wasn't I?"

"I know you loved me. I think you tried your best. We made a lot of great memories. Paris. God, we had some great times in Paris."

"Paris, France?" Her tone lightened.

"Oh, yes, you traveled the world. Paris was your favorite."

Maeve's eyes sparkled. "I went to Paris on a regular basis?"

"Once a year for fifty years," I told her.

She clutched her chest. "My, my. Paris definitely gives New York a run for the money."

"Well, you preferred getting your antiques first-hand. Paris or nothing, you used to say."

Maeve smiled. "I said that?" She clapped her hands together. The happiest I'd seen her in weeks. "Do you have pictures? Of my travels?"

"I made you a huge scrapbook for your eightieth birthday." Finally she showed some enthusiasm for it.

Maeve placed her hand over mine. "I'd love to see the photos."

I patted her hand, thankful we'd turned a corner— she normally didn't thank me for anything. I stood and sipped my coffee, the aroma filling my nose.

"I'll gather them up for you and you can finish your coffee on the sofa and look at them. I'll ask Jervis to sit with you while I run to the store. I thought perhaps we could bake some of your favorite foods."

"Apple pie like my mother used to make," Maeve said. "Flakiest crust you've ever tasted."

Pleased I could make her smile, I began to leave to retrieve the albums when Maeve's voice trailed behind me. "I can't imagine how you must've taken the news."

I turned around. "The news?"

Maeve's hand smoothed over her robe, her eyes crinkling in the morning light. "Why that Canty was your father, of course."

My china cup hit the floor moments before I did.

"What do you mean you had a suspicion?" Gwen asked Kelly as they stood above me like mother hens, treating my goose egg with an ice pack.

"In Tulsa, the old pictures looked like, well, you, me, and...her," Kelly said defensively.

Their voices sounded hazy, far off, but I could make them out and when I opened my eyes, there they were like angels in the light. I hadn't died at all, but if I had, they would surely be my heaven.

"Don't bicker," I whispered. So much for being the Don't Mom.

"I thought she knew," Maeve said, pacing back and forth. "Should we take her to the hospital? From what Bess said, I can afford to pay the bill."

"I'm fine," I said, focusing on the three of them. "As fine as a woman who found out her whole identity is a lie can be." I looked at Maeve with a dead glare. Too much shock to cry or shout.

"I said I'm sorry," Maeve said again, taking the ice pack from Gwen's hand and smacking it back harder onto my bruise. "If I had known you didn't know, of course I wouldn't have blurted it out like that. I can't imagine why I wouldn't have told you."

"I think I have a clue," Kelly said, pulling me from my place on the wooden floor to the kitchen seat. The blood began rushing back. "Maeve, you decided to marry Henry Apple, and whether or not you knew it at the time, you were pregnant. But I have a feeling you did know. That you do know."

Maeve winced. "I'm not a harlot. I'm not sleeping with anyone but Canty. It's definitely his child. Henry and I haven't even made it to third base. I think he wants to wait until our honeymoon, sweet sap that he is."

"You didn't take the car for a spin before buying back then," I said stiffly. I couldn't bear to look at my mother. She made me sick, keeping a secret like that. I wasn't mad at the Early Maeve. I was mad at the pre-Alzheimer's Maeve who had decades to tell me the truth and years to tell me after Henry died. What was she thinking?

"Depends on who's test-driving," Maeve said with a smirk. "Anyhow, I thought Canty would come back for me someday. I thought our love was strong enough."

"Canty's wife is pregnant, too," Kelly said. "Due in a few months. I mean, back then. I've been doing some research."

"My father is sounding like a real stand-up guy, alright," I muttered, before the realization hit. I didn't have a father I didn't know about. I had an entire family. A sister.

"Don't talk about your father like that," Maeve snapped. "You've got him all wrong. He's a good man. He married too young. Married for the wrong reasons. I know he's staying with his wife out of obligation. To do the right thing. I haven't been certain of much in life, but this I know: Canty and I are meant to be together. If we didn't spend our lives together, then it was because he couldn't."

"I don't think he knows," Kelly said. "I think that's what Maeve meant when she said she had regrets, that she wasn't honest. I think she kept it a secret from everyone. She was going to take it to the grave."

"Dear child, don't talk about a grave in my presence," Maeve interjected. "I'm still here, you know. But I could see how I wouldn't want to hog-tie Canty into leaving his wife. I want him to leave for me."

"I've got a sister," I whispered. A bona fide, flesh-and-blood half-sister. Anna. Just up the road! Would she want anything to do with me?

"She's the reason your father didn't leave," Maeve said. "I just know it."

"Does this mean you didn't tell my father? I mean, either of them? How could you let Henry believe I was his child?" One wave of shock followed another, like jolts of electricity.

"I don't know if he knew or not, because I haven't even said I'd marry him yet," Maeve said. "But he wants to settle down and start a family right away. But as I was telling you earlier, I'm going to do things differently this time. I'm going to New York, pregnant or not! Why, I'll be a modern woman like Kelly."

"But you've already done it," Kelly reminded her. "You've already made your choice. You chose Henry and he became a powerful politician and businessman, and you became a well-loved governor's wife and fashion icon and antiques dealer and philanthropist. You did it all."

"Why bother, Kelly? It's useless talking any sense into her now. She thinks she gets a do-over!"

Gwen nodded. "I think it's sweet. Trying the path untaken. You were a cool chick, Maeve. Still are."

Maeve placed the ice pack on the table. "Nice to know, ladies, but that was Round One. It's a new day and I want a new future. Show me to Canty." She glared at Gwen. "You've been away with him, haven't you?"

"No. Ax has made it very clear he wants nothing to do with me." Gwen's smile faded.

Maeve may still be confused as to who was who, but that weekend Anna would return and we could find the real Canty. Would it be too late? Fear rose up like a geyser gurgling underneath the surface. Not the bone-rattling nerves at meeting my biological father, but the fear that my mother might be a blip on the radar of his life. That she wasn't the star in his heart she thought she was.

Chapter 16

Gwen

"Can't make it," Victor said as I peed on the toilet and watched him shave Saturday morning. I used to love to watch him shave. (Let's not even mention that pivotal moment in the relationship when you decide you can piss in front of him. For the record, he did it first.)

"What do you mean you can't make it? I need you there for moral support," I said, washing my hands beside him. I used to love that we had to share his lone sink, an intimate way to begin and end the day, but I wanted my own damn sink.

"I'd sit there and listen to you," he said as though I'd asked him to watch paint dry. He patted aftershave on his skin, a scent I used to love. I tried to get him to change things up the last few years, but he was a creature of habit.

"That's kind of the whole point about moral support. You don't do anything. I'm nervous."

Victor turned to face me, his plaid boxers pressing up against my polka-dotted cotton undies. "Can't I give you my support now?" He put his hand on my ample bottom and squeezed.

"No, thank you." I pulled my pelvis away. We'd made love the night before for the first time in two weeks, but alas, it wasn't Victor on my mind. I tried the dead celeb fantasy again, but no one was getting me hot until I replaced Charlton Heston (Ben-Hur, full Greek regalia) with Ax Ellis in full knight gear, only his armor wasn't the hardest part of his body.

In my fantasy, Ax had whispered naughty, medieval sweet nothings in my ear before nibbling it and working his way down my neck and chest and breast, and by the time he got my dress and corset off, Victor and I came together. Ax was probably nothing like my fantasy. He was probably better.

"Look, I agreed to switch the time of the wedding. I've been taking on more of the reality show. Isn't that support enough?" Victor said, trying to pull me into him again. "I've got a big mall meeting with the new ad agency, so I can't take time off."

I pointed my toothbrush at him. "Now you're working Saturday mornings, too?" I crossed my arms, so my breasts weren't up against Victor's hairy chest. "What's the matter? You've been acting strange ever since you got back from New York and I told you about Canty being mom's father."

"It's big news, Gwen. We can't let it get in the wrong hands. People may start treating you differently. Especially your extended family. The whole blood-is-thicker-than-water thing. You were heir to Oklahoma royalty. Knowing you're descended from some B actor from the '50s may knock you out of your throne."

"So you're saying the only reason we got asked to be a part of *Luxe Weddings* was because of my mother's maiden name?"

"Of course it was! It's the reason we've been invited to the Smithton's summerhouse in the Hamptons. It's the reason we get free invites to the best parties around town. Because it matters for us to be seen there. Because of who we are. Who you are."

"You mean what my name is, not who I am. Because I am more than that name." Maybe I was the delusional one. Maybe this was the one way I could remove the shell of my name once and for all. I could be the real me underneath.

I stormed out of the bathroom to get dressed. Victor

followed me and I spun around. "Wait a minute. You're disappointed Henry isn't my biological grandfather, aren't you?"

Victor leaned on the doorframe. "I'm not going to lie, Gwen. A bloodline is important. It would've been great to pass down to our kids. Besides Will Rogers and Wiley Post, he was probably the most influential figure in Oklahoma history. That name is synonymous with success in Oklahoma City."

My heart fell to my feet. Why hadn't I figured he would see it that way? He'd always loved my grandfather, wanted to be just like him. "I see. Well, I'm sorry you're disappointed I didn't get genetic gold. Maybe it does explain some things about me."

Victor tried to reach out to me, but I backed away. "It's good to be prepared," he said. "Know the worst-case scenario. That's a 'Henry Apple Golden Rule.'"

Golden Rules in Life & Business was a New York Times bestseller back in the '80s. My grandfather had written it after he survived his first bout with cancer, and he'd always dreamed of writing a book. Victor kept the book on his nightstand where most folks keep their Bible. He had it memorized by heart. Maybe it was time I took another look at the book before I made a total mess of my life.

"Know the worst-case scenario, huh? So Papa said that should apply to both your personal and professional life?"

"That's right."

I slipped on my shirt dress, thinking:

Victor/Gwen Wedding Worst Case Scenario: You'll spend your life with a man you're not totally in love with. A man who thinks your dreams are less important than his. We'll grow distant, sex will become non-existent, we'll shift attention to our children, replacing our own dreams for theirs. One of us will leave. Or we'll die first. Alone. Wondering how the hell things could've turned out this way.

How old would I be when this worst-case scenario plays out? Thirty-five? Forty? Sixty like Bess? Or what if I'm Maeve's age when that "a-ha" moment hits that I want to change my future, but I've reached the end of the line? The road no longer provides a fork, but a dead end. No turning back.

My heart raced, and I slipped on my boots and grabbed *Henry's Golden Rules* from Victor's bedside table and stuffed it in my oversized Chanel bag.

"Hey, what are you doing with that?" Victor asked.

"Reading it. With fervor this time."

"Don't drink or eat anything while reading it. And no reading on the toilet, and definitely no bubble baths with it," he commanded.

"It's *my* signed copy. Don't you have a boxful of them as backups on your bookshelf?"

"Still. That's my favorite copy. It's gotten me to where I am today."

I kept my mouth shut. Where I am today in the office next to the corner office, next to my Daddy's office, engaged to the president's daughter. Yes, Victor had fused his personal and professional life really well, hadn't he?

"Don't forget you're meeting with the trainer after work," he said as I hurried to the door. "Skylar said the crew would follow you from your auditions to the gym."

"Stupid show! I swear if I didn't need the money so badly, I'd call the whole thing off." Oops.

"What did you say?"

"Not that, honey. Not the wedding. I meant the show. Just the show. I'm sorry. All this stress is getting to me. And you know how I hate to sweat on camera. The message boards will have a heyday making fun of me." One thing I know for sure: I wasn't going to spend the rest of my life trying to be thin.

Victor grabbed my arm. "What did you mean about needing the money?"

"I'm sorry, Victor. I haven't been totally honest with you about my financial situation. Don't freak on me. It's nothing we can't work out. I'll bring it all to the financial planner's office, okay? And so I know—worst-case scenario—if my finances aren't what you thought they'd be and I don't lose the weight you and the rest of the TV viewers think I should, will you still love me?"

Victor shrugged his shoulders. "Of course. But that's not gonna happen."

"What if after our first child I can't shed the new 40 pounds I've gained? What then?"

"Come on, Gwen. Golden Rule #5: If you believe, you can achieve."

What he didn't know is I wasn't auditioning for a role. I was auditioning for a different future altogether. If I could do this, I could do anything. Be anything. But what role, if any, would Victor play? And did I mean what I blurted out? Would I call off the wedding if it weren't for the golden carrot at the end of the I do's?

Chapter 17

Kelly

Don't tell me people go to Sonoma Valley for the wine.

People go to Sonoma Valley for the sex. Sure, it's called "Real Wine Country," but if I were creating a secondary tagline, I'd call it "Real Sex Country."

I'd never been, which is perhaps why I'd never had great sex. John wasn't bad, but I thought that had more to do with me. Women start coming into their own sexually in her 30s — sexual peak and all that — which is why it's a bit ironic I've given up on men, and thereby given up on sex with a man, when I'd reached my peak and I'd entered the sex stage of my pregnancy. If people didn't intentionally come to Sonoma Valley for the sex, it was a natural by-product; the wine and lush landscape an aphrodisiac for incredible, unencumbered lovemaking.

I knew why my grandparents had regularly visited the Valley. Sure, my grandfather was a wine connoisseur, but I'd bet he'd enjoyed Maeve more than he'd enjoyed the wine.

"Wine is magic," he'd told me when he gave me a rare bottle of Pinot Grigio for my twenty-first birthday. "Life, like a fine glass of wine, should not be rushed," he wrote in my birthday card. "Sip it. Savor it. Make it last."

This is exactly what I had in mind. Sipping and savoring every moment of sunshine, moonlight and Edgar McGuire.

He may not have ever been in my bed, but more and more he was showing up in my dreams. When I catnapped on the couch after our lunches, the dreams went from weird (Edgar holding an egg, which I assumed was my baby, in his cupped hand while I went to a meeting) to wonderful (him kissing my huge bare belly before tucking me into our bed). Again, I blamed the dreams on his presence and the hormones, not that I was developing genuine feelings for him.

"What do you think?" Edgar said, a bottle of his first wine Grey Sky, a red varietal, between us as we looked out over the gorgeous countryside.

"The view is breathtaking," I said, taking in the kaleidoscope of God's green country, and the lavender field Edgar had added in memory of his mother, whose favorite scent was lavender. In the middle of the field was a cleared area, though I couldn't tell from that far away what it was.

As Maeve always says: If it sounds too good to be true, it probably is. I think this applies to men, too, though I'd never met one. But Edgar in this moment? Complete Mr. 2G2BT.

Despite my telling him I didn't drink wine, I did take a sip and savor it.

"I meant what do you think of the wine," he said, disarming me with his smile again. I liked seeing him out of my office, out of the business environment.

"It's good," I said lifting my glass in the air. "No wait. I know you expect more from a wordsmith. Let's see." I concentrated on the taste and let the words rise to the top. "A mellow fruity ensem with a woodsy after note."

"Nice. I'm impressed. For someone that doesn't drink wine, you seem to have the lingo down."

"Henry. My grandfather. He was an amateur wine taster. He'd try out new descriptions on us at holiday gatherings. It was a rare glimpse at the softer side of Henry Apple."

"Speaking of, did I ever tell you I got a signed copy

of *Golden Rules* for my high school graduation?"

"A signed copy, huh? Well, he did do a national book tour. And what high-achieving kid didn't get one for graduation, right? Question is, did you read it?"

Edgar scrunched up his face. "Will you hate me if I admit I never read it? Think I may have sold it at a garage sale in college. Needed beer money."

I laughed. "I don't hate you. In fact, I admire that you told me the truth. Pretty standard stuff — you know, a mix of what Jesus, Buddha and your mother told you. My sister was up reading it last night, in fact."

"She on a self-help kick?"

"More like a prerequisite to her marriage to Victor Prescott. He's a bit of a Henry Apple groupie."

"Hard not to be in that town. His legacy lives on."

"I like to remember him as the guy who sliced the turkey on Thanksgiving. The guy who sprayed my skinned knee with Neosporin after I tried to ride my bike for the first time and he said 'anything you try is going to hurt a little bit, but then the pain goes away and before long you've mastered it.'"

Edgar cut a slice of Brie and spread it on crackers and handed it to me. He was making it awfully difficult to think of him as a client. What was it with Edgar feeding me all the time? Habit forming. Him feeding, nurturing, me, eating and eating and eating. Would I even remember how to feed myself when our project was through?

With his good looks and good manners and good food, he was making it nearly impossible for me not to like him more than. We were compatible, this much I knew. But I couldn't ruin a good business relationship even if I was attracted to him and my hormones were shouting, "Just do it" every nanosecond. Since I retired the Apple Urban account and my client's budgets were nose-diving, I needed this wine business more than ever. Sleeping with the client was never, under any circumstances, a good idea. Not that I'd ever tried it in the past.

And even worse than sleeping with a client, what if I developed deeper feelings for him after? What then? God, I'd be one of those secret baby Harlequin romances come to life.

"Shall I give you a tour?" Edgar stood first, and ever the gentleman, held out his hand to help me up. In a few months, I'd need that sort of help to get out of the chair. I knew I'd tire quickly after the long walk through the winery and vineyard, but with the cheese and crackers, hopefully I had some energy to burn.

I tried to call my mother three times on the tour, which defeated the purpose of the "only for emergencies" promise I'd made to myself, but Bess getting a hold of Anna, her long-lost sister, was an emergency. Time was of the essence. Every day we were aging, Maeve could regress even further, and who knows what sort of condition we'd find Canty in.

I'd left Gwen in good spirits after her amazing audition, which *Luxe Weddings* aired on the show the very next day. I'd never been a fan of reality shows, not much reality to them in my view, but I liked that they showed that a bride could have a thought in her head that wasn't about tulle. That she could have passions beyond that of her groom.

The producers would be posting the cast on Sunday night, so I'd be back in time to be there for moral support, whichever way it went.

We passed by couples on the tour, couples living out the fantasy I'd played out in my head, the get-drunk/make-love-anywhere rendezvous, and eschewed the thought that I could have that one day. Been there. Dreamed that.

When we finished the tour, Edgar walked me to my cabin, one of six on the property, used as a bed and breakfast and for weddings and family reunions.

"Thought you might want to rest before dinner," he said as he unlocked the door.

I'd barely made it the last hundred meters. Fortunately, the nausea had subsided, but I was bone-tired, every muscle waving the white flag to drop onto bed and sleep. Even if I'd wanted to ravage him, I was too damn tired to do it. "How could you tell?" I asked wearily.

"The yawning was a pretty big sign."

"I'm sorry." I brushed by him in the doorway, as he opened it for me. Even tired, my body responded to the touch. "It's not the company, I promise."

"You've been working too hard," he said, his grey eyes locking with mine. "What do you say we don't talk about work tonight? We'll have a nice dinner and you can turn in early if you like. There's something I want to show you."

"Thank you." In that moment, I wanted to tell him my fatigue wasn't overworking, but my body doing a triathlon for the growing baby inside of me. But would he understand? Could a man identify with the desperation a woman of a certain age feels when she wants a child, but hasn't found a man to give her one? To share a life?

Edgar's cell phone rang and he looked at the caller and smiled. I knew before he even said the word who it was.

"Leslie," Edgar cooed. "How are you?"

My heart thudded, the chemistry vanished into thin air. His attention was on Leslie, whom I figured was somewhere in California. He probably wanted me to turn in early so he could meet up with her. Big fool. It wasn't out of kindness at all, but a way to get rid of me so he could have his own private rendezvous with his long-distance sweetheart. He was like the rest, a wolf in designer clothing. If I'd thought he'd invited me here for anything other than to see his winery and vineyard, I was sorely mistaken.

Too tired to be angry, I was out before my head hit the pillow.

The next thing I knew, Edgar was at the screen door, the sound of a spoon rattling against china in the breeze. Stirring what smelled like a very aromatic tea.

"Get in here," I said, groggily. "Especially if that's for me."

"Sorry if I woke you," he whispered, setting the tray of tea and two cups on the bedside table. "I wanted it to be here when you woke up. My mother used to drink this during her chemotherapy. Works wonders for exhaustion, too."

Had I been that obvious? I'd tried to hide it all day. "Talk about room service. You do this for all your guests?"

Edgar lifted his teacup to his lips. "Just the pretty ones."

"This is a first," I said. "Tea in bed with a client. Sorry, I didn't mean it to come out that way. Still sleepy."

"I know what you meant. I needed a cup to clear my head. Tasted too much wine while sipping it with customers today."

"I thought you weren't working this weekend?"

"Trick is, you have to know how to balance the two. And working out here doesn't feel much like work, wouldn't you agree?" He took a sip of tea.

"I'll give you that. But the nap was very nice, thank you. If you hadn't offered, I may have fallen asleep in the vineyard with grapes as pillows. Tourists would've had to walk around me." I laughed. Felt good to laugh with a man again, no agenda, no expectations. I could be me, warts and all.

"Dinner will be ready in a half hour unless you need more time," he said, standing. I wanted him to sit back down, to curl up beside me and tell me more about his life. How hard would it be to grab his arm and pull him back down?

I lifted my hand, and grabbed for my teacup instead. I sat up, but Edgar was too quick for me and lifted the teapot and poured me a cup. The lavender aroma filled my nose. "Don't tell me, you make this here, right?"

"I can't take credit, but I do provide the lavender."

"It's delicious. Thank you." Why was he being so nice? Buttering me up so I'd say yes to branding his wine? He'd been nothing but a gentleman, but since I'd never actually dated a true gentleman, he'd thrown me for a loop. What do you do with a nice guy?

"I'll see you at 6:30 on the lavender field then. Come hungry."

I smiled. "When am I not? Thanks to you I'm packing on the pounds."

"You look good with more meat on your bones," he said, and I told myself anyone could say that to anyone, even work associates.

A half hour later, I arrived to the edge of the lavender field, the purple flowers waving me a greeting in the wind, the lavender lulling me into a peaceful state. Hard to be wound up here, heavy workload or not. I wore a blue slip dress, a color that complemented my strawberry blonde hair and fair skin. Pregnancy had turned my disdain for dresses upside down. Dresses were absolutely the most comfortable attire on Earth. I may never wear pants again.

No sign of Edgar or the food, and I very much wanted both.

I called out his name. I could hear the faint sounds of a band playing in the distance, but the property was so large it could've been a half-mile away. The hunt for the Californian hunk was on.

"In here," he hollered back. The sweet lavender was nearly four feet tall. When he stood, I could see his head in the distance and his arm waving madly above him.

"How do I get to you?" I yelled back.

"Follow the path on the east."

I walked around the field, and saw a path where green grass and stones made a walkway straight through the lavender. As I entered the floral sanctuary, it reminded me of my grandmother's garden maze I'd played in as a child. I smiled that my own child would get to visit Victor and Gwen and run in the maze when we visited them.

"Coming," I announced, feeling like a giddy little girl myself. "Is this a trick?" I asked when I'd been walking for more than a minute.

"Keep coming, you're almost here," he called back, yet he didn't stand again. He wasn't making this easy for me, which made it all the more fun. Playing hard to get, perhaps?

A few more turns and I reached him, nearly taking my breath away. In the middle of the field lay a wide circle, nearly 25 feet in diameter, the floor a grassy carpet. Two stone benches and a stone fountain of a mother with a bucket on her shoulders pouring water and two children at her legs holding on to her skirt sat in the middle of the opening. The sight of mother and child tugged at me.

The fountain was beautiful, but didn't compare to Edgar, who sat at a small folding table covered with a white tablecloth. He wore a blue-grey button-down shirt and blue jeans. Fresh flowers and candles sat on the table. He stood to greet me. "You found it."

"I felt like Little Red Riding Hood. Glad to see it didn't lead to a trap." As if I would've minded that at all. Trapped in a lavender prison with this guy. "This is, wow."

"Pretty cool, huh? I wanted to show you how I balance work and life in one day."

"This is living, all right," I said, taking a seat across

from him, and sipping the lemon water wondering if he brought Leslie here, or other women he'd seduced with lavender tea and wine and a view as sexy as the man himself. "But if you want to discuss business, I'm up for it. After that power nap, my brain is working again."

"Well, I did want to make a toast to everything you've accomplished. The Medieval Fair downtown for opening weekend is brilliant. And the float for the 4th of July parade is coming along nicely. I would've never thought of it."

I raised my water glass. "That's why I charge the big bucks."

"Not to mention the big lunches," he added.

"My grandfather always said there's no such thing as a free lunch," I said with a teasing smile.

"I guess he's right. And you've worked hard, but for me? Hasn't felt much like working."

"It hasn't?" My arm, still in mid-air, began to burn. I cleared my throat. I would not toast to us, to free lunches or lavender or calm, cool, collected blokes like Edgar. "To *Princess and the Pauper*," I said.

"To *Princess and the Pauper*." Our glasses chimed in the evening air.

Mozart played from the hidden speaker in the stone bench while he uncovered the dish before us, tantalizing my nose and taste buds. Lamb and potatoes and fresh-baked bread. My stomach churned in anticipation.

"Looks delicious. Please don't tell me you made it or I might have to hit you," I said.

"No. I don't cook much, but I'm learning. Taking some gourmet classes in Downtown Oklahoma City actually. You should join me."

"For cooking classes? I guess a bachelor better know how to cook to some degree."

"So do bachelorettes," he added. "Especially the top ones."

"Oh, please. I survive on PB&J and I think the barter

with you has worked so well I might try to get breakfast and dinner worked out with some of my other clients."

"And here I thought I was a special case." His gaze held mine until I had to look away. I kicked off my shoes underneath the table and ran my toes through the short cut grass. Heaven.

"So I overheard you telling one of the producers you have a place in New York, too?"

"Place I share with my cousin. We both do a lot of business in New York so it's better than having to worry about booking hotels."

All the better to bang chicks on every corner of the globe, said the Big Bad Wolf.

He buttered a chunk of Ciabatta bread and handed it to me. "I try to spend time there around the holidays. Can't beat shopping in New York and the whole pomp and circumstance of it all. Rockefeller Center and the whole bit. Used to take my mom there after Thanksgiving each year and the tradition kind of stuck. I'd like to take my family there someday." His expression changed.

"So you'd like kids some day then?" I asked, wishing I hadn't. Because I knew what would come next. You can't volley out the questions without them coming back to you and smacking you square in the face.

"Me? Oh, I don't know. I've never seen myself as the fatherly type. I travel so much I don't think I'd be very good at it." My expression must've changed, because he quickly added, "I'd love to settle down with someone though. But there's plenty of time for all that."

My throat thickened. Perhaps things had gotten serious with Leslie, and why did I care, anyway? I knew what he was out of my league from the moment I saw him. Work was his life, and I happened to fit into it at that juncture.

"What about you? Why aren't you married yet?" He leaned in, waiting for my answer.

I gave him a look, and he promptly added, "I mean because you're so beautiful and successful. Top Bachelorette thing and all that. Oklahoma is such a family-friendly state. Especially your family."

I exhaled. The question, smack, right between the eyes. No use being coy. "What I am amazingly successful at is picking Mr. Wrong," I said honestly. "So after my last male companion moved out, I decided I was done searching." Then I added hastily, "It's amazingly freeing not to be looking."

He leaned back in his chair, surprise on his face. "But what if precisely when you stop looking is when love finds you instead?"

His eyes bore into mine, sincere and longing. It was all I could do not to jump over the table and kiss him right there. I took another drink of water, feeling myself flush; my whole body igniting with yearning. Surely he didn't mean him, but how could I answer? I hadn't thought in a million years love would find me. I was always the one who'd had to be in control, to steer the ship. "I don't think a person has to be half of a couple to be happy."

Edgar leaned forward, refilling my lemon water. "Certainly not completely, but wouldn't the company be nice?"

Company. Code word for sex, or simply companionship? "You don't need a certificate of marriage to keep good company," I told him. "Most marriages fail anyway."

"Any of this stemming from your parents' divorce? Because your grandparents had a long, happy marriage, didn't they?"

"Due to her dementia, she doesn't remember Henry, but from the outside looking in, I thought they had it all. But she's so fixated on Canty that it's all she can think about."

"Well, don't you think you can love more than one

person?"

"Serially, maybe. Simultaneously, I certainly hope not. You believe in the possibility of two soul mates?"

"Two or four or ten. I don't know. I'm not saying that you get married to all of them or even that you are in a romantic relationship with them. Don't you ever meet someone, say a friend, and you connect with them on this deep level that has nothing to do with shared personality traits or circumstances? Things just click. And when you don't see them for a long time and then see them again, it's as if no time passed. That's a soul mate."

A man who believes in soul mates. Even multiple ones. At least I believed in the "mating" part. "I don't know. I'd like to believe it. Now my sister Gwen believes. She thinks if we find Canty it'll prove that true love can survive anything, even a separation of 60 years."

"I think she's right." He stuck out his hand and I was afraid to touch him, to feel any electricity. I may not be able to turn back.

"I get it. You want to bet on it?" I asked.

"Of course I do. If I'm right, then you brand Grey Sky for me for free for six months, and if you're right, then you get to take me to New York after Thanksgiving to see the tree lighting at Rockefeller Center."

"How can you sound so sure? So you win either way."

"No," he said, his hand still in mid-air. "I'd pay for the trip, not that you're going to win. I haven't known Maeve long, but from what I hear, she and Canty had the real deal."

"Three months, not that you'll win." I shook his hand, feeling the electricity pulse through me, but when I pulled back, he didn't let it go. "What are you doing?"

"Come with me. I want you to see something." His voice deepened, became hypnotic. I'd follow him anywhere, this I was sure of.

I let him hold my hand as he led me to the bench. He

pulled a blanket out from inside of it—a clever storage container. He spread the blanket out on the lawn, and lay down. He patted the space next to him so I joined him, laying flat on my back next to him, our arms inches apart. We stared up at the purple-blue crayon marks hanging in the horizon above the lavender field.

"It looks like a Monet painting," I whispered. If anyone could pull off the Mozart/Monet evening, Edgar could. How did he make it all seem so effortless?

We stared up at the sky for a long time without saying anything. I was afraid whatever might come out of my mouth would screw up the too-good moment.

The sky continued to swirl and change as the light left us completely, and the moon moved squarely above us. How long had we been lying there? Thirty minutes? An hour?

"Close your eyes," he said. "What do you hear?"

I relaxed, and concentrated on nature's soundtrack. "The water fountain, the wind rustling the lavender, birds farther away. Crickets. And you. I hear you breathing."

The next thing I felt were lips on mine, warm, soft, then firm, and I didn't protest. I wrapped my arms around him. *What do you feel?* I wanted to ask him. *My skin, my arms around your neck, running down your back, under your shirt. Pulling you on top of me, kissing you back, harder, longer.*

What do I feel? Your warmth on top of me, your manhood pressed up against me, our bodies settling together, fitting perfectly, my heart beating out of control, your skin igniting mine as I remove your clothes and you remove mine.

I hear you say, "we should stop," as if you thought it might end with the kiss, ever the gentleman, but I say, "no," and when I open my eyes I see that you want this as much as I do, and I hear myself say, "I don't want a relationship," and you say something back, something like "okay," or "alright," but I'm not hearing anymore because I'm too busy feeling.

The stars sprinkle the sky and the moon casts a spotlight on two lovers, and I feel tears fill my eyes because we are those lovers. I stare up at the moon as if I'm looking right through it as you kiss my breasts and my body cannot remember ever feeling this good. I've lost my mind, giving over to carnal desire, and as I moan and gasp with pleasure, I don't recognize myself at all.

I've lost her, lost me, inside of you, and I'm not ready to find her again.

Chapter 18

Gwen

The Orpheum was alive, half of what it would be, but twice as good as it had ever been. The cast announcement was tacked carefully to the bulletin board in the unfinished lobby as if a surgeon had meticulously inserted a new heart. A theater was a lifeless vessel without the lifeblood of the show — the cast, pumping it to life at curtain call.

The actors who had tirelessly rehearsed for the auditions for weeks had gathered around the paper heart like bees swarming around flowers. They flitted, tittered, screamed, sighed, squealed to see if their names were imprinted on that heart. I knew them by name — we were all different, yet we were one. Speaking the same lines, singing the same songs, dreaming the same dream.

I'd arrived later than most, slipping away from a baby shower for Victor's cousin. Victor waited outside in the car, idling and reading the Sunday business pages as if it was our typical Sunday evening.

I tried to ignore the camera stuck in my face, recording my reaction. Would the audience be able to hear how loud my heart was beating?

In the crowd, I saw Ax, beaming as he looked into the heart, and then hugged and high-fived his friends and received a congratulatory kiss from Tabby, who never seemed to leave his side. When he turned and saw me, his smile fell away, his eyes telling me all I needed to know. I didn't get the part.

He was the Pauper, but I would not be his Princess.

Chapter 19

Bess

"I can't believe I'm sitting here with Bess Apple-Barton," Anna said, as we nervously made our introductions early Monday morning before she had to go in to work. My sister is a nurse. I don't know why, but I liked the sound of it, or maybe I liked that she was someone who liked to take care of other people. Nurses saw people at their worst, yet gave them their best.

We met in public at a local bakery, with two steaming cups of coffee sat between us as groups of businessmen and stay-at-home moms chattered around us.

Gwen offered to come with me since Kelly was out of town in Sonoma Valley, but I didn't want Anna to think we were ganging up on her. I told her on the phone that I wanted to discuss the revival of Princess and the Pauper, which was at least partly true.

Anna was simple, yet pretty, dressed in a three-quarter-sleeved blue cotton shirt and khaki capris with sandals. I guess she'd opted out of meeting me in her scrubs. Her nails were painted coral and her make-up was fresh and natural. Her strawberry blonde hair was cut in a bob around her round face, her blue eyes sparkling underneath her bangs. I think this may be what I would've looked like had I not been raised with money. I don't know if Anna was noticing our resemblance, but I couldn't help but stare at her right dimple and her bright blue eyes, which mirrored mine. As for her square face, she looked like Kelly, or rather, Kelly looked like her. At a glance, I look much more like Anna than I ever did my mother. Canty's recessive Irish genes somehow became dominant. I don't see how any gene could've overpowered Maeve's, but it had, nonetheless.

I considered for a split-second making up another lie, because I was afraid the truth would be too much to swallow over coffee, but I had a mission and my "just do it" mantra applied to meeting my long-lost sister, too.

"It's lovely to meet you," I said, nodding curtly.

"When I told Frank, that's my husband, that I was meeting you here, he was as tickled as I was. I've followed you your whole life. In the papers, I mean. Society section and whatnot and of course my daughter and I are glued to the TV each week to watch *Luxe Weddings*. Must be so much fun to be able to organize a fairytale wedding."

Fairytale. That's what it was, all right. All make-believe. Pretending we were royalty that could pull off a fairytale wedding. Phillip had scolded me again for wedding bills. Since he'd shut off the credit card, I'd asked the vendors to send the bills to him. It wasn't fair I had to deal with it alone. Let him talk to his future son-in-law about paying part of the wedding. Gwen made it sound as though Victor didn't believe her that we'd welcome his help paying for the wedding. Let his boss tell him. See how serious he takes it then.

If it were a fairytale, then why did I feel more like Cruella DeVille than the queen of a princess?

Anna gushed. "My Daddy used to show me pictures of you when you were in the newspaper and magazines even when I was a young'un."

"He did?" My throat caught. "He kept up with us?"

"Sure as all get out. We're only a few months apart, so it was fun to see a girl my age living in the governor's mansion. And my mom and I would curl up on the couch on Sundays and read the society section and see where you and your mother had been. All those trips to Paris!

My mom and I would fantasize that we'd get to do that someday, but time and money were two things in short supply. Not that I have much of it now, either."

"Wasn't your father in New York and L.A., though?"

"Oh, off and on, but my mother had family back here and whether it was a play or a movie, he'd be gone into the wee hours of the night or sometimes weeks or months at a time. Mama never felt safe in a big city so we ended up moving back here when I was little. He came back as often as he could, but I was glad when he gave up acting, even if a part of him changed after that. Seemed to have lost some of the glimmer, you know? Course he's always been in one band or another. We moved up to Tulsa and took over an antique store. Lived above it like I hear you're doing now. Isn't that something?"

"Yes, that's something alright." I took a sip of coffee, thinking how sweet and honest Anna was. She was right. I did have many wonderful memories of trips with my mother. Why couldn't I appreciate them fully? They were mine and mine alone.

And if her father was keeping up with me, did he know I was his daughter? Sitting there, it seemed obvious that Anna didn't know, and that perhaps Canty hadn't, either. Who was I to turn her whole world upside down? Maybe she doesn't want to think of her father as a philanderer who got another woman pregnant while Anna was in her mother's womb. Why had I been so selfish? Honestly, I'd not given a thought to the implications this might have on Anna.

Nothing worth telling is easy, Henry used to say. The goldest of all his golden rules. A rule I'd been famously bad at. Tough talk was never my strong suit. I'd rather sit and stew than take action. How else to explain my years in a lifeless marriage?

"I'm sorry to hear about your divorce," Anna said. Sincerity. Something I hadn't heard from most of my so-called friends. The day before, I'd found out my little outburst at the Choral Society meeting had resulted in not getting an invite to Betty Smithton's huge summer gala. I hated that I cared I'd been cut off so easily.

"Thank you, Anna. It's been hard. But I'm picking up the pieces again. I let Gwen help set up a profile for me on 2gether.com. I guess a lot of people at the company have met their significant others there. Feels strange, though, getting back out there after so many years."

"You'll have no problems finding dates," Anna said. "You're so beautiful, and well, you."

"Well, when I was young, being me made it hard to find a real man, and I obviously couldn't keep him. Now that I'm older, I can't see how it'll be any better or easier."

"I'll tell you why," Anna said, wagging her finger, something I catch myself doing all the time. "You've got wisdom now. You'll smell a rat out. My cousin Rae met her third husband on 2gether.com. Said if the technology would've been around years ago, it would've saved her two bad starter marriages."

"Starter marriages?" I relaxed and laughed. "Well, we'll see. I've gotten a few e-mails, but I didn't use my hyphenated name. Barton. I did use a real recent photo, though. Hopefully, they'll be as honest."

"That's a smart idea," Anna said, nodding enthusiastically. "See, you're already putting your wisdom into action. How's your mother, poor thing? I've been keeping up with her progress."

Her decline, she meant. And the only way Anna could be keeping up was by reading OI. "Well, she has her good days and her bad days."

"I was so tickled when I read *Princess and the Pauper* was coming here. My heart dropped straight into my shoes when Gwen didn't get the part of Princess last night. And that it was taped! The look on her face killed me."

"Gwen wants it more than anything," I said. I was at least thankful that the world could see the sweet daughter I'd known all my life. That they hadn't edited away her feelings.

Anna's smile widened. "But then to get your call! I can't wait to see how my father got his start."

I liked Anna. I didn't want to hurt her, didn't want to turn her world upside down. And yet. I withheld a smile. "You're so right about that, Anna." I paused. "See, my mother's Alzheimer's has advanced. She's remembering bits of the past, and talking about it more. The thing is ... my mother ... oh, Anna, there's simply no pleasant way to put this. My mother says Canty is my father."

Anna smiled, a pasted on grin. "What?"

I whispered, for fear of being overheard or for all I knew an OI mic tap nearby. "Canty. Turns out your father is my father."

Anna titled her head, confused. "Oh, my. This is ... oh, my."

"I know. My mother never told me until now. I don't even know if she told my father," I said.

"My father?"

"I meant Henry. But I don't know if she told Canty, either. It's all a big mess."

"But then, that means we're sisters." She shook her head in tiny movements. "And that our mothers were pregnant at the same time."

I nodded. It sounded too dreadful to be true. I felt the shame for the both of us.

"How could my father do that to my mother?" Anna's face cringed in disgust. "My mother always worried he'd leave us for the stage – not come back one day, but he always did. I think she was more worried about that than other women. Or else she just turned her head."

"I'm sorry to come to you with this, but my mother's disease has brought on a series of unexpected events, and finding Canty is a top priority. Not for the show, Anna."

"She wants to see my father again?" Her tone changed, hardened.

Incredulous, she must be thinking. That I could waltz in here and buy her coffee and slap her in the face with a secret from the past. I didn't blame her for hating me. I hated myself at the moment.

"With her disease, her timeline is all screwed up. She doesn't remember much about her past. Nothing in fact, after her time with Canty. She still thinks she's going to New York and hoping for a life with him." I paused, giving her time to let it sink in.

"I see. So you want me to march to his retirement home and tell him that he's a father again?"

Why did it sound so ludicrous coming from her? Well, it was preposterous. Dredging up the past, messing with his peaceful retirement. But I knew he was alive. That he lived in a retirement home. A start. And I was tired of sweeping things under the rug, tired of sweeping up everyone else's problems. If it was a mess, it was a mess and should be dealt with outright. Some things time couldn't change. Like the fact that he was my biological father, and I, his daughter. He had an entire family branch he knew nothing about.

"Maeve doesn't remember telling him. You don't have to do it," I said. "I'll do it. Once I explain to him what my mother is going through, I'm sure he'll want to see her again. And if he doesn't want to sing in the show with Maeve, that's fine. No pressure. On any of it."

Anna stiffened. "You know my mother died twenty years ago," she said. "He never dated again after that. The old ladies still pursue him like crazy, but he said he doesn't have eyes for another woman."

"Of course. It's not like I'm trying to set them up." But I was, wasn't I? He lived in a retirement home and he was still the catch of the day. I hadn't even considered that he could've gotten remarried. "A reunion of sorts. It would mean a lot to her. A lot to me."

"They never had any more children," Anna said thoughtfully. "All my life, I thought I was an only child."

Tears filled my eyes. "So did I," was all I could say.

"This changes everything, doesn't it?" Anna said, her eyes brimming with tears. She reached across the table and squeezed my hand.

"How can it not?"

Anna wiped the tears in her own eyes. "They say the past always catches up with you. Life has a funny way of whacking you in the ass when you least expect it."

I smiled at her humor. "I know. But you can see I couldn't keep this to myself."

"If I were in your shoes, I would've done the same thing. But then, maybe that's because we're sisters."

I curled my lips together and nodded, trying to be stoic in the face of a meltdown. "Perhaps."

Anna made the first move. As we stood to leave, when I stuck out my hand, she pulled me in for a hug. "I'll be in touch," she said, and I watched my sister walk out the door.

After eight hours of arduous reorganization, I reassembled the Apple board, every apple back in its proper place, including Phillip's. I'd made him a new one, and not black like I'd threatened, though I did it with a heavy heart. He was president of the company, the patriarch of the family, and the father of my children. I had to be the bigger Apple here. He could stay on the tree. While I still pined and whimpered every now and then, when I needed a boost of self-esteem, I logged on to my account on 2gether.com and read the e-mail responses.

Amazing how many people my age are looking for love. Why had I thought it was a bygone emotion? That love is for the young? For the wrinkle-free?

But according to my inbox, looking for love, or at least companionship, was very much a top priority. And I vowed to meet more people, people not in the "in crowd," and so I said yes to first dates in safe places. When I thought of Samuel, and of that kiss, I felt a warm glow. But I couldn't spoil a great friendship by taking advantage of an old friend, even if we did have mutual attraction. Besides, we lived in two different worlds, though I began thinking I was the one who'd been living in the wrong one all this time.

I wasn't even a blood Apple. My heritage had all been a lie, and at once I believed I didn't deserve any of this, the whole opulent life my mother had so carefully carved out for us.

Yet people didn't know the truth. I suppose I could ease right into the grave with my secret identity if I really wanted. While I was still living this role, as the sole heir of Senator Apple, I was expected to date a certain type of man—monied, well respected, appropriately positioned in the community. I hated judging the men who responded to my 2gether.com profile, whether they were too old or too fat or too blue collar. Surely they were doing the same about me.

What would it hurt if I gave someone, anyone, a chance, to see where it went? And if I did, why couldn't I give that chance to someone I felt completely myself with? Someone like Samuel. I'd depended on him too much already, but it didn't mean I stopped thinking about him, and wondering if I was being presumptuous to think he might want to kiss me again. Every time I went outside to check on him, he was strangely absent. Had I scared him away with my bold move? Run him off? I didn't dare call him, though I had all his numbers. I'd already put the man's hand on my breast for god sake. I'd let him make the next move if there would be one at all.

I'd risen early, too much on my plate to sleep in. Since Victor was also an early riser, it might be my single chance to spend some alone time with him before my girls awoke. Gwen had called in sick, so while I was the nursemaid to Mother, I'd have to nurse Gwen's broken heart, too. The whole blogging community was talking about Gwen's audition; the moment where she found out she didn't get the part was the top viewed video on YouTube.

Ax had handily won the part of Pauper, and I'd never seen her this upset, which means I've never been this upset. When your child hurts, at any age, the sword may as well have gutted your own belly. You can't win 'em all, my father told me time and again, but you still wish for your children to win most of the time.

Victor had shrugged it off, and he'd come across unsympathetic on television, making me think perhaps that was the real Victor. Not the one that was polite and mannerly and helped with the dishes when he was around me, but the guy who didn't give a shit that the love of his life was hurting.

I didn't blame her for running home to her mother. I'll tell you what I'd do with that sword, right where I'd stick it. Off with his head! Couldn't he see how badly she'd wanted it?

When I walked out the back door, two bikes sat against the railing. One was old, dirt still in the tires, but the other was brand new and shiny purple. My favorite color.

"You're up early," Samuel said, as he turned the corner wearing blue jeans and a fitted black T-shirt, his favorite look. "You up for a morning ride?"

He'd returned. Maybe I hadn't scared him off after all. "Oh, Samuel I haven't been on one of these in years." I thought of my girls, but decided they could get on without me for a bit. I left Gwen a note to get breakfast for Maeve. Even the heartbroken could manage coffee and eggs. "What the hell. Let's get out of here."

I perched on the bike, thinking how nice it was that I'd shared my childhood favorite things list with Samuel and he'd taken action on it. That he'd gone to all this trouble for me. Half an hour later as we rounded corner after corner of the historic neighborhoods in Midtown, I forgot my troubles.

My blood pumping, I stared at the back of his head. I wanted to see his face. I mean, I'd kissed him, but that was for old time's sake. We were friends. Good, old friends. The thought of getting naked with the man, any man was bad enough, but Samuel? Lord, I'd be so self-conscious. He had such an incredible, fit body. I was glad he couldn't see my face, either; because I was most certainly blushing the color of the roses we passed by.

"Let me know how much I owe you for the bike," I said as I caught up to him at a stop sign.

"It's a gift. And I've been working on the rest of your list, too. You know I have two horses, don't you? Thought we might ride this weekend."

I tried to hide the surprise in my voice. Samuel owned horses? He'd never mentioned it, but until recently we'd mostly talked of business, and of course, the wedding. I had no idea about his private life or where he lived.

My stomach pitted. This weekend I already had a date. A 2gether.com date with Kelly's fertility specialist, Dr. Spurlock. The one she called TV Doc, very respected in the community. I figured if he helped give my daughter a child the least I could do was share some pasta with the man. Why didn't I tell Samuel about my date? Couldn't I tell him anything?

"I'd love to," I said hesitantly. "We'll figure out a time," and by the time we stopped for iced coffee we'd worked up a sweat. I knew I looked dreadful, sopping probably, and my muscles were already revolting.

Samuel and I parted ways at the nursery, where he

took our bikes to lock up in the garage. He paused as if he might lean in to kiss me or grab my hand, but I was so sweaty I wanted to leave before he could really get a good look at me. When he raised his thick brows and said, "I'll call you," I could've sworn he'd read me a love poem for how my heart pitter-pattered out of my chest. Even as my thighs screamed at me with each painful step to the loft, my heart acted like a balloon and got me to the top.

"Board looks good," Gwen said, her eyes puffy from crying as she pulled her leopard print robe tighter around her as I joined her at the table. "How do you know Maeve's not going to destroy it again?"

My heart lurched at the sight of her. What I wouldn't do to take the heartache from her. "I don't, but I'm going to lock it in the craft room to be safe."

Photo albums littered the kitchen table. Maeve must've brought them into the kitchen during the night. I wondered when she awoke if she'd remember anything. What questions about her past she might throw my way. "Camera crew will be here in a half hour so I best get in the shower. You might consider some cucumbers for your eyes."

Gwen rolled her pretty green eyes. Green like my mother's. Cat eyes, my father used to call them. "Can you tell them I'm not here?"

"Running away from your own wedding show?" According to the production schedule, Gwen had to decide on a wedding dress that day. Crunch time. Wedding in a month, and half a dozen couture designers around the globe were waiting on her decision.

Gwen's red hair fell in curls around her arms as she banged her head against the table. "I still haven't lost enough weight. And all that dancing was for nothing. Understudy," she said, tears welling in her eyes.

I sat across from her. "Do you know how many brides out there would give their right eye teeth to get a free dress from a couture designer? It's the one thing you don't have to pay for! And the designers will make it fit you like a glove."

"I know, but ..."

"But nothing. So Victor wants you to be thinner. Tough shit," I said. My head clear from the ride, I felt I could say anything.

"Mother!"

"Yes, your mother knows how to curse. It's stupid to try to lose weight for a wedding. Then what? You'll go on your honeymoon and drink high-calorie drinks and gain it all back."

"But the photos, the TV show. The footage will last forever. If I look good on that one day, then that's what people will remember," she said.

"Phooey. Your size is who you are, and no offense to you, honey, but the show will come and go. Three more couples will get national attention next year. Victor is marrying you because he loves you as is, right?"

Gwen shrugged her shoulders. "I don't know."

"You don't know? You better know. This is a huge commitment, Gwen."

"I know that. But I don't know if he loves me for me. I think he loves the idea of me, and maybe he loves the me I've been showing to the world, but is that really me? He doesn't seem to be too crazy about the acting, singing, dancing Gwen. She doesn't fit in with his neat, organized planned-out life. Honestly, I care more about working on my vocals than my abs, and definitely more than planning a mall."

"So do that. Work on your vocals."

Gwen snapped her fingers. "That easy, huh? Dad is counting on me. To prove he had some faith in me, he's given me even more responsibility, but I think I've made a mistake. I should've never worked for the company in the first place."

I placed one of Barbara's blue-ribbon cinnamon rolls

in front of her and that got a smile out of her. "I know you want to make your father proud. I did the same thing all my life. But, I think your grandfather would agree with me when I say, screw all that. Do you know how much energy I wasted trying to please the family? To do things and go places expected of me? Mother wanted me to be a great hostess like she was and a great board member — but that's not who I am. It took me way too long to figure it out. Take my word, Gwen. If you don't want to do it, don't do it. You're young. Please don't waste a single minute of it."

Gwen eyed me evenly. "You regret saying you'd help with the wedding, don't you?"

"I never said that, but it's a lot more intense than I expected."

"So you said yes, when you really wanted to say no."

"But you're my daughter. We all make sacrifices for family, Gwen. We have to learn to know when to make them and when to put our foot down."

"If I quit now, he'll never agree to the extra money for the wedding."

I sat down. May as well tell her while she's already upset. "I'm sorry, but your father said with all his money tied up with investors in New York, he won't be able to put more into the wedding account. But I'm sure if you talked to Victor ..."

Gwen's peachy complexion whitened, the last bit of color gone from her face. "Victor's investing everything we have into the mall concept, too. He even wants to use our show money to invest more."

"Well, as much as I hate to say it, your father suggested you get a credit card to cover anything else."

Gwen wrapped her arms around her belly, a chuckle beginning in her diaphragm and bursting through her mouth until she was laughing so hard she had tears pouring from her sockets "Credit card. Good one."

I couldn't help it. Her laughter was contagious, and even though I had no idea what was so funny, I began laughing, too. My whole body shook. "What's so funny about a credit card?"

She could barely get the words out through her laughter. "Because I already have twenty of them."

"You what?" I stomped my feet, the laughter a force field of its own.

"Twenty! Cards! With ninety thousand dollars of debt!" Gwen splayed back on the chair, completely spent.

Now my face drained, the last laugh erupting through the room. "Gwen Apple-Barton. Did you say you have ninety thousand dollars of credit card debt?"

Gwen's shoulders stopped shaking, her smile evening into a thin line of despair. "Well, thanks to Kelly's idea to return some of the tagged merchandise, I returned about $5,000 worth. All those boxes you've been telling us to get out of the hallway are for the designer sale we're having next week out in the extra storage garage in the nursery. Victor said we could use it for the day. So I'm hoping, fingers crossed, that I can make another $10,000 on Craigslist and the sale before the wedding."

"Jesus, Gwen. So that's what you were selling in those paper bags? Shoes and handbags?"

"What did you think I was selling? Drugs?!"

"I have no idea what to believe anymore. Everything is turned upside down, and I'm no better." I exhaled, then grabbed a notepad from the desk. "Tell me all your sizes, beginning with your shoes and working your way up."

"What do you want that for?"

"Do you possibly think you're going to sell all that stuff having people slink in and out of here with paper bags? You need to target the big spenders, Gwen. Let's do a list, attach pictures and I'll send it out to my address book."

"But then everyone will know. I've been trying to sell the stuff off on the QT."

"The QT won't get your debt paid off any faster. Besides, I think my circle already knows I'm not the wealthy woman I thought I once was. Why not go for broke?"

"Bad choice of words, Mom. But what happened to putting your foot down?"

"This is far more important than picking out a wedding cake, my dear. And as the saying goes, a mother's work is never done. Now give me your sizes."

With a quick note to send out the items later that day, I began cleaning up the table, returning photo albums, picking up the glass of half-drunk green tea Mother must've made herself in the night. As I carried the albums to the living room, a courier envelope fell to the ground. I picked it up and studied the stamp and return address. Johnston Estate Planning. Must've arrived while I was out with Samuel. The contents of my future. Mother's will.

I'd canceled the last two meetings with Johnston due to conflicts with the show and suggested he send over a copy for me to review on my own before we sat down. He'd been hesitant, preferring we go over everything in person, but I was the sole heir to my parent's fortune. I was aware of her cash situation, but there were so many properties and assets, I'd be well taken care of, even without Phillip's alimony payments. Mother had mentioned that she changed the will after my father had died, but not since she'd gotten Alzheimer's. She always was more generous than my father, so I assumed it would be pretty cut and dried. I would get everything.

I wished I'd remembered Henry Apple's Golden Rule Number Nine: *Never assume. It only makes an "ass" out of "u" and "me."*

Chapter 20

Gwen

I swore I heard Bess crying in the shower when I'd snuck in to grab my flat iron, yet I didn't say anything. The shower is a sanctuary, the one place where your tears can mix with the water and disappear without the world ever having to know. I'd done the very same thing thirty minutes prior. I let her be.

Skylar looked ravishing in a deeper tan and a lemon yellow dress with stilettos when she arrived on time with Shadow, the cameraman. I could barely remember a time I loved the camera. It may as well have been devil horns protruding from his head. You don't need to wear your heart on your sleeve when you've got a camera stuck in your face to do it for you.

Skylar flitted about the family room, setting up the confessional. Once a week, the brides were supposed to enter the black box and confess to the world some deep feeling about our nuptials. I tried not to compare, but Nantucket confessed things like wishing she could've had more bridesmaids (as if twelve weren't enough) and California had confessed how she could never truly express her enormous love for her groom. (Which is funny since she was confessing it to thousands of viewers. Gah.)

I, on the other hand, used the confessional for it's true purpose. In fact, if Catholic confessionals were anything like this, perhaps I should convert. The confessional had gotten me into hot water over the past few months because I hadn't really thought about what I would say when I entered the secret chamber.

Before Skylar called me into the booth, where I would sit alone staring into the camera, Mom proudly handed me the box of invitations (one of seven), which had arrived from Paris. She suggested, with her newfound confidence, that she would not address a single one, offering instead to invite my gaggle of bridesmaids for a martini party to take care of it. Nantucket and California, of course, were sending theirs out to a professional calligrapher, which I had priced at $2 per invite. Martinis would be way cheaper.

"Ooh, very hands-on," Skylar said, taking note of it. "We can get you all to dish about love and life. You know very Sex in OK City."

I nodded, knowing full well my girlfriends were nothing like the girls from *Sex and the City*. Martinis on camera would be disastrous. As I held the gorgeous invite in my hand, smoothing my finger over Victor's name, it hit me: I didn't want to send out the invite and it had nothing to do with the manual labor.

I knew, as I stared into the camera, that it wasn't the show that caused my jittery nerves. It wasn't even the luxury wedding I couldn't afford. It was the marriage part, the "I do," and "'til death do us part" part.

This was my chance to set the record straight. That although I loved Victor and always would, we weren't right for each other. He needed a pretty corporate wife to plan his parties and raise his kids and head up the PTA, not an actress and singer who'd be traveling the country and coming in at ungodly hours. I'd tell them that the trick to knowing if you really want to marry someone is if you'd be as happy going down to City Hall. If you want the fancy wedding more than the fiancé, think twice.

And then I'd tell them to swing by for some really great deals on luxury brands this luxury bride could no longer afford to keep. Hurry! Hurry! Hurry! Everything must go!

"We're rolling," Shadow said from the other side of the black curtain. The tiny red light on the camera blinked, so I blinked back the tears, put on my best cheerleader smile and shoved the invitation into the camera lens.

"Lookie what I got in the mail. Direct from Paris! Aren't they fab?"

Too bad I hadn't paid attention to the *Luxe Wedding* contract nine months earlier when I'd been so gung-ho to share my once in a lifetime fairytale wedding with the world. If I had, I would've known all along that to break the sacred contract for any reason, including breaking the sacred promise to marry, had substantial financial consequences. First off, I'd get absolutely no money for any of the shows aired to date, and secondly, I'd have to pay the producers $100,000 in damages.

After all, if there's no wedding, there's no wedding show.

Breaking off the wedding would put me in double debt, not to mention the social repercussions. Victor and I weren't the "it" couple of Oklahoma City, it seemed, according to People Magazine, we were the "it" couple of the country, with plans to put our wedding photo on the cover with Nantucket and California getting only small squares on the cover. This should've brought me extreme glee. My big chest should be bursting with pride.

Instead, I headed to the financial planner's office with my secret tucked in a manila envelope ready to lay it all out on the line. Every last borrowed penny. So maybe Victor had failed me a couple of times — first with the audition and second when he practically did a Snoopy happy dance when he heard that I hadn't gotten the part of Princess. He had one final chance. How he handled the news that his princess was a pauper with a useless platinum card would determine my fate. Maybe I had a case of cold feet. Maybe these last six years did mean I was supposed to spend the rest of my life with him.

I grabbed a shiny gold pair of Gucci heels from my row of sales shoes in the hall. If I were going out, by God, I'd be going out in style.

Chapter 21

Kelly

Had I floated back from Sonoma Valley or had I actually flown on a plane? Funny, I can't remember. The weekend with Edgar already felt like one of those fuzzy dreams you have where the details begin to blur; yet the feelings linger long after you wake up.

I had sex with Edgar McGuire. In the middle of a freakin' lavender field. Under the moon and stars. What the hell was I thinking? And is it a good thing not to think sometimes? To let your body take over? Isn't this how stupid mistakes are made? I'd always been a thinker. And I was over thinking it.

The fight or flight instinct was still working, only I could no longer fight my feelings for Edgar so I had to flee. I left for the airport without so much as saying goodbye. He left a message for me on my cell phone about wanting to bring me breakfast in bed and then join me. Thank God I got away when I did. I texted him back, saying I had urgent business back home, but that we were okay. A small part of me (very small) had wanted him to be a terrible lover so I'd never desire him again. Fat chance.

Once the plane landed at the Will Rogers Airport in Oklahoma City, my brain seemed to reconnect to the stem. Edgar would not be a "friend with benefits." Even worse, a client with benefits. How would I feel when I billed him $3K at the end of the month? Gross, that's what. I'd literally screwed myself out of my best client days after dropping my number one client. I could blame my hormones on a lot of things, but this was a doozy.

It was time to present him my brand concept for getting modern America to dash to see a musical about a medieval knight who was really a pauper and a princess who was willing to give up her fortune to be with the man she loved. I'd then have to hand over the account to an associate as well as give up the Grey Sky wine account.

Not to mention, he'd slept with a pregnant woman, which would likely disgust him. How much longer would he be a nice guy after I was so horrible?

Three calls from Richard Hunt, the PRiah. I didn't have a chance to return his call before he called me again. "You sure live up to your name," I told him in place of a hello.

"I'm worried about you."

So Phillip did tell him. Dammit. "Right. You're worried word will get out before you'd had a chance to spit and polish it, you mean."

"No. I mean I'm worried about you, Kelly. My wife and I could never have children. We ended up adopting later in life, but if we'd had this technology around when we were younger, we'd have probably done the same thing."

Talk about catching a gal off guard. "Thank you. I appreciate that."

"I'm ready to meet whenever you are."

He was good. Reel me in with emotion and then throw me on the fryer. I exhaled. "Can't we slap the gossip rags with a libel suit or something?"

"It's tricky, because you are considered a celebrity now that you're featured on a hit television show. You know the gossip sites eat up those reality shows."

"I know. Fine. I'll be in touch soon."

"Take care, Kelly."

I'd called the kitchen meeting because I'd obviously gone off the deep end and needed some perspective and a lot of carbs to get my head back in the right place. Give my heart one weak moment and look what happens?

The smell of cinnamon bread filled the loft and there was Maeve standing in the middle of the kitchen wearing an apron. For most people, seeing their grandmother in an apron would be as common as the morning sunrise. Seeing Maeve in an apron was like witnessing the passing of a centennial comet.

"Just in time," Maeve chirped.

Not much for chirping, either.

"Just took her meds," Bess said in my ear as she kissed me. She stood back and studied my face with a scowl. "Have you been crying?"

Also as infrequent as a comet. Even at Henry's funeral, I hadn't cried, though inside I was most certainly bawling like a baby.

Gwen hugged me next, and before I knew it, even Maeve joined in. While Maeve served us, Bess whispered, "She forgot that she doesn't serve people," and winked.

We may be fellow boarders to Maeve, but it was nice being in the same room together, three generations of well, whoever we were. Scratch that, four generations.

Over the next two hours we laughed together, cried together, and ate and ate and ate. Maeve kept the comfort food coming, like little pieces of heaven delivered straight through the oven. Peach cobbler and apple turnovers and cherry tarts. Coffee to wash it down. Decaf for the preggo.

I told them about Richard and my father's quest for spinning the pregnancy. "I have a feeling Dad wants option number three—to get me married off before the baby is due."

"Oh, poo," Maeve said, serving us a piece of coffee cake with caramel drizzle. "You're a beautiful, bright woman with a good chunk of her life ahead of her. And that baby will have a great life because she or he, Lord help us, will have all of you, man or no man."

"And we'll have you, too, Maeve," I added.

"If I haven't flown the coop by then," Maeve said.

Gwen gasped.

"Not dead, darling. On a tour. With my band," Maeve said, and we laughed.

I'd never taken off this much time off of work to chat with my family, but it felt good. I wished I'd let myself confide in them sooner.

The phone rang and Bess took the call in the other room for privacy. It wasn't any call; it was the call. From her sister, Anna. When she didn't come back quickly, we knew it couldn't be good news.

She pasted on a grin, but her one quick shake of her head when Maeve wasn't looking told us that our dream to find Canty and reunite them might not be a reality.

"Go to your meeting," Bess said walking me down the stairs. "And try talking to Edgar the way you talked with us. Don't assume it was a one-time thing unless that's truly what you want."

"I could never talk to a man the way I can with you all. You're family," I said.

"But how does a man go from being a man to being family?" Bess asked.

"I have no idea. I'm not married, remember?"

"A man makes the transition to family when you start treating him like family. You open the door to your heart like you would your home." She made it sound so simple.

"I really think no matter what happens; I've screwed things up royally."

"At least if you're honest you won't hate yourself later. And if it's …"

"Meant to be, it'll be," I finished.

"So you have been listening all these years?" Bess pressed her hand into mine.

"You're a broken record, but I'll never stop

listening."

We stood on the back patio and waved to Samuel in the nursery. I could see my mother's posture change in front of him.

"Tell me what happened with Canty," I said.

"He hasn't forgotten her, but he hasn't forgiven her, either. Something about Arthur giving Maeve the role of Princess if she'd go to New York, and then she backed out at the last minute. Anna apologized profusely. Said she did her best, but Canty refused to talk any more about it with her. Said she's never seen him so upset."

"Upset? Mom, if he's upset that's a good thing. Maybe Maeve didn't go to New York because she knew she was pregnant and decided to marry Henry instead."

Bess put a fingernail in her mouth. "I suppose. But it still doesn't sound like the Maeve we've been around the last few months to give up the chance to star on Broadway. Something is still fishy."

"Maybe she'll remember. But as far as Canty goes, if he's upset that means he still cares. It means there's still a chance," I said.

"You think so?"

"We have to change our strategy. It's not a reunion we're after, but a reconciliation." Not a wish, a plan. Something I could get behind.

"I don't know, Kelly. If you've carried sixty years of resentment and hurt, wouldn't it be like a time bomb going off?"

"Maybe, but we'll prepare for the worst case scenario. Did Anna say whether or not he knows he's your father?"

"Couldn't get beyond saying Maeve's name before she got a door shut in her face, so she didn't get to ask him. Or tell him. When the time is right," Bess said, and I was so thankful we had each other for support. When one column collapses, the others hold the fortress up.

Edgar was waiting for me when I arrived back at my office. Ten minutes late. Extremely rare for me. I'd reapplied my makeup and combed through my hair. He wouldn't have to know about my earlier meltdown. He held up a sandwich bag. Turkey and avacodo, I bet. My latest craving besides him.

"Hey," he said, standing to greet me next to the couch. Instead of sitting next to him, I sat in the side chair across from it and tore open the sandwich bag.

"I've got some good news," I said, as I unwrapped the sandwich. "Your days of schlepping sandwiches are through. I'm finished with your campaign." I made a big ta-da move with my arms, but his face twitched.

"Really? I didn't think we were through."

"Yep." I motioned to the black boards behind my desk. "My designer delivered those mock-ups from the printer this morning. Wait until you see it. New logo, new look, new campaign theme and the grandest grand opening you've ever seen. It's everything we've talked about."

"Super," he said. "Can't wait to see it. Then we can get started on the Grey Sky launch, right?"

I swallowed, wanting to tell him I couldn't concentrate on another campaign because that would mean being around him, and I couldn't be around him because I was afraid of developing deeper feelings for him, of becoming dependent on him in my life. Hadn't I already?

But I couldn't say that.

"I thought about that on the way home yesterday, Edgar. I don't think I can launch right back in to another campaign right now," I said, all business-like. "Even if it was a one time thing, our being together makes it impossible for me to work with you again. I can't make a commitment."

He nodded, his posture hardening like a Greek statue. "Are we going to forget Sonoma, is that it?

Pretend it never happened?"

Forget Sonoma? Not on my life. I had two choices. One, rush into his arms and tell him about the baby and my feelings for him, or two, keep things professional, which we could both be comfortable with, no messy feelings getting in the way. I had to tell him the truth, but how? "Forgetting would be pretty hard to do. I really did have a wonderful time — especially Saturday night."

His face softened, his brows rose, hopeful.

I swallowed hard. "But."

"There's a but?" His shoulders dropped.

"It was all so magical, so out of this world amazing. I mean, stargazing? Lavender? And you, God, you were incredible."

"Still can't believe there's a 'but' in that scenario."

"But it's fun and make believe, and while it's perfectly okay to have a dream date once in awhile, it's not reality. I have so many personal, family things going on."

Edgar nodded slowly, then exhaled. "Reality. Right. Can I see your phone?"

He grabbed the iPhone from my desk. "Hey. What are you doing?"

"I want to know my song," he said.

"Your song?" The color drained from my face.

"You assign everyone in your contacts a song. I want to know what mine is."

I lunged over the table, magazines falling to the floor. "I didn't give you a song."

Edgar shot up from the couch, busily fingering my iPhone for the contacts database, but I was right behind him, bear hugging from the back and snatching the phone from his hand.

Disaster, averted. Thank God.

"You wanna play like that?" He asked, his back still to me.

I smoothed my skirt, when his image appeared on

my iPhone a half sec before the song started.

He spun around, a huge grin on his face, his cell phone held out.

Before I could stop it, Michael Bublé sang out his rendition of "Fever." Dammit, dammit, dammit.

"That's what I thought," he said, clasping his phone closed and stepping towards me.

"It means nothing," I stammered. "I like the song."

"It means this weekend wasn't a spur of the moment fantasy, Kelly. This weekend was far, far from make-believe, and you know it. I do think I give you fever and I want to give it to you again."

He'd called my bluff. I was ready to tell him what was going on inside, physically and emotionally.

Justin rapped on the door. "We're ready when you are," he said.

"We better get in there," I said cheerily, my heart nearly exploding in my chest. No time for baby talk now. My staff was waiting. When we were alone, yes, but not before a presentation my team spent two months creating. Afraid I'm having a baby, will you still love me, now let's go see that amazing campaign wouldn't cut it.

"Why can't you admit it? What are you so afraid of?"

"It's complicated. We'll talk later," I said evenly, then grabbed the boards to carry into the conference room. Betrayed by a song! Why, oh why, couldn't I have given him the safe ringtone? Like, say, a dog barking?

I stood at the head of the conference table, a place of comfort for me, like my La-Z-Boy recliner, where I could be in charge of the remote on the business world and call the shots. Besides Justin, an account service rep and a media buyer joined our meeting. I was thankful to not be in the room alone with Edgar a second longer.

"We want to bring in lovers of all ages," I said with confidence, but choking on the word "lovers." "We're going to make the musical fresh and cool and happening."

I clicked play on the remote to the flat screen where fast-moving quick clips of medieval armor, archery interchanged with corsets, a sultry eye, a passionate kiss and pounding rock music. Fast, frantic, full of passion, sex, lust, pulsating to the beat of the modern rendition of one of the world's oldest tales of love. Would it turn on the viewers or was it my blasted hormones again?

When the commercial finished, the lights came back up revealing Edgar staring at the blank screen and then back at me. "I don't like it," he said flatly.

Surprise jolted through my body. It's not like I haven't had clients not like my work before, but this new image of dark passion was perfect. "What precisely do you not like about it?" My staffers tried to hide the horrific disappointment on their faces.

"Not sure," he said, adjusting his jacket. "Something doesn't feel right. I don't think we're done here."

"I assure you, we were done." My staffers looked confused.

He looked at his watch then got up. "We'll talk about it later. Got another meeting. Those lofts you were so fond of," Edgar said. "Closing the deal."

"With Phillip?"

Edgar shook his head. "Decided to go solo on the deal. Sometimes solo is the only way to go, don't you agree, Kelly? Now if you'll excuse me."

He left the room and it seemed to darken without his presence. My staffers looked at me, waiting for a debriefing as was our usual modus operandi, but instead, I flicked my hands and sat there dumbfounded that Edgar wasn't blown away by the campaign, and hurt by his solo comment. We'd worked so hard. He was going to go move into the Get Laid Lofts and live in the penthouse suite where Leslie could come visit him and he'd have his pick of the litter of the young darlings living in the eight floors below him. King of the hill.

I gave up trying to work the rest of the day. Every cell of my body revolted. A thousand thoughts fought for the spotlight. The traveling. The baby. The mysterious Pauper. Edgar hating my campaign. The damn Bublé song.

After sending the staff home early (you should've seen the shocked look on their faces) I closed the blinds to my office making it as dark as a tomb. Even if I'd had the energy to go back to the loft, Bess took the afternoon off riding horses with Samuel and Gwen was off trying to work through things with Victor. What do you do if something feels off, but you can't place your finger on it? (And your finger has a diamond that means you best figure it out soon.)

I awoke to a rapping at the door. To my surprise, the sun had already gone down and it was after nine. I'd slept for nearly seven hours. I'd had my phone on vibrate and I had two text messages from Gwen.

Where are you? We're ordering pizza.

I texted her back on my way to the door, and when I hit send, Edgar was on the other side of it. I unlocked the deadbolt. "Come back to further humiliate me?" I asked with a snarky smile, when I really should've asked a client, may I help you? Proof I'd let him rattle me.

He jangled some keys. "Thought I'd let you be the first to get a tour of my new digs. Fully furnished."

"New digs. I've actually seen them. I planned a big VIP party when they opened. Nice place. I'm sure you'll be very happy there." Remote, professional.

"Come on. I ordered some take-out from Nonna's. Enough food for two."

Or three? A real dinner and not leftover pizza? "You can't lure me around with food you know," I said, knowing very well he could do that in my condition.

"We can debrief on our meeting today. And talk."

Talk. Meaning *the talk*. Was I ready to put out the

fever so soon? "Let me think on the campaign some more and I'll call you. Tomorrow." Yes, tomorrow I'd be stronger and have the perfect speech lined up. I'd stay up all night writing it.

His gray eyes pleaded with me. "Please, Kelly."

"Fine. I'll go grab my briefcase." Food and business and a quick confession. An hour, tops. *This is going to hurt me more than it hurts you. I'm pregnant. Nice knowing you. Have a nice life.*

Late June in Oklahoma is already hot and sticky, yet a cool breeze made the quick walk to his high rise bearable. Getting some fresh air and circulation through my system improved my mood considerably, especially when, to my surprise, he grabbed my hand and held it the rest of the way.

The final ingredient improving my mood was the food, a full table of pork meatloaf, mashed potatoes and gravy, dinner rolls and seasoned asparagus.

"So you're not the only one who gets her picture in OI," Edgar said as he watched me scarf down the incredible gourmet food. "Ax shot a profile of me here in the loft today." He looked at me with a critical eye. "Everything going okay? You don't seem yourself tonight."

"I guess I was surprised, okay shocked, that you didn't like the campaign. I thought we were in sync on everything," I said.

"I've felt since the beginning we were in sync, Kelly."

Didn't sound like he was referring to the campaign. I cleared my throat, but he continued.

"Perhaps I judged too quickly. Maybe a few tweaks will do the trick. It was a little too dark. Music sounded angry, not romantic," he said.

"We can soften it up. So there were some things you actually liked about it?"

He crossed his arms, his crisp white dress shirt open

at the collar. "I may have been harsher than necessary because you refused to work on Grey Sky."

"So you were getting back at me," I said pushing back my empty plate.

"I think you're pretty brilliant, Kelly. And pretty and brilliant."

I was relieved the day would end better than it started. "Thank you. And I'm sorry I was so short with you earlier. It's just that now is not the best time for me to take on a new project or a new relationship."

I followed him to the floor to ceiling view of downtown Oklahoma City. We had a bird's-eye view most people would never get to see. We could see the Bricktown Canal with a boat full of conventioneers and the lighted walkways with couples taking a stroll after their late night dinner.

He took my hand gingerly in his. "Truthfully, I wouldn't mind not working with you again."

"You wouldn't?" My heart thudded.

Edgar stood beside me, his arm brushing up against mine. "I'd like to try not working when I'm with you. I get that relationships are tough. But is work really all we have?"

"For workaholics, that's kind of the rub." I had to look away from the panoramic view. Too romantic, this evening, this place, this close to someone like him telling me he wanted less business and more pleasure. Even if I did want that, I couldn't.

He faced me, and stuck his hands in his pockets. "I don't think it's fair you get to call all the shots."

"I don't. You're the client."

"I meant about us."

My eyes met his. "There is no us."

"That's a problem." He leaned into me, turning me so my back was against the cool glass, pinning me. "Tell me you don't want this and I'll stop." His kiss melted every thought, every ugly moment of the day.

When our lips parted, I could barely get the words out. "We don't always get what we want."

He unbuttoned my shirt, and slid his hands from my collarbone down over my breasts. I shuddered under his touch. "You are a modern woman," he breathed into my ear, before nipping at my ear lobe, then kissing down my neck. "Only sex. I get it. I can deal with that."

I ran my hands through his hair then pulled him in for a longer kiss, the fever growing hotter. Letting him go was the farthest thing from my mind.

We stumbled to the big bed in the big modern loft and christened the Get Laid Lofts in the appropriate manner. Twice.

I snuck out sometime in the middle of the night, walking the streets of Downtown Oklahoma City in my business suit and sensible one-inch kitten heels. I couldn't wake him and say goodbye, and I didn't allow myself to watch him sleep because every moment I looked at him, I felt myself falling into him. I hated myself for not telling him about the baby at dinner, for letting him play me like a fiddle. But I'd wanted to be played, hadn't I? If it was really about the sex, then I could drop him at any time.

Only when I crawled into my bed and realized Gwen wasn't sleeping in hers, did I wonder what it might be like to wake up beside Edgar and actually cook for him for a change. Scrambled eggs and bacon and black coffee. Decaf for the preggo. Only we weren't a family and the baby wasn't his.

Funny how the normal stuff seemed like the biggest fantasy of all.

Chapter 22

Gwen

Victor stared at me, clasped his hands together, and turned to the financial planner. "Well, that was unexpected," he said with a laugh.

Where were the daggers? The curse words? The raised voice?

The financial planner, Hilton Blaney, stared at us over the rim of his glasses, completely unphased. I'm sure he'd seen much, much worse. It's not as if I invented the concept of living beyond one's means.

"It's only money," Victor said with a throaty laugh.

Why the hell was Victor being so calm about all this? Mr. Tightwad? Mr. Save-it-for-a-Rainy-Day? My news should've sent him over the fucking edge.

The fact that it didn't meant only one thing.

He had a secret far bigger than mine.

Chapter 23

Bess

I stared at the gorgeous hybrid roses Samuel had grown especially for Gwen's wedding, trying not to give in to the sadness pounding behind my eyes. I'd waited for two hours for his return, barely moving a muscle except for the rapid beat of my heart, which apparently I had no control over. Never had. Never would.

He announced himself with a whistle, nearly causing me to fall off the big barrel I'd used as a seat. I screamed, and he caught me as I tumbled down to the ground.

"Sorry, Bess. Didn't mean to scare you."

"Lordie. You should know better than to sneak up on a woman like that."

He helped me up and smiled. I suspected his smile would only grow bigger as our conversation went on.

"What brings you out here this time of day?"

Lunch. Yes, I should be getting back in to Maeve, but at that moment I couldn't stand to look at her.

"I have some news for you. About the nursery."

"Is there a problem?" He waved a glove through the air.

"Not a problem. Actually it's quite good news. For you, I mean. It will be yours. Maeve left the Apple Urban Park to you in her will. I thought it's the kind of thing a person might want to know for their retirement purposes." I smiled, but thinly.

Samuel's mouth opened, then closed, then opened again. He put his hands on his hips, and shook his head. "Bess, why in the world would she give this place to me?"

I stood, my knees feeling shaky. "Samuel, you should know the answer to that. My mother and father loved you dearly. This place is your lifeblood. Your passion. She knew no one could care for it like you."

"But I assumed it would be yours," he said, wiping his thick neck with a rag. "I planned on working for you to my dying day, God willing."

I held my tongue from telling him what my father said about assumptions, but I am most certain Henry had given Samuel that speech when he was a child mowing our lawn. He had tried out all of his golden rules on us before he put them on paper.

"Mother knew what she was doing. Now I better be off to tell Jervis his good news. The antique store and the loft will be his someday, which means good news for him and bad news for the buyer I had on the hook for it."

Samuel's smile disappeared. "Wait a minute, Bess. You live in the loft. That should be yours. I think there's been some kind of mistake. Perhaps you could talk to your mother."

I shook my head and smiled through the pain. "It won't do any good speaking to her about it. She did the will years ago, when all of her faculties were functioning. I dare not go against her wishes. Besides, she probably thought I'd be taken care of by Phillip, and I'm no businesswoman. We still have the urban planning company and oil and gas, though my shares are a lot smaller than most of the board of directors now."

Samuel slapped the glove on his thigh, clearly upset. "If I may be so bold to ask, please tell me she left you something. Something good."

I shrugged, feeling better by Samuel's compassion alone. "She left me her estate in Nichols Hills. The one she wanted me to pass down to the girls, but I was planning on giving it to Victor and Gwen as a wedding gift and make it up to Kelly by giving her profit from the nursery. I don't know what to do. I know. First-world problems."

"Now don't go putting yourself down. Whether you're from poor kin and don't have a dime to your name or wealthy and lose it, it hurts all the same. But please tell me you'll be taken care of."

"My father used to say, you win some and you lose some. He's right. I've lost inheritance and my biological father doesn't want to see Maeve again and still doesn't know I exist. Do you think some secrets should stay hidden?"

"You know how Henry felt about honesty," Samuel said. "If you want to know what I think, it's that Maeve did tell Henry the baby wasn't his and he married her anyway. I've never seen a man adore a woman more than your father adored your mother. He was a good man. Sure, Maeve made the sensible choice back then, but it doesn't mean it was the wrong one. When she told you she had regrets, I think it had more to do with not telling Canty you were his father. She could've been afraid of what he'd do."

"Should I drop it then? Not tell Canty the truth?"

"I think your father would want you to tell Canty the truth. Honesty can be painful, but necessary."

I exhaled. "You're right. I think this calls for apple dumplings with cinnamon ice cream. Care to join me?"

"Two scoops," he said with a wink. "And don't be stingy."

As I re-entered the house, Darla, my second cousin, grabbed me by the arms. She'd stopped by to visit Maeve, as she did once a month.

"Where were you? I looked everywhere. Maeve's been crying hysterically for a half hour. Recalled a memory from your childhood. Did you ever get lost in Paris?"

The knots in my stomach tightened. "I did. But I was only lost for a few minutes. In an antique store."

"She said she must've been a terrible mother to lose

you like that. Been practically tearing up the antiques store hollering for you. She thinks you're lost down there. Now."

"Oh, dear. I'll go right away." When I'd gotten lost in Paris the first time around, she had spanked my bottom and sent me to bed without dinner. I couldn't believe this time she'd cry for me, that she'd remember it any differently.

She must've been frightened to death, fearing she'd lost her only child in Paris. She would never believe I was that lost child.

I dialed my cousin's number to see if her 5-year-old granddaughter would like to play hide and seek in an antique store.

Do you know what's worse than getting a root canal? Going on a date with a man who performs them. I'd never been good at small talk, a skill my mother had tried to pound into me from the time I was six, but I had been shy all my life. Being in the spotlight only made me want to crawl further into my shell.

The date with Dr. Spurlock—the doc who'd "gotten" Kelly pregnant—had been dreadful the week before. Perhaps it was second nature to him, but the man went straight for my vagina. Not literally, but he'd suggested, before our meal was even up, that he give me a tour of his home with a wink that said he meant bedroom, bed, sex. Sex on the first date! Can you imagine? I may miss physical intimacy, and the doctor may be sexy, but what kind of girl did he think my mother raised?

Yet Gwen convinced me to try again, so here I sat with Dr. Peters, a dentist. I figured if he were going to make a play on anything, his first inclination would be my mouth. Much safer first-date material. He was attractive in the same way that Phillip was attractive: well-groomed, nice clothes, but not naturally handsome.

Or rugged. During our meal at Red Prime Steak, my mind kept wandering to the memory of riding bikes with Samuel. I hadn't seen him in days due to some big summer projects with his landscaping company, and I missed him. Without him there, I had no one to talk to when my girls weren't around. I couldn't tell this affable dentist anything other than the superficial, could I? All of the big news in my life was private.

You know your date isn't going well when you feel like you're sitting in the dentist's chair instead of in a cool restaurant. Just enjoy your merlot, I kept telling myself, instead of catching glimpses at my watch to see how much longer the extraction would take. It was hard for me to call him Andy. He didn't seem like an Andy to me. He may as well have worn his white dentist jacket to the meal. The only place I could envision his hands were in other people's mouths, not anywhere on my body.

Oh, Lordie. He wouldn't try to kiss me, would he? As expected, he commented on my teeth. He droned on about why more old people should get their teeth whitened to make them look younger, when I stopped nodding my head pretending to listen. I wasn't sure if he was saying my teeth needed to be whitened, but I'm fairly certain he wanted them whiter.

My eyes suddenly had Bionic Woman capabilities and had locked on to a target: Diana and Phillip dining in the private cubby, cuddling like teen lovers. My face felt as red as that merlot looked. Who did they think they were? I threw my napkin on my plate. Andy's eyes followed mine. He laughed nervously. "Unfortunate," he said. "The evening was going so well."

Because you love to hear yourself talk, I wanted to tell him.

"You're a lovely man, Dr. Pe ... Andy, but I think I'd like to skip dessert if that's okay with you."

Andy dropped some cash on the table, a hopeful look on his face. Crap! Not that kind of dessert!

"How about a nightcap?"

I'm not sure if his suggestion should've made me feel flattered, but one more glance at Diana and Phillip, and it wasn't anger that washed over me—it was something else—jealousy. Not jealous of Diana, but of the chemistry between them. Phillip had never looked at me that way, even when we were young. They were in love.

"I'd rather go home," I told Andy politely. "But thank you for a lovely evening." More white lies. Pearly white lies! Getting so good at them.

Maeve fell asleep watching *Dancing with the Stars* on TiVo. She'd already watched the same episode four times that week, yet each time she acted like she didn't know who would be kicked off. Some days I wished she did have a case of amnesia and not Alzheimer's, but I held on to the hope that she would remember more. I knew in my heart of hearts that the time was drawing near. I wouldn't be able to take care of her forever. I'd cried when she found my grandniece in the antique store, thinking she'd found the lost me in Paris. "You're the most important thing in my life, darling," she'd said. "I don't know what I'd do if anything ever happened to you."

And that's when it hit me that Samuel was likely right. Though Mother didn't show it, she likely gave up Broadway and Canty to ensure I had a good life. It didn't mean having the easy life had been easy on her, though. Some wishes we never grow out of.

Slowly, I let go of the hurt over the will. Giving away her assets to those she thought best deserved them should make me proud of her, not angry. Most of all, I was angry with myself for expecting it, for believing it would save me from an uncertain future. I would have to figure it out on my own.

I shifted her body down on the couch to a sleeping position and covered her with the afghan her mother had made. She'd been digging in the attic again; trying to rediscover the things we thought meant nothing to her anymore. She recognized the afghan, remembered her mother had made it for her as a wedding gift and had held on to it like Linus with his blanket ever since.

Mostly, Maeve cried over Canty. When will he come back? Will he leave his wife? She wanted to tell him she was pregnant with his child. I wished it hadn't mattered one way or the other, but of course it made all the difference in the world whether or not your father knew you and refused you or had no idea you existed beyond the photos of you in the newspaper. Was I just a headline to him?

I couldn't sleep with so much up in the air. I'd been so apprehensive about Gwen's wedding and she was leaving me nonetheless, only not for a man, but for a dream. I had no idea where she would go or when, but I had to toughen up and be ready for it. Prepare for the worst-case scenario.

I worried about Kelly the most, which in the end surprised me. She was the one I never had to worry about much growing up. I began to feel excited about her baby, my grandbaby. All my years of being a Don't Mom meant that I'd saved up all my do's for my grandchild. We would go on wild adventures together. I would see the world anew through that child's eyes, and I knew without a doubt who the child belonged to. A gift from God, plain and simple.

I wished she'd open her heart to the possibility of a man. No mother wants to see her child alone, especially when her own child would need a father figure. I'd suggested she put up a profile on 2gether.com, too, but after that disaster, I would stop shelling out the dating advice like I was some cheesy game show host. Dating was not a game.

Nearly drifting off to sleep next to Mother, my cell phone rang in my pocket. "I'm sorry to be calling so late," the familiar voice said. It took only a moment to recognize Anna's cheerful lilt. "My son and daughter are coming over for brunch tomorrow so I thought it might be nice for you to join us. Thought we could go see my father, our father, afterwards."

My throat caught. To Edmond. To see my sister. My niece and nephew. And meet my biological father for the first time. No time like the present.

Just do it. "I'd love to, Anna. I'll see you tomorrow."

Chapter 24

Bess

After a lovely brunch — bright kids, a neat home, a sweet husband — Anna and I stood in front of Canty's door at the Grace Living Center. Anna's family had accepted me lock, stock and barrel. If the roles were reversed, I am certain the Apples would have demanded a DNA test to confirm that I was Canty's flesh and blood before so much as offering a slice of bacon. They would have to get clearance by Richard Hunt first. It was only a matter of time before Richard would find out that he had a much bigger story to spin than a sperm-bank pregnancy.

"Are you sure this is a good idea?" I asked as Anna rapped softly on the door.

"Only one way to find out."

To think, Maeve's love of her life had lived twenty minutes from her all this time. Had she known about it before Alzheimer's began washing away her memories like sand on the shore?

I held the stack of pancakes in my hand, covered with foil. Sunday ritual for Anna to come and visit her father with pancakes. Something about a loved one making them for you made it taste so much better.

"Come in already," Canty said.

I half expected to walk in and find Canty the way my mother remembered him, like I'd walked through a sliver of time back to the 1940s.

Canty sat at his window, staring out at the already

hot summer afternoon. I hadn't expected to be so overcome with emotions at the sight of him, yet there I was, barely able to keep hold of the pancakes as my eyes misted over.

"Handsome devil, isn't he?" Anna said, going over and planting a kiss on her father's cheek.

Canty returned her kiss and laughed. His blue eyes twinkled, the spark not yet extinguished from old age. His hair was the same jet black as the photos I'd seen him in, though thinner and receding. A redhead who had dyed his hair black because he thought it looked better on stage. A man like this would look good in any hair color, I suspected. Everything about him seemed stretched like an image on Silly Putty.

He eyed the pancakes and then me. He searched my face, but nothing came to him. Blank. I don't know what I expected.

"Daddy, this is Bess Apple-Barton," Anna said, speaking louder while her father cupped his ear.

"Is that so?" He said holding his hands out for the pancakes. Anna went about heating the syrup in the microwave.

Nothing.

He uncovered the foil and handed it back to me. Canty shook his finger at his daughter. "What are you trying to do? Give an old man a heart attack?" He turned to me. "I don't much like surprises with my pancakes," he said with a scowl. "Though good company is good company all the same."

"It's nice to meet you," I said, willing my voice not to crack.

Anna poured his syrup and we sat in the two empty seats opposite him, staring out at the gardens in the lawn. Two women were walking with walkers and turned around to wave at Canty. He waved back and they looked at each other and giggled. I hoped I still had giggle in me when I was their age.

"Smitten, every damn one of 'em," Canty said. "Can't even go to the dances anymore. Like I'm some kind of rag doll the girls can pass back and forth. Think I should get a body guard?" He teased.

I smiled. "Most men would love to be in your position. How long have you lived here?"

"Too damn long," Canty said. "But I'd rather be around people my age and have things to do than sit around watching Jeopardy! with my daughter. No offense."

"He's always been a social butterfly," Anna said. "And he gets to play in a band here. Every Tuesday, Thursday and Saturday evenings."

"Old folks go to bed by nine," Canty said. "But let me tell you, I used to play into the wee hours of the morning back in the day."

"What do you play?" I asked.

"Better question is what do I not play?" He smiled, and even with his wrinkles, the dimple on his right cheek and the cleft in his chin were still there. Just like my girls'. "Over the years, I learned to play about every instrument. But with my old lungs, I tend to stay away from the wind instruments. Stick to piano mostly. Course my fingers don't always cooperate. Little arthritis flares up now and then."

"He's still very good," Anna said proudly.

"So you're the governor's daughter," Canty said as he sat his plate down on the table. He crossed his fingers on his lap. Not a question, really. A statement. Did he mean for me to respond to that? Was it a trick to get me to tell him, no, you're my father? Not difficult to pick up on the fact he didn't mention my mother.

"Yes. Henry Apple. Governor and then senator and then ambassador." Why did I do that? Spit out all those titles? Canty knew who he was. I was fumbling all over my words. Nervous as all get out. I looked at Anna for help.

"Daddy, Bess came to me last week asking if I might talk to you about setting up a reunion between you and Maeve for Princess and the Pauper. But you wouldn't talk to me about it, so I thought I'd let Bess try to talk to you."

"Ack," Canty said, swatting the air and turning his face away from us. I couldn't see his expression, but he began wiggling his foot.

"It would mean so much to me if you would talk to her," I said. "Maybe she could come and listen to your band one evening?"

Canty got up, no need for assistance, and walked over to his closet and pulled out a hat. "Time for my morning piano," he said, putting on a vintage hat.

Could he dismiss me that easily?

He turned to face me. "I see your mother in you," he said. "Hard for me to look at you."

I nodded. Hardly anyone ever said they saw a resemblance. What exactly did he see?

"Walk with me," Canty said. "We'll be back shortly," he said to his daughter, leaving his pancakes half-eaten.

Canty's back was bent, but he was still tall, nearly six feet. Lanky, but well fed. His complexion had a healthy glow.

We walked in silence, the women all smiling when we passed by, making eye contact with him, not me. "See you at dinner," one said. "Come to water aerobics this afternoon," said another.

"I guess they've got you outnumbered," I said as we reached a darkened reception hall with no windows, metal chairs stacked against the wall, a small dance floor, and a stage with a piano. The lights were off, but one flick of the switch and the stage light came to life. I followed him to the stage where he sat at the piano. I imagined it might be the place in the world he felt most himself.

"Thank you for not throwing me out," I said, taking

a seat beside him on the piano bench.

"Your mother meant a lot to me at one time. How's she holding up?" He began playing something I didn't recognize, but it was slow and sweet.

"She thinks she's 25 again. It's the disease. Won't stop talking about you."

His fingers rested on the keys, but he didn't look at me. Then he reached around to his dress pants pocket and pulled out his wallet and plucked out a picture. He handed it to me.

"That's us the day before she told me she was going to marry Henry Apple," he said. "I remember it as if it were yesterday." He made a stabbing motion to his heart and turned it.

The photo was of the two of them, Canty and Maeve, cheek to cheek. Happy as larks. "So you didn't expect it?"

"I knew she'd been seeing him. It was all over the papers of course. Senator's son dating a local actress. But I thought she was trying to make me jealous. Trying to get me to see I could lose her if I didn't leave my wife. But then my Anna was born a few weeks early. Precious little thing. Back then they didn't have the technology that they do now. And my wife didn't ad well to having a newborn. Baby blues, they called it then. Think they take it more seriously now."

"Postpartum depression?"

"Something awful. Anna cried all the time. My wife cried all the time. Neither of us was getting any sleep. One day," Canty paused, then cleared his throat, "my wife said she was going to kill herself." Canty grabbed a hanky from his other pocket and dabbed at his eyes. "Still hurts like hell to think of it."

"I'm so sorry. That must've been terrible. So you ended things with Maeve?"

"I could never end things with Maeve. The plan was my wife and baby would stay with relatives in Tulsa while I was in New York. Best salary of my life, so I could send the money home. I told Maeve it was until the baby was a little older. Maeve was beside herself. Said there wasn't any time and she couldn't go to New York, end of story. Next thing I know she's telling me she's going to marry Henry, and Arthur hired a new Princess. Talk about a daily reminder of the one you love. I was never the same after that. It's funny, but I didn't care to be Pauper if Maeve wasn't my Princess."

"But you made a name for yourself."

"A name?" Canty smiled. "A name is just that: a word. But I kept tabs, as much as it hurt. You were on your way by then and every week in the society section there the two of them were. Parties and elaborate baby showers and whatnot. Made me sick, but I couldn't stop looking."

"But you never saw her again?"

"About fifteen years later, I came back to Oklahoma. Gave up acting for good, though I'd never give up my music. Started an antique store in Tulsa and the week after it opened who walks through the door?"

"Maeve?"

"As gorgeous as ever. But better. Mature. Happy. Regal. She looked, even smelled, like a queen. I swear I turned to stone when she looked at me." He patted his chest.

"What did you do?"

"I asked her if I could help her and she said, yes, indeed, I could. Said she was looking for a particular piece for a client—a European chest and had heard I'd gotten one in and thought I might have something."

"And did you?"

"I did. Sold her the piece and when she kissed me on the cheek, I nearly broke down. Told her how sorry I was. How much I missed her, but she smiled that smile that always brought me to my knees. She said, 'What's done is done. We both had to do what we had to do.' And she was gone. Never saw her again in person."

"That's all she told you? She didn't mention anything about me? Not before you went to New York or after?"

He dabbed at his eyes again, shaking his head. His feelings were so raw, underneath the surface. I felt relief that he'd never been told about me, that he hadn't avoided me all these years like my mother had avoided telling me the truth.

"So then you don't know why she couldn't wait? Why she didn't go to New York?" I said after awhile.

Canty looked at me, his blue eyes the same color as mine, the same color as Anna's. I could still see the pain in his eyes.

"She was already pregnant with me, Canty. With your child."

He hunched over, deflated. He bounced his balled fist against his mouth, and shook his head, not looking at me. He needed a moment. I could give him a moment. I could give him all the time he needed.

I tried to be strong, really I did. I didn't want to cry in front of this stranger, but even though he'd been real to me three months through Maeve's story, he didn't feel strange to me. I could feel his love for my mother going all the way back, building like a snowball, packed and stronger than ever.

"I swear to you, I had no idea," he said, and I believed him.

He got up and left the stage. When I thought he was leaving me for good, he turned around. "You coming?"

I followed him behind stage to a row of locked storage cabinets. A sign that read Keep Out had been taped to it. He reached into his pocket and pulled out some keys and fumbled for a good minute until he found the right key and opened the door.

Inside the cabinet were ten leather photo albums. He ran his fingers over them and pulled out the first one. Heavy. I grabbed a chair and sat down with it. I expected photo albums, but after the pictures of the actors from The Orpheum and another photo like the one I'd first seen of Canty and Maeve on her nightstand in the Early Century department, the rest of it was news clippings. Scrapbooks. The first one, 1949. Then nothing for a year. And then, 1950, 1951. From that time on, each scrapbook contained five years worth of news and magazine clippings. The Apples kept historians on staff to keep news clippings about the company and its executives, but these were stories I'd never seen before. The news wasn't about Henry Apple at all, though he was in a lot of the pictures. Each one was Maeve.

Every publicized party she'd ever hosted.

Every board she'd ever governed.

Every trip, award and news bit the society section reported on. Recorded there for posterity. I was in some of them, too, the ones with my mother in them. My first birthday party. Pictures of me giving the press a tour of the Governor's mansion. My graduation from OSU. My engagement to Phillip. Our wedding.

With each scrapbook, I watched my mother age, but I felt something else, too. I could feel the love Canty had for my mother deepened with each passing of the page. "You couldn't let go of her entirely."

"It was all I could do. I kept a subscription of the paper so no matter where I was in the country; I knew that she was okay. Something in me told me I should save them. Now I know why. My family doesn't know about them, except for the first one. I was afraid I'd have to throw them out."

"So you really didn't have a clue I was your daughter then? Even with my hair and skin color?"

"No. I don't know if it's because I have a thick skull or because I would've assumed Maeve would've told me something that important. But I can see why she wouldn't have."

"You do?"

"She did for me what I couldn't do for myself. When I told her my wife was sick, she knew the right thing for me to do was to stay with my family, even if that meant in marriage and money only. I was still gone an awful lot when Anna was little. Maeve knew how to take care of herself. How to take care of you. Look at the life you've lived! Maeve knew what she was doing all along. And as much as I hate to admit it for my heart's sake, she did the right thing."

I opened the final scrapbook, the one only two-thirds of the way through. Most of the latest clippings were from OI. The large photo of Maeve singing on stage at Downtown Blues. "This one made me happiest of all," he said, pointing to her picture. "She's back doing what she loved the most. And she's still the most gorgeous woman I ever laid eyes on."

"So you'll agree to see her again?"

Canty shook his head as we walked back to the stage. "I was so angry at her for so long, for not choosing me. For not waiting for me, but with what you've told me, it all makes sense. She wanted to give you a family. To give you a chance to have a better life than the one Maeve had growing up. But I'm not the man I once was."

"How so?" I asked.

"I'm old, if you haven't noticed." He cracked his smile again.

"But you're still Canty."

He rubbed the back of his neck. "I'd love to see Maeve again, if my ticker can take it."

"Do you have heart problems?"

"Only where she is concerned," he said softly.

"I know this is a lot to take in. But she's been wearing the promise ring you gave her."

"Know this about me, Bess. I'm a man of my word. And that's a promise I intend to keep." He began playing another tune, more upbeat, faster.

I was amazed his fingers could move like that.

"That's all about to change, Bess." After a few more bars, I recognized the song, "Everything's Coming Up Roses." I hoped beyond all hope, that he was right.

Chapter 25

Gwen

The viewers voted Vera Wang with sixty-two percent of the vote. Finally, with the help of my loyal and backbiting blogging fans, I had a wedding dress. Vera's people were busy stitching it to perfection, while I dealt with laying to rest the other mysteries that plagued those final weeks to the wedding.

Four days since the big debt reveal and Victor still hadn't chewed me out. Either Victor had really won the test and loved me for me, despite my shockingly high interest rate, or something was up.

Fastest credit card in the West, the future Mrs. Gwen Apple-Barton Prescott, had become her own detective. I'd leafed through Victor's sock drawers, desk drawers, cell phone records, credit card receipts and briefcase, looking for anything suspicious. I was sure his wanker had been wandering. How else to explain my get out of jail free card?

But nothing. Nada. Zip. Not one suspect call or purchase or cocktail napkin with a lipstick smudge and phone number. Victor was as reliable and predictable as ever. The paper trail of his life included only business and the wedding. I tried not to let it bother me that he texted my father more than me, but other than that, he only called his friends, Skylar and me.

The only place I hadn't searched was his office and if I found nothing, then I swore to myself I'd marry him and life would go on. My mother said lots of brides have wedding jitters, but I wondered how many of them regretted going through with the wedding.

I knew Victor was in a weekly staff meeting, so I leisurely sauntered into his office, closed the door and sat at his massive desk, which I noticed was a good two feet longer than mine. I took a good look around. This was the guy I was going to marry. The space represented him much more than his home did. His walls were covered with plaques and awards. Leadership Oklahoma City, Leadership Oklahoma. What next, Leadership World?

His neat desk and bookshelves were full of photos of him with important people—the mayor, the governor, the Richie Riches of the business world. Finally I spotted the photo of Victor and I in our high school graduation cap and gown, with my grandfather between us, and it hit me that Henry would always be between us. As if Henry was a conduit that bonded us together. No wonder Victor was upset Henry wasn't my biological grandfather.

I'd finished reading Papa's book. The rules were about doing what's right and living your dreams and taking risks to get the reward. They were about being big enough to take apologies and bigger still to admit mistakes.

As painful as it was, I knew in my gut what I had to do. Someone as amazing as Victor Prescott deserved a girl who'd appreciate the awards and business ambition and his willingness to let his wife stay home and raise the kids.

Victor was a great leader, a determined businessman, a caring corporate citizen. He wasn't for me. My grandfather's advice to follow your heart, had to be most important when dealing with matters of the heart, right?

My cell phone vibrated again and again. Bess. Then Kelly. I let them go to voice mail. I knew there was nothing here to prove Victor wasn't the stand-up guy the world believed he was. Maybe, after all, I was looking for the easy way out. An excuse. Far better to go through with the wedding and give the whole marriage thing a chance. I wouldn't know what it was like until we'd tied the knot. Pauper and Ax would be long gone and I could concentrate on making a life with Victor. A wave of nausea coursed through me. How could a thought have so much power? If I couldn't even think it, how the hell was I going to do it?

Nothing worth the telling is easy.

Besides the Wall Street Journal, Victor's favorite reading material was Oklahoma Insider, typically because he was in every week's issue. The man couldn't get enough of himself. I thumbed through the society section, and sure enough, they we were at Macy Billings' hello to summer pool party and Chef's Feast and the Underground Arts exhibit. To the outsider, we looked like we had it all.

Then, an unexpected face stared up at me from the glossy pages.

Actor Ax Ellis parties at the Skirvin with long-time squeeze Tabby Mathews.

No way. Ax was going steady with the choreographer? Why wouldn't he tell me all those times we'd been together? How had they kept their relationship quiet in front of the cast? Actors loved to gossip. I remembered how Tabby had kissed him when he found out he got the part of Pauper. It had seemed like a friendly cast kiss, nothing more. My heart sunk in disappointment.

A hard rap at the door nearly made me jump out of his pricey leather seat. I wiped away my guilt at snooping where I shouldn't and rolled my shoulders back. "Come in."

Shadow emerged, wearing his usual grungy button down western shit and baggy jeans. Mid-40s if I had to guess, with permanent stubble on his face. I'd never seen him clean shaven, even on our early morning shoots.

"Didn't expect you," he said, "though it's better than the alternative."

"I thought you weren't shooting anything until the best man planning the bachelor party tonight?"

Shadow sat in the seat across from the desk and put his boots up on the desk. I nearly swatted them away, but thought better of it. Shadow was the guy who could put really unflattering shots of my ass on national television, after all. "I do what the boss tells me," he said.

"How was New York?" I asked. I hadn't gotten to talk to him after the confessional, too shaken up about the arrival of my invitations.

"New York is New York," he said scratching his whiskers on his neck. Shadow wasn't exactly vile, but he'd grown on me nonetheless. He was like a mole you get used to after a while.

"How long have you been shooting *Luxe Weddings*?"

"Too damn long. If I never saw another wedding again, it would be too soon."

"Wait. Don't tell me. You probably don't believe in happily ever after do you?"

Shadow slid his boots off the desk and leaned forward onto his elbows eyeing me. "You know this is all fantasy, right? Sure, you're a rich girl getting a princess wedding, but once the cake is all eaten and the wedding dress is put away, even rich girls realize marriage is nothing like what they imagined. It's like Cinderella in reverse."

He smiled, proud of his Aristotle moment, and got up to leave.

"You don't like Victor very much, do you?"

"I know his type," Shadow said. "Hell, I was his type. Used to be a Wall Street broker in my twenties, engaged to a CEO's daughter."

I blinked hard, disbelieving my ears. I couldn't picture Shadow in a snazzy designer suit or anywhere near Wall Street. How had he gotten from there to here?

Had a broken heart done this to him?

"All I'm saying is, you can stick a penguin suit on a man, but you can never change his stripes. You get my drift?"

Shadow left, Victor's cell phone vibrating under some papers on his desk. A text message. Curious, I picked it up.

Thank u 4 the flowers.

Skylar. A prickly, hot feeling spread through my face. I scrolled up, reading the ongoing conversation between the two of them the last several months. Nervous and shaky, I decided to start at the top and read my way down, noting any that sounded above and beyond the call of duty for *Luxe Weddings*, beginning in March.

VP: downtown is not where the action is.

ST: action sounds good.

VP: I'll set you up.

ST: not interested in your friends.

April

VP: wear the mini dress.

ST: I love a naughty groom.

May

VP: told G I would take over more wedding planning

ST: knew u were a smart guy

VP: G has rehearsals every nite this wk. plan on my house 7p. bring red nightie

June

CP: going to NY. Think u could work it into show so u can go?

ST: done and done.

So he sent her flowers after he fucked her silly in New York. What a gentleman. I took his phone with me, possibly the only proof I'd have that his relationship with Skylar was anything other than producer and groom.

I left the office, feeling like such a fool for not

noticing what was happening right under my nose. I'd seen the way he looked at her, but didn't all guys look at her that way? Victor had never been unfaithful to me in all of our six years together—that I knew of. What if Skylar was the final note in a chorus of liaisons? I rushed out of the office, tears pounding behind my eyes, but I wouldn't give him the satisfaction. I debated storming into his meeting, but as I saw Shadow in the break room getting coffee, I had a better idea.

"Loft. Impromptu confessional," I said.

Shadow's usual languid demeanor morphed to concern. I probably looked like I'd seen the ghost of the future. "Sure," he said. "I'll call Skylar."

"No. Just you and me. Can you get it to New York without her knowing?"

"You saw the stripes, right?"

I nodded, holding back the rage within me, and we headed for the loft.

Chapter 26

Bess

Samuel had the horses saddled and ready to ride when I arrived. I was a little late and apologized profusely. I caught him up on Canty, that we were going to arrange a time for he and Maeve's reunion on opening night. He was happy for me, of course, but he didn't seem himself.

We hadn't gotten together the weekend before because Maeve wasn't feeling well, and I couldn't leave her. Samuel and I walked the horses from the stable out into the field. I don't know what we were thinking riding horses when it was nearly 90 degrees outside. I was sweating before we'd even mounted them, but he assured me the wooded path was cool and shaded. I could hear the creek somewhere within those woods, and I had no idea Samuel lived on such a property. He didn't have a neighbor for miles that I could see, and the land was beautiful.

"What's the matter?" I asked him. "Everything okay? If you don't want to ride, we don't have to."

The horses snorted and shook their heads. Even they seemed agitated.

"I called over last night," Samuel said. "Gwen answered the phone. Said you were on a date."

Guilty as charged. My chest caved. "I did. I'll tell you all about it," I said lightly.

"Nope," Samuel said, helping me up onto the horse. "The last thing I want to hear about is your date."

"Samuel. Really. It wasn't anything."

He mounted his horse. "Hee-yah, Louie." He clicked

the reins and my horse Nichol followed obediently. Samuel spoke loudly from his position in front of me, but I'll admit I didn't mind the view one bit. I couldn't see his expression, but his tone was harsh, unusual for him. "If you expect me to sit here and listen to you recount your evening with another man, then I'm sorry, I can't do it. I can handle a lot of things, but that wouldn't be one of them."

"I'm sorry," I said, feeling both ashamed and happy at the same time. I had no idea I'd made Samuel jealous. Not my intention at all. "I should've told you I had a date. It was a silly thing to do. I'll never make that mistake again, believe me."

Samuel stopped his horse and my horse sidled up next to his. "You mean the part about not telling me or the part where you go on a date with another man?"

"Both, I guess," I said. "I didn't think it would bother you. I mean, we're good friends, right? Very good friends."

"Hell, Bess. For a smart woman, you sure don't see it, do you?"

"See what?"

"That you can't kiss a man and expect that to be the end of it. I want more than a scoop of ice cream with you. Much more."

I could feel my toes tingle. I hadn't had more than ice cream in a very, very long time. I nodded, for words seemed superfluous.

"Then I hope you don't mean the part about not dating again," he said.

"You do?"

"Well, what do you call this here? I'd say we're on a date."

"If I'd known that, I would have freshened up my makeup. Though what I started with this morning is already melted off." I tried to laugh, but I could see Samuel was serious.

"I mean it. You'll know it's a date when it ends with a kiss."

I could feel myself blush. "Oh, my."

"And not one, either."

"Samuel!" I laughed.

He backed his horse up and the horse brushed up against mine, until we were so close; our legs were touching in our stirrups. "As a matter of fact, I don't think you technically have to wait until the end of the date, either." He leaned over and kissed me, but I wasn't content with a peck. I let go of the reins and put my arms around his thick neck. He smelled of musky aftershave, and his chin was already growing whiskers. I kissed his chin to feel the whiskers on my lips. Then his soft mouth. An ageless mouth.

"I don't think I want to ride horses anymore," I said, breathlessly.

"Happy to oblige."

Sometimes the best things in life, the ones that seem like the biggest disasters of your life, end up being the best things that ever happen to you.

I never expected I would get a divorce and live with my mother and daughters again. I never expected that I would fall in love again. Never expected that passion plays no favorites to age.

That what some people might consider the tail end of their life could also be the beginning.

When I arrived home two short hours later (the saying time flies when you're having fun still applies at my age), Kelly greeted me at the door with a huge smile on her face, though I don't see how it could've been any bigger than mine.

"She's remembered," Kelly said.

We walked together into the living room to find the photo albums again littering the floor, and Maeve sitting in the middle of them like the funnel of a tornado. "I miss Henry," she said, holding up a photo of them from a cruise in the '70s. "Where's Henry?"

Chapter 27

Gwen

There was a small chance in the far corner of Hell that I would forgive Victor for cheating on me with Skylar. I'd confronted him that night, after the confession of my findings had already been transmitted to the head honchos at *Luxe Weddings*. He'd denied it until I'd read him back his text messages, and then the apologies and explanations couldn't come fast enough.

He swore he loved me, only me, and his tryst had only been a case of cold feet. After all, he'd said, you were the only one I was going to have sex with for the rest of my life. So he blamed it on sowing the final rows on his wild oats, while it hit me that the prospect of having sex with only me for the rest of his life shouldn't have sent him straight into the vagina of the hot producer. But maybe that's me. And I'd thought I'd had a case of cold feet, too, but it was more than that for both of us.

While my people talked to the show's people to work out the legal and PR mess that would result, I concentrated on being the best Princess understudy I could. I knew every word, every note, every dance move by heart. I may never get to show anyone on stage, but I became her just in case. At least Maeve would get her finale with Canty, and the chance to finish whatever they had started so long ago.

While I watched Ax play the piano and the actors slowly dispersed for an afternoon excursion to the lake, I decided the best way for me to learn how to be an understudy was to study under Ax. In his bed. In his camper. In his tent. Wherever.

Victor and I hadn't been right for a long time, and his wrongdoing only made me want Ax more.

Only he was taken. I was tired of skirting around the issues, beating around the bush. Tabby was home sick in bed, a case of a severe summer cold, so I could confront him without her around.

"Not going with the gang?" he asked as I gathered up my bag.

"Think I'd rather die than hang out in a swimsuit all day with my fellow actors," I said. "Especially skinny Princess."

Ax scowled. "Have to disagree with you there, Gwen. I like a girl who fills out her bikini top. Is it always this hot in Oklahoma?"

Only when you're around. What was that about the bikini top? "So you're going with them, then? Or maybe to go take some cold soup to Tabby?"

"Tabby?" His lips twitched.

"Why didn't you tell me you two were seeing each other? I saw it in the paper."

"I'm not dating her. We're friends," he said sheepishly. "I started freelancing for OI last month and the guys in editorial thought it would be a gas to put us on the society page. Because we're not society. Get it?"

"So you're not sleeping with Tabby?"

Ax shifted uncomfortably on the piano, which I took as a yes. "Tabby and I have known each other off and on for a long time. She came in from New York with some of the other actors. Look doll, I feel like I'm being read the riot act here. I'm not the one that's engaged."

I resisted crying in front of him. But he was right. I was engaged, or else he thought I still was, and all Ax and I had done was danced together. Slowly. Closely. Intimately.

"I'm not going back to teach at the reservation in the

fall. I guess what you said hit me. This is giving me the motivation to try for real this time. If 'real' means quitting your day job to pursue your passion."

I blinked back ears. "So New York, then?"

"Actually, L.A. A couple of agents called me and said they could use a few more insanely handsome Native American types, so ta-da!"

"That's our Ax, the '50s lingo-speaking Native American triple threat. You'll be a smash, dollface," I said, affecting an accent.

He stood, but I didn't budge.

Ax reached into his duffel bag and produced his camera, something I rarely saw him without. He pushed several buttons then handed me the camera. "I know it doesn't matter, but while we're laying it out on the line, here's the gal I'm crazy about."

I sucked in my breath. It was me. Every last one of them. Photos from rehearsals and auditions and goofing off with other actors. Swing dancing and singing on stage. Extreme close-ups and moody images with blur and gorgeous lighting. Artistic. Memorable. I wasn't wearing designer clothes or posing for some party pic. He'd captured what I'd looked for all these years. The real me.

The hairs on my head stood on end. "Why did you take these?"

"Because." Ax looked down at his hand on the table and then back up at me. "I wanted to remember this time in my life. To be perfectly honest, dollface, I've had a thing for you from the moment I laid eyes on you. I knew you were engaged, that our worlds were so totally opposite. But I wanted something to remember you by. Pauper will come and go, and I'll be back in L.A. and you'll be here married to your king in your castle in Nichols Hills. This will all be a distant memory, but I'll always have these."

I shook my head slowly. "I don't know, Ax. I don't

think I'm done making them yet."

Next thing I knew, Ax had locked eyes with mine, and I felt his gaze pulling me into him until I realized it was him coming closer, then kissing me, softly, and I was so shocked I didn't do anything, but my heart beat so fast I was sure it would combust. Our eyes opened, and he was real, an inch from my face, his hot breath on my lips and I let him kiss me again, because angry or not, unsure or not, it's the one thing that felt right.

"That's real," Ax said as he pulled away from me.

Breathless, I regained my composure, resisting the urge to kiss him again, longer, harder. Ax swung his arm, gesturing to the door. I descended the stage steps, his kiss still tingling on my lips and walked into the hot morning. I tried not to think about how much I wanted to share the stage with him, both in work and in life. How much I wanted to get to know him better.

"You're right—in this heat, I think getting wet is mandatory," I told him. "I know the place."

He opened the car door for me and I resisted a repeat performance of our kiss.

Ax leaned closer. "I'm sorry you didn't get the part," he said. "I really, really wanted you to be Princess. I think the producers made a huge mistake."

Funny how I'd never been sure about anything, not where I should go to college, or what I should major in, or what kind of napkins I wanted at my wedding, but singing I felt sure of. It felt like the most natural thing on Earth. Did not landing the part mean I should give up before I'd even really tried? And did I dare venture out into a world where I was a nobody? Where my name meant nothing?

An hour later, we were drinking margaritas in my grandmother's pool at the swim-up bar, the whole place to ourselves, no skinny Princesss or jealous Tabbies or slit-eyed Maeve's to get in our way.

Ax slicked back his thick hair and I tried not to stare at his wet six-pack abs. I grabbed a bottle of sunscreen and rubbed my hands on his shoulders and then he turned his back to me so I could lotion his broad back.

"This I could get used to," he said, referring to the massive house in front of him. "It's like Camelot."

"Not exactly."

He turned to face me. "Rumor has it your grandmother wants the house to go to you as a wedding present, right?"

I'd been wanting to tell him about Victor all week, yet it wasn't as if Victor had disappeared from my life. He was desperate to win me back and pleaded for forgiveness. "There are some things you should know about me, Ax. First off, I owe about $70,000 in credit card debt after selling off about 20 Gs in couture this summer and trading in my car for a cheaper model. Until recently, I was a shopaholic. A big majority of my closet is for sale, which is actually a lot more painful than it should be. I have a hard time letting things go, even if they're bad for me. My fiancé, a job I loathe, and clothes I can't afford."

He raised his brows. "What else?"

"My family isn't as wealthy as they seem. I mean, we own a lot of property, but we lose money on some of it and my grandmother willed two of our businesses away. Most of our money is in investments that may or may not pay off. So even though it's at a higher level, it still feels like working paycheck to paycheck."

"Far from eating ramen noodles every night. And?"

"Turns out Canty, the original Pauper, is actually my biological grandfather."

He shook his head. "This keeps getting better and better. More?"

"I'm afraid so. This estate was going to be a wedding present as you said, but since there won't be a wedding, then there's no present."

Ax raised a brow "Wait a minute. Back up to the part about the wedding."

I handed him the sunscreen and turned my back to him. He began rubbing the sunscreen slowly along my spine, my shoulder blades, my neck. Too softly. I cleared my throat. "Victor's been screwing our wedding producer, but I was thinking about calling it off before then. Only there's a hefty price tag with calling it quits on the show." I waved my ringless finger in the air as proof.

Ax's hands moved over my shoulders, pulling me back against his chest. "I'll start saving my pennies," he whispered into me ear. "I'm not sure you should've told me that, dollface." His fingers caressed my neck, my throat and then splayed out to the top of my chest. I put my hand over his to stop their descent.

At least if my body was on fire, I knew how to put it out. Plenty of water to extinguish it. I turned to face him. "Why not?"

"Because you being engaged was the only thing coming between me and that bikini."

My heart practically leapt out of my top. "You like it, huh?"

"Very much. In fact, I like the whole package. Every last inch."

No, Ax Ellis was not a fashion plate. He didn't care that my bikini was Chanel. He liked me, my voluptuous body, which was 100 percent Gwen Apple-Barton. They say if you give them an inch, they'll take a mile. Ax could have every millimeter.

I slid my hand up his strong thigh. "I'm sorry the show only plays four weeks." He leaned in closer, our lips nearly touching.

Four weeks and he'd be gone, to try to make it in L.A., hopefully with the acclaim of critics on his resume and his phone buzzing with jobs. Yet I would trade four weeks of rapture for a lifetime of monotony.

Beginning with this: I leaned in and kissed him and

let myself go, melting into him. Things got so heated I swore when I came up for air we'd turned the majestic pool into a hot tub.

My home girls were eating again when I got back to the loft, a FedEx package setting in the middle of the table along with a plate of cinnamon rolls. Who knew I'd ever be able to eat carbs during swimsuit season?

"Open it," Kelly said, handing me the mid-sized box.

The return address listed a boutique in California. Thanks to the Internet, every luxury brand worldwide was still available to me, but I couldn't remember what I'd ordered.

I ripped open the box and pulled out a plastic bag full of cute white flip-flops. "My bridal flip-flops!" I squealed. My pair had tiny crystal studs along the band and a huge diamond at the toe. I'd planned on surprising my bridesmaids with them. Perfect for dancing at the reception.

Oh. My face fell in disappointment.

Maeve, Kelly and Bess looked at me sadly, waiting for my response, as if I'd crumble at the sight of them.

I smiled, tearing off the tags. "Why the glum faces? As far as I know, it's flip-flop season and there's no law that says you can't wear bridal flip-flops even if you're not a bride." I passed the flip-flops around the table. One for each of them.

"Perfect, because none of us are brides," Kelly said. "And I think my feet are already starting to swell in this blasted heat."

Maeve squealed. "I've never worn flip-flops before," she said, and for once she was right. We'd never seen her or Bess in a pair before.

"They're darling," Bess said. "They may be my new everyday shoes." She showed off her red painted nails and the gems sparkled in the sunny kitchen.

Maeve tapped her feet back and forth. "Wow, they're comfortable. Where have they been all my life? I think I've died and gone to shoe heaven."

Bess kissed me on the cheek. "Thank you for finding the silver line, darling."

Maeve began spinning around the room. "Did I ever tell you about the time I danced with President Reagan at the White House?"

She had, but the story got even better with every telling. I was thrilled she'd remember it. The best part, she said? Dancing with Ronnie to Ella Fitzgerald after dinner. And Nancy seemed the slightest bit jealous.

I excused myself, but Kelly grabbed my arm. "Almost forgot. Ax called. Something about a big break."

An hour later, skinny Princess, who was laid up in a hospital with a broken leg from a water skiing accident, was replaced by her understudy, one curvy Princess who understood with all of her being why she had the hots for the pauper, the most handsome make-believe knight in all the land.

What was that Phillip said about it not being meant to be?

Chapter 28

Kelly

"Oh, my God, you're showing already," my best friend, Taylor, said as she wrapped me in a hug in the loft that afternoon. When she had told me she was coming up for the Fourth of July with her hubby and daughter, I'd taken off for the rest of the week, much to my staff's surprise.

I didn't take off work. Ever. I was the one who was typically late to our Christmas Eve dinners because I was trying to finish something up at the office. So three days off that weren't around a winter holiday seemed extravagant. And I'd never been into Fourth of July activities like a lot of people. The only reason I'd liked the holiday was for a day to get caught up on my work because my clients wouldn't be calling. There. I said it. But did I sort of look forward to dressing up my baby in patriotic gear and sweating in the heat to see a parade like a regular mom? You bet.

I patted my belly as Taylor's three-year old Emily ran in circles around my legs like an excited puppy. "Showing? It's because I'm eating like there's five of them in there."

"You? Eating? I'll have to see it to believe it," she said.

"Well, you'll get your wish. In fact, I could use a snack right now. I bent over and kissed Emily's blonde head of hair. Big Shirley Temple curls. "Want some peanut butter and jelly?" I asked her.

"Yes, please," she said then tore off to explore the loft, out of earshot, but within eye line.

"Please. Impressive," I said to Taylor.

"We're working on it," she said, handing over an oversized gift bag. "As long as she doesn't blurt 'eff you,' I'm thinking I deserve a 'Mother of the Year' award."

"Still tough to slay the cursing dragon, huh?"

"I like to blame it on advertising. Take the boring words from my vocab, but please let me keep my F-bomb. Unfortunately, Pig Latin has saved the day," she said.

"Well, advertising gets the blame for everything else, why not your potty mouth, too?" I held open the huge bag of goodies. "This is where I'm supposed to say you shouldn't have, but that would be a lie."

"Perks to having a friend with a baby clothing account," Taylor said.

"My first baby clothes. And from Studio Baby, no less! I hope they gave you a discount."

"No, but considering their account pays my mortgage and most everything else, I can't complain. But you'll be pleased to know I stuck to my promise I made at the Mojo retreat. I'm only taking on new clients if one leaves and I work from home on Fridays. I even leave my phone in the car when I get home so I'm not tempted to answer it."

"Why do I feel like we're not workaholic besties anymore?"

Taylor smoothed her shirt. "Would you settle for preggo besties instead?"

I stared at her nearly flat stomach, a smile creeping onto my face. "No way."

She grinned. "You didn't think I'd drive all the way up here for a parade, did you? I'm four weeks behind you."

We jumped up and down, squealing like sorority girls on bid day.

She followed me to my bedroom where I put the bag in my oversized closet. For once both Gwen's and my things fit easily in the closet. I'd spent the entire day before at the designer sale, nearly getting trampled from women who'd come in from all over the city to grab up Gwen's designer splurges. She'd raked in $8,000 by sunset with more Internet offers coming in. She still had a long way to go to be debt free, but I believed she'd think twice before using a credit card again.

Taylor clutched the Prada tote she'd bought from Gwen, planning to use it for baby and business. "Please tell me you're going to take some time off when the baby comes. Don't be one of those sick women who work right up until their due date and then they're back on their laptop the second day their home."

"Like you, you mean."

"Hey, I wasn't that bad. I was at home for six weeks and I only checked my e-mail once a day. You'll find you could just as easily slip into momaholism, where you become obsessed about being a good mother."

"Shoot me now," I said, rolling my eyes.

"Oh, you'll find yourself on the grocery aisle debating the merits of organic versus the ease of frozen meals like the rest of us."

"I can't wait," I said, my eyes misting. "I mean that."

"I know you do. Now when do I get to meet the sexy client?"

My body tensed. Edgar, the client I seemed to be playing emotional ping pong with: I can't be near you, we need to stay apart; oh, hell, how did we just have sex again ping-pong. "I'll take you on a tour at the Orpheum. Maybe he'll be there."

"Maybe, my ass. You know he'll be there."

"It's frightening how well you know me," I said.

"Still nothing beyond the physical?" Taylor stuck out

her bottom lip.

"I'm telling you what I told him: I can't be in a relationship right now, and you're the one who knows the real reason why."

"And why are you so sure he wouldn't be okay with you having a baby?"

"You're kidding, right? This may be modern times, but he's still an old dog. He's a jet-setting adventurous CEO. He doesn't want to be tied down, believe me. I'm convenient for him."

Taylor nodded slowly, a skeptical scowl on her face. "Well, from the look of your pooch, you can't keep it a secret much longer."

"I've decided Independence Day should be just that. Telling him about the baby, which will make me independent of him from here on out. Besides, as soon as The Orpheum opens, he'll be off to his next big conquest."

"Other women?"

"Other real estate. Other cities. But, yeah, probably other women, too. I told you about Leslie, right? She calls him practically every time I'm with him."

"You think they have an open relationship?" Taylor asked.

"I'd like to think he's not a cheater, but who knows. Asking him would be crossing the no-strings line. You staying for opening night?"

"Wouldn't miss it. Especially when your new campaign says Ax Ellis is the hottest swordsman in all the land."

"Believe it or not, that change was Edgar's idea. Thinks we'll bring in more young single women if we put more of Ax in the promo. But to be fair, he also suggested adding more shots of my sister's breasts to bring in the guys."

"See? Men can put their cavemen sensibilities to good use in advertising. He knows when he's got a hot property. And I don't mean the show."

Emily bounced on my bed like a trampoline. "Jump! Jump!"

"There you are, Bess," Maeve said, entering the room and bending down to Emily's level. "I've been looking everywhere for you."

I mouthed "sorry" to Taylor and we walked closer to them.

"She loves to play hide and seek," Maeve said to us. "Lost her in Paris in an antique store last week. Scared the living hell out of me. Now let's get up in your seat like a big girl and have our snack."

Emily clapped her hands. "I want peebudder jewwy."

"That face," Maeve said. "Could there be a more beautiful thing in the world?"

I wished my mother were here to see Maeve's maternal affection. Maeve busied herself making the sandwich in the kitchen, while Taylor and I sat on either side of Emily and caught up.

After serving Emily her sandwich, Maeve picked up the phone and hit redial and placed it to her ear. "I don't know what's wrong with these blasted phones today. I've been trying to reach Henry at the office all morning."

I exhaled. Bess had told Maeve a dozen times that week that Henry was dead, but after a few swear words and the slamming of doors, Maeve would re-emerge as if the whole thing never happened. And ask again for Henry.

Bess was handling the whole thing a lot better than I'd imagined. After two months of searching for Canty and finding him, she had nowhere to turn to appease Maeve's mind of the moment. That particular day, Maeve believed she was the mother of a three-year-old. The day before that she was packing for a trip to the Cayman Islands ... a trip she took in 1978. While my heart was on the fritz, Maeve's mind was playing ping-pong with the past.

Who knew how she'd react when she saw Canty again? Would she even recognize him? What would Mae the Princess see? Would she remember to tell him about their child?

According to Bess, Canty braced himself for anything.

The Orpheum would reopen in less than a week, with a reunion of a lifetime coming. I couldn't wait to meet him, my biological grandfather, and it had nothing to do with the bet between Edgar and me. Believe me, the bet would be off as soon as I told him about the baby. I wanted Maeve and Canty to still be in love after all this time. I didn't see how it was possible. It was beyond impractical. Beyond reason.

An hour later, we felt like we had been transplanted to the past, the 1940s, with glamorous crystal chandeliers, red carpeting and mirrored tables and black chairs at the Orpheum. I could imagine how gorgeous the candelabras would be glistening in the atrium.

Edgar, dressed down in denim and a lavender button-down Ralph Lauren shirt with his sleeves rolled up, greeted us warmly, and pulled me in for a kiss on the cheek. Unlike most men, he bent down and stuck his hand out for Emily to shake.

"And who is this pretty young lady?"

"Emily!" She said, putting one finger in her mouth and the other inside Edgar's palm. She shook it hard.

"Whoa! Big grip for such a little girl." He let go and shook his hand, as if it hurt, making Emily laugh.

"Like kids, huh?" Taylor asked.

"Honestly, I've never been around them much. My brother doesn't have kids and most of my friends are through business. I am a Big Brother back in California, though."

Taylor gave me the eye. Of course a guy wouldn't admit he didn't like kids.

I'd only been away from him for a few days because he'd had a business trip on the East Coast and there was no way I was going to tell him about the baby over the phone. My body was shaking like I was in withdrawal. Telling him about the baby would be, God, why couldn't I text him like asshole John had texted me about our split? He'd probably be relieved. Could move on to his next bachelorette.

"Can I get you a drink? Regular or I could pop open a bottle," he said. I wished upon those shiny lights on the chandelier that he'd stop being so nice, so unselfish.

"It's only one o'clock, but what the hell. I've been dying to try Grey Sky," Taylor said.

"So Kelly's been talking about me, huh?"

"Just your wine," Taylor said.

The last time I'd seen him, he'd been lying naked on his sheets in his new loft. I'd hated to leave him and thinking I may not ever see him that way again. I swallowed the lump in my throat.

"You know Taylor here is a brand strategist," I said. "If I win the bet, then perhaps Taylor might be interested in branding your wine. We used to office together in Dallas."

Taylor shook her head. "Got my hands full already."

"She's always trying to dump me on somebody," Edgar said. "Mind if I speak with you a moment?" He took me by the elbow and led me backstage to Maeve's dressing room. In Maeve's honor, he'd had Mae Moore put on the black door in gilded gold letters. For as long as this building stood, the dressing room would be branded with her stage name.

The room had also been renovated with some modern twists. New leopard print carpet had been installed on the floor, a sleek black sofa sat against the wall, behind a mirrored coffee table with a red bowl full of green apples and a smaller bowl of lemon drops, Maeve's favorite.

"Nice room," I said. "Hope your finicky star likes your changes. What did you need to see me about?"

Edgar locked the door behind us and pulled me into him with one swift jerk. "This." He pressed his lips against mine, leaving me wanting more.

I backed away. "What was that for?"

"I've missed you."

"It's only been two days." I said, versus what my heart wanted me to scream: I missed you, too.

"Two days too long. Stay the night tonight. All night. I'll make you bacon and eggs. Pancakes even. You a syrup girl or a butter-only girl?"

I backed away. "I'm a girl who said she wouldn't stay the night, remember? And what did I say about no more food?"

"I refuse to remember what I don't like to hear," he said.

"Sounds familiar," I said, thinking of Maeve. "Doesn't change the fact that I said it."

"I don't think you mean it. What's so wrong with dating me? We don't need to sneak around. We're not vampires. I'm fairly sure we can be seen together in the daylight and not turn into dust."

"It wasn't supposed to be like this. You were supposed to be a client. That's it. Maybe even a jerk client, because that I'm used to," I said.

"You're mad at me because I'm not an asshole?"

"Yes! And not only that, but you end up being a really nice sexy guy who comes along at the worst possible time."

"Wait a minute. If we've learned anything from the theme of the musical, isn't it that love knows no boundaries? Not of time or place or position?"

I looked away, catching sight of the framed photo of Mae and Canty, the stars. "The musical, yes. But look what happened in real life? Mae and Canty could never go beyond playing pretend. They even called each other by their stage names."

He shook his head. "I'm still going to win the bet," Edgar said. " Just because they couldn't be together then, doesn't mean they don't still love each other. So she chose the single prince over the married pauper she was madly in love with. You don't have to choose, do you?"

"I do." Wrong choice of words. "I mean, I slept with you in Sonoma Valley on false pretenses."

"False? You mean you've got a boyfriend?"

"There is someone else. Someone I don't even know yet." My hands began shaking.

"Let me see if I'm following you. There's someone else that you haven't met but who will keep us apart."

I willed myself not to cry in front of it, but damn if a tear didn't fall despite myself. "The someone I haven't met yet is a baby."

"A what?" He folded his arms and walked closer, as if to hear me better.

My shoulders shook, losing all composure. When I'd rehearsed it in my mind, I'd sounded so rational, so eloquent. The blubbering queen? Not in the plan. "I'm pregnant."

If I'd have announced I was a Ken instead of a Kelly, he couldn't have looked any more shocked. "Right now?"

"I'm so sorry. I do have a plan, or else I did have a plan, and this wasn't it. The baby was the plan. But what I never planned on was you."

Edgar held his hand up for me to stop, and I hated myself for falling to pieces in front of him. Really, I think a text would've been a much better way to go. I wanted him to yell, but what he did hurt far worse. He stayed calm and even handed me a box of tissues.

"It's obviously not me, so who's the father?"

"Number 61894."

He closed his eyes, his nostrils flaring as he inhaled, then opened them again. "I think I met him in a bar once."

I threw a wadded tissue at him. "Not funny."

"I'm sorry. God, wow. I don't know what to say here. Very hard not to freak out with this bit of news." He looked down at my abdomen as if he didn't believe me.

"I really am sorry, Edgar. I don't know what else to say. I've wanted a baby for so long, and when John left me and I went to Hawaii, I made a promise to myself to have a baby at 35."

He ran his tongue over his teeth, nodding and then pacing back and forth. He opened his mouth to speak several times but stopped each time and paced some more. After a few minutes, he looked at me, the saddest look in his eyes. "Well, I guess I know how my uncle felt. Loving a woman who would never return it."

That night I awoke to the sound of Gwen crying in her bed. My alarm clock clicked 2:37 a.m. and I hadn't slept yet, pretending that Gwen's tears were my own. I let her cry them for me.

"Gwen, you okay?" I asked, knowing full well she wasn't. Gwen had told Victor her decision was final. She wouldn't take him back so the show had the arduous task of figuring out how to break the news to the viewing public. With ratings higher than they had been in their five-year history, they didn't want to lose their star couple — or publicly admit that it was their own producer who had contributed to the break-up.

With the help of our family's legal eagles, they had hammered out a deal. Gwen and Victor would still get the show money in exchange for not publicizing the affair between Skylar and Victor. Victor and Gwen would each have their turn in the confessional, giving a watered-down version of the truth that still amounted to: we weren't right for each other. In the end, it either works or it doesn't.

Since Gwen was crowned Princess and the premiere was the same day as all three weddings were supposed to be, the executive producers were going to show some of Gwen on stage versus at the altar. In her Princess gown versus Vera Wang, and next to the man I suspected she was really in love with—her co-star, as our grandmother had been.

Phillip had no qualms about firing his number one guy. Victor was terminated on the spot, asked to pack up his office that night and not return the next day. My father might be all business, and his magic malls concept was his new baby, but it would never replace his real one. Gwen would always be his princess. And, oh yeah, don't ever think of working in this town again.

"Shouldn't I be relieved by all this? I mean, I'm getting the money without having to marry the man," Gwen said, pounding her fists onto the mattress.

"We both know it's not about the money. You're hurt, and he risked a lifetime with you for a few rolls in the hay with a hot-to-trot New Yorker. You have every right to still be pissed."

"Maybe I'm crying over Vera Wang."

I threw the pillow at her. "Well, you can take the labels out of the girl's closet you can't take the label lover out of the girl."

"Hey, I haven't bought anything in, like, three weeks."

"Good. You shouldn't. You're broke."

"Thank you for all you and Mom did. I think I can get what's left paid off in the next two years if I don't slip up."

"Kind of hard to do since you quit your job, though."

"Well, it was easier to quit when I had Daddy's sympathy. Think my being on national TV playing Princess might help me land some roles in L.A.?"

"Couldn't hurt. Some reality stars end up stretching

their 15 minutes. And, besides, you have real talent. Even without *Luxe Weddings,* I think you'd make it." Thinking of her moving away caused another stabbing pain in my heart. Damn sentimental hormones. "You may be a messier roommate than John was, but you were a helluva lot better to live with in the long run."

"Thanks. I think." She laughed. "I'll miss the way you line up your products like little soldiers on the vanity."

"You will not."

"Will so. It's cute. A little anal, but cute. But I feel bad about going away with your baby coming. You promise we'll stay close even if we're far away?" Gwen asked, her voice cracking again.

"Promise. Did you hear tickets are already sold out for opening night?" I rested up on my hand, proud I'd had a lot to do with ticket sales being so smashing.

Gwen slapped her hands together. "Oh, now I'm not nervous at all! I know I shouldn't with the play opening in a few days, but will you eat some of Maeve's peanut-butter-and-chocolate-chunk cookies with me?"

"Right now?"

"Is there a better time to eat cookies than the middle of the night?"

"That's what sisters are for," I said, throwing the covers back.

"I like the fatter Kelly. You're much nicer."

I poured the milk as Gwen opened the cookie jar and retrieved a handful of cookies. "This isn't a one-cookie kind of night," she said with a smile.

I handed her a tall glass as we nestled around the kitchen table. The cicadas chirped outside our open window.

"Think Edgar will call you?" she asked.

"I think there will be some awkward wrap up stuff to do on the account. I'll see him at opening night and at the after party where we can barely muster 'hello,' let alone eye contact, and then, whoosh. He'll be like a distant memory. An amazingly hot memory."

"Do you regret it? Sleeping with him?"

I could feel my throat close up. "No regrets, but I should've known he couldn't be a sex buddy. I knew him too well, and I don't think it works for me. I'm chalking it up to sucky timing. Look what happened to Maeve? Her big chance to make it on Broadway, and she's pregnant out of wedlock. What choice did she have? The show ran for two years in New York. Can you imagine being a single mother in New York in the late '40s?"

"Hell, I can't imagine being a single mother these days! I don't know how you're going to do it."

"Even with losing Edgar, I know I still made the right decision about having a baby now. I don't think there's one more thing I need in the universe."

Gwen looked at me thoughtfully. "It's not about needing, is it? It's about wanting. About getting what you want. But you have to ask for it."

"Sometimes the asking is the hardest part. But really, enough about me." Better to begin the forgetting now. "You heard Mom come in yet?" It wasn't like her not to call and tell us if she'd be late. "Think we should be worried?" I asked, as I dipped my cookie in the milk."Nah. She's a grown woman. If she can't stay out past curfew now, then, when?"

"Mom's favorite saying. Have you noticed we've all started saying it? If not now, then, when?"

"Well, she's right. Mom's always right. Just don't ever let her know it," Gwen said, shaking a soaked cookie at me.

"She out on another 2gether.com date?"

"You didn't hear? She took down her profile. Guess her dates with the dentist and your doctor were all she could take. Nothing like a couple bad dates to make you appreciate what you have."

"What she has, meaning Samuel? Is she with him?"

"Horseback riding. On Samuel's ranch."

"Little late for riding horses, isn't it?" I asked.

"Yeah. Think they could be riding each other instead?"

"Ewww! Thinking about our mother being intimate makes me break out in hives."

Gwen laughed. "I want her to have passionate sex. Gives me hope for our golden years." She reached into the depths of the cookie jar and pulled out the last cookie and raised her glass. "I propose a toast. To taking chances. And getting laid in our golden years."

"Is this a trick toast? I can't even get laid in my creeping into mid-life years."

"You have, and you will again." Gwen forced the clink, and then we laughed at each other's milk mustaches as if we were ten again.

The tinkling of far-off laughter drifted in through the window. "Mom?" Gwen wondered aloud as we walked to the window and looked out below at the nursery. The lights had all been turned off, but the moon was bright and high in the sky. Another July scorcher.

We heard her voice again, and our eyes followed the moonlight to the path inside the nursery. A naked white body, running through the trees. In a moment, her white skin was covered as she and a man fell to the ground. Samuel?

"Oh. My. God," Gwen said, covering her mouth.

"My eyes are burning," I whispered. Then we looked at each other and burst into hushed laughter, trying not to wake Maeve.

"I say again," Gwen said, lifting her glass. "To the golden screw."

I rolled my eyes. "Fine. To taking chances." If a toast was a promise, I had my work cut out for me.

Nothing like a trombone to get you up and at 'em on

a holiday. A high school marching band warmed up for the parade outside of our store, the clanging cymbal piercing my sleepless brain as I zombie-shuffled through the halls. Maeve soundly snored in her bed. Gwen's voice sang out "Give Me One Knight" from the shower.

Happy uckingfay Independence Day. You got your wish, dearie. You're as independent as the day is long. And I'd had about enough of the whole charming, dashing, and romantic musical. If I never heard another love song again, it would be too soon.

The next moment a plunk/slide/thud noise sent me to my balcony where the punk OI paperboy had thrown the Special! July 4th Edition! I almost hurled it back at the kid's head, but out of my peripheral vision, my own picture on the cover caught my eye. It was small, about two inches square, but it was clearly me with a huge smile on my face. What now?

The cover teased: See who's welcomed Oklahoma's hottest new bachelor to town with open arms.

And legs. Hell's bells. No uckingfay way.

My heart thudded louder than the drum section outside my window. I flipped to page 24, where the photo of me from the Bachelorette issue sat next to the sexy black-and-white photo of Edgar from one of his corporate web sites. The one I used on my iPhone.

New Oklahoma heartthrob and wealthy businessman Edgar McGuire has found his own welcoming party in the form of his event planner, wealthy bachelorette, Kelly Apple-Barton, owner of Appleseed Events. Our insiders say the two have been lunching together for two months and even went on a romantic weekend getaway to Sonoma Valley. Sorry, OI readers, looks like our OI Bachelorette may be off the market for good.

I raced into the kitchen full of shocked faces, their noses in another copy of OI. Bess. Samuel. (She hadn't kicked him out in the middle of the night). Gwen dressed in her Princess costume, getting ready to be in the parade. Taylor, and her husband, Jake.

"You're all … up," I said. They looked as guilty as if they'd been caught with porn.

Taylor gave me a sympathetic shrug. Gwen didn't try to hide anything.

"On the bright side, this should squelch those lesbian rumors once and for all," Gwen said.

"There were lesbian rumors?" I asked.

Gwen put her hand on her hip. "Oh, so what if a few people thought John was your mustache?"

"You mean beard," Taylor corrected, as I stared at them incredulously.

"Whatevs. I've always got your back, Sis," Gwen said. "I routinely bring up that hot Hawaiian masseuse you had an island affair with."

I joined them at the table. "Who is this insider that's been talking about Edgar and me? Victor?"

"No way," Gwen said. "I think he's in enough hot water as it is."

"Oh, I'm sure they're saving him for next week," Bess said.

"Gotta run, gang. I'll wave to you all from the float," Gwen said, waving to us regally. So she had her Independence Day, free from Victor, and she'd get to spend it with Ax.

"I have a sneaky feeling about this." I left the group as I punched Richard Hunt's ugly mug on the screen of my phone.

"I wondered how long it would take you to call me," he said. "Happy Fourth!"

"Happy nothing. So you've seen the magazine?"

"If you look at it the way I do, you'll see this bit of PR is a blessing," Richard said.

"A blessing? Are you nuts? The article outed us and makes us look like an item when we're not. So when people find out that I'm pregnant … oh, my God, it was you!"

"Isn't that better than the alternative? Victor threatened your father. Said he would go to the press with the news of your pregnancy, plus the news of Canty being Bess's father to try to weasel his way back into the company. So we beat him to the punch on the smaller story and threatened Victor that we'd give OI our blessing to publish the story of his affair with the producer if he said anything about Canty. We gave OI an anonymous tip that you were seeing someone important. So when people find out that you're pregnant, they'll assume it's Edgar's child."

"But it's not!" I said hotly.

"That's a story for another day," Richard said smugly.

My heart stung, but I'm not sure if it was because Edgar wasn't the father or because we did look so damn cute together in the magazine.

"We've known about your lunches with Edgar from the beginning. All we needed was to plant the seed that you were seeing him outside of work. The fact that you actually were sleeping with him was icing on the cake."

My head buzzed; my voice cracking. "Plant the seed is a bad choice of words. But whatever we had is over."

"And time marches on." Richard's voice was drowned out by the marching band, which had reached our store. Everyone but me stood on the balcony to watch the band pass. Emily cheered from her perch on Jake's shoulders. In that instant, I felt a pang of sadness that my child would not have paternal shoulders to ride on. But my shoulders would work just fine. It was no time to let my confidence slide.

With a quick change of clothes, I left the apartment in search of Edgar.

No answer at his new loft.

No answer at his old loft.

Not a single construction worker at the Orpheum, but on the way out, I spotted one of the New York producers getting into her car.

"If you're looking for Edgar, he's picking up Jamie at the airport," Rebecca said.

Jamie? Who the hell was Jamie? And worse, why did I care? What about Leslie? Hadn't I assumed all along he was dating other women? And, besides, we weren't dating. We were pathetic ex-lovers, and I was the great pretender here, not him.

I smiled through my disappointment.

"Don't tell me you're working today," Rebecca added. "Aren't you going to watch the musical troupe in the parade?"

The parade. Surely Edgar wouldn't miss the parade. His big chance to show off his first production. My stomach knotted. I hated feeling jealous, especially when I had no right to be.

"On my way there now," I told her. "Thought Edgar would want to be in some of the press photos is all. He's not answering his cell."

"So you are working. Take it easy, Kelly. And Happy Independence Day," Rebecca said.

Happy independence. Was there such a thing? I'd thought so. But was it possible to be independent and share my life with someone, too? Was all this fantasy knight stuff getting to my head?

A full day passed—the parade, a picnic at the Apple Boathouse followed by rowing in the sweltering sun (I watched, the non-preggos rowed), and cooled off with a pool party and cookout in Nichols Hills. No sign of Edgar. We swam with Emily, and Jake manned the grill while Gwen cooed on her cell phone with a guy in tights and an armadillo shield. Ax as Pauper finally arrived at our loft later that evening after taking pictures for hours with parade goers and giggly girls and he shot some freelance photos of his own.

He carried a single yellow rose, removed his helmet and bent down on one knee and kissed Gwen's hand, while the rest of us watched slack-jawed. They oohed and ahhed.

I didn't know if I should cry or be sick. People in love always made me feel like an extra-terrestrial.

We settled on the rooftop of our loft, armed with rocket popsicles and lemonade as the sun went down. Taylor's family wore patriotic outfits. Again, sickeningly sweet. Taylor asked me to take a picture of them, and when I snapped it, something clicked in my head. What if I'd told Edgar the truth upfront? Would he have even given me a chance? But I'd made the choice for him.

"Go," Taylor said, as I plopped back down in my lounge chair, a frown on my face.

"What do you mean? It's almost dark. The fireworks are going to start."

"You need to go find Edgar. I've seen you calling him all day. You've been here, but not really here."

"What kind of a host do you think I am? I'm not leaving my company."

"No offense, sweetie, but you're about to get upstaged by fire in the sky, so sneak off. And come tell me everything when you get back," Taylor said.

I'd never believed in seeing stars when you kissed someone or fireworks going off in your brain. I'd never believed in soul mates or happily-ever-afters, but seeing Samuel holding hands with my mother, who was so sure that her love life was over when she'd signed those divorce papers, made me think just maybe.

And when the door to the loft opened and Ax took Gwen in his arms and spun her around, how could I not? How could I not believe?

In the possibility.

Someone for everyone.

No matter how messy or imperfect.

I tore through the packed crowd and finally made it

to Edgar's loft, all the way up to the eighth floor, as the first firework shot into the sky.

"Kelly?" He yelled as he saw me through his sliding glass door of his balcony. He came inside to greet me, as a firework burst behind him. No sign of this Jamie woman.

"Edgar. I've been trying to call you." I tried to calm down, but seeing him made everything in my brain fuzzy. What had I planned to say that was so brilliant? That would make him not hate me?

"I lost my phone. Can you believe that? I told you I never liked it anyway." He shifted uncomfortably. I don't think it was nerves. I think he wanted to get out of this situation as fast as possible. Get back to the fireworks and Jamie and a life uncomplicated by a crazy pregnant woman.

"I've been trying to call. A lot," I said, trying to hold it together.

"Okay." He raised his brow. "And?"

"And? And, yes. I was wondering if you'd seen OI today."

"You came all the way over here to ask me if I'd seen the society rag you claim you don't read?"

"Right. Well, you're in it."

"My feature story was in last week's issue," he said.

"It's a new story. About … you and me."

His brows rose. "I see. Do you happen to have a copy of this on you?"

"No. I figured you already had one."

He crossed his arms. "Since I don't, would you mind giving me the synopsis? We aren't naked in them, are we?"

I smiled through the tension. "Nothing like that. But they said we've been seeing each other."

Edgar looked unamused. "So? We were and now we're not. You've made that abundantly clear."

"Well, I wanted you to know I'm sorry they put that

in there. I'll ask them to print a retraction," I said, all business-like.

"You'll ask ..." Edgar put his hands on his head and turned around, his body tense.

"What? A retraction is the proper thing to do in this situation, right?" I got up to leave.

"Where do you think you're going?"

My eyes stung with tears. "I'm going to let you go so you can enjoy the fireworks with your lady friend."

"Lady friend?"

"Jamie. I hear you talking to Jamie on the phone...and mostly, Leslie."

Edgar rolled his eyes, then calmly walked to the sliding glass door. "Jamie, can you come in here, please?" He yelled to the empty terrace. Two lone lounge chairs. I hadn't seen anyone.

Up popped a bald head.

"Kelly, I'd like for you to meet Jamie, my other uncle, Arthur's only brother. He came to see the opening of *Princess*," he paused. "Uncle Jamie, this is Kelly, a work associate."

Jamie stuck out his hand for me to shake. "Is this the mystery woman I've been hearing so much about it?"

Edgar shifted uncomfortably. "Yes, uncle. She's the one."

"It's nice to meet you," I said weakly, while 'she's the one' echoed in my head. "You go on back to the fireworks show. Looks like it's time for the big finale."

Edgar stared at me like one might a rare artifact. "You thought I'd been seeing someone? Or several for that matter?"

"Leslie calls you every day on the phone. You always say 'I love you.'"

Edgar crossed his arms. "Unbelievable. I told you I had a brother. I was hoping you could meet him in Sonoma Valley, but you took off. He has Downs Syndrome and calls me every day to tell me how much he loves me. I swear he's the one thing that keeps me going some days."

"I see," I said, but I hadn't seen at all. I'd had my eyes wide shut.

Edgar laughed through his anger. "So I have family members with unisex names and you assume they are women I keep on the string?"

I had to sit down. He'd talked about his brother during our lunches every now and then, and maybe even after getting off his calls, but I couldn't remember him ever saying his name and he definitely hadn't told me about the Downs Syndrome, which explained why he talked so sweetly to him. "I feel stupid. I don't know what to say. Thinking you were with someone else was the only reason I thought it was safe to have lunch with you."

"Safe? You wanted me to be taken?"

"I guess I did. I had the IUI treatment the day we met, actually. And then I took the pregnancy test the day that you knocked on my door at my office. I wasn't going to tell anyone about the baby until the second trimester. I never counted on ..." My voice dropped off.

"So what you're saying is I've been there all along, but you didn't want to trust anyone with the news, because..."

"I was afraid."

"And now?"

"Afraid for a different reason."

"Weren't we recently talking about lessons learned from the past?" He came closer, inches away, our bodies almost touching.

The fireworks exploded behind him and I could feel them exploding within my chest. "The past hasn't exactly been kind to me in the romance department." I bit my bottom lip.

"I'm tired of talking about the past, Kelly. Why don't we focus on the future? Even better, the present."

I nodded shyly, the glass rattling from the powerful booms of the fireworks.

"I'd like that," I said, as Edgar placed his hand behind my neck and pulled me into him, his lips lightly touching mine.

My lips sealed his with a kiss, a promise, to taking chances and forgetting what everyone else thought about what we should or shouldn't do or be.

Maybe, just maybe, he wasn't Mr. Too Good to Be True. Maybe there was a chance he was the real deal.

Only one way to find out.

Chapter 29

Canty

What does one wear when you're seeing your sweetheart again for the first time in sixty years? When you're reprising the role that started your Broadway career, you find yourself in armor and tight pants. I can't say I mind the armor a bit since age has stolen the muscular build I had in my youth. If Maeve refuses me, or God forbid, doesn't remember me, at least I'll have my coat of armor to shield my heart.

Isn't life the damndest thing? You're going along eating your buffet meals at eight, eleven and five, but life itself is no longer a buffet. You get what you get and feel lucky each day you open your eyes and don't have shooting pain somewhere in your body. The things you're most thankful for are your meds and the sunrise. It means you've made it another day. Oh, I'm healthy enough, knock on wood. Nothing like watching the roller-coaster ride of health in a retirement community to make you appreciate the bones and muscles and organs that string you together.

But this? The chance for that woman in the scrapbook to come to life again? It's as if I'd stepped out of a fairytale, but look at me—I'm no knight in shining armor, though I'd pretended to be one to steal the Princess' heart. In truth, I always related more to being the Pauper, even after I became a star. I never could let go of the one who got away, though I'm certain she did what had to be done. Those were the times.

Truth is, after my wife died, I tried to date again. I

was Bess and Anna's age. Thought I was too old to find love again, and after being with one person for so long, your life runs in sync with them. I never did become a household name like some of the stars back then, but the people who meant the most knew me. They knew I had to have music to breathe. I had to have the stage and an audience to come fully alive. Sharing that with Maeve had been one of my greatest joys.

My wife never liked how much time I spent with my music, but I fit it into our lives and she dealt with it, even after I left the big stage and screen for good. Only woman who ever loved music as much as I did was Maeve. I swear if you would cut us, notes would pour out instead of blood. I think that's the way it is when God plants some seed of passion within you, and it sprouts inside and can take over if you don't carefully prune it.

I tried to leave my room five times, but my knees were knocking so hard I had to sit down again. Not sure if I'm strong enough to see her again. I might crumble before her eyes.

Gave up driving a few years back, but Bess and Anna said they'd pick me up. My heart nearly explodes every time I lay eyes on Bess. I see the resemblance clear as day. Funniest damn thing about that dimple. She inherited it, and I hear my granddaughter, Gwen, got it, too. Isn't it wild a thing like a crease in the skin can be passed down from generation to generation? And Bess has my eyes. Blue as the wild blue yonder.

I can't take any credit for bringing my daughters together, but a part of me feels like I've given each of them a gift, however belated. Anna begged her mother and I for a sibling for years, but we were so afraid my wife would get the baby blues again and she suffered from depression as it was.

I choose to believe what happened was meant to be. Who's to say that one wrong turn won't lead to a beautiful surprise way down the road?

Finally, the girls arrived. Anna and Bess clasped their hands at the sight of me. They don't know it yet, but they have very similar characteristics. Bess may be a bit more cautious, but each time I see her, she seems more comfortable and happier.

"Don't look at me like that," I told them, still sitting on the edge of my bed.

"Why ever not? Can't a daughter be proud of her handsome father?" Anna said, reaching out her hand for me.

"I can't get up. Believe me, I've tried. Could be my blood sugar."

"Pooh. You're blood sugar is fine. You know the play starts in over an hour. We'll watch from the balcony so you can see Gwen perform and then we'll go down when it's time for you to get ready for your finale," Anna told him.

"The stage, ha! I'll eat up the stage. I'll make them want to get up out of their chairs and dance. It's not the stage or the crowd that scares me."

Bess sat down on the bed next to me. "She's having a good day today, Canty. She's in a good disposition and she thinks she's young again. She seems to be happiest when she believes she's back in that time. I used to worry about it. I wanted her to be the woman who had lived all those years with me, but I'm not worried anymore. And you shouldn't be either. I'm not going to say that it'll be easy, but let's take it one step at a time."

I raised my finger in the air. "With Maeve, it's one song at a time."

Bess's idea was for me to see Maeve on stage. That if Maeve came on first as the duet required, she would know who I was in my armor. But I had to get over the shock of seeing her in private. No offense to Bess, but I tend to do what I want, even though most of my days feel like I'm a piece of cattle prodded this way or that.

The dressing room door could've been made of ten tons of steel for how hard it was for me to open it. It wasn't the weight, believe me. Was my damn nerves getting the best of me again.

Seeing Maeve's name on the door made my heart do a do-si-do. I knocked softly at first, but I could hear her doing her vocal warm-ups. Same as I remember. *Do-re-mi.* I knocked harder.

"Come in," her sweet voice rang out.

I opened the door and well, what do you say? I've never been a poet. Wasn't ever a very good songwriter, but seeing her sitting there in that emerald green Princess gown and her full figure spilling out of her dress? I had to lean back on the door behind me to keep me from fainting. She was gorgeous.

She gave me her smile in the mirror, and batted those big black lashes. Thank God He doesn't change our smiles as we age. It was her. God Almighty, it was her.

"I wondered where you've been," she said putting on her earring.

I didn't know what to say. So much I wanted to tell her. *You may not have known it, but I've been here with you, darling. Always with you. You were never farther than the middle of my heart.*

"It's good to see you," I stammered, holding my helmet in my hand.

"You could never get enough of me," she said, swiveling in her chair.

I remember this, how flirtatious she always was with me. Like she could swallow me whole with one look. I can't tell you how much I wanted her to.

"Here, latch this for me, will you?" She held out a diamond necklace that was probably worth more than a car while I placed the helmet on the chair.

She stood inches in front of me and faced the mirror. My fingers trembled as my skin brushed against her neck and thankfully I fastened the necklace, but couldn't keep my eyes off of her in the mirror. We'd had a ritual. Every night before we performed, I would come in and latch her necklace, then I would kiss her neck right there, underneath the clasp, then put my hands around her waist (okay, sometimes they roamed north—I could never resist) and then she would spin around, and ...

Her eyes met mine in the mirror. She seemed to be waiting.

And so I kissed her right there, underneath the clasp. I put my arms around her, every muscle in my body turning to mush. She felt so soft, smelled so nice, and I looked at us in the mirror as if we were a mirage. I could've never dreamed up this day. I'd given up on the dream of us being together again so long ago.

She brushed her face against mine and held my hands in hers about her waist. The diamonds and jewels on her fingers sparkled, including the simple promise ring I'd given her. "I knew you'd come back for me," she said. "Where have you been?"

She turned around to face me, her eyes twinkling with mischief.

I knew I couldn't confuse her with the truth. Yet I couldn't lie. "I've had an extended gig," I told her. "Great place. Great people. And they're looking for a new headliner. They'd go crazy for you."

"Of course they would," she said with a tiny shrug of her shoulders.

It always drove me crazy when she did that. Still does.

"Does it pay well?" She practically purred.

I swear I'm putty in her hands. Pure putty. "The pay is great. Free room and board and more parties and adventures than you could believe. You get to spend all day with friends and you even get your own dressing room."

"With seltzer water and lemon drops?"

How could I be so happy she was still a diva? God,

the women would sure talk about her. But they would grow to love her. Everybody does. "For you, anything."

Maeve wrapped her hands around my neck, and her lip brushed against my ear lobe. "I wish we had time for a quickie before we go on stage."

I laughed. Nothing in my life was quick anymore, especially that. "We'll have time for that later."

"Aren't you going to ask me?"

"About what?"

"My decision. About Henry's marriage proposal."

"Oh, right." My heart tripped up. I remember this moment like it was yesterday. The moment she ripped my heart in two. I'd lived with half a one for so long. I didn't think I could bear to hear it again. "We don't have to talk about that right now."

She straightened her shoulders. "I've decided not to marry him. Whenever you get things figured out with your wife, then I'll be here for you. However long that takes."

"However long?" My eyes welled up. "Well, the thing is, she left me. Went to a better place. I'm all alone now."

"Alone? Canty, why so dramatic? With me, you'll never be alone again." She stood on her tip toes and kissed me; and it's like someone hit rewind and I was right back there in 1949, kissing my lover in the dressing room at The Orpheum, only this time I had every right to be doing it.

A rap on the door. I hated to pull away from her, afraid to lose her again. Would she wake up the next day and forget this moment? Forget me altogether? I couldn't think about tomorrow. Moment by moment. When you're our age, believe me, it's all you've got.

The door opened and the owner popped his head in. Arthur's nephew, eh? "You lovebirds ready for the spotlight?"

"Arthur, darling, we were born in the spotlight," she beamed.

I smiled at the memory of Arthur. I could see the resemblance. How could I forget the face of the man that gave me my big break? The man who brought Maeve and I together once, and once again? God bless you, you old sonofagun, wherever you are.

"And Arthur," she said, holding my hand tightly in hers. "I've thought a lot about your proposition. About Broadway. I'm sure your aunt is a very lovely woman, but I decided I couldn't give my child up for adoption. As scared as I am to have a child, and as much as I want to go to New York, I can't do it. I'm afraid I've already fallen in love with the child. I have a feeling it's going to be a girl."

Edgar stood dumbfounded, and it took everything in me not to crack right in front of her. All this time I'd assumed she hadn't gone to New York to get back at me. I had no idea she'd had a life inside of her, and that the baby was mine. That she had decided not to give up our child made me fall in love with her all over again.

"The show won't be the same without you," Edgar said, playing along. "So that makes tonight even more special. Your big finale."

"It's now or never," I said, resisting the old phrase "break a leg," because at my age, you never know.

"Don't forget, there's an after-party at my loft," Edgar said. "I want my stars to be there."

"Miss a party? You don't know us very well, do you, darling?" Maeve gushed.

"Looking forward to it," I told him, then looked back at my Maeve. "All of it."

Chapter 30

Kelly

I don't believe in living a life with regrets.

I am a modern woman with her own money and her own dreams. I could be independently wealthy and independently happy. I had my family. My business. My baby on the way.

Pulling off the grand reopening of the Orpheum had told the community I still had it, and new business calls poured in. It seemed whatever recession I'd been in began to lift.

It seemed we'd all stepped outside of the armor we'd been wearing and let our true selves in the spotlight. No more pretending. No more secrets.

I didn't ask for, or need, that retraction in OI after all.

"You owe me a trip to New York," Edgar said looking up at the stage, where Maeve stood singing in front of her pauper. She didn't forget a single word, as if they had been imprinted on her heart.

"How do you know?" I asked.

"Because I walked in on them kissing," he said. "They've still got it after all these years."

I was so happy for them, so relieved that at least for the moment, they had this. Maybe, maybe, true love could really withstand the test of time. "So you think she got to tell him what she wanted to all those years?"

"I do."

I do. Funny choice of words, given the circumstances.

Shadow, who after that night would be Gwen's

shadow no longer, videotaped the whole evening for the world to see the bride-to-be turned off-Broadway star. Skylar, sent packing to New York after Gwen's confession, was replaced with a gay male producer who purchased half of Gwen's designer scarf collection.

"I won't be able to travel at Christmas," I reminded him.

"I'll take a rain check on that," he said.

I met his eyes. "You will?"

"Yeah, next year works for me."

He took my hand and pulled me against the wall, the notes of the age-old Princess soaring through the air. "Remember Me," she sang. And, really, how could we forget?

He nuzzled my neck. "Looks like we've got some celebrating to do."

"I think we're finally on the same page."

"I knew you'd come around eventually. I didn't think it would take quite so many sandwiches, though."

"I come from a long line of strong, independent women who happen to be foodies," I said, running my fingers through his hair.

"Your eyes do sparkle when I say, 'let's eat'." Edgar's face softened, the fine lines around his eyes crinkling as he smiled.

Maeve had fallen asleep on Canty's shoulder in the short car ride from The Orpheum to the party at Edgar's loft.

"She gave it all she's got," Canty said as he held her.

"She always has," I told as him as I turned around in the passenger seat to look at them. So peaceful.

Edgar pulled into his parking spot and shut off the engine, leaving only the lights of the garage streaming in through the window.

"Thank you for doing this, Canty," I told him. "It means so much to all of us."

He wrapped his other arm around her and nodded. "It's me who should thank you. It's all I ever wanted. A second chance with her."

Edgar reached across the seat and slid my hand into his. He turned to face Canty. "You're always welcome at The Orpheum. Special feature performance."

"We'll see if we can fit it in our schedule," Canty winked. "They keep us pretty busy at Grace."

"I know it won't be easy with her," I said.

"Love never is," Canty said. "But let me tell you young 'uns one thing. Every bit of heartache and pain is worth it for moments like this. Just breathing the same air. I wouldn't trade it for every bit of my youth back. I've never been happier."

There I went again. Crying. How did it come so easily after so many years of not being able to cry at all? "Oh, Canty. You're welcome at our house anytime. I hope we can make it a regular thing."

"I wouldn't miss it for the world. Besides, you're carrying our first great-grandchild."

Edgar reached over and brushed away my tears. I took his hand and kissed it. "Maybe we'll name him Orpheum for bringing us all together," I joked.

"Whatever we call him, we'll spoil him rotten," Canty said.

With love, I thought, not money.

"Or her," Edgar added.

Canty tapped him on the shoulder, with three thrusts. "You promise me you'll take good care of them."

"The best," Edgar said. "Easiest promise I've ever made."

Maeve stirred, her eyes shot open. "Did I pass out again? Must've been too many cocktails."

There were no cocktails. But I wasn't about to take the party out of the party girl.

"Arthur, you go in first and announce our arrival," Maeve said to Edgar.

"Will do," he said, as he got out of the car.

"We've got a little celebrating to do," Maeve said, snuggling closer to Canty as Edgar came around and opened my car door. "We'll be up in a bit. Make sure my champagne is chilled."

"We'll be waiting," I said, as I took Edgar's hand and left them alone.

Edgar and I walked to the elevator. "They going to be alright?" I asked, peeking back to see them kiss.

"I don't think they've ever been better," Edgar said. "In fact, I think they've got the right idea."

As the elevator closed behind us, we kissed again, and didn't stop until the elevators swished open and a flash went off.

"Don't panic," Edgar said, smiling for the camera. I guess it wasn't so bad not to be photographed alone. By morning, our photograph would make it on the society page, and I would be smiling.

As we walked over to Bess and Samuel, I asked Edgar if he'd be interested in seeing Maeve's house in Nichols Hills. Told him offhandedly that I might consider moving in after the baby came. "I'd love to see it," he said as we walked up to my family at his cool bar. "Tired of loft living already, huh? Time to plant some roots?"

Before I could chew on the idea that he could be talking about him planting roots in our garden, Samuel approached and shook his hand. "You two talking about my favorite topic?"

"Sort of," I answered. "I'm going to show him your gardens at Maeve's tomorrow. Have lunch on the terrace."

"He's nothing slight of a miracle worker with his hands," Bess said of Samuel, and from what I saw at the nursery, I knew she could mean besides gardening. "I like the sound of that a lot better than Gwen's move."

Gwen approached with her co-star beside her. "Come on, Mom. Don't start laying the guilt trip on me now."

Bess shrugged. "She had to fly the coop eventually. Doesn't mean I have to like it. Now, where's Maeve? You can't leave her alone," she said to me. Like I'd forget to lock the door again.

"She's not alone. She's with Canty. Wants to be fashionably late," I told her.

"Never has been on time all of her life," Bess said. "Why start now?"

"She wants to make an entrance. It's kind of romantic if you think about it. Like making their introduction as a couple," I added.

"I can't believe you said something was romantic," Gwen said shaking her head. "And, Mom, try not to worry so much. We're all going to be fine."

"It'll take me awhile to get used to not being needed. Whatever will I do with myself?"

Samuel said, "I'm sure if we put our heads together, we'll think of something."

Bess blushed. "Canty stuck his head in, then closed it."

"Oh, the announcement," Edgar said, pointing to the stage with the mic and piano.

"I'll do it," Gwen said. She grabbed the mic stand and swung it around. "Ladies and gentlemen. Draw your eyes to the door and join me in welcoming the past and present stars of *Princess and the Pauper*, Clarence "Canty" Shaw and Mae Moore."

The hundred or so guests clapped, whistled, and cheered as Canty and Maeve walked through the door. Maeve gave us her best beauty pageant wave and did flirtatious quarter turns so the photographer could shoot her at every angle. We lined up, Bess on the other side of Maeve when I heard her turn to Bess and say, "You're growing on me, you know that?"

Bess kissed her cheek. I'd relayed what Maeve had told Edgar about not wanting to give her daughter up.

"Ditto, Maeve."

"Watch the rouge, darling," Maeve said as she stuck one hip out and smiled. "Let's make this one for the record books."

"Now, come on, Canty," Maeve said, grabbing his hand. "Let's give the people what they want. An encore performance." She led him to the stage.

Canty turned and tipped his hat to us. "What can I say? You only live once."

THE END

About the Author:

Malena Lott is a married den mom and dance mom in the Midwest. Her novels include *The Stork Reality, Fixer Upper, Dating da Vinci* and the popular beach novellas, *Life's a Beach* and *The Last Resort*. She writes young adult under the pen name Lena Brown. See her full bibliography at and read her creativity blog at www.malenalott.com.

Connect on Twitter, Instagram and Pinterest: @malenalott and on Facebook at www.facebook.com/malenalottbooks

Did you know? Kelly was first introduced in The Last Resort as the event planner at the Mojo in Maui conference.